Dark Protector
A Standalone Mafia Romance

M. James

PNK Publishing

Gia

I'm so excited, I can hardly sit still.

It's just one week until my wedding. But it's more than just the wedding itself I'm excited about. Like so many other mafia daughters, my marriage is arranged. But unlike others, I had a hand in picking my future husband. A prince of the Bratva—the *pakhan's* heir.

As I sit at one end of the long dining room's breakfast table, picking at my plate of poached eggs, fruit, and toast, I can't stop thinking that today is the last time I'll get to see my fiancé before our wedding day. With the date so close, an entire week feels like an eternity. My skin prickles with anticipation, my mind filled with memories of all the moments we've spent together over our courtship. Of small touches and near-kisses, whispers that hint of everything still to come. My pulse flutters in my throat, imagining the moment when we won't need to stop short of a kiss any longer —when we won't have to stop at all. Just last week, I bought my lingerie for my wedding night while out shopping with my friends.

Now, all I can think about is the moment that my new husband will undo my dress, and see what I chose for him.

I've been lucky so far; I know that. Most girls in my position either don't even meet their husbands until their wedding day—or they know who they'll marry, but it's not a match that they're excited about. I've been to three weddings this past year alone, and all of the grooms made me feel all the more fortunate that my father cares about my choice in the matter.

Cared, rather. I swallow hard at the reminder that instead of my father sitting to my right at the breakfast table, it's now my godfather and guardian, Salvatore Morelli. He glances up at me as I shift anxiously in my seat, raising one dark eyebrow.

"You're energetic this morning," he observes idly. "Something to do with the Lasilov heir coming by in a few hours?"

I bite my lip, unsure of how to respond. "You don't always have to be so irritable about it," I mutter, unable to keep as quiet about it as I know I should. My excitement dims just a little as I look at the stern expression on Salvatore's face, and my irritation grows. "I know you don't approve of Pyotr, but my father made the decision, not you."

My petulance doesn't seem to affect him. But then again, not much does. I look away from him, wanting to return to my daydreams about my wedding day, my first kiss at the altar, Pyotr's lips finally touching mine after so long. His mouth has always looked warm and soft, and I've thought a hundred times at least about what it would feel like to be kissed. To be kissed by him, the man I'm promised to.

Salvatore's voice breaks through my fantasy again, and I grit my teeth.

"I served your father loyally for all of his life," Salvatore says calmly. "I will continue to do so. A part of that is honoring his wish that I be your guardian until your marriage vows are said. Whether you like me here under your roof and at your table or not, Gia, that's how things will be."

I don't like it. Every time Pyotr Lasilov is mentioned, or the Bratva in general, I can *feel* the tension in him. I can see the way his expression darkens. And although the mafia has long had no love for the Bratva, and vice versa, he seems to especially dislike them.

"My marriage is supposed to bridge the gap between the two families," I remind him. "That can only be a good thing, right?" Improved by the fact that I'm looking forward to my wedding day, rather than dreading it.

I stab irritably at a piece of strawberry on my plate—part of a spring fruit salad that our cook has made a regular part of the breakfast rotation for April. Since Salvatore came to live here, he's quizzed me on things like that—how much I know about running a mafia household. Apparently, he thinks my future husband will expect me to be well-versed in managing the staff, directing the menus for the week, and generally overseeing the running of a mansion. I don't actually think Pyotr will care about that at all—as far as I'm concerned, what's the point of having a staff if I have to manage all of it? My father never insisted that I learn any of that, and our household has seemed to move along just fine. But my godfather appears to be of the opinion that was a major oversight in my education as a future mafia—or Bratva—wife.

If I'd grown up with a mother, maybe that would have been different. But she died when I was young, and my father remarried. He didn't seem overly concerned about finding someone to teach me the things she would have, either.

Salvatore makes a noise low in his throat, one that seems disapproving to me. "You'll have security for the meeting, as always. Don't try to slip out of the gardens or sneak off anywhere private with him. Stay in full view of the guards at all times. Do you understand me?"

I let out a sharp, frustrated sigh. "Yes. I understand."

He frowns. "You're blushing, Gia. Whatever you're thinking about your fiancé, it's not appropriate for the breakfast table. Truthfully, it's not appropriate for you to think about things like that at all."

"Do you always have to be such a wet blanket?" I snap, pushing my plate away. My appetite is gone, because Salvatore seems intent on taking my anticipation and turning it into a lecture on good behavior. His reminder about the guards is just another way of doing that.

When it comes to that, at least, Salvatore and my father are similar—there's always been a heavy guard on me and instructions that I *not* try to get away with sneaking off into dark corners with my intended. But my father was worried about things going too far, the natural desire of two young people who will eventually be married getting out of hand—and even I had to admit that was a possibility. The extent of it was one uncomfortable conversation where he pointed out to me that the Bratva could back out of the marriage if my innocence was lost before the vows were said, and I didn't want that, did I?

Since I very much want to marry Pyotr, I agreed. We've *mostly* kept our hands to ourselves. He hasn't so much as gotten away with a kiss. And my frustration and eagerness to get to the wedding night has only been building with every week and month that has passed.

"Good." Salvatore cuts a bit of sausage on his plate, looking at me levelly, with his dark, serious gaze. "The Bratva are dangerous, Gia. You need to be protected until the treaty is complete."

I'm going to be the heir's wife. They wouldn't dare touch me. Pyotr would kill them. I bite my tongue because we've had this conversation before. Salvatore doesn't trust the Bratva, seemingly believing that every interaction is an opportunity for them to cut us down in our own home instead of honoring my father's arrangement. And I don't understand why he thinks they're one step away from being feral beasts.

It's all the more evident when they arrive. We're waiting in the formal living room when Giorgi, the head of the house's staff, shows Pyotr and his entourage in. I feel my heart leap in my chest the moment I see my fiancé—he looks as handsome as always, dressed in black wool suit trousers and a dark red button-down with the sleeves rolled up over his muscular forearms. His honey-blond hair is swept back from his face, dark blue eyes immediately lighting on me the moment they walk in, as if he's been anticipating this moment just as much as I have. A half-smile curls his full mouth, his lips the only soft part of his otherwise strong, chiseled face. I feel a swirl of butterflies fluttering in my stomach when I remember that in one week, I'll get to kiss those lips for the first time.

Or sooner than that, maybe. A part of me wants to try to sneak a kiss today, just to get back at my godfather for how strict and cold things have been since he's arrived. He's said over and over again that he's only concerned for me, that he wants to make sure I'm protected and ready for my future. But I'm used to more freedom, and his way of doing things feels restrictive and oppressive.

My closest friend, Rosaria, thinks that it's Salvatore's way of handling his own grief over my father. He's always been a dutiful man, I know that, and I can see that she might have a point—that he's channeling his own sadness into making sure that nothing goes wrong for me.

I, for my part, have been trying to remain hopeful, as much as I miss my father. Trying to look forward to the life he arranged for me, rather than allowing myself to be mired in grief. I don't think he would want me to lose myself in sadness, and I've tried not to allow that to happen. The first few months were terrible, but in the past weeks, especially as the weather has warmed and I've been able to get out of the house a little more, I've started to feel my heart lighten a bit. And seeing Pyotr today will only help.

"Are you ready?" Pyotr glances at me and then at Salvatore. I can see his expression darken a little as soon as he looks at my godfather

—it's clear there's no love lost on his side, either. "Where am I allowed to spend time with my *dorogoy* today?"

Dorogoy. Sweetheart. He taught me that word early on in our courtship, and I taught him the Italian word for the same—*tesoro,* or *treasure.* It was one of the sweet, romantic moments that I've held onto these past months—especially as the visits have been fewer since Salvatore has been in charge of things. His caution has meant I haven't been able to see Pyotr as often—he felt that my father was too lax in allowing it as much as he did. He's leaned on tradition heavily to justify it—that mafia daughters typically don't see their husbands-to-be outside of formal events until the wedding, if at all—but it has felt overprotective to me, instead. That overbearing need to keep me safe from an imagined threat that's hung over me since he came to live here.

"The gardens are fine," Salvatore says, his voice clipped. "I'll be in my office. My personal security will keep an eye on Gia, while the two of you spend time together."

There's a warning in his voice, and I look at him sharply. "Don't be rude," I whisper under my breath, a now-familiar fear springing up in my chest. Every time Pyotr has been here, Salvatore has been just-this-side of what seems rude to me—cold and sharp and just a hint of threatening. I've been afraid that Pyotr will take it badly, and that he or his father will call off the wedding, feeling insulted.

"Don't forget your place," Salvatore returns, his voice low and flat, his gaze still fixed steadily on the Bratva. He nods to Pyotr and then to me. "You may go."

I feel my jaw tighten. I don't like being told what to do, ordered around and dismissed, reminded of my *place.* Slowly, I stand up, and look nervously at Pyotr.

"Of course, your men may watch over her," Pyotr says easily, from where he's been standing since he and his entourage walked in. "Mine will come too, of course."

"Of course." Salvatore stands as well. The tension between the two men is thick and palpable, and I swallow hard. All I want is to be left alone with my fiancé.

Pyotr takes my hand, and I instantly feel more at ease as his fingers curl around mine. He looks at Salvatore, a hint of challenge on his face, as if to dare him to say something about Pyotr holding my hand. My father didn't mind such things, but technically, Pyotr shouldn't so much as touch me.

I see Salvatore's gaze flick to our joined hands, and the muscle twitch in his jaw. But he says nothing, letting us walk out of the room as he and his guards follow.

I lead Pyotr to the back garden—he knows the way by now, since last summer when we first started courting after the marriage was arranged. But he lets me lead the way, which only makes me like him more. We walk through the house, to the large glass French doors that lead out to the paved walkway, and into the garden that's beginning to bloom with life. It's a bright, sunny day, warm with the fresh smell of last night's rain and new flowers filling the air, and I breathe in deeply, turning to look at Pyotr with a smile on my face.

"I'm so happy to see you. It feels like it's been an eternity."

He chuckles, an amused expression on his handsome face. "It's only been three weeks, *dorogoy*."

"I know." I pout teasingly, walking backward along the path as I lead him further into the garden. Behind him, Salvatore's personal security and Pyotr's bodyguards follow, looking ill at ease next to one another, watching us with a scrutiny that I try hard to ignore. There are always eyes on us, and I can't wait for the day that there isn't. "But we used to see each other more often. I don't think we went longer than two weeks, while my father was alive."

"Your godfather seems to prefer the old ways." Pyotr catches up to me, his long stride easily eating up mine. He catches me with an arm around my waist, pulling me a little closer than he should, and my heart flutters. This has been the extent of our physical contact—

moments where he pulls me close, his hand in mine, my leg touching his as we sit on a bench side-by-side. It's only made the anticipation that much more intense—I can spend days after we meet, imagining what comes next. What would happen if we were ever alone.

"But that doesn't matter, *dorogoy*," he murmurs, leaning down to whisper in my ear, as if daring to see how far he can push it before Salvatore's men intercede and warn him away from me. "Soon, I'll have you all to myself. Less than seven days now, and you'll be mine. *Milaya nevesta.*"

Sweet bride. I feel my skin tingle, a flush of warmth filling me as I look up at him. There's a dark gleam in his blue eyes, one that makes me feel that hot, curling anticipation low in my stomach.

"*Mio marito*," I murmur. *My husband.* I touch his arm just above his elbow, where he's holding me, feeling the firm muscle under my fingertips. I feel almost dizzy with want. There's so much I've imagined, and so much that I don't really know yet. *Only six days left.*

I hear one of the guards, a little further down the path, clear his throat. Pyotr loosens his hold on me a little, allowing a sliver of space between us, but he doesn't take his arm away from my waist. He grins at me, a mischievous glitter of rebellion in his eyes, and an answering smile spreads across my face.

This has always been what's attracted me to him—what I've been drawn to since our very first meeting. My father knew it would, and he told me as much, when we first spoke after Pyotr and I were introduced to one another.

"It doesn't matter what Salvatore thinks, either," Pyotr continues as if reading my thoughts. "Your father wanted us to marry, and that's all I or the *pakhan* care about. *He* arranged the treaty, he and your late father, not your godfather. He simply stood by and advised. We'll honor the old don's wishes, not the new one."

"My father thought we'd be good for one another." A mafia princess and Bratva heir—the new ruling couple of a joined family. I've always been outspoken, disliking the structure and rules of the mafia. Instead of trying to stifle that or force it out of me, my father encouraged it instead. He told me that he would try to find a husband for me who would both benefit the family and who would appreciate my brazenness, someone who could allow me to be an equal with him rather than a subservient bride. "That we'd challenge one another," I add, glancing at Pyotr. "He said you and your family are strong-willed, and so am I. He felt we'd complement one another, rather than clashing."

It's a conversation we've had before, but so close to our wedding, I want the reassurance once more that I'm truly what Pyotr wants. And he's doing a good job of making me feel better, as always.

Pyotr chuckles, turning to face me. "I'm looking forward to having a strong-willed bride," he murmurs, reaching down to touch my chin. His fingers are a little rough, his thumb sweeping over the edge of my jaw, and a shiver runs down my spine all the way to my toes. My knees feel a little weak, my skin tight, my heart racing faster than it should as I look at his handsome face above mine. I want him to kiss me so badly that it almost hurts. "I'm looking forward to finding out what it's like to have your will match mine, *dorogoy*."

There's an edge to his voice that I can only interpret as desire. His gaze is dark and hot, and I can feel the world narrow down around us, almost to the point that I can forget that the guards are so close, watching us.

But they *are* there, and I can't forget it entirely. More to the point, I don't want them to report something back to Salvatore that will earn me a lecture, or give him a reason to argue that Pyotr is taking advantage of me, and push back against the wedding. *I can wait six more days.*

Even if, right now, I feel as if I'm going to die from waiting.

"I can feel how much you want me, *dorogoy*," Pyotr murmurs, his thumb brushing over the back of my hand. "Our wedding night can't come soon enough."

"It's not just that." I look up at him, feeling that shiver of excitement in my veins again. "It's—this is the last thing that my father wanted. He spent his last six months alive arranging this marriage, seeking out peace between our families, trying to ensure that my godfather would inherit a stronger mafia by creating peace instead of war." I bite my lip, hoping that he'll understand, that he won't think I'm being silly. "It feels like this marriage is the last thing I can do for my father. I can do one last thing to honor his wishes. And I'm hopeful that we'll be happy, too. I'd like to be happy, after so much sadness these last six months."

"I have every intention of being happy." Pyotr smiles at me, as we sit down on a bench opposite the large garden fountain together. "Our marriage will join two families, and we'll no longer be in conflict with one another. I can't imagine why your godfather bucks against it in the slightest. It's been decades since the Italians and Russians haven't been in open conflict with one another."

"It's quite an achievement. My father's last achievement." I lean back against the carved stone back of the bench, my fingers still laced with Pyotr's. "Is there a garden like this behind your house? I still haven't seen it." There was some talk, in the early months of our courtship, of my being allowed to visit Pyotr's family mansion with an escort of guards. But the visit never happened, and Salvatore quickly vetoed that idea the moment he had a say in the matter.

"No garden. I have a penthouse in the city. It's very luxurious and grand; I'm sure you'll enjoy it." Pyotr glances at me, and I think I see a small flicker of annoyance at the disappointment I can't quite hide. "You'll be pleased with it. You won't want for anything—I have a full staff, and they'll be at your disposal."

"Of course." I hadn't thought that Pyotr might live somewhere very different from what I'm used to—a huge mansion outside of the city with sprawling grounds. I'm not sure how I feel about living in the actual city, but I tell myself that the novelty of it will outweigh anything I might miss. And there's no reason I can't come back here to visit, if I want to get out of the noise and bustle of the city for a little while. Pyotr would never tell me that I can't come back home. "I'm excited to see it."

"You'll see it in a week, *dorogoy*." His voice lowers to something darker, more intimate. "I have plans to take you home for our wedding night. I thought I would surprise you, but I can see you're a little disappointed, *sladkiy*. Instead of an impersonal hotel, I thought you would like our first night to be in our own bed. Where we'll spend every night after that."

I can't help but smile at that. "That's very romantic," I murmur softly, squeezing his hand. "You're right. There's no reason I'll be anything but happy, so long as I have you."

The look he gives me makes my heart flutter wildly in my chest. I spent so much of my early teenage years worrying that I'd be given to some old man, or married to a stuck-up, uptight mafia son, one of the many irritating boys I encountered over the course of growing up, at dinner parties and events that I was allowed to attend. But instead, I'm being given to the Bratva heir—a rebellious, handsome man who fits every sexy bad-boy fantasy I've ever had. A husband who will encourage my wildness, my stubborn streak, my willfulness, rather than try to break and mold me into what he wants. A man who will desire me all the more for it because we're the same.

Marriage is the end of happiness for so many mafia daughters. But for me, it's the beginning of everything I've wanted—a fantasy I was afraid to believe in until my father gave me the choice of marrying Pyotr.

A little while later, one of my godfather's guards approaches, clearing his throat. "It's getting late, Miss D'Amelio," he says, glancing between the two of us. "Don Morelli will want you to be ready to join him for dinner, soon."

I'm not ready for Pyotr to leave. But he's right, of course—I need to change for dinner...the floaty blush pink sundress and white denim jacket that I wore for my "date" with Pyotr won't be acceptable.

"Alright." I look at Pyotr, who is already standing up, tugging me up from the bench with his hand still firmly entwined in mine. "I'll see you in six days?"

"On our wedding day, *moya nevesta*." He smiles at me, that dark, heated gleam still in his eyes. I feel a quiver of anticipation—and a flicker of disappointment, mixed with longing, as I look at his full, smiling mouth. I wanted that kiss, but we lost our chance. I didn't push the issue, and Pyotr seemed inclined to wait, testing the boundaries in other ways.

He lets go of my hand as we walk back into the house, giving me one final nod before he follows his entourage to the foyer, and out of the front door. I'm left with Salvatore's guards, who are standing awkwardly nearby, watching the Bratva leave.

"You can go now," I snap, feeling irritable as the door closes behind Pyotr. A week feels too long, and I'm filled with anxiety; the moment of our marriage is so close but still so far away. The last six months have felt strange, uncertain—getting used to my father being gone and someone new watching over me all at the same time. I'm ready to move forward with my life, and what was planned for me. "Unless my godfather ordered you to come upstairs with me while I get ready, too?"

"Of course not, Miss D'Amelio." Josef, the one in charge of Salvatore's personal security, motions to the others. "Let's go."

I let out a sigh as they walk away, turning to head upstairs. I have an hour to get ready for dinner, and I want nothing more than to lie down for at least half of that.

Salvatore is tense and silent at dinner. We're served formally, something that my father often eschewed, feeling that a typical four-course dinner brought in course-by-course for two people was a little ridiculous. He saved the formalities for dinner parties. But

Salvatore seems to like the structure of it—or at least, believes it's important that I get used to it.

"Is this how the Bratva structure their days?" I ask, a little testily over the first course of lemon and crab soup. "Formal meals? Dressing in business casual at the table?"

Salvatore glances up at me, tearing a corner of his bread off and dipping it in the saucer of herbed olive oil in front of us. "I don't pretend to know what Pyotr Lasilov does at home. You'll be living alone with him, his staff, and his guards at his penthouse. Has he told you that?"

"He mentioned it today, yes." I drag my spoon through my soup, feeling my appetite beginning to fade. I wish I could simply fast-forward through the next six days, and wake up on the morning of my wedding.

Salvatore's expression remains neutral. He's a difficult man to read, and after so many years of closeness between me and the only other person I lived with—my father—I often find it frustrating. "And how do you feel about that, Gia?"

I shrug, taking a small bite of my soup. "Fine. I'm sure it's beautiful. It probably has a gorgeous view of the city—maybe even a spa in the building. A rooftop pool. A concierge. Whatever I could possibly ask for."

Salvatore nods. "Well. You'll be expected to attend family dinners with the Lasilov heir's family, I assume. I gather even the Bratva have events, from time to time, dinner parties. You will be expected to behave in a way that befits the future *pakhan's* bride, and in a way that suggests you've been raised as a don's daughter, not a feral child. So you should know how to dress and act formally at the table."

"My father didn't completely neglect my education." I narrow my eyes at him, feeling the sudden and almost undeniable urge to take my frustration out on him. "Anyway, who are you to be lecturing me about manners? You were *rude* to Pyotr earlier. Don't pretend you weren't."

"I was firm." He finishes his soup, pushing the china bowl back slightly as we wait for the next course. "I made certain he understood you would be supervised, and that attempts to harm you or take liberties with your person would not be permitted. I won't allow that boy to take an inch with you, until he's said his vows and made good on his father's promises."

"He wouldn't." I lift my chin, a little defiantly. "Pyotr is a gentleman."

Salvatore's eyes darken. "You have no understanding of the Bratva, Gia. Your father sheltered you, even if he did spoil you—"

"I'm not spoiled," I mutter, and Salvatore chuckles.

"You are a mafia princess, Gia." There's a hint of tenderness as he says my name, and I look up at him, seeing his expression soften slightly. "You were always going to be spoiled, one way or another. Your father allowed you to run a bit wild, and that was his prerogative. But it's *mine*, now, to ensure you're protected. That means letting me concern myself with your future, and how it's handled. My interactions with the Bratva are not for you to worry about."

"I'm the reason for the treaty." I know I sound petulant, but I'm not entirely sure I care. "My choice to agree to this marriage is why there will be peace. And you're meant to honor my father's wishes, too," I add, leveling my gaze at him. "*He* arranged this, and you know it. So you shouldn't endanger it by being rude to my future husband."

"Your future husband, indeed," Salvatore muses. His gaze flicks to my right hand, holding the silver spoon still trailing through my soup. "Pyotr didn't give you an engagement ring, did he?"

"You were there for the betrothal ceremony." I shrug. "You saw the whole thing. It's not their custom."

"But it is ours." Salvatore's voice is even and cool. "It would have been a gesture of goodwill, for him to respect our customs and give his future bride a ring. But then again, I suppose the Bratva would see it as poor taste to give away a gem when they could profit off of it."

I'm vaguely aware of what my godfather is getting at—the Lasilov family owns a number of foreign mines, not all of them operating strictly legally, most likely. But it's not as if our family operates with any concern for the law, either. "Or I could respect theirs, and not expect one."

"Fair enough." Salvatore looks almost amused, sitting back as one of the staff comes to collect our soup bowls while another replaces them with salads. "You should be cautious, Gia. Not so trusting of your new husband. The ring is just an example. They will stick to their ways, and expect you to forget all of yours. You will be one of them, but they won't try to behave as one of us at all."

"This is a *treaty*. It goes both ways." I stab my fork into a tomato, feeling frustrated with all of it. I don't really want to talk family politics over the dinner table with my godfather. "Anyway, I won't be your problem in a week, any longer. I'll be married, and you can focus on business, like you always have."

Salvatore frowns. "You're not a problem, Gia." His voice has softened again, slightly, and I glance over at him. He almost looks a little hurt by what I've said—although I can't really imagine anything hurting him. He's always been unflappable, impenetrable, the solid wall between my father, me, and anything that might dare to threaten us. My father's voice if need be, his pen if necessary, and his most trusted friend. My father and Salvatore have always been two halves of one ruling man.

Which makes me wonder, yet again, why Salvatore seems so uncertain about this decision now.

"I'm meeting with them tomorrow to discuss the wedding," he says, sitting back and looking at me. "I want to be sure that without your father here, the terms of the treaty will still be upheld."

"What do you mean?" I feel that flicker of fear again. "A meeting? Why wouldn't they—"

"It's a precaution, Gia." Salvatore sounds suddenly tired. "I'm looking out for your own best interests."

"My best interests are that this wedding happen, *as planned*." My throat feels tight, and I swallow hard, trying not to let my panic show. "Salvatore—"

"We don't need to discuss it any further. We'll talk tomorrow." He turns his attention back to his plate, and I can see from his posture and the shuttered look on his face that the conversation is finished, whether I like it or not.

I don't like it. And if my godfather thinks he can stop me from marrying Pyotr at the last minute—

He'll find out that *willful* doesn't begin to describe how I can behave.

Salvatore

I'm not looking forward to my meeting with the Lasilov Bratva in the slightest.

This marriage between Pyotr Lasilov and Gia, has been planned for a long time. I've been aware of it from its inception, since the late Enzo D'Amelio—Gia's father—first thought of the idea to try to put an end between the Italian and Russian contention by arranging a marriage. An old solution, and often, a good one. *Back to the basics*, he said. A wedding ring or a bullet—those are the only two solutions that families like ours ever seem to know. And normally, I would have agreed.

But I've known Gia all her life. I've watched her grow into a beautiful young woman that any man would be fortunate to have as his bride, and I've often felt protective over her. When Enzo suggested the marriage, my response was so quick that it startled both of us. *The Bratva are animals.*

His suggestion was to let them meet. To see if Gia took a liking to Pyotr. He argued that most of the mafia sons who would have been worthy of marrying her—through name, wealth, or potential power—would only stifle them. That none of them were capable of handling a bride with so much willfulness in her, a woman incapable of being quiet and subservient, as mafia wives are so often expected to be. That the Bratva heir would challenge her, and she, him. That a Bratva son would prefer a bride with some fire in her.

I've worried since the start that Pyotr will want to tame her, instead. That his interest in Gia's rebellious spirit isn't because he wants a bride who can rule with him, but because he sees her as a challenge to overcome. A wild filly in need of breaking.

I'm afraid he'll destroy her. That Enzo's only fault was ever seeing the best in even his enemies—that he was a man who wasn't brutal enough to hold the title of don. I loved him like a brother, but in this, I think he was wrong.

Today's meeting is my last chance to try to discern if that's true—and put a stop to it if so.

Pyotr, his father Igor, and their guard are already in my office when I arrive, shown to their seats by Georgi. They're talking quietly as I walk in, and both Pyotr and Igor go silent and stand up as I step into the office, showing that much respect, at least.

"Don Morelli. It's a week before my son's wedding. I assume there's a good reason for this meeting?" Igor gives me a dark, level stare. His expression tells me that he's perceptive enough to gather at least some part of why I've asked him and his son here, and that he's biding his time to decide how offended he should be.

My only concern with their perceived offense is how much blood might spill if the wedding is called off. If there is some other way to prevent violence between our families, I want to find it.

"The late don was quick to agree to this marriage because it pleased his daughter. But I want to ensure her safety. It is my job now, as her guardian, to be prudent in all things concerning her—especially her marriage."

"You don't need to worry about that." Pyotr leans back in his chair, giving me a careless wink. "I'll *please* her."

Igor casts an irritated look at his son, and I feel my temper rise. "Gia is going to be your wife," I bite out in his direction. "You should speak of her with respect."

"She'll be my wife soon enough." He shrugs. "I'll speak of her how I please." Pyotr chuckles, sitting up a little. "Don't tell me you haven't thought of what you would do with that pretty young body if you got your hands on it. She's grown up beautifully, hasn't she?"

He's needling me now, and I have no intention of falling for it. "Gia is my goddaughter," I tell him coldly. "My interest is in her safety and protection. And right now, she remains under *my* roof. If you can't keep a civil tongue in your head—"

"Threats?" Igor breaks in, his accent thick as he leans forward. "This marriage is to quell the violence, *da*? So I suggest you not encourage it, Don Morelli. Or else we will think this marriage is not in good faith."

"We have customs. Ways a betrothed couple is meant to behave. Your son already treats her without respect. My men reported that yesterday—"

Pyotr snorts. "Your precious *goddaughter* was all over me. Whatever your men might have reported to you, it would have been twice as much without my *restraint*. She was so wet for me I could practically taste it." He flicks his tongue lewdly against his lower lip, and my teeth clench together, hard enough that I can hear the bone grind.

"I will warn you once more—"

"Don Morelli." Igor's voice cuts through the conversation, sharp and pointed. "Excuse my son. He's an eager groom ready to take his wife to bed. And this meeting, so far as I can see, is unnecessary. Unless you plan to break off the arrangement—"

My gut tightens. Pyotr is still looking at me with an intractable smirk on his face, not an ounce of respect for his future bride or even affection there. Whatever he has promised Gia, whatever she has imagined between them, I see none of it in him at this moment.

He's not asking me to allow the marriage to go forward—as far as he's concerned, Gia is already his. And I know all too well how Bratva men treat their women.

I'd like to think that she would be treated better. That he wouldn't dare hurt the daughter of a mafia don, one-half of a treaty preventing bloodshed between our families. But I don't believe for a minute that the Bratva want the treaty as badly as Enzo did. I don't believe that they care if the streets between their skyscrapers and our mansions run red again. And I don't believe that Pyotr won't hurt Gia.

He believes she already belongs to him. And when she truly does—

I tried to turn a blind eye to it when Enzo arranged the marriage. He was set on his daughter's perceived happiness, pleased that he'd found a match she was excited for, a man she wanted to marry. He thought it made him a better don, a better father, that he'd arranged a marriage for her that she was happy to agree to. It was always my job to back him up, to advise him only when he asked for it, and he felt confident enough about the match that he didn't think he needed my advice.

It's been harder to ignore since his death. Since all the responsibility for Gia's happiness, her safety, falls on my shoulders. I've tried, in the months following his passing, to focus solely on upholding his legacy and his wishes. On keeping the mafia that he led together, rather than allowing it to fall apart at the seams, as sometimes happens during transfers of power.

But now, looking at Igor Lasilov's cold expression and his son's mocking smirk, I feel with every instinct in my body that this is wrong. That if I allow this marriage to go forward, I will regret it. That even though Gia doesn't realize it now, *she* will regret it, when she sees Pyotr's true colors.

He will break her heart. I feel certain of it. And I worry that he will break *her*, too. Her spirit—and quite possibly, her body as well.

What I need is a compromise. A way to give both myself and Gia more time—myself time to find a solution to this, and time for Gia to see Pyotr's true colors. He's managed to play the game of eager and doting fiancé for nearly a year now. Still, I imagine he can only continue pretending for so long. Particularly if he's denied what he wants a little longer.

"I'm not breaking off the arrangement. What I want is a postponement."

Pyotr sits up straight, outrage on his face, but his father holds up a hand. Igor's expression is still unreadable.

"Gia's father died barely six months ago," I continue. "She hasn't had time to properly grieve. The date should be pushed back by at least another six months. She's not ready to be a wife, or to take on the responsibilities that entails. What if she and Pyotr were to conceive on their wedding night?" The thought of his rough, careless hands on her makes my gut clench once again, but I push the feeling down, focusing on business, not emotion.

"That is usually the desired result," Igor says wryly. "Make your point, Don Morelli, if you have one."

"Usually. Yes. But Gia isn't ready to be a mother. A child, fifteen months after losing her father? The pressures of motherhood so soon? Give her time to grieve, to adjust. Their marriage will only be improved by knowing one another better in the meantime. And when they do marry—"

Igor's expression tightens. "Don D'Amelio arranged this marriage. The contract was signed, in front of witnesses, and your priest. Promises were made, blood exchanged, according to our ways and yours. Now, you suggest a postponement? You suggest I'm a fool, Don Morelli—"

"I haven't said—"

Igor stands up abruptly, motioning for his son to, as well. "It does not need to be said aloud, Don Morelli. Only a fool would believe that this *postponement* will not lead to a breaking of the promises between our families, before the wedding can happen."

I stand up as well, preparing to speak, but Igor continues before I can. His voice is flat and hard, his eyes flinty, and I have no doubt that he means what he says.

"Gia D'Amelio will be at the altar this coming Sunday morning, as arranged. She and my son will say their vows, and she will become his wife. And if she is not there, and the wedding does not happen—" Igor looks at me pointedly. "You know what the consequences will be, Don Morelli. The Bratva are not afraid to spill blood, when our honor is offended."

He stalks out of the room, Pyotr on his heels, surrounded by his men. *The Bratva have no honor*, I want to snarl, but he's gone before I could say it, and nothing would have been gained by it anyway. It would have only meant potential violence here, in this house, which would be unacceptable.

For the first time, I'm unsure what to do. I have no doubt that Igor Lasilov will follow through on his threat of consequences if I fail to produce Gia on her planned wedding day. But I'm not sure I can stomach the potential consequences of handing her over, either. I asked for this meeting seeking reassurance that my fears are unfounded, that my suspicions that the Bratva will be cruel to her are just that. But if anything, I feel more instinctively than ever that this is wrong.

That I'm sending Gia into the lions' den to be devoured.

I drop my face into my hands for a moment, breathing deeply. There's a solution to be had here; I just need to find it. But I only get a few moments to think before my office door slams open, and I look up to see Gia standing there in the doorway, her cheeks red with fury, nearly shaking with it.

"What are you *doing?*" She pushes the door shut, stalking further into the office to stand in between the chairs in front of my desk, her hands clenched angrily at her sides. "You said this was just a precautionary meeting, that I didn't need to worry about it—"

"It was, and you don't. We can talk about this later, Gia—"

"We can talk about it now." She glares at me, her chest heaving furiously. She's wearing workout clothes—a loose white tank top and tight black leggings, sneakers on as if she were about to go for a run. "I was headed outside and ran into Pyotr. He said you asked for the wedding to be postponed!"

"I did." I lean back in my chair, gathering my composure in the face of the angry spitfire that is my goddaughter, standing in front of my desk. "It's only been six months since your father died, Gia. You need time—"

"Don't tell me what I need!" She shakes her head. "What I need is for my life to keep moving. To have something to look forward to—"

"Marriage into the Bratva isn't something to look forward to, Gia!" My voice rises before I can stop it, frustration and worry tightening my chest. "You have no idea what they are. What they're capable of—"

"Pyotr is a good man. He wants me to be his wife. He's been nothing but kind to me, looking forward to our wedding, to my happiness—" Gia grits her teeth, still glaring at me.

"Men can be liars, Gia. They're often exceedingly good at it." I run a hand through my hair, letting out a sharp breath. "Particularly men in our world. Particularly the Bratva. I could tell you stories that would give you nightmares about their brutality. The Bratva are cruel—"

"My father wouldn't have promised me to a cruel man." Gia looks at me defiantly. "Pyotr is different, then. And I *want* to marry him."

"You wouldn't, if you understood. Your father's desire to please you, to give you what you wanted, overrode his better judgment. But I won't allow it to cloud mine—"

"You don't give a shit about what I want!" Gia's voice rises, and I narrow my eyes at her.

"Watch your mouth, Gia—"

"No." She crosses her arms, her cheekbones still burning red with stubborn fury. "I won't. I'll say whatever I fucking want. You're not my father, Salvatore. You're just his friend. His second-in-command. And my *father* arranged this marriage. *This* is what *he* wanted. *Your* job has always been to follow *his* orders and fulfill *his* commands. And in this, my father and I were in agreement. He thought this was best for me, and I want to marry Pyotr Lasilov. There *is* no argument, Salvatore, because it's already been decided. Or are you going to defy him now that he's in the grave?"

I feel my teeth clench, my own anger rising to meet hers. I only barely keep it in check, reminding myself who it is that I'm talking to. Not one of my men, not someone who works for me or someone who is a peer, but Gia—my goddaughter, my responsibility. A young woman who imagines herself in love, and has no idea what she's throwing herself headfirst into.

I force myself to breathe deeply, to calm down. To manage this the way I would if it were my own daughter who were in this situation. It's difficult to imagine—I've never married, never had children. My entire focus, all my life, has been serving this family. Supporting and serving my best friend, my don, Gia's father. There were chances, over the years, women who I briefly dated, or who wanted more. But I was never able to give them enough, to give them the focus and devotion that a relationship—let alone a marriage—required. I was married to my job. To the mafia. And now, it's difficult for me to think of how to communicate to Gia what she needs to understand.

I care about her safety. Her happiness. I want to honor Enzo's wishes, but I see what he was unable to. I feel certain of that. And I can't help but think that I would rather have Gia hate me than see her broken at Pyotr Lasilov's hands.

"I'm trying to keep you safe, Gia." I let out a long breath, running a hand through my hair. "To make sure that this is carefully thought through—"

"You're suggesting my father didn't *think things through?* What kind of friend are you, anyway? Let alone his underboss—"

"I am *don* now!" Briefly, my voice rises before I can keep it in check. "*I* am in charge. And *you* have not thought this through. Are you ready to do what this man expects of you, regardless of how you feel about it? To obey him? To give him children, within the year, possibly? Are you prepared for all of that, at barely eighteen, Gia?"

"Pyotr will listen to me. If I don't want to do something—"

"You are impossibly naive." I shake my head, ignoring the utter fury that blazes in her expression at that. "You can't think that the Bratva heir will take your opinions into consideration, that he thinks you're his *equal*—"

"I'll be his wife—"

"That means nothing to them!" I stare at her, willing her to understand, but I can see that she won't. She's set on this, and nothing less than a ring on her finger in six days will make her happy.

"I could go to them now." Gia raises her chin defiantly. "Tell them I want to honor my father's wishes and marry Pyotr despite your reservations. Stay with the *pakhan* until the wedding, and—"

For a moment, I feel as if my blood has turned to ice. The only thing worse—more dangerous—than Gia marrying into the Bratva would be her going there now, alone and unwed. I don't believe for a moment that they would shelter her and uphold the treaty, following through on the marriage intended for this weekend. Pyotr would take her innocence and discard her—or the *pakhan* would, or both. My stomach turns at the thought of it, of Gia unprotected, a lamb among wolves.

I'm at an impasse. She's in danger; I feel certain of that. But she's right in that it was her father's last wish. It's clearly hers, as well.

I could put a heavy guard on her every day for the next six months, until I find a solution, or someone else to marry her to. But I don't believe the Bratva will wait six months to retaliate, or that Igor will agree to the postponement. They could try to kidnap her, and they might even succeed. There would be no marriage then, only ruin for her, and possibly worse. And if she tried to run, if she somehow snuck past my security and went to them—

What choice do I have?

I can feel my heart sinking as I look at the defiant young woman in front of me, her arms folded and her eyes snapping with fire. There is no convincing her. There's danger if I agree, and danger if I refuse. And I have no idea which path will keep her safe.

So, despite my better judgment, I follow the path I always have.

I follow Enzo's orders, his wishes. I do as he asked. One last time.

"Fine." I let out a slow breath, feeling the weight of dread settling over my shoulders. "You will marry Pyotr then, on Sunday. As agreed."

Gia doesn't thank me. She doesn't say anything at all. She just nods and pivots on her heel, stalking out of the office, the door shutting hard behind her as she goes.

And I can't help but feel that I've just signed her death warrant.

Gia

The day of my wedding is as impossibly beautiful as I could have hoped.

There are no clouds, no rain, nothing to suggest the impending doom that my godfather seems so sure is coming for me. He's been cold and quiet over the past week, speaking only to me when necessary, immersed in work and managing my late father's affairs. When we have spoken, it's only to briefly discuss the wedding, to go over protocol, to finalize last-minute details. Even the formal meal times have fallen by the wayside, with Salvatore keeping to himself, spending long hours and late nights in his office. I can feel the tension in him, the dread, and I don't understand. It's as if he's living in a different world, with a different view of the Bratva than I have—or that I suspect my father had, given that he arranged this marriage.

I'm sitting on the edge of the bed when Rosaria knocks on the door, followed by my two other close friends—Angelica and Cristina. They're already dressed, wearing the rose-pink bridesmaid gowns that I picked out months ago. Most of the planning was handled by a hired wedding planner—my father having no intention of dealing with any of it—and she would come to me with anything that required my opinion. The only thing that my father *did* insist on was that I be involved as much as possible. So, while Angelica didn't have the slightest say in her wedding two months ago, I actually got to pick out parts of mine. Flowers, cake flavors, things like that—and, of course, what my bridal party and I would wear.

One of the maids comes in behind them, with a tray of breakfast pastries, fruit, and mimosas. Rosaria immediately hands me one, and Cristina takes a small, floral china plate and starts to put a piece of raspberry danish and a scoop of sliced fruit onto it.

"Here, you need to eat something." She hands it to me. "*Before* you start drinking," she adds, glancing reprovingly at Rosaria.

"She's marrying the Bratva heir today." Rosaria glances at me nervously. "I think she needs the champagne."

"Why would I?" I take a sip, following it with a bite of strawberry to pacify Cristina, even though my stomach is so full of anticipatory butterflies that I'm not sure how I'm going to manage to eat. "Pyotr is wonderful. He's been romantic, and kind, and—"

"You just don't *know* him." Rosaria bites her lip. "Not really. Or what his family will be like—"

"I spent time with him twice a month for the first half of our courtship. And then every few weeks after that. It's more than most girls like us get." I take another tiny bite of the danish. "I'm excited to marry him."

"It's okay to be nervous, too." Angelica is getting my makeup bag out, setting out items to help me with it. "I was *terrified* on my wedding day."

"You were married to a Sicilian man you'd never met," I point out. "I know Pyotr. We've gotten to know each other. There's no reason for me to be anything other than excited." I hear a tinge of frustration in my voice—I don't want anything to mar this. I don't *want* to be anything other than happy. Salvatore has been a dark cloud over the topic of my marriage for months, and all I want from my friends today, is excitement.

Caterina seems to pick up on my mood. "We just want to reassure you if you need it," she says quickly. "But it doesn't seem like you do! And I'm glad you're happy."

"I am." I get up, taking the small plate of food and my mimosa glass with me as I go to sit at my vanity, so that Angelica can help me with my makeup and hair. "Can you bring me my bouquet?"

I reach into my jewelry box as Caterina goes to get my bouquet—a gorgeous spray of huge peonies in various shades of pink, mixed with white roses and greenery. I have a locket that my father gave me years ago, with a picture of him and my mother in either side of it. I wrap the chain around the ribbon holding the stems of the bouquet, tucking it into place. I want my father here with me today, in some small way, and this was the best way that I could think of to manage it. And I want my mother here, too, though I never knew her well enough to feel the same attachment that I do to my father, or have the same deep pangs of grief that she can't be here today. I was only five years old when she died—not enough to remember her well. I grieved the loss of the relationship we could have had, when I was older, more than my mother herself.

Angelica plugs in the curling iron, handing me a tube of makeup primer as she waits for it to heat up. Caterina is sitting on the edge of the bed, alternating bites of danish with sips of her mimosa. Rosaria goes to the closet to get my wedding dress. It was delivered two days ago, zipped into a pink garment bag, and the butterflies in my stomach take off in a cloud of excitement as she hangs the bag on the front door of my closet.

"You're going to look like a princess," Rosaria says as she unzips the bag. "Absolutely beautiful. The most stunning bride there ever was."

I'm enjoying every moment of my transformation. Angelica curls my long, dark hair, leaving it thick and heavy around my shoulders as she sprays it with product, then starts to twist and pin it up into an elegant updo studded with pearl-tipped gold pins. She keeps my makeup light, leaving me looking almost bare-faced to the untrained eye, with a hint of blush and an expert dusting of champagne and rose-colored shadow across my lids. A rosy lip stain is swept over my lips, and I look like the picture of a blushing bride—innocent, sweet, and virginal.

The thoughts running through my head, as I picture Pyotr getting ready at this exact moment miles away, are decidedly *not* virginal.

"What was your wedding night like?" I ask Angelica, glancing at her as she tucks the makeup bag away. "Was it good?"

Angelica makes a face. "No." She looks up at me quickly, wincing. "I mean—I don't want you to think yours won't be. Or to scare you. But he was—it was fast. It didn't feel particularly good. And it hasn't really, since. He doesn't really seem to be very—good at it, I guess? Or he's enjoying it, so he doesn't care if I do. I don't know. I think he's mostly worried about getting me pregnant. It's been two months, and he seems concerned that nothing's happened yet."

"That doesn't mean it's always like that," Rosaria adds quickly, but I see her and Caterina share a worried look. "One of our maids started sleeping with one of the bodyguards—they think they're being sneaky about it, but they're not. I'm *always* catching them in corners, kissing, touching, looking at each other when they think no one sees. So it must be good sometimes, for anyone to get that obsessed with it. They could get in trouble, but they don't seem to care."

"You haven't told your father?" Caterina looks at her curiously, reaching for another mimosa, and Rosaria shakes her head.

"It's entertaining. I'm always so bored at home. If one of them got fired, or sent away, where would be the fun in that?"

Angelica rolls her eyes, going to my dresser to get the tissue-wrapped lingerie that we bought on a shopping trip a few weeks ago. "I'm sure it will be fine," she says soothingly. "My husband was never going to be an exciting match for me. But you've talked before about how Pyotr makes you feel, and it seems to be mutual, from what you've said. So your wedding night will be different, I'm sure."

"Does it hurt?" I bite my lip, toying with the belt on my robe. All of the romance novels I've read with virgin heroines suggest that it hurts. But all those heroines also end up wildly ecstatic with pleasure by the end of the night, and Angelica's account of things is *very* different.

"A little," she says, although the hitch in her voice makes me think that, for her at least, it hurt much more than that. "But again—my husband wasn't exactly slow or gentle. It sounds like Pyotr cares about you, enough to take his time."

I think of the last afternoon I spent with Pyotr in the garden, of the way it felt with his arm around my waist, the way I wanted him to kiss me so badly, the desire that I saw clearly in his expression as he looked down at me. Just holding his *hand* made my skin tingle and my heart race. I can't imagine how tonight could be anything other than good for us both—*better* than good.

He makes me feel all the things that I've read about, all of that breathless, shaky, passionate longing. He's straight out of my fantasies, and tonight, he'll be mine.

And I'll be his. Just the thought makes my skin heat. He might be a brutal man with others. He might be Bratva, through and through. Maybe *that's* true. But he'll be gentle with me. He'll make it good, because he cares about me. I have no reason to think otherwise.

I take the lingerie from Angelica and go into the adjoining bathroom to change. Part of it is a white satin corset that goes under my wedding dress, with silver rose embroidery along the sides. I hold it up to my breasts as I go back out to the bedroom so that one of the girls can help me lace it up. Rosaria helps me, deftly tightening the ribbon at the back of it. It's a fashion corset, meant for aesthetics and not much else, but I still can't help but think that I *look* like a princess as I glance in the full-length mirror in front of me. My hair is perfectly done with a few small tendrils around my face, the smooth white embroidered satin of the corset outlining my figure and pushing up my breasts, the matching panties clinging to my hips and emphasizing my long legs. Another flutter of excitement ripples through me as I think of Pyotr taking off my wedding dress tonight, and finding this beneath it. Of him looking at me with that desire on his face that I always see during our 'dates,' and knowing this time that we don't have to stop.

That I can finally find out what it will feel like to be kissed. For *him* to kiss me.

Rosaria brings me my wedding gown, holding it as I step into the cloud of satin and tulle. It's stunning—a fitted satin bodice and a full tulle skirt spangled with tiny diamonds, the bodice fitted perfectly just above the corset with delicate tulle straps that hang just off my shoulders. Angelica helps with my chapel-length veil, slipping the sapphire-and-silver comb that holds it into my updo. The fragile tulle of the veil floats around me like a cloud, edged in delicate lace, and I reach up gingerly to touch where it's fastened to my hair.

The sapphire comb—my *something blue*—was my mother's. She wore it on her wedding day, as well as the pearls that are sitting on my dresser—a matched set of drop earrings and a strand necklace. I touch the pearls gently as Caterina clasps them at the back of my neck, remembering what my father told me about their wedding day.

His marriage to my mother was a love match. Unusual for mafia—but he fell for her, and luckily, she was an advantageous marriage for him as well as one they both wanted. It's why he never remarried, and why he tried to arrange the same for me—a husband that would both benefit us and also make me happy.

He succeeded. And today, I have them both with me in spirit, as I walk down the aisle and fulfill his final wish. That I be *happy*.

"Are you ready?" Rosaria hands me my bouquet as I step into my white satin heels, taking a deep breath. My pulse is fluttering in my throat like a trapped bird, and I feel giddy with excitement. "The driver is downstairs with the car." She checks the time, biting her lip. "We should probably go, so there's no chance of traffic making us late on the way to St. Patrick's."

There's a bottle of Dom Perignon on ice waiting for us in the limousine, and Angelica pops it open as we all pile into the back of it. I know I should be careful how much I drink—I don't want to be a tipsy bride going down the aisle, and I've very rarely been allowed to drink at home, other than a glass of wine with dinner. But I take the flute from her, the fizz of the bubbles exploding on my tongue, matching the buzz of excitement in my veins. With each mile, as the driver heads towards St. Patrick's, I feel my heart beat faster in my chest, the distance closing between me and my future husband.

Between Pyotr and I.

The girls are excitedly chattering, the back of the limousine a cloud of pink satin and white tulle, the floral scent of my bouquet mingling with the flower and vanilla perfumes we're wearing, and the bright, sharp tang of the champagne. I look eagerly out of the window as we enter the city proper, fussing nervously with the ribbon of my bouquet and the locket attached to it, as the cathedral comes into view.

"We're almost there." Angelica touches my hand, smiling at me. "You're the most beautiful bride, Gia. Everything is going to be perfect."

The limousine pulls up in front of the church steps, and the driver comes around to open the door, helping each of us out. I'm the last one to slide out of the car, my skirts puffing out around me as Rosaria and Caterina arrange them and my veil, Angelica helping me with the blusher. As we walk into the church, I'm immediately struck by the warmth of it, the dry scent of incense filling the air, and I see Salvatore standing in the nave waiting for us.

He's wearing a bespoke charcoal suit, elegantly fitted, his dark hair swept back from his face, smoothly clean-shaven. He's the one who will be walking me down the aisle today in the absence of my father, and I can feel the tension in him as I take his arm.

"Are you ready?" He glances down at me, and I can't help but think that he's hoping I'll say no. That I'll balk at the last minute, asking for him to postpone the marriage after all. "If you've come to your senses about marrying into the Bratva, all you need to do is say the word." His dark eyes are filled with worry as he says it, confirming exactly what I thought. "You won't need to take any of the responsibility, Gia. I'll handle all of it."

I shake my head, quickly. "No. I'm sure. This is what my father wanted." And what I want. I shift impatiently, looking at the double doors in front of me. I don't want to talk about this any longer. I want to say my vows and leave the church with my husband. I want to be alone with him. My skin heats at the thought of everything to come, of being able to finally make good on our desire.

Salvatore lets out a sharp breath, but he says nothing else. I can hear the music change, and a moment later, the wide doors that lead into the church open, the three members of my bridal party leading the way as we begin the slow walk down the aisle.

With every step, my heart beats faster, fluttering in my chest. It leaps when I see Pyotr waiting for me at the altar, his dark blue gaze fixed on me as I glide down the aisle, and I imagine I can see the barely-concealed desire in his face. My cheeks heat a little, thinking of the first time he'll kiss me at the conclusion of our vows, and I'm glad for the veil's blusher to hide my face.

I almost wish that we could skip the reception, as beautiful and fun as it will be, so Pyotr and I could be alone together sooner.

Salvatore leads me up to the altar, placing my hand in Pyotr's. I see him glance at me out of the corner of his eye, but he gives my hand to Pyotr without hesitation, as if he's finally accepted that there's no going back from this. That now, at this moment, it's too late to change what my father set in motion.

Relief washes over me as I feel Pyotr's fingers close around mine. He's an arm's length from me, and my pulse flutters, seeing how handsome he is. He's wearing a dark blue suit that is only a few shades darker than his eyes, and the errant piece of dark blond hair that so often falls into his eyes looks as if it's on the verge of slipping free. I have to fight the urge to reach up and push it back, to touch his handsome face.

Soon, I'll be able to. Whenever I want.

I smile at him, biting my lip and tasting lipstick. His hand is warm around mine, and I barely hear anything the priest says as he begins to speak. I want the ceremony to go by as quickly as possible, to move past all the formalities so that Pyotr and I can be husband and wife. I feel like I've been waiting so long for this, and it's finally here.

The guests are all seated, watching us. The music has gone silent; the only sound is the priest's droning voice as he begins to speak about the sanctity of marriage. A moment later, he asks if anyone has any objection to Pyotr and me being wed.

I tense impatiently. The time for objections is past—and who would dare, anyway? Here, at the altar, with the ceremony already having begun—no one would speak up now. I swallow hard, waiting for the moment to pass so that the priest can continue.

But instead, there's a soft gasp from the congregation, just as a sharp, clear voice cuts through the air. A voice that I know.

"I have an objection."

Salvatore's voice.

Salvatore

The sound of a collective gasp fills the church, the shock of a hundred guests reverberating all at once. I can feel my skin prickle, the hairs on the back of my neck rise, and every pair of eyes turn towards me to see what will happen next.

I've never been a man to act on impulse. Not in all my forty years of life.

But seeing Gia standing in front of the Bratva heir, her hand in his as she looks innocently up at him with such anticipation, is the last straw.

I know I'm undoing what Enzo arranged by stopping the wedding. I know I'm disobeying his wishes. I know I'm going to anger Gia, and that the consequences of all of this could be dire.

But none of it stops me from standing up when Father McCallum asks if anyone objects, and speaking up.

I see Gia flinch as my voice rings out through the cathedral. I feel everyone around me go absolutely still. As I step forward, walking around the other guests in the front row and striding towards the couple at the altar, I can feel the prickle of oncoming violence in the air.

It was all I could do not to force her to go back out to the car when I saw her walk into the cathedral's nave in her bridal finery. It took everything in me to place her hand in Pyotr Lasilov's, knowing what I do about the Bratva, knowing what they're capable of.

The priest's question was my last chance to put a stop to this. And I couldn't stop myself.

I can't allow her to be handed over to them. I know the fantasy she's crafted in her head, who she imagines her fiancé to be, and the thought of how that will break her when she understands that it's all a lie shatters me.

I'm the only one left who can protect her. I might fail her father by doing this, but it's better than failing her, when I'm all that remains between her and misery.

And there's only one way that I can think of that will mean the Bratva cannot take her. That Igor can't come to me tomorrow, and demand I give her back, that the wedding agreement be fulfilled. Only one way to ensure that Pyotr Lasilov will never have her, until I can think of some other way to mollify them and prevent bloodshed.

I can see, out of the corner of my eye, as I stride to the altar, three of Pyotr's security moving towards him from where they were stationed in the right corner of the church. I twitch the fingers of my left hand at my side, a signal for my own security to move out of the pews, towards me. Protection for myself and Gia, as I see the Bratva beginning to move, readying themselves for violence. But I have no intention of any blood being shed today.

"What is the meaning of this?" Igor Lasilov walks quickly forward to meet me, his blue eyes blazing angrily in his face and his expression set in hard, furious lines. "You *dare* interrupt this wedding, Don Morelli? The time for objections was when we last spoke—"

"And I raised them. You refused to hear me." I feel my jaw tighten as I stare him down. "This marriage was arranged by the late Don D'Amelio, but *I* am the don now. Don Morelli leads the New York mafia, and I do not agree to this marriage. If I say so, the former betrothal is null and void."

Igor's eyes glitter dangerously. "And you say so?"

I hear Gia's soft, shocked gasp to my right. Out of the corner of my eye, I can see her trembling, staring at me in horror, her hand still in Pyotr's. I want to snatch it away, to stop him from touching her this very moment, but I wait. I can feel the tension radiating off of him, too, and I wait a beat, and another, until my security surrounds us. Until Igor's men are outnumbered.

And then I face him and speak, my voice calm and even.

"I do say so."

"Salvatore!" Gia cries out, and I see Pyotr pull her towards him. The click of the safeties on a dozen guns echoes in the church, and the priest steps forward, his expression dismayed.

"This is a house of God," Father McCallum says sharply. "There will be no blood here."

"So it is. And a marriage is meant to take place here, today." I turn, reaching for Gia's hand—the one still clasped in Pyotr's. He tries to stop me as I take her hand, turning her away from him, but two of my men step forward, their hands on their guns. "*Pakhan*, if you want to leave here alive, with your son, I recommend you tell him to take several steps back."

Igor's jaw is clenched so tightly with rage, I can almost hear his teeth grinding. "Don Morelli, I will give you one more chance to think better of this, out of respect for your predecessor and our agreements. Stand down, and give my son's bride back to him. We will continue on as if nothing has happened." He smiles tightly, baring slightly crooked teeth. "After all, I can understand. Your goddaughter is a beautiful woman. Any man would desire her. And you are the new don, now—you might be jealous that Don D'Amelio did not hand her over to you. According to the old ways, it would have made sense—you are his heir, she is his daughter. But he chose differently." Igor's gaze meets mine, unflinching. "You feel cheated, perhaps, of the pretty young bride who should have been in your bed."

I feel Gia flinch. A hot anger burns in my chest, and it feels difficult to think clearly. I want to grab Igor by the front of his jacket and feel the satisfying weight of my fist meeting his jaw, the sound of bone crunching, to feel hot blood on my fingers. It's been *years* since I've been in a bare-knuckle fight, since I've so much as pulled a trigger. Since I've been in the position to engage in the kind of violence that I enforced, once, when I was a younger man. When Enzo needed me for different things.

But that violence, today, will only make things worse. I can protect Gia with words, better than I can with my fists.

"Desire has nothing to do with it, *pakhan*," I tell him tightly. "But you are right in one thing. I *am* the new don. And whatever I might have been party to before when Don D'Amelio made these agreements—I have changed my mind. The old deals no longer stand."

Igor chuckles darkly. "So you have no plans to take her for yourself? You claim you don't desire her? That you don't think of my son in bed with her, and feel such jealousy that you would stand up and break the treaty Don D'Amelio so carefully crafted?"

"Not out of desire." I grit my teeth. "But Gia was entrusted to me to protect. And I will accomplish that here, now. No one will touch or harm her once she's mine."

Gia gasps, trying to pull her hand out of my grasp. "What? No—Pyotr!" She turns, looking frantically for her former fiancé, but Pyotr has already been backed away from the altar by my security, he and the other Bratva guards being slowly herded towards the church doors. Several more of my men move towards Igor, urging him back as well.

"You're outnumbered, *pakhan*. Go." I nod towards the doors, my hand still wrapped tightly around Gia's. "There will be no bloodshed today if you leave now."

"Maybe not today, Don Morelli. But there *will* be blood for this. You can be sure of that."

The look on Igor's face is murderous. I have no doubt, not in the slightest, that there will be consequences for this—and that those consequences will come soon.

But for now, all that matters is making sure that Gia is safe. That they will not take her. That Pyotr will no longer want her—that she is not valuable to them or this alliance. And there's only one way that I can accomplish that—to make certain beyond a shadow of a doubt that she is mine to protect.

I have to marry her instead.

Gia

My head is spinning. It feels impossible to sort out everything I'm feeling—shock, anger, heartbreak—as Salvatore turns me back towards the altar and stands opposite me. He has both of my hands in his now, and I look dizzily between him and Father McCallum, waiting for the priest to put a stop to this. To say that this is impossible, that I've already been promised to Pyotr, that Salvatore can't simply step up and take his place.

"Father." Salvatore nods to the priest. "There's been a change of plans. Gia D'Amelio will marry me here, today. Please continue."

My knees nearly buckle, nausea sweeping through me. Only Salvatore's grip on me keeps me upright—the last person in the world that I want supporting me in this moment.

What I want is for him to stop touching me. For time to rewind, and go back to the way things were. The way everything was supposed to be.

"Don Morelli—" Father McCallum hesitates, just long enough to give me a moment's hope. But Salvatore gives him an even look, and I see the priest's gaze flick from Salvatore, to the back of the church where the Bratva are being forced back out to the street by Salvatore's men. "Very well," he says, after a moment. "A change in groom doesn't mean that we can't celebrate the blessed union that was intended to be held here today."

"What?" I stare at him, at Salvatore, and back again. "No! I haven't agreed to this. I didn't agree to marry him!"

"Gia." Salvatore looks down at me, his face calm, though I can see the angry tension in his jaw, feel it radiating from where his hands are gripping mine. "Don't cause a scene. It will do no good."

"A *scene*? Where is Pyotr? Where—" I twist around, looking to see if he's still in the church. I catch a glimpse of him as the broad doors leading out to the nave open, his face furious and his hair mussed as he and his men are forced back. "No! I'm supposed to marry Pyotr. I want this wedding to go ahead as planned! I don't accept another groom, I don't—"

Salvatore's hands tighten, and I swallow hard, feeling hot, angry tears filling my eyes. Father McCallum has already returned to behind the lectern, preparing to begin the ceremony again, and everything feels as if it's spinning out of control. It's all moving too fast.

"I'm not doing this." I set my jaw stubbornly, narrowing my eyes at Salvatore. With every bit of strength I have, I yank my hand free, shoving my blusher back so that he can see my face fully. I don't care about propriety any longer, or how this is *supposed* to go—I barely cared about that in the first place, and only because I was marrying the man I wanted. Now, I don't give a shit about any of it. "I'm *not* marrying you."

Salvatore lets out a sharp breath. "I'll explain later, Gia." He glances up, over my head, to where I can hear the guests becoming restless. There's no requirement for an audience for the marriage to continue; only two witnesses to confirm it. However, it would reflect poorly on Salvatore for the guests to run from the wedding he arranged. To my right, I can see that Rosaria and Caterina are still standing there, pale-faced and nervous; Caterina's bouquet has fallen on the stairs at her feet. But Angelica has retreated—either back to the pews, or pulled away by her husband.

"There's no explanation!" I stamp my foot, shaking my head. "You can't make me marry you—"

A muscle jumps at the side of Salvatore's jaw, impatience in his expression. "I know you're used to getting your way," he says in a low voice, his dark gaze fixed evenly on mine. "Your father spoiled you, I understand that. You've been told that what you want always matters, more than anything else—"

"You're betraying my father!" I raise my voice, not caring who hears, ignoring the dark look that passes over Salvatore's face at that. "You're going against his wishes, breaking the agreement you both made. He didn't want violence—what the hell do you think will come of this?"

"Watch your mouth," Salvatore snaps, reaching for my other hand and catching it in his. I can tell from the way his lips press together that what I've said landed a sharp blow. But he presses forward, and my heart trips unsteadily in my chest as I begin to realize that there might be no way out of this.

Salvatore is my guardian now. Short of Father McCallum refusing to perform the ceremony, there is no one to speak against it. No one who outranks him who can put a stop to this. And even if Father McCallum were to try, there are other priests. Other ways of making sure that the marriage is both legal and sanctified by the Church, the two requirements for a marriage to be recognized according to our traditions.

Aside from the third—the wedding night.

My knees nearly buckle at that. "I'm meant to be in Pyotr's bed tonight, not yours," I hiss, the *pakhan's* accusations that he flung at my godfather a moment ago still ringing in my ears. "I don't want you!"

"It's not about wanting," Salvatore says tightly. "You were given into my care after your father's death, Gia. I intend to do what's best for you whether you like it or not."

"I don't like it!" I shake my head, feeling my cheeks blaze hot, my face flushed with anger. "I'd rather die than marry you!"

I hear Caterina gasp. I hear Rosaria let out a small, frightened squeak. And a moment later, I hear the *click* of a gun's safety, and see a dark shadow out of the corner of my eye as I hear Josef, Salvatore's second-in-command, speak.

"That can be arranged, Miss D'Amelio, if you refuse to listen to the don."

Salvatore flinches, his eyes narrowing. "Stand down, Josef," he says sharply. "I didn't ask you to threaten her. But it's not necessary, in any case. Gia will obey." He looks at me evenly. "Good mafia wives are obedient. And now is as good a time as any for her to begin to learn that."

I feel hot tears brimming at the edge of my lashes, my heart racing almost painfully with fear, the loss of Pyotr, and the shock of all of it, feeling as if a fist has reached in and crushed my ribs. I glance back towards the doors—the Bratva are gone. Pyotr is gone. The guests sit stiff and silent in the pews, all of them seemingly uncertain as to what to do. There are no more Russians in the room—the congregation is half-empty, only the mafia guests remain. And they all answer to Salvatore.

I hear Caterina whimper. I look at Rosaria, and see the wide-eyed, frightened expression on her face. And I realize, my stomach plummeting, that there is no way out of this.

Father McCallum clears his throat, confirming my fears. "May I continue?"

"You may," Salvatore says through gritted teeth, and for the first time since he stood up and objected, I say nothing.

There's nothing for me *to* say. Nothing that will change what is happening, as everything I envisioned for my future is wrecked in front of me.

It's over. Everything that my father and I planned, everything that I wanted.

And I have no choice in what lies in front of me.

If I could, I would run. I would try to find shelter with the Bratva, with Pyotr, as I'd threatened to when Salvatore and I argued a week ago. I almost wish he'd refused me then, gone ahead and forced a postponement, so I could have tried to evade his security and run then. Now it's too late. The doors are blocked by his men, his grip on my hands is iron-hard, tight as chains. There's no escaping. And I have no idea what will happen if I stand my ground, if I stubbornly refuse to say my vows. They can't be pried out of me; the marriage can't go on if I refuse to say *I do*, but this is new territory for me. I look at Salvatore, and I no longer recognize him.

I resent being called *spoiled*, but my father would never have hurt me. He would never have forced anything out of me, never coerced my agreement to any arrangement. He would certainly have never held me at *fucking gunpoint*. Even if that was Josef acting out of turn, it doesn't change the fact that I'm just now realizing, as I look up at Salvatore's hard, angry expression, that I don't actually know what he might do.

He's always been a brutal and commanding man; I know that. My father's right hand, willing to enforce what my gentler father could not. I've heard stories about who Salvatore was as a younger man, things that he did for my father before others took up those roles, and Salvatore filled a more diplomatic position at my father's side.

I never thought of Salvatore as a threat to *me*. And even now, he claims he wants to protect me. That he's doing this *for my own good*.

But he's taking everything from me. And at this moment, I hate him for it.

I feel tears drip from my lashes as Father McCallum begins to read the vows. Salvatore's hands are warm and broad around mine, his long fingers holding me firmly in place, and I feel myself tremble at the thought of what's ahead. Of what he will be to me—once my godfather, and soon my husband.

Salvatore speaks his vows clearly, firmly, his deep voice resonating in the absolute quiet of the cathedral, silent as the grave except for his voice. *'Til death do us part.* I've never wished for that to come true as much as I do at this moment, as I numbly repeat my own vows, feeling sick.

Everything has changed too quickly. The panic recedes to a blissful nothing as I look up at Salvatore, repeating what I'm told to say, his words and mine a low hum in my ears as I struggle to keep my composure. My fingers shake as he takes my hand and slides a thin gold band onto my left ring finger, and I nearly drop the thicker match to it as I start to put it on Salvatore's hand. It's too small, sticking at his knuckle, and Salvatore closes his hand into a fist to hold it there until Father McCallum can finish the rite.

"That ring wasn't meant for you," I whisper under my breath. "That was Pyotr's."

If he hears me, he says nothing. And then Father McCallum's voice cuts through the fog, as he announces us man and wife.

You may kiss the bride.

I stare up at Salvatore, feeling my heart crash into my ribs. *He won't. He won't. He can't.* Resentment boils up in my chest as he steps towards me, my hands still clasped in his, as he leans down to steal yet another thing that was meant to belong to Pyotr.

My first kiss.

The shock of his mouth against mine reverberates through me. It's the barest brush of lips, the ghost of his mouth against mine, so light that I barely even feel the warmth of it. But it stuns me all the same, as much as if he'd crushed me to him and slid his tongue into my mouth.

Or, at least, it feels that way.

My eyes close without thinking, as his lips touch mine. I feel that hint of warmth, briefly, that momentary caress, and something sparks over my skin. A recognition of touch, of intimacy, that my body recognizes even as my mind and heart cry out that this is wrong. That all of this—my vows, my kisses, my emotions—were meant to be for someone else. That I was meant to be feeling excitement, pleasure, anticipation…instead of fear and dread.

The guests are on their feet, Salvatore turning me with him as we walk down the aisle, man and wife. Dizziness washes over me again, making it an effort for me to walk without my knees buckling, shock rippling over me in waves that hit me again and again, the realization of what just happened freshly painful each time. But I don't want to trip. I don't want him to have an excuse to catch me, to touch me.

He'll be touching you far more, in a few hours.

My stomach twists, fear snaking down my spine. Angelica's warning comes back to me, her disappointment with her wedding night. Only pain, and no pleasure. And in a way, now, that almost seems better. I don't want pleasure from anyone other than Pyotr.

From the man I was *supposed* to marry.

The car is waiting outside. I blink in the bright sunlight, feeling as if I've walked out into a dream. None of this can be real. It can't be happening.

But it is.

Salvatore opens the door for me as if nothing is wrong, helping me with my skirt and veil as I slide numbly into one side of the car. "Given the upheaval," he says calmly as he joins me on the other side of the car, as if nothing were wrong, "I think the wedding reception will be canceled."

"Where are you taking me?" I hear the thread of fright in my voice, feel my pulse beating hard in the hollow of my throat, anger and fear and numbness all taking over by turns. The volley of emotions is dizzying, and I clutch my hands together in my lap, digging my nails into my palms to try to ground myself.

"To a hotel." Salvatore glances at me, his dark gaze sweeping over me as if to assess my mental state. "I've arranged for a suite at the Plaza."

"For what? To take advantage of your new bride?" I snap at him, narrowing my eyes. "I hope you have enough security there for what you've brought down on yourself, Salvatore. Pyotr will come for me—"

"The Bratva may make a move, yes." Salvatore sounds almost tired as he says it, as if the gravity of what's happened is finally settling on him. "But it won't be because Pyotr cares for you, Gia. I need you to understand that—"

"You're lying. All to get what you want." I wrap my arms around myself, fingers digging into the stiff satin bodice of my dress as I look out the car window. We're moving slowly through the afternoon traffic—too slowly for my liking. The large interior of the limousine feels cramped and small, this close to Salvatore, after what he's done.

Salvatore lets out a slow breath. "I'm sorry for the lack of a wedding reception, Gia," he says slowly. "I know you did a great deal of planning. I'm sorry that you'll miss it."

"You think I'm angry over a *party*?" I sneer at him. "You think I'm that much of a spoiled brat?"

"It would be understandable for you to be disappointed—"

"I'm not *disappointed*," I hiss. "I'm fucking furious. You *stole* everything my father and I planned. You've ruined my marriage, taken away my chances for happiness—"

"I know these changes are a lot to take in, Gia." It's clear from Salvatore's tone that he's struggling to stay calm, and keep his voice even. A part of me almost wishes he'd lose his temper and lash out—I could be even angrier with him then, even more justified in my fury. "We'll go to the Plaza, and you can rest. We'll talk later, after you've had a chance to calm down—"

"I won't *calm down.*" I tilt my chin up, looking at him defiantly. "You think you know what's best for me, but I was looking *forward* to being Pyotr's wife. I wasn't dreading any of it. I wasn't afraid. I was looking forward to tonight." I lean forward, seizing on a possible opportunity to hurt him, to drive a knife in and twist it. "Do you know how many times I've imagined what Pyotr might do to me tonight? How he might kiss me, and touch me, the things I could do to him? If he would want me on my knees, or be so eager to fuck his new bride that he—"

"*Enough!*" Salvatore's voice thunders in the small space, making me jump backward, and I see a vein pulse in his temple. "Enough." His face is taut, angry, but he laughs darkly as he shakes his head. "You have no idea what you were marrying into, Gia. No *fucking* concept of what the Bratva are like. Your father knew, but he was blinded by his desire to please you. Convinced that perhaps the young heir would be better. He's not, Gia. Pyotr was not the romantic hero of your dreams. And when you are finished being a silly, petty child about all of this, we can discuss the future."

I sit back, narrowing my eyes at him, arms still crossed over my chest. "Don't patronize me," I hiss. "If I'm a 'silly, petty child,' then I'm the one that *you* married."

Salvatore gives me a dark look, one that suggests he might have begun to regret it. *Good*, I think, turning away so that I don't have to look at him, my chest tight. The atmosphere in the car is so icy, I can almost feel the chill.

"You're my wife now," Salvatore says calmly as the car pulls up in front of the Plaza, though I can hear the edge in his voice. "There's no changing that, Gia."

"Of course not." I smile at him sweetly. "But you might come to regret it."

Salvatore lets out a slow breath, waiting for the driver to open the car door. He steps out and comes around to open mine, holding out his hand to help me, but I ignore it. I gather up my skirts, stepping out of the car with my train and veil rumpled around me. I felt like a princess earlier, like a beautiful, stunning bride, but now I can't wait to get the dress off.

Except—my pulse flutters in my throat again with anxiety, thinking of what taking the dress off will mean.

"I sent a message to one of the staff at the mansion, to have some things sent here for you," Salvatore says as we walk to the doors. "They'll be here before this evening."

He holds open the door for me, and I walk in. The hotel's interior is gorgeous—marble pillars surrounded by frothing green plants, a high patterned glass ceiling, the entire place smelling faintly of citrus and vanilla. Salvatore walks to the check-in desk, all business, and I follow just behind him, my anxiety growing by the moment. I watch as he's handed a slim keycard, and he looks back at me, nodding towards the elevator.

I have no choice but to follow him. I can't dig my heels in, refuse, or make a scene. It would do me no good—who would defy him? Who would come to help me? Anyone with the authority is in Salvatore's pocket already, and my future has been decided for me.

I never realized just how quickly everything could change.

The room itself is equally as beautiful as the hotel's interior—cream-colored carpets, glass French doors leading out onto a balcony framed by layered drapes of gauze and velvet, a Baroque-style couch on one side of the room in cream and gold with a sleek wooden desk on the other side. There's a matching wardrobe, and I see a door to the left that undoubtedly leads to a similarly gorgeous bathroom. The bed—

I can't quite bring myself to look at the bed. My heart is beating hard in my chest as I turn to look at Salvatore, who is setting his wallet and phone down on the nightstand next to it. "I'm going to order room service for you," he says calmly. "Some food will be good for you, to help settle your nerves. Try to relax. I have some business to attend to, and then I'll return. Stay here," he adds, his voice firm. "You might think of trying to run, but I assure you, I have security posted everywhere. You won't get far, and you will only make things worse."

"So you're my jailor now." I press my lips together, willing them not to tremble.

"No, Gia." Salvatore lets out a slow breath, as if willing himself to remember to be patient. "It's my duty to keep you safe. You're making this more difficult than it needs to be. But I understand you're in shock and need some time to understand. I'm going to give you that space, while I go and handle what needs to be taken care of. And then I'll return, and we can talk."

"*Talk?*" I narrow my eyes at him, my gaze flicking briefly toward the bed, and I see Salvatore tense ever so slightly.

"Get comfortable, Gia. Take a bath. Eat. You'll feel better soon." He looks at the door, as if he's already eager to be out of the room and dealing with matters he feels more equipped to handle. *If he doesn't want to deal with me, then he shouldn't have married me,* I think bitterly.

"I can't get comfortable. I can't get out of this stupid dress on my own." I know I sound petulant, but it's my only recourse right now. It's that, or anger, and I can feel the anger slowly beginning to drain out of me, replaced with exhaustion.

Being so furious is tiring, I'm beginning to realize.

"I'll help you with it." Salvatore takes a step towards me, and I reflexively move away. "I'm your husband, Gia." There's a note of exasperation in his voice. "I'm not going to ravish you on the bed like an untamed beast. I'll help you with your buttons, and then I'll go."

Something flickers deep in my belly, a mingled heat and resentment tangling together. I'd imagined Pyotr doing just that, after all—filled my head with imagined visions of our wedding night, where he was so overcome with finally being allowed to touch me that he all but devoured me, before we enjoyed a gentler second round. Now I have no idea how my wedding night will go.

Igor accused him of lust, of taking me for his own selfish desires, but he doesn't look like a man overcome with lust. He looks, if anything, tense as he steps towards me once more, this time circling around behind me to reach for the buttons at the back of my dress.

His fingers brush against the back of my neck, at the very top of my dress, and I stiffen. The touch, feather-light, sends a tingling sensation across my skin, making me catch my breath. For a brief moment, I can imagine that touch skimming down my spine as the dress opens, slowly building that flickering heat that I'd hoped for.

But Salvatore only tugs at the buttons, undoing them one after another, quietly cursing under his breath when he realizes how many more there are to go. "Who made this blasted dress?" he murmurs, irritation lacing his tone.

"Dior." I stay facing forward, trying not to think about what's beneath the dress. About what he'll see, in just a moment, when he—

His fingers go still at the top of my corset. I hear him breathe in slowly, unsteadily, for a brief second. And then, as quickly as the moment came, it passes.

He keeps going, undoing one button after another until the dress is laid open down to my hips. I feel his hand linger again, once more, at the bottom of the opening. I feel his fingertips graze, lightly, against the very base of my spine, the thin strip of flesh between the edge of my corset and the white silk of my panties. I reach up, reflexively, to hold the sagging wedding gown against my breasts, not wanting it to fall, and let him see me in my lingerie.

"Do you need help with this, too?" He touches the corset, his hand brushing beneath my dress just against the curve of my waist, and I hear a hoarseness that wasn't there before. His fingers press, just barely, against the stiff embroidered satin, and I feel myself go very still.

The tension in the air is so thick I could cut it with a knife. I feel my pulse beating, hard and heavy, against the side of my throat. The man I wanted isn't the one standing behind me, and I *don't* want the one who is—but something about his touch sends that flicker of heat spiraling through me, my skin warming.

With embarrassment, I tell myself. *Because my godfather is undressing me.*

But he isn't that, any longer. He's my husband. And tonight—

I shake my head quickly. "I can manage it." My voice sounds strange, too, higher than usual, catching in my throat. "I'll be fine."

Fine isn't the word I would use, not really. But it might be what gets Salvatore out of the room, and gives me a moment alone.

He withdraws his hand, stepping back. "Alright, Gia. I'll return when I'm finished with business. Food will be sent up to you shortly."

I don't move. I don't speak. I stand there, clutching my wedding dress to my chest, until I hear Salvatore's footsteps heading towards the door, and the click of it opening and shutting again.

And then, I let my hands drop. My dress falls to my waist, the tulle sleeves sliding down my arms, the weight of the skirt pulling it down over my hips until it becomes a pool of silk and lace and tulle at my feet. I stand there in my bridal lingerie, shivering, my arms wrapped around myself as I try to think about what to do next.

I *can't* run, at least not yet—unless I want to try to make a break for it in nothing but a Plaza Hotel robe. Numbly, I reach behind me for the ribbons of my corset, tugging them loose and pulling them apart so I can take it off. It, and the rest of my lingerie, lands in a pile with my dress as I walk to the bathroom. I leave it all there—someone else can deal with picking it up.

My stomach growls, reminding me that I haven't eaten since the little bit of danish and fruit that I had this morning—although I'd happily take another glass of champagne right now. I go to the closet, finding one of the soft, fluffy robes, and wrap myself in it as I sink down on the edge of the couch and wait for the room service that Salvatore promised.

It arrives after only a few minutes—a grilled chicken sandwich with avocado and lemon aioli, and a pile of thin, crispy fries salted and tossed with parmesan. Disappointingly, there's no additional champagne with it, but even as anxious and exhausted as I am, I devour all of it. I haven't had a full meal since last night, and I'm starving. It doesn't hurt that, as much as I don't want to enjoy anything about this entire situation, the food is delicious.

I also don't want to follow any of Salvatore's suggestions, but either a hot bath or a nap is all I want, and I don't want to be in the bed when he returns. So instead, I opt for the bath, leaving the room service tray and wandering into the bathroom.

It's every bit as elegant as I would have imagined—all white and gold, with a huge soaking tub. I go straight for that, turning on the water as hot as I can stand, and looking through the toiletries arranged on a pretty golden tray until I find vanilla-scented bath oil.

I pour it in, breathing in the sweet-scented steam and feeling myself relax just a little. I close the bathroom door and lock it, and sink into the tub, pulling the pins out of my hair one at a time until it drapes long and loose over the back of the tub, and I sink down into the hot water.

Despite myself, I can feel my muscles starting to loosen. I close my eyes, imagining myself anywhere else—somewhere far away from

Salvatore and his machinations, from what's going to happen later tonight, from the rioting emotions still tangled up in my chest.

I imagine that my father is still alive, and that I'll still have everything I wanted. That my wedding day hasn't fallen apart spectacularly, and that I'm not trapped now, in a marriage I don't want, to a man who seems to be an entirely different person than the one I believed him to be.

And for just a little while, I can almost believe it's true.

Salvatore

What a time to begin acting on impulse.

Even when I was a younger man, and might have wanted to, I always kept a rein on myself. I never allowed myself to indulge my baser impulses, to be anything less than a man who was capable of upholding the wishes of the don I served. I didn't live like a priest, by any means, but I've always avoided excess in all things—including desire.

I clench my fists at my sides as I step out of Gia's room, trying to shake off the feeling that lingers on my fingertips, the sensation of touching her for the first time. I had meant it when I told Igor that my interruption of the wedding had nothing to do with lust. That I didn't desire my goddaughter. That I was only looking to protect her from a fate that I couldn't willingly hand her over to.

But I felt her momentary intake of breath when I touched the nape of her neck. I saw what she was wearing beneath that dress—lingerie fit for a princess, for a virgin bride. One who was meant to be sacrificed to the Bratva tonight, even if neither she nor her father saw it that way.

They did.

My jaw tightens. But that means that someone else will have to take her to bed tonight—*me*. The only way to make the marriage stick is to ensure it's consummated. Even the blessing of a priest and signatures on paper won't stop an annulment, if Gia were to escape and go back into the Bratva's hands. Not unless it's clear that the marriage has been made complete in *all* ways.

I'll think about it later, I tell myself, sucking in a deep breath as I head to the elevator. First, I need to speak with Josef, my second-in-command, who is in charge of my security. He's the closest thing I have to an underboss—I hadn't gotten around yet to appointing someone to fill the role that I once filled for Enzo.

There will be consequences to what I've just done. The fallout could be severe, and we need a plan to mitigate it. To know what we will do when the Bratva come to take their revenge.

It's not a matter of *if* they will. I don't doubt the sincerity of Igor's threat, not for a moment.

I'd be a fool to do so.

Josef is waiting down in the lobby. "I've done what I can to ensure you and your wife's safety," he says, his forehead creased. "I've doubled the normal security detail on your suite, and there's more discreetly placed around the hotel and its grounds."

Your wife. Hearing Gia referred to in that way startles me. It hasn't entirely sunk in yet—what I've done. What this will mean for us both.

"I'm adding security at both her family mansion and yours, as well, Don Morelli," Josef continues. "The *pakhan* could choose to retaliate in a number of ways—we should make sure that we're prepared for any potential outcome. And depending on which home you plan to take her to, after tonight—"

"Mine." It comes out a little more sharply than I intended. "She is *my* wife, after all, as you said. She'll come back to my home, with me."

Josef nods. "Of course. I'll make sure the bulk of the security is stationed there, then, and that they're all aware of the situation. If the Bratva attacks, we're not to hold back, are we?"

I shake my head, feeling the weight of it as I do. The peace with the Bratva was carefully crafted; for all that I don't agree with the means, and I've just shattered it with one decision. "No. There's no quarter, if they attack. I won't risk anyone harming Gia."

"Understood." Josef looks at me somberly. "There will be bloodshed, Don Morelli. A lot of it, I think."

"I know." I rub a hand over my mouth, and for a moment, I wonder if I've made the wrong choice. But I reject the thought as soon as it forms. I would never have done it if I hadn't felt sure that the Bratva posed a threat to Gia. That she wouldn't have been safe with them.

That they might have enjoyed taking out decades of resentment and strife between our families on her, and it would have been too late to save her, by the time she realized her mistake.

"The focus is on protecting her, at all costs," I tell Josef firmly. "She should never have been promised to them in the first place. I've done what I can to right that mistake, and we'll deal with the consequences from here."

He nods, but I can't help but wonder what he's truly thinking. I've put a great many people in danger, to protect one person. It's not that I think their lives are worth less than hers—but I can see why he might think that. Why Josef might look at my choice and think, to himself, whether or not it was worth what will come.

I have to believe that this was the right thing to do. That the peace wouldn't have lasted, once Pyotr grew tired of his new toy.

That one way or another, lives would have been lost, and Gia would have paid an unnecessary price.

"I'll report back to you as soon as all of the men are in place," Josef says, and if he disagrees with what I've done, there's no trace of it in his voice. "You're going to take her back to your home tomorrow?"

I nod. "Mid-morning, probably."

"Everything will be ready for you, then. I'll notify the staff, as well."

"Thank you." I pause, wondering if I should say something else to him, some reassurance. But I'm not sure what, exactly, I could say that would make the situation better.

If anything, saying more might only make it worse.

As I head back to the hotel—and Gia—my thoughts are a tangle of conflicting desires.

I know I need to consummate the marriage. The validity of the union—and thus her safety—depends on it. Beyond that, I'll need an heir eventually. Enzo's death came with a mountain of duties, and a transfer of power that needed to be carefully handled, lest someone see the chance to slip in and take the title from me—and with it, everything Enzo had built. I hadn't had a chance, before today, to consider what else I might need to do in order to secure that future—if I would marry and produce heirs, or if I would pass the title on to someone else. I hadn't had time to consider it. And in the past—

I can recall thinking, at times, that I would like to marry. The idea of a wife, a more domestic home, children—all of it held a growing appeal for me as I got older. But my life, and my devotion to Enzo and his legacy, left no room for a family of my own.

As the don, I had the opportunity to have that at last. And in time, I would have begun to consider it. But now, all those considerations have come to a head.

I *have* a wife, now. And if I want to truly continue her father's legacy and mine, I will need to have a child with her. It's as much my duty as it is hers—and if there's one thing I've always been devoted to above all else, it's the concept of doing my duty.

Of ensuring that those who depend on me are not let down.

But what it takes in order to do those things—

I feel my jaw tighten as I see the hotel come into view, the minutes ticking down until I see Gia again. I shouldn't want her. I shouldn't think of her with so much as a flicker of desire. I've watched her grow up, seen her turn into a beautiful young woman without even the beginning of an indecent thought in my head. I've been her godfather, her father's best friend, her guardian.

And now I'm meant to be a husband to her—and all that entails.

If there's one downside to being a man, I think grimly as the car pulls up in front of the hotel and I step out, *it's that I will need to feel desire, in order to make this night work.* I will have to want her, in order to consummate the marriage. And I'm not sure if I can allow myself to feel what I need to, in order to go through with it.

Gia isn't in the bedroom when I walk in. Her dress and lingerie are in a pile on the floor, her room service tray abandoned on the cart. I'm pleased to see that she's eaten, at least, but I feel a flash of anxiety at not seeing her there in the room. And then I see the light under the bathroom door, a bit of steam feathering out, and I relax.

She'll come out eventually, and I'm in no hurry to face her. I pour myself a glass of cognac and call for someone to come and take the tray away, studiously ignoring the pile of silk and lace next to the bed. It's a reminder of just how beautiful she looked today, of what she was wearing beneath the gown, of how much less she's wearing right now.

My cock twitches despite myself, and I take a bracing gulp of the cognac. I don't know whether I want my arousal to be difficult, or not. The quicker I can find it within myself to desire her, the faster this can all be over—but even that twitch has caused a knot of guilt to settle in my stomach, threatening to grow with every moment that I try to distance my thoughts from the naked woman in the adjoining bathroom.

It feels both like an eternity, and all too soon when I hear the click of the door. Gia steps out, wrapped in one of the thick hotel robes, her dark hair loose around her shoulders. Her cheeks are slightly flushed from the heat of the bath, and she stops when she sees me sitting on the couch, her expression instantly turning wary.

"Someone brought your things up." I nod to the quilted travel bag sitting next to the wardrobe. "Everything you might need should be in there."

"Including the husband I was meant to marry?" Gia asks tartly, and I feel my jaw tighten.

"Do you want a drink?" I ask her, hoping to change the subject, and she presses her lips together.

"How was your *business*?" she asks instead, every word barbed. "Did your time away from me help? Did you have a chance to think about how you're going to manage to please your pretty young bride? I have expectations, you know."

Her voice is high, arched, full of petulance, but I can hear the nerves underneath it. She claimed to have been looking forward to her wedding night, but I've never heard of a virgin mafia bride who wasn't terrified of the act. Her father allowed her some liberties with Pyotr—let them court and visit at home—but I can't imagine she's all that well-versed in what's meant to happen tonight. No decent mafia daughter would be.

I take a slow breath, ignoring her question as I sip my drink. Gia stands there for a moment, clearly at a loss as to what to do, and then crosses the room towards her bag. She's about to unzip it when I stop her, forcing myself to speak up.

"We can get this over with now, or later, Gia. Whichever you prefer."

She straightens, her hand going to clutch the front of her robe. "You tell me," she says flatly. "After all, you're the one who forced me to marry you."

"You understand what needs to happen tonight, don't you?" I stand up, going to refill my glass. I'll need at least one more drink, if I'm going to get through this. "I'm asking your preference, Gia. Pyotr wouldn't have given you as much."

It was the wrong thing to say, and I knew it before it came out of my mouth. I've never been one to lose control of my tongue, but the tension in the room has me on edge as much as Gia, making it hard to remain calm.

"You don't know anything about Pyotr." Gia's shoulders tense, and she wraps her arms around herself. "We talked about tonight. We—"

I don't want to hear about what lewd things Pyotr might have whispered in her ear. "Do you want a drink, Gia?" I ask again, and she bites her lip, looking at me with a sudden uncertainty flickering in her face.

"Yes," she says finally, and I can hear a little more of the nervousness slipping through.

"Wine, or liquor?" The bar is well-stocked with the latter, and I wait for her answer. She hesitates for a moment more.

"Wine," she says finally, letting out a breath. "I don't know what kind of liquor I would enjoy."

"I'll order up a bottle, then. A good one."

Gia says nothing as I call for a bottle of wine, still hovering near the wardrobe. She seems unwilling to come and sit down, so I sit instead, watching her from across the room.

"We don't need to be enemies, Gia," I say slowly, trying to think of how to diffuse the tension. "We've been on good terms all your life. I care for you. I always have. I've only done this to—"

"If you say 'to protect you' again, I'll scream." Gia's lips press together, and she glares at me. "You're doing this for your own ends.

Your own desires. I don't want to hear about how it's for my own good."

"What can I say to convince you that I'm telling the truth?" I take another sip of my drink, hoping she'll answer me, and not just bite back with another attempted jab. Our marriage can't be one of contention and strife for all of it. And I would rather it not begin that way at all.

"There's nothing." Gia turns her face away, her arms tightening around herself. A moment later, there's a knock at the door, and she goes to open it, clearly eager for that drink she was promised.

I watch her as she opens the bottle before I can even offer to help, pouring herself a glass. She moves stiffly, every inch of her body strung taut, and I question whether this has to be done tonight. Surely, I could give it time—give her a chance to become accustomed to the idea of the marriage…and myself time to come around to the idea of desiring her.

No. It has to be done tonight. Tomorrow, I need to have proof of the consummation to send to Igor, evidence that there is no point in him trying to take back his son's bride. Without that, Gia remains vulnerable, still a potential match for the Bratva heir, their marriage embattled but not entirely impossible.

Once she is mine—in every way—they won't be able to touch her. Not like that. And whatever violence comes of it, that will be a different matter for me to settle.

I'll make it quick, I tell myself as I polish off the remainder of my cognac and stand, setting the glass aside. *Brief, for us both. It will be about duty, and not lust.* I'll imagine what I need to in order to be aroused, and I'll find enough pleasure in it to finish. I'll hope that tonight will give us an heir without any further need to fuck her again. It will be done, and from there, I'll decide how our marriage will be managed. If I need to find pleasure outside of the marriage from time to time, it's not unusual for a mafia husband to do so—

though I don't relish the thought of being unfaithful. But I've never been a man with such strong lust that I can't make it a rare occasion—

"What are you thinking about?" Gia's voice cuts through my thoughts, sharp and curious. "Trying to get up the nerve to touch me? Or maybe just get it up?" She sets her glass aside, her chin tilted up defiantly, her lip curling as she glares at me. "Here. I'll make it easy for you. Since you were so intent on stealing what wasn't meant to belong to you."

Before I can fully register what she's saying, she undoes the belt of her robe, and lets it drop to the floor.

She's naked underneath. Completely, entirely bare. Deep down, I know I should look away, that I shouldn't take pleasure in devouring the sight in front of me. But she's utter perfection. Glossy, thick dark hair tumbling around her shoulders, a full-lipped, rosy mouth, round, high breasts that would fit perfectly in my hands. Her waist nips in softly, her hips a perfect slender curve, her legs long and smooth. Her skin is pale, flushed ever so slightly, and I feel a ripple of lust go through me at the sight of the soft brown curls between her thighs, hiding what I know would taste as sweet as honey.

I feel my cock swell, stiffening against my thigh, and I feel entirely ashamed. But she's remarkably beautiful—maybe the most beautiful woman I've ever seen.

And she's *mine*.

Looking at her, I can't help but think what a painful irony it is that I'm seeing her like this, and shouldn't relish the knowledge that I'll be the one to sink into her soft, perfect heat tonight, making her mine entirely. I can't imagine anyone else would look at her, and think: I *have* to fuck her tonight.

But I shouldn't want this. I can't.

Gia reaches for her wine glass, taking another drink. A droplet clings to her lower lip, and I feel a shiver run over my skin. She stands at the foot of the bed, the two of us at an impasse, and I see her gaze flick down to the front of my suit trousers.

"Maybe you aren't having as much trouble getting it up as I thought you would have." She tosses her hair, finishing off her wine, and putting the glass down before turning towards me. "Well? Aren't you going to tell me what to do, *husband?*"

I shouldn't let her get to me. Her bravado is hiding her nervousness, her fear—I feel certain of that. But as she steps forward, walking towards me brazenly as she leaves her robe puddled on the floor where she stood, I begin to wonder if I've misjudged her.

Before I can gather myself and think of what to say, Gia walks up to me, pressing her palm against the front of my trousers.

Right against my thickening cock.

My body reacts before I can think to rein it in. A beautiful, naked woman is pressing her hand against me, and my cock stiffens instantly, hard and aching under her touch. Her eyes narrow, her lips curving in a mocking smile.

"No desire here, hm? No *lust?*" She cocks her head to one side. "It's bigger than I thought it would be."

I grab her wrist, jerking her hand away and doing my level best to ignore the throbbing ache where her palm was a moment before.

I *have* misjudged her. I thought of her as barely more than a child, sweet and innocent, if capable of standing up for herself when she found something she thought she wanted. But the woman in front of me seems to have more of an idea about what she expects to happen tonight than I would have thought.

"What are you doing?" I tighten my grip around her wrist for a moment, before letting go and stepping back.

"Making sure my *husband* will be able to do his *duty*," Gia smirks at me. "What's next? You tell me to lay back on the bed—or would you rather have me bend over it? Do you want me down on my knees? What filthy things did you fantasize about, that made you decide to steal me away *literally* at the altar?"

Each word comes out like a hiss, dripping venom, her body coiled tight as a snake ready to strike. She intends to make this into a fight, I can tell. My head is swimming with a desire that I wasn't prepared for, with urges that I know I shouldn't give in to.

"How do you even know all of this?" I snap, retreating to more comfortable territory—outraged that Gia seems to be so well-informed about her wedding night. "Did your friends tell you all of this? What you should expect from your husband?"

"My *friends* all told me it was terrifying and painful," she snaps. "But it wouldn't have been for me. I know how I felt with Pyotr, those afternoons that we spent together, how he made me feel. It wouldn't have been like that with him—"

I close the space between us before I can stop myself, my hand on her arm as I glare down at her. "You will *stop* speaking his name in our bedroom. Do you understand? I don't want to hear what fantasies *Pyotr* spun with you about your wedding night—"

"No?" A cruel smile curves Gia's mouth. "Don't you want to know what I'll be imagining while you fuck me?"

"*Christ*, woman!" I nearly snarl it, taking a step back as I shake my head, trying to rein in my anger. In a matter of moments, she's managed to rouse me more quickly than anyone ever has—in more ways than one. "Are you even a virgin? Or was your father more of a fool than I thought, to allow your Bratva fiancé to court you in half-privacy?"

"Why does it matter?" Gia shoots back. *God, but she's beautiful when she's angry,* I can't help but think, seeing her dark eyes snapping with fury, her full mouth pursed, her body poised as if she's half-thinking of lunging at me. Everything I've ever thought about her, all the ways I've seen her all her life, crumble in the face of this woman in front of me. This Gia is someone I've never met before. I caught a glimpse of this side her, maybe, in my office when she demanded that the marriage be allowed to go forward. But not like *this*. "Why should any of that old-fashioned nonsense matter? Who *cares* if I'm a virgin—"

She's being difficult on purpose. I'm sure of it—there's no way she and Pyotr could have gotten that far, but I'm past thinking clearly. I move towards her, and I see her quick intake of breath as I back her towards the bed, looming over her, my expression taut with anger and frustration.

"*I* care," I growl. "You are my *wife*, Gia. I have a right to know if—"

"I'm a virgin," she hisses. "There you go. Does that turn you on? That's what you want, isn't it? Knowing there's a tight little hole waiting for you that no one else has fucked before?"

"Watch your mouth." I clench my hand into a fist, trying not to touch her until I have a rein on my emotions, on my arousal. I'm stunned to hear her speak that way, to hear that kind of filth coming from her pretty, innocent mouth—and at the same time, my cock is harder than it's ever been. It feels as if all the blood in my body has taken up residence between my legs, throbbing with a near-painful ache, demanding relief.

"What are you waiting for?" she taunts, taking another step back, until her thighs hit the edge of the bed. One movement, that's all it would take to topple her onto it. I'd worried that I wouldn't be able to find it within myself to desire her, that I might not be able to get hard, that I'd both make a fool of myself and fail to protect her all at once. But *this*, I hadn't expected.

I want her with a ferocity that shames me, and makes me nearly feral with need all at once. I can see everything that I want to do to her in my mind's eye, the way I could turn her mocking taunts to mewling cries in moments, just by spreading her legs and showing her how it feels to have a man's tongue on her sweet pussy. I could make her come again and again before I finally fuck her, leave her breathless and gasping, and make her apologize for all the things she's said before I give her what she wants.

I could make her beg for me.

I could make her forget that there was ever supposed to be another man in her bed.

Her brazenness, her fire, is completely unexpected. It's almost enough to make me want to rewind time and give her back, because I can see the ways in which she might very well make my life hell over the coming days and weeks.

But it's also turning me on beyond anything I've ever felt before.

"Well?" She taunts again. "Are you trying to remember how to do it? Where it goes, maybe? I can't imagine very many women are lining up to jump in bed with you, *Salvatore*. You're so far past your prime, after all. Maybe it was different when you were younger, but —" She shrugs, sliding back onto the bed, her tongue flicking out over her lower lip as she leans back against the pillows. "Should I just go to sleep now? Maybe it won't matter one way or another. You'll spend all night making up your mind, and Pyotr will come for me in the morning—"

I should gag you. I should find another use for your mouth. I should show you all the things I could do to you, and you'd forget every insult you're thinking of right now, lining them up to fling at me like knives. I bite my tongue against everything that springs into my head, knowing that engaging with her mockery won't make this any better, or easier.

She frustrates me to no end. I grit my teeth, sucking in a breath as I look at her slender, naked body on the bed, and reach for the buttons of my shirt. By the time I undress, I tell myself, I'll have this under control. I won't engage with her taunts that Pyotr is coming to save her; I won't—

I see her eyes flick to my chest, as my shirt falls open. I've kept myself in good shape over the years—far better than most forty-year-old men. I see her gaze sweep over my muscled chest, down to the hard lines of my abdomen, lower, where the lines on either side of my hipbones disappear below the edge of my belt.

The warring urges within me are enough to drive a man mad. The dance of seduction is familiar to me, the rhythms of lust, the things I would say to her if she were *any* other woman in the world. My cock strains against the fly of my trousers, utterly insensible to the fact that *this* woman, we're not supposed to want. *This* woman should have been off-limits.

But I've made her mine, and now I have to follow through. Even if it feels as if I might damn myself in the process.

I let my shirt fall to the floor, and I see Gia look away, as if trying to pretend that she didn't notice—that she didn't find me attractive for a moment. I start to reach for my belt, and then pause.

"Hurry up." Gia lets out an exasperated breath. "I'm bored." She rolls towards me, propping her head up on one hand, her body exquisite as a painting from this angle. "I should have known you wouldn't be man enough to fuck me, even after you stole me. After all, you're not man enough to keep your promises, are you? Why would you follow through on this?"

The words are sharp, slicing at me, stinging. I made a promise to her father, to uphold his decisions, his legacy. I made a promise to protect his daughter. Those, in and of themselves, were at odds with one another. And now, to protect her—

I have to do what should be unthinkable.

But my body is all too eager to do what has to be done. And my bruised and battered ego is tired of taking her blows.

I move onto the bed, grasping her hip with one broad hand. Gia gasps, startled just long enough for me to easily roll her onto her back. She stares up at me, her eyes widening as I sweep my hand down the outside of her thigh, nudging her legs apart so that I can kneel between them.

"What are you—" Gia sucks in a breath as I place my other hand on her knee, slowly sliding it up her inner thigh. Her mouth trembles, just a little, as my fingers slide higher, and I feel her muscles tense under her touch, see her abdomen tighten as the unfamiliar sensation washes over her. "What are you doing—"

She looks utterly stunning, laid out for me like this. *Keep it brief. Quick,* I remind myself. *Pleasure her enough that she won't be hurt by the act, but don't draw it out for your own enjoyment.* I cling to that thought, to the idea that what I'll do next is for *her*, not for my own gratification. I'm well aware of my own size, and the effect it might have on a virgin. I've never taken a woman to bed for her first time before, and it's paramount to me that I don't hurt Gia.

This is for her, not for me. I repeat it in my head like a mantra, as I slide my hand up to the dark curls between her thighs, clinging to it as the means to get through this. I'm not doing it for my own arousal, or because the sight of her with her legs spread and her breasts shaking with each breath makes my cock throb with an excruciatingly pleasurable need. I'm not doing it because I'm aching to feel the wet heat of her on my fingertips, to find out what sound she'll make when I graze her clit for the first time.

It's all *necessary*. Unavoidable. A part of my duty to protect her. To keep her safe. To keep her from harm.

"Preparing you," I murmur softly, brushing my fingers over the outside of those soft curls, not delving between her folds just yet. "I don't want to hurt you, Gia. I want you wet. Ready for me."

Gia snorts, turning her head away, but I see the hitch of her breath in her throat. "You're not *that* big," she taunts, but I don't miss the way her eyes quickly flick to the shape of my cock in my trousers, and away again before she thinks I can see. But I see everything. I'm watching her, making certain I don't harm her. That I don't frighten her.

That she's protected in this, as in everything else.

I promised, I think as I slip my fingers between her folds, grazing a fingertip against her clit for the first time. *I promised to keep you safe. That's all this is.*

But her eyes widen, and she gasps, her hips arching up as she feels the touch of a man's finger against her most intimate, sensitive spot for the first time.

And I know I'm lying to myself, if I say I don't want this.

Gia

You bastard. You fucking bastard.

I've been repeating it in my head all afternoon, all night, since the moment Salvatore brought me here. Salvatore, the man who I always thought saw me as a ward, an untouchable princess, someone for him to protect and guard, but never desire. And here he is, shirtless with his hand between my legs, kneeling over me on the precipice of taking the innocence he swore to protect.

You lying bastard.

I've been robbed of everything. My promised husband, my wedding, my wedding *night*. So the only revenge I could think of was to ruin it for him, too. The only enjoyment I'd be able to get out of it—mocking him, getting under his skin, reminding him that he's nothing but a perverted old man who is getting off on taking his best friend's daughter to bed.

But the man kneeling over me, his hands sliding up my thighs, could hardly be called *old*. And the look in his eyes—

He looks tortured. Torn, as if he both wants to be anywhere else, and is being driven mad with desire all at once. If he truly believes that he doesn't want me, he's lying to himself as well as me. I might be a virgin, but I'm not as innocent as he thought. I know how this is supposed to work. I know at least enough to see that Salvatore wants me desperately. That I've turned him on to the point that it looks visibly painful.

"I don't want to hurt you, Gia," he murmurs, his hand sliding higher, up my inner thigh. "I want you wet. Ready for me."

The way he says it, his accent thickening, his voice dropping to a husky rasp, makes my breath catch in my throat. I feel a throb between my thighs, a blossoming warmth, and my chest tightens.

"You're not *that* big," I snap, turning away, but I can't help but glance, quickly, at the thick ridge straining against his suit trousers. A flicker of fear trickles through my veins—he looks *huge*. Too thick to fit inside of me, no matter what I've read in the romance novels I used to hide in my room. We both know there's no truth to my taunt. He looks as if he could split me in half.

His fingers slip between my folds, and I feel fear. Not fear of *him*—I don't believe he'd actually harm me, not physically. But fear of what he could make me want. Because as his finger slides over my clit, touching me where only I've ever touched myself before, I feel arousal shudder through me, down to my bones.

I can't help my response. The feeling is electric, pleasure rippling out from that one spot where his fingertip glides, and then presses down, rubbing in small circles as I gasp and arch upwards, instinctively wanting more. I watch as his jaw tightens, his eyes narrowing with focus as he moves his finger over the swelling flesh.

I want to be disgusted by him. I want to be horrified that this man is touching me. But the man leaning over me seems like someone entirely different than the uptight, terse man I've known all my life, in his pressed and tailored suits, his expression always stern and forbidding, always perfectly put together. This man, the one with his fingers stroking between my legs, looks like something carved from stone, chest broad with rippling muscle, dark hair dusted over it, down to the line running from his navel to the edge of his trousers. His hair is falling forward a little in his face, his jaw set, his eyes dark with lust as he looks down at me, a man at war with himself, fighting off the urge to throw all his restraint aside and fuck me the way a man like him was meant to fuck a woman like me—a powerful man, who has taken what he wants.

No. I close my eyes, fighting off the heat blooming through my veins. *That's not what this is. That's not it at all.* But the soft friction continues, his fingers stroking me, and I open my eyes to see him draw in a shaky breath, the shape of his cock twitching against his fly.

My hips arch upwards again as I gasp, my fingers tangling in the sheets. I want to pretend that I'm not enjoying this. I want to lie still and silent, to make him feel guilty for what he's doing. I *want* him to feel as if he's forcing both me and himself, but the sensation is more than I thought it would be. It feels good, *so* good, and I can feel wet heat forming between my legs—

"Good girl," Salvatore breathes, his voice low and dark, hoarse. "That's it. I want you wet and ready."

The words jolt through me like electricity. I jerk under his touch, a moan slipping from my lips before I can stop it, my legs parting wider despite myself, as if to allow him more access. Salvatore looks up, startled, his focus momentarily broken by my reaction. Something crosses his face, some realization that I don't understand, and he draws in a shaky breath.

His fingers slide lower, circling my entrance, spreading the slick arousal back up to my swollen, aching clit. My body feels strange, hot, my skin too tight, and my nerves frayed. I felt something like this with Pyotr, before, those afternoons when we would tease and flirt—but this is so much more—

No! I try to resist it, try to fight back. I don't want to enjoy this. I don't want to give Salvatore the satisfaction—but his fingers feel so good, soft, and urgent at the same time, the sensation heightening with every stroke, and my body craves what my mind wants to deny us.

"So wet for me," he murmurs, splaying his fingers on either side of my clit, rubbing just next to it, but not directly where I need him. "This feels good, doesn't it? Do you think you could come for me, Gia?"

I shake my head viciously, back and forth, refusing the idea. Refusing to think that he could coax that from me, too, my first orgasm at someone else's hand, the pleasure I was meant to have tonight and wanted so badly. But I *want* it. I want him to stop stroking me everywhere but where I need his fingers, for him to make me come, with his fingers, with his tongue—

I'm panting now, arching into his touch, another sobbing moan slipping out as Salvatore groans.ABizzily, I see him reach down, adjusting himself, the thick line of his cock standing out in sharp relief. "Just fuck me already," I hear myself mumble, a last attempt at a taunt, to force back the pleasure that he's determined to inflict on me.

"No, *principessa*," Salvatore murmurs, and the sound of the pet name rolling off his tongue makes a shudder ripple through me. He chuckles, low and dark in the back of his throat, his fingers hovering over my clit. "You'll come for me first. Won't you, sweet girl? Just like that—" He strokes his fingers over my clit, and I whimper helplessly. "Yes, you will. Come on my fingers, *principessa*, and then I'll give you my cock."

I feel his index finger, thick and long, press against my opening as his thumb replaces it on my aching clit. Slowly, he starts to push it inside of me, and I squeeze around him instantly, gripping his finger as Salvatore lets out a shocked, pained groan.

"Oh, *fuck*," he murmurs, and I see his jaw clench, his eyes close briefly. "You're so fucking tight. You'll feel so good around my cock. So wet and tight—"

The praise flows over me, rippling over my skin, pushing me higher. I've forgotten to be angry, to fight back, to hate him for this. All I want is the pleasure, sweet and thick like honey, sliding over me, in me, so, so *fucking* close.

"Do you want another finger? You'll need to take that, at least, to take me. Can you take another, my good girl?" His voice slides over me, crooning, his thumb keeping up that slow, rolling slide on my clit, and I whimper, nodding as my hands fist in the blanket beneath me.

"Yes," I whisper. "*Yes, yes—*"

"Good girl," he breathes, and I feel a second finger join the first, sliding deeper. There's a stretch, a burning pain, and I moan as I clench around his fingers, arching back for a second. But the pleasure is still there, so close, and I lean into the friction of his thumb, letting out another sobbing moan.

"Right there. Oh, you're so close, sweet girl. My sweet *principessa*. Just let go. Come for me, Gia. Come all over my fingers. Right there—"

His voice is pulling me deeper, further, into a whirlpool of pleasure that I'm helpless to resist. It drags me down, swallows me whole, the words repeated over and over as the heat blooms outwards and—

The orgasm crashes over me, and my head tips back, my mouth opening on a breathless cry as I feel his fingers push deeper, his thumb press down, and I come unraveled. My hips arch upwards, grinding on his fingers, bucking, writhing, the pleasure so much more intense than any orgasm I've ever given myself, consuming me. I hear myself crying out *yes, yes, please, god, yes,* and I've forgotten that I'm not supposed to want this, that I hate him, that there is any emotion or feeling in the world other than the ecstatic bliss consuming me at this moment.

And then, it starts to fade. I slump back onto the bed, breathless, shocks of pleasure still rippling over my skin, and I blink, my eyes refocusing. I watch dimly as Salvatore slides his hand from between my thighs, and I can see the sweat beading on his brow, his own chest heaving, his cock so hard that it looks like it might tear the fabric it's straining against.

He swallows convulsively, his hand reaching for his belt. My heart stutters in my chest, fear and anticipation mingling together because, in my dizzy haze of arousal, I've forgotten that I don't want to give my virginity to this man. All I can think is that I want to know what comes next, that I want to see his cock, thick and hard for me, that I want to know how much better it can feel when it's him spearing me instead of his fingers. I look at Salvatore, dark and handsome, looming over me like some forbidden thing, and I shudder with a fresh wave of anxious need.

And then his face shutters suddenly, and he draws back, his gaze fixed on something between my thighs. His hand drops to his side, his trousers still zipped up, and I blink at him in confusion.

"What's wrong?" I manage, feeling as if I'm swimming up through a thick fog, my mind still muddled from the force of my orgasm. "Salvatore—"

The sound of his name on my lips seems to jolt him out of whatever fog *he* was in. His expression goes cold, and he moves off of the bed, shaking his head as he takes a step back. "That's enough," he says, his voice thick and rough, but firm.

"What do you mean, *enough*?" I demand, my voice turning suddenly high and petulant again. "We haven't—"

"Look." He gestures towards the bed, the space between my thighs. "It's good enough to prove that the marriage is consummated. We don't need to go further."

I blink, pushing myself up slightly. I see what he means almost immediately—there's a splotch of red blood on the white duvet, barely the size of a quarter, but enough to prove that I'm no longer a virgin.

"You bled." Salvatore bends down, reaching for his shirt. "You won't need to suffer any more of my attention tonight, Gia. That will be proof enough that you're mine."

I stare at him, hardly able to believe what I'm hearing. A moment ago, I was angry that he was going to be my first, that I was being forced to accept him—but now I'm angry for an entirely different reason. "You're going to cheat me out of my wedding night *again*?" I nearly shout, my voice high and sharp with disbelief.

He's forcibly married me, demanded we consummate it, awakened the first taste of pleasure in me, brought me to the cusp of unlocking all of the mysteries I've only imagined so far, and now he wants to *stop*?

My emotions are a flustered tangle. Now, I want to keep going, to find out if it could have continued to be that good. And I'm confused as to why Salvatore, who so clearly is aroused, would stop before he has his own pleasure.

"That's enough." Salvatore is buttoning his shirt, his expression closed off and hard. "I'll leave you be for the night, Gia."

Anger surges through me. I'm furious that I'm being *managed*, told what to do, treated like I'm something to be maneuvered, and then told to be silent when my opinion isn't wanted. "What?" I mock, pushing myself up as I glare at him. "Afraid you won't be able to keep it up long enough to come?"

Salvatore gives me a look that says I'm being ridiculous. And I know I am—all it takes is one look at the strained front of his trousers to know that there's no question about his virility. An unexpected shiver of desire goes through me again, a longing to know how this all ends, and I narrow my eyes. "You can't leave on our wedding night."

"I can." Salvatore gathers his tie and jacket. "What needed to be done has been done. We're finished here. In the morning, I'll take you home, and we can discuss your new role." He strides towards the door, his attitude dismissive, and I want to scream. To throw something.

He pauses, just before he opens it. "Good night, Gia," he says calmly. And then he's gone. I hear the door lock behind him, and I know there's no escaping.

I'm all alone on my wedding night. And I'll stay that way until tomorrow.

When my jailor will return to take me to my new prison.

Salvatore

I can't say that I regret what I've done. Not when I believe that it is necessary for Gia's survival. For her future safety.

But for god's sake, does she have to make it so fucking difficult?

I hadn't expected her to be grateful, or even to fully believe me. It was clear from that afternoon when she came into my office that Pyotr managed to thoroughly make her believe he wanted her for herself. That theirs was some kind of forbidden romance. But I hadn't realized just how deeply that went until tonight.

It's a struggle to get my emotions under control as I go into the bedroom adjoining Gia's. I hadn't intended to spend the night with her—this isn't a marriage of love, or one where I expect us to share a room and a bed. The quicker it was over, and the sooner she saw this as the necessary arrangement that it is, the better.

Or so I had thought.

Things had spun out of control. I grit my teeth as I close the door behind me, rubbing the flat of my palm over my stubborn erection. I'm angry that I let an eighteen-year-old girl's taunts get the better of me. That I let her foolish fantasies about Pyotr make me jealous, as if I'm a deceived lover instead of her guardian and protector.

That, when it came down to it, I *wanted* her with such ferocity.

My cock throbs, refusing to ease. My pulse throbs along with it, beating hollowly in my throat, and I stride to the bar, pouring myself another shot of cognac. I down it in one gulp, and pour another.

A small part of me feels guilty for leaving her alone on her wedding night. She's no doubt confused and emotional, still angry from what happened today and frustrated with the way the night was so abruptly cut off. But with the proof of the consummation there, I couldn't bring myself to go further.

I'll have to, eventually. In order to get her pregnant, I'll have to finish what we started tonight. But I can't do it while I want her as badly as I do right now. The guilt will eat me alive.

I need to cool down first. When emotions have settled, and I have a clearer head, I'll be able to make it about the business of getting an heir, and nothing else. I'll stop as many times as I need to, I tell myself, if it means not fucking her in the throes of lust.

I'm a grown man, not an animal. I can control my own desires. And when I have myself under control again, I'll finish taking Gia's virginity.

I toss back the second shot, pouring a third. It's easier said than done. My head aches. My cock is hard to the point of pain. And I can't stop thinking about the woman in the next room—my wedded *wife*—lying naked in bed, still wet between her thighs.

Fuck. I undo my belt angrily, flinging it to the floor, jerking down my zipper. My cock pushes free of my briefs and trousers almost immediately, impossibly hard, nearly touching my abdomen. I wrap my hand around it, hissing at the contact against my sensitive skin.

I can still smell her arousal. Still feel her wetness on my fingers. Hear the high, mewling cries she let out as she experienced pleasure at someone else's hand for the first time.

My hand slides along my cock, my arousal heightening. I feel as if I'm going a little mad with how she makes me feel, visions of her naked and arching up to meet my touch flooding my mind no matter how hard I try to think of anything else as I stroke myself.

She's going to make my life a living hell if I don't get her under control. If I don't get myself under control. I should be turned off by her brattiness —*that* has never been my kink—but with her, every word she spits back into my face only seems to drive me wild with desire that I didn't think I could feel for her.

I would laugh at the irony of it, if I didn't feel so much guilt. Just a few hours ago, I'd been worried I wouldn't be able to physically consummate the marriage. And now I'm standing alone in a hotel room, feverishly stroking myself to lustful thoughts of my unwilling bride.

Except she wasn't so unwilling when your fingers were in her.

I suck in a breath sharply between my teeth, my hand tightening around my cock. Every inch of her perfect, naked body is burned into my mind; more beautiful than I could have imagined. I can see her shuddering with the realization of pleasure when I touched her clit for the first time, feel her hot, tight heat wrapped around my fingers. She sounded sweeter than anything I've ever heard when she cried out for me, when she came—

I can see streaks of her virgin blood on my fingers, as I look dizzily down at the hand wrapped around my length. I should be disgusted with myself, but it only makes me harder.

Mine. My wife. Mine. My pulse throbs in time with the words repeating over and over in my head, my hips thrusting forward into my clenching fist, as I give up and give myself over to desire for a moment. I imagine her arching against my mouth as I teach her the pleasure of my tongue for the first time, her sweet, slick arousal on my lips, how good she would taste. The softness of her thighs wrapped around my head. I groan, stroking faster, letting myself think of what it would have been like to finish what we started, to sink into that tight heat, to give her my cock. To teach her what it feels like to have a man inside of her.

She's untouched, except by me. I could teach her everything. Every pleasure, every sensation, every *single* thing that can be done between a man and a woman. All of her is mine, if I want it.

If I let myself have it.

I feel my cock stiffen in my hand, veins pulsing as my balls tighten, and I grab a bar napkin just in time to cover my cockhead with my other hand, my cum spurting out with a force that nearly makes my knees buckle. I lean against the wall, groaning, eyes closed as I erupt into my palm, the cum that was meant for my bride wasted.

Because after all these years of discipline, of duty, one woman has already begun to unravel my self-control.

Guilt fills me the instant the pleasure begins to recede, everything coming back into sharp relief as the lust abates. I go to the bathroom to clean up, anger mingling with the guilt. Anger with Enzo, for making the deal with the Bratva in the first place, when he should have known the danger he was putting his daughter in. Anger with myself, for not stopping him. All of this could have been avoided, if I'd tried harder to make him listen to me when the marriage was arranged.

Except, I *had* tried. He just hadn't listened, because he wanted to please Gia. And as much as it pains me to think of my late friend as too tender-hearted, too short-sighted—those things were true when it came to his daughter.

Who is now my ward. *No*. My *wife*.

I strip out of my suit and get into the shower, intent on washing away all traces of the day that's now behind me. Tomorrow, I'll take

Gia to my home. She'll settle in, and we'll go about the business of finding a way to live together. She'll take on her duties as a mafia wife, and when her indignation about her 'ruined' marriage fades, we'll be able to handle the problem of an heir. With any luck, she'll be pregnant after a few nights, and that will be that. If she gives me a son, I'll never have to touch her again.

My cock twitches, frustration filling me instead of relief. *I don't really want her,* I tell myself. *It's an irrational reaction.* But it's hard to mistake what I'm feeling for anything other than genuine desire.

A desire that feels as if it will only worsen, the longer I deny it.

My cock stiffens, throbbing, and I grit my teeth. It's been a long time since I've gotten hard again so quickly. *What the hell is wrong with me?* I should have eased it, and that should have been that. *Is that all it takes? One forbidden young woman, and you're as horny as a teenager again?*

I thought better of myself than that, but maybe I shouldn't have.

I let out a sharp breath, and resignedly wrap my hand around my cock, bracing my other hand against the tiles. And no matter how hard I try to keep Gia out of my head as I stroke, sharp, hissing breaths of pleasure escaping me with every pass of my palm over my too-sensitive cockhead, she fills my mind anyway. The woman who I should be lying next to in bed right now, taking my pleasure with *her* instead of jerking off alone.

When I'm finished—both with my stubborn cock and the shower—I dry off and change into a pair of soft black pants and a T-shirt. My bag is sitting next to the couch, delivered along with Gia's, when I asked someone to send her things, and I get out the book lying on top of my clothes, retreating to the bed.

Tomorrow I'll be home, I tell myself again, hoping that if I reinforce it enough, it will be true. *Things will go back to normal.* Gia and I will sleep apart, and I'll maintain the same routine I have every night, the one I'm doing right now. An hour's reading, then to sleep, before the business of the next day. Gia will go back to being a part of my life, instead of a disruption.

It was simple enough, living with her at Enzo's mansion, after I took over her guardianship. She could be stubborn, frustrated with my attempts to fill in the gaps in her education on how to be a good mafia wife, but she wasn't impossible. We managed well enough.

She'll settle down, and my head will cool. Tonight was a product of the day's near-violence and fraught emotions, that's all.

I have to believe that, because the alternative—that my fractious bride will continue to try to make my life a living hell and my desire will continue to drive me insane—isn't a future I'm willing to accept that I've created for myself.

That with one impulsive decision, I've shattered my own personal peace as well as the future peace between families.

It's hard to focus, as I try to read. My thoughts keep drifting back to Gia—if she's calmed down or if she's still angry, if she's able to sleep, if she's safe. The latter I shouldn't worry about—her room is very well-guarded, and Josef was instructed to make certain everything was secure. But it's difficult not to worry.

I meant it when I said I took my responsibility to protect her seriously.

Frustrated, I close my book and set it aside, resisting the urge to go and check on her. If she's still awake, there's the possibility of another argument. And if she gets under my skin again—

I need to have myself fully under control, before I face my new bride in the morning.

I slide beneath the covers, switching off the light, doing my best to clear my head. The exhaustion of the day catches up to me quickly, and I'm on the verge of sleep.

And then, an all too familiar *crack* jolts me abruptly back from the edge.

Another, and another. I sit bolt upright, scrambling out of bed and instinctively grabbing for my gun. I know the sound of gunshots.

Moreover, I know them well enough to know the difference between the guns that my mafia are armed with—and the ones that the Bratva use.

They've come for Gia. And I was a fool to leave her alone.

Gia

I lay in bed, awake, for a long time after Salvatore left. I thought about trying to run, even though I knew it was impossible. I seethed. I plotted ways to make his life miserable, once we leave here tomorrow.

And eventually, I fell asleep.

My dreams are a tangled mess—fractured visions of my wedding gone wrong, heated flashes of Salvatore's hands on my body, of Pyotr walking with me in the garden. I half-wake once or twice, tangled up in the sheets, only to fall back into the dreams again.

And then, I'm snatched out of them by the sound of gunshots.

The sound is so close that it hurts my ears, bolting me awake. I sit up, stifling a scream as I leap out of bed on instinct, clutching the sheet against myself. I fell asleep naked, and I don't want anyone to burst in and find me like this. My heart is hammering in my chest, blood roaring in my ears as I run for the bathroom, closing the door and locking it behind me as more of the shots ring out in the hall.

I'm shaking as I lower myself to the floor in the darkness, wrapping my arms around myself, my teeth sinking into my lip as I fight back the urge to scream. *It's Pyotr,* I tell myself, trying to keep calm. *He's done exactly what you told Salvatore he would do. He's come to rescue you.*

But as much as I believe that, the violence that I'm hearing—the shots and the shouts and the faint *thud* of something hitting the floor—chills me down to my core. I've never been exposed to any of it. Our home was never attacked. My father kept me sheltered from the violence of our world. And as I huddle there, quivering, I feel vaguely as if I'm going into shock.

Terror spreads through me, my mind running away with itself, crafting a dozen horrific scenarios that have nothing to do with Pyotr or what we promised each other. Visions of the Bratva cutting Salvatore down, of the men set to guard me killed, blood everywhere in the hallway of the hotel. I want the husband I was promised—but I don't want anyone to die on account of it. I don't want Salvatore hurt, even though I'm furious with him, even though I feel betrayed.

My marriage was supposed to bring peace, not bloodshed.

None of this is your fault, I remind myself. *You had every intention of going ahead with what you promised. This is on Salvatore, not you.* But as the seconds tick by, I feel the cold fear spreading through me.

The sound of the door to my room slamming open jolts me, making me jump as I cover my mouth to stifle a scream. I scramble to my feet, looking for an escape as I hear more gunshots, this time in my room, inches from the door. A new fear floods me—the fear that I'm going to catch a stray bullet, that I'll get caught up in the crossfire and injured or killed while the Bratva are trying to come and rescue me.

Or maybe they're not, a tiny voice whispers in my head. *Perhaps you're worthless now to them, and they just want revenge.*

I shake my head, holding the sheet around myself as I frantically look for a way out. Those are Salvatore's lies about Pyotr and the Bratva poisoning my mind, not anything grounded in truth. If it is the Bratva, it's because Pyotr wants me back. What happened between Salvatore and me tonight is something that can be figured out.

Anyway, he didn't even really consummate the marriage. Technically, I'm still a virgin. Pyotr will believe me, if I tell him that. He has to.

My heart sinks as I scan the room, my eyes adjusting to the darkness. There's no way out, only a small window too high up for me to reach. One that I wouldn't fit through, even if I could get to it. And we're on a high floor—more than likely, it only leads to a deadly drop.

There's another rattle of gunshots, startling me, and this time, I *do* scream, feeling the blood drain from my face as I spin toward the door. I hear a groan, that heavy falling sound again, and then suddenly the rattling of the doorknob. I back up, shaking like a leaf, frightened tears springing to my eyes.

Another shot, the *ping* of something striking metal. And then the door swings open, and I see Salvatore, standing silhouetted in the doorway. His white t-shirt is covered in blood, spatters of it on his arms and face, his hair disheveled, and his face dark with rage.

Just beyond him, scattered across the now bloodied and ruined carpet of the hotel room, I can see at least four bodies. Maybe more.

I feel myself sway in place, my head swimming. "You're not doing a very good job of protecting me," I say thickly, just as he starts to stride towards me. "If that really is why you married me."

The room spins around me. My vision narrows. And just as I feel my knees give way, and the darkness rush up to claim me, I feel Salvatore catch me as I fall, his strong arms wrapping around my body.

And then, I pass out, as my vision narrows, both the room around me and the solid feeling of Salvatore's arms fading away into nothingness.

I wake to sunlight streaming through gauzy curtains, in a huge four-poster bed, in a room I don't recognize. My eyes feel sticky, and I blink several times, reaching up to rub them as I sit up. I'm still naked, and I reflexively clutch the blanket against my chest, as the events of last night start to come back to me.

The duvet I'm holding feels like velvet. The sheets underneath me are impossibly soft, the kind of astronomical thread count I'm used to at home. The room I'm in is huge, the bed in the center of it, a stone fireplace to my left. There are furnishings that match the bed frame—a wardrobe, a dresser, a vanity. A closet with double doors.

A wing chair next to the window to my right—that Salvatore is currently asleep in.

He's not wearing the bloody clothes from last night any longer. He's wearing dark grey sweatpants and a black t-shirt, and his hair is falling softly around his face, shiny and clean, as if he washed it last night. As I breathe in, I can smell the scents of soap and shampoo lingering in the air—he must have showered here, in the bathroom that I'm pretty sure is past the door next to the closet.

He didn't want to leave me, after what happened. It's the logical assumption, and I wait for it to soften something inside of me, to make me believe his story that all of this is for my own protection. My own good. I think of the violence last night, the blood and bodies that I saw, and shiver as my stomach churns with a sudden nausea.

I glance over at him again. He looks younger in the early morning light, asleep and relaxed as he is. I shift in the bed, biting my lip as I wonder if I should wake him—and then I see him start to stir, as if that slight movement was enough.

He opens his eyes, sitting up as he rubs a hand over his face. "Good morning," he says, his voice rusty, and I tense. His dark gaze meets mine, and the rest of yesterday comes rushing back to me, resentment filling me to meet it.

"Is it?" I cross my arms over the blanket I'm still holding to my chest. "Theft *and* murder in one day. You really are everything a mafia don aspires to be, aren't you? But nothing like my father."

Salvatore's lips thin momentarily. "Do you always wake up so combative?" he murmurs, sitting up straighter as he runs a hand through his hair. I try to ignore how soft it looks, spilling through his fingers as he looks back at me.

"Only when I wake up in a strange room, with the man who literally stole me away from my fiancé at the altar sleeping across from me." I glare at him. "What *happened* last night?"

He lets out a slow breath. "I'm sorry for leaving you," he says tersely. "It won't happen again."

I try not to make assumptions about what *that* might mean, yet. I have a feeling it's not something I'm going to like. "Why?" I ask instead, still glaring. "Why *did* you leave me?" I hadn't wanted him to stay—to sleep next to me—but it feels like the next logical question to ask. I have the distinct feeling that decisions about me are being made *around* me, without my input, and I don't like it. I like it even less when it seems like those decisions led to a shootout in my bedroom.

Salvatore sighs. "I thought it was better to put some space between us. With emotions as—heightened, as they were." He runs a hand through his hair again, watching me warily, as if I'm something he expects to pounce. "I planned to arrange for us to have separate bedrooms here. But now I've reconsidered."

"Where is *here*?"

"My home. *Our* home now, I suppose. Your things will be delivered today from your family home, don't worry," he adds, as if my primary concern right now is *anything* material.

"So you just decided that I would live here?" I feel my teeth grind together. "Am I going to be asked my opinion about *anything*, any longer?"

Salvatore lets out a long-suffering breath. "A wife moves in with her husband after marriage," he says slowly, as if speaking to a child. It irritates me, because not only am I *not* a child, but he certainly didn't seem to see me as one last night.

"Your wife." I press my lips together. "You should decide if you're going to look at me like that, or patronize me as your ward. You can't have both."

Something sparks in his eyes, dark and irritated, and I can tell I'm starting to get under his skin. *Good.* "So we're not going to have separate bedrooms?" I make sure he can hear the disappointment in my tone.

"No," Salvatore says tightly. "We'll share a room at night, so if there is an attack here, I'm better able to protect you. And when I'm not here, you'll have a heavy guard on you at all times." He says the last pointedly, as if to remind me that there's no use thinking about trying to escape. Just because we've changed locations doesn't mean it will be any easier for me to slip away, and try to go to the Bratva.

Frustration wells up in me. I had a chance to go back to Pyotr last night. I feel sure that he would have believed me, once I was able to tell him that Salvatore hadn't actually fucked me last night. But the more time that passes, the more likely it is that won't be true any longer.

Last night, I'd been frustrated at having my wedding night interrupted, aroused and not thinking clearly, wanting to find out all the rest of what I'd been promised would happen. But now, I'm back to dreading it.

Once Salvatore finishes what he started, there is very little chance that Pyotr will want me any longer. And then, any possibility of our marriage will be shattered.

"It was the Bratva, last night," Salvatore says quietly—as if I would have thought it was anyone else. "Trying to take you back, possibly. Or just seeking revenge."

"I told you Pyotr would come for me," I snap. Salvatore says nothing, and my stomach tightens. I'm angry with him for putting me in this position, and angry with myself for doubting Pyotr last night—for believing that the Bratva had come to kill me, too. In the light of day, my fears seem foolish. I remember everything we talked about, all the things we said to each other, and I'm ashamed I doubted him.

"What happens now?" I tilt my chin up defiantly, daring Salvatore to tell me what else he has planned. "What else have you decided *for* me?"

He breathes out slowly again, another long-suffering sigh, as if even sitting here and telling me is too frustrating for him. *You have no idea how frustrating I plan to make things*, I seethe inwardly, gritting my teeth.

"The sheets from last night will be sent to the *pakhan*," he says calmly. "Proof that the marriage was consummated. I doubt it will stop their plans for bloodshed. But it should stop any attempts to reclaim you, personally."

Something in his voice falters when he says it, as if he's not entirely sure. I grab onto it, wanting to exploit whatever I can. "It wasn't consummated," I point out. "Not really. You were too much of a coward to finish the job."

Salvatore's jaw tightens, and his eyes darken, his gaze sweeping over me once in a way that makes my skin prickle before he seems to regain his composure. "We'll get to it in time," he says stiffly, his tone harsh enough that I know I'm not supposed to argue.

It pisses me off. I'm not used to being sidelined, to not being heard, to being treated as if my opinion comes second to those around me. I'm not used to decisions being made *for* me. And I resent *this* decision, the decision about what happens to *my* body and how it's used, being made for me most of all.

"Are you sure about that?" I taunt, flinging the covers back. Dimly, in the back of my head, I'm reminded that if I taunt him into fucking me, my chances of going back to Pyotr are shattered. But I'm too angry to think clearly, and I want to get under his skin. I want to hurt him, to make him feel as frustrated and furious as I do.

It feels worth it, because I see Salvatore flinch, ever so slightly, as my naked body is entirely revealed to him once again—this time in the bright morning light. "Because if you can't manage it now, I'm not sure I believe you ever will. I'm going to be a virgin forever, aren't I?"

"Stop, Gia." Salvatore stands up, his face impassive, but I see the muscle in his jaw twitch. "You're acting like a child."

"Am I?" I lean back against the pillows, slowly spreading my legs an inch apart, and then another. "Or am I acting like a woman whose husband showed her how *pleasurable* marriage can be, and then left her cold?" I let my hand slide down the flat of my stomach, down to the soft curls between my thighs. "It sounds like you're going to leave me like that more often than not, now. I'm just going to have to take care of it myself, I guess."

I reach down, my fingers slipping between my folds, spreading them enough that if Salvatore looked, he could see all of the soft pink flesh between my legs. "Are you scared of your virgin bride?" I taunt, rubbing my fingers on either side of my clit. A rush of warmth passes over my skin, a tingle of adrenaline following it, and I realize I'm enjoying this. *Really* enjoying it. I feel wetness against my fingertips, my clit throbbing, and an ache begins to build. *I could get off like this*, I realize, and I rub my fingers against the sides of my clit again, letting out a small, mewling whimper. "That's okay," I tell him, enjoying the look on his face. He looks like a man tormented again, like he did last night. *Good*. If I'm going to endure this, so will he. "My fingers feel better than yours did, anyway."

I lock eyes with him, moving my finger so that it's rubbing against my clit, and toss my head back as I reach down and start to slide two fingers into myself, ready to give myself up to the pleasure—

—and feel Salvatore's hard grip around my wrists as he snatches my hands away from my body, pinning them over my head.

I let out a frustrated moan before I can stop myself, my teeth gritting at being denied. Salvatore is leaning over me, his jaw tight, and when I look down, I can see that he's hard. "So you're just a coward," I taunt. "You do want me. You're just so guilty that you won't do anything about it."

Salvatore lets out a frustrated growl, deep in his throat, and despite myself, I feel a shiver go down my spine. His hands slide down my arms, still pinning them in place, and for a split second, I think he's going to join me on the bed. That this is the moment he's going to give in, and take what he stole yesterday.

My heartbeat quickens. For a brief moment, I'm not entirely sure if it's out of fear or anticipation.

And then Salvatore grips my arms, more roughly than he has before, jerking me up out of bed and onto my feet. He shakes me once, his gaze dark and angry, and I flinch with surprise. He's never been this rough with me before, and this time, the quick skip of my pulse in my throat *is* fear. I wonder, briefly, if I've pushed him too far.

"What exactly do you think you're doing, Gia?" Salvatore growls, and I tilt my chin up, refusing to let him break me. To let him frighten me.

"You broke my father's trust," I hiss. "He *never* intended for me to marry *you*. For me to be naked in your house, for you to—" I break off, because Salvatore's grip on me tightens, his face taut as he glares down at me.

"Don't you dare." His mouth presses into a thin line, and I feel the edge of the bed press into my thighs, his body close enough to mine that I can nearly feel the texture of his clothing against my bare skin. "*Everything* I have done is to protect you, Gia! You can continue to protest, to call me a liar, to be ungrateful—but *I* know the truth. I know why you're here, and it has nothing to do with these...these perverted fantasies—"

"*My* perverted fantasies?" I try to wrench out of his arms, but his grip is too tight. "*You're* the one who had your fingers in me last night, you—"

"To keep from hurting you!" he roars, his voice filling the space between us until I can't help but shrink back. "You're nothing but a foolish girl who is naive enough to think your precious Bratva prince would have taken even a moment to consider your own body's limits before fucking you *exactly* as he pleased."

"Don't talk about Pyotr that way!" I scream back in his face, still struggling in Salvatore's grip, and he lets out a disgusted snort before letting go of me, taking a step back.

"You're deluded." He shakes his head. "Your father indulged you too much, but now I'm your husband, and I'm not going to do the same. Last night was about duty. The pleasure I gave you was to prepare you, so that I wouldn't hurt you when I took your virginity. It wasn't about my own desire."

A muscle leaps in the side of his jaw, and I still don't believe him. "Your cock is hard," I hiss. "You're a fucking liar."

He looks at me with something, that, for a brief second, almost looks like a flicker of contempt. *For me, or for himself.* "Your ignorance clearly extends to how a man's body works, Gia, despite your filthy mouth and overactive imagination." He takes another step back. "I've had enough of this. There's no argument to be had here, and I won't waste my time bickering. You don't understand, clearly, but you don't need to. You are my wife now, and I will handle things."

Rage boils up in me again, spilling over. "I won't be—*handled* like this! You can't just tell me what to do, make these decisions—"

Salvatore chuckles, but there's no mirth in it, as if he's not enjoying this any more than I am. "I can, and I will, Gia. Now get dressed. I'll give you a tour of your new home. *Our* home," he adds.

And then he turns, walking away from me and striding out of the room. I hear the lock click, and I let out a frustrated scream from between my teeth as I grope for the nearest thing on the nightstand —an alarm clock.

I throw it against the wall, and watch it shatter.

Gia

An hour later, I've managed to at least make myself look as if I've calmed down. But I'm still angry, my frustration simmering just below the surface. But I shower and dress and put my hair up. When Salvatore knocks on the door, unlocking it and stepping inside a moment later, I wait for him to say something about my choice of clothing.

"I didn't know if you expected formal dress *every* hour of the day in your own home," I snipe. "But at *my* home, I'm used to dressing mostly how I please."

Salvatore ignores me. He already knows that his insistence on dressing nicely for meals irritated me. I watch his gaze sweep over me, taking in my dark skinny jeans and soft teal-colored t-shirt, my makeup-less face, and the messy bun atop my head. "You can dress however you want," he says coolly. "I'm not going to give you a list of rules, Gia."

"Of course. You'll just make them up in your head and then reprimand me when I fail." I smile sweetly at him, but it doesn't reach my eyes. "Are you going to spank me when I'm bad?"

There's that twitch in his jaw again. A tell, but I haven't yet figured out if it means he's aroused or angry. Or both. "I don't have goalposts for you, Gia," he says tersely. "But I do expect a proper mafia wife. So I'm going to show you your home, and then you'll meet with the staff. All the things I said you needed to learn before your marriage will apply here. I expect you to oversee my household, arrange and plan the dinners and parties that will be expected, and make friends with the wives of my associates. And I expect you to do it pleasantly, and without constantly reminding me how *dis*pleased you are to be here."

"I can't promise anything." That sweet smile is still on my lips, but my tone is venomous. "Although I suppose you could find some way to force it. You're good at forcing promises out of women, apparently. Just yesterday, you managed to make me say vows I didn't mean."

Salvatore draws in a slow breath, and for a moment, I think he's going to shake me again. He certainly seems to want to. But instead, he turns and gestures towards the door. "Let's get on with the tour."

I step out into the hallway. We're on the third floor of the mansion Salvatore lives in. The floors are wood, the walls a soft blue, edged with matching dark wood. The room I just came from has a double door, and I see another matching suite across the hallway. They appear to be the only two rooms on this floor.

"The master suite," Salvatore says from just behind me, making me jump. He steps forward, opening the other doors. "I put you in the suite reserved for important guests. I intended it to be your room, once I brought you home. But as I said, the attack changed my mind about our sleeping arrangements."

Important guests. Home. I'm not a guest; I'm his wife, but this isn't my home. My home is a few miles away, a rolling green estate with lush gardens and a gorgeous mid-century mansion as the focal point of it all. This place feels strange, unwelcoming.

But I follow Salvatore's lead, and walk into the master suite, because I'm beginning to realize that I'll need to pick at least some of my battles.

It's a huge room. There's a fireplace at one end, French doors leading out onto a balcony, and a bed bigger even than the one I woke up in. It's very similar to the suite across the hall, except decorated in darker tones—deep greys—and with some of Salvatore's possessions neatly visible. An uncomfortable sense of intimacy fills me—I see his watch on the nightstand, the closet door cracked open just enough for me to see suits hanging inside of it. The air smells like him, like the woodsy cologne that he wears, and my stomach tightens.

He's going to expect me to sleep with him in that bed tonight, and every night that comes after it. He'll expect more, too—whether it's tonight or further in the future, but eventually—

Salvatore clears his throat. "Follow me," he says curtly, as if he saw my gaze linger on the bed for too long, and wants to put a stop to my line of thinking.

He leads me down a long, curving wooden staircase. It gleams in the sunlight coming through the tall windows from the top floor, down to the second floor. "The guest rooms are here," he says. "A few of them have en-suite bathrooms; others are simply bedrooms, with another large bathroom on this hall. If we have guests at any point, you are expected to assign rooms based on their status within the Family. I assume I don't have to explain to you how to determine that."

I shake my head. Truthfully, I'm not all that aware of which families hold the most status, which should be favored over the others. But I don't want to hear another lecture on holes my father supposedly left in my wifely education, so I keep my mouth shut, and let Salvatore assume.

"I don't think I need to show you through each and every one. Most of what I want to show you is on the main floor." He gestures to the staircase, and I follow him down to the stone-tiled entryway that leads into the remainder of the house.

"My study is there." He motions to the first door down a hallway to the left. "I prefer to be left alone when I'm working, but if you need me, you can usually find me there during the day. There is a library down here as well." He leads me down the hall, past the door that I assume goes to his study, and into the library.

It's a large room with another fireplace, leather seating scattered across the space, and floor-to-ceiling bookshelves. Salvatore looks at me, clearly expecting my approval, and I find that I don't want to give it.

"What? You think just because I mentioned once that I like to read, you'll win me over with this?" I shrug. "It's fine. The one I'm used to at *home* was bigger."

Truthfully, it's lovely. The library in my father's house was airier and more modern, but there's an old-world beauty to this room that catches my eye. Those same blue tones and dark wood, the leather seating all visibly buttery-soft to the touch, the stone fireplace built with varying shades of grey that give it a rustic elegance. But I'm not about to admit that to Salvatore.

Nor do I want to admit how gorgeous the rest of his home is. He leads me through a similarly decorated formal living room—only with fewer bookshelves and velvet seating, the rugs tufted in a rose pattern—and a semi-formal living room with a long, soft-looking sectional couch that has thickly knitted throw blankets folded over it, inviting me to curl up with a book in front of the fireplace.

"Did you tell them to put a fireplace in *every* room?" I ask sweetly, crossing my arms. "Or was that an accidental design choice?"

Once again, Salvatore ignores me. I press my lips together, forcing myself to keep my expression smooth, not to show how irritated it makes me that he can ignore me so easily, without consequence. I'm sure if I ignored something he had to say, I wouldn't hear the end of it.

He's clearly not willing to let me bait him any longer, but I know it's only a matter of time before I manage to get under his skin again. He can try to bolster himself against it, but I'm not going to let him have any rest. Not when he's taken me away from everything I wanted.

He shows me both dining rooms, the smaller one where we'll take our meals and the larger one where the dinner parties he talked about will be held. And then he leads me out of the glass doors at the back of the house, to the estate beyond.

"There's a swimming pool there." He gestures to where I can see a small building, and a fenced-in deck. "And the gardens and greenhouse are that way. My cook likes to grow some of her own produce, so she puts it to good use." Salvatore pauses, taking a deep breath, as if he's trying to summon his goodwill back. "I saw how much you enjoyed the gardens at your father's home, Gia. I thought you would like to see the ones here. You can make whatever changes you like. In fact, if there's anything about the house you would like to change, feel free to give me your ideas. I'm not so overly attached to any of it that I won't listen."

"I'd like to change the fact that I'm expected to live here." I pivot towards him, refusing to give an inch. Inwardly, I couldn't help but feel a small pinch of emotion that he remembered how much time I spent in the gardens at home once it was warm again, how happy it made me to be outside. But I won't let him manipulate me with it. "You can show me whatever you want, Salvatore. It doesn't change that this is a very beautiful prison."

His mouth twitches, ever so slightly. "So you're admitting you do like it."

"No!" I glare at him, taking an angry step forward. "I *don't* like it. I don't like being here. I don't like *you*. And I don't like anything about this situation that you've *forced* me into."

His jaw tightens. He looks down at me, and I can tell that he's close to his breaking point. I'm pissing him off, and I imagine the sexual frustration isn't helping. He can say he doesn't want me all he likes, but I can see the way he's looking at me.

"We're not going to do this every day, Gia," he says quietly. "I'm not going to indulge your desire to make this marriage one of utter misery—"

"Then you probably shouldn't have married me." I give him that falsely sweet smile again. "After all, despite watching me grow up, you really don't know me all that well, do you?"

"I know that even your father wouldn't have allowed you to be such a brat!" Salvatore snaps, and then instantly tenses, taking a step back. His anger is rising, and I can see him trying to control himself. I see him swallow hard, see his hands flex, see the way his eyes darken as he looks at me. He might *say* he doesn't like my attitude, but it's not only anger that's making him look as if he's on the verge of snapping.

And despite myself, a flutter of curiosity makes my pulse throb in the hollow of my throat, my own heartbeat quickening. The memory of Salvatore's long, deft fingers sliding over my heated flesh, the pleasure that rippled over me, the expert way he made me come—it all comes back to me, and I feel my breath catch in my throat.

I don't want him. *I don't.* But it had felt so good. Better than anything I've ever done alone, despite what I said to him earlier. And I can feel warmth spreading through my veins, a faint ache forming as I wonder what it would feel like if he did it again, and didn't stop. If he replaced his fingers with his tongue. His—

I shake my head to clear it, taking a step back. *It doesn't matter,* I tell myself sharply. *What matters is that I figure out how to exploit this. How to make his life miserable for what he took from me.*

Salvatore clears his throat. "Come with me, Gia," he says tersely. "It's time for you to meet the staff." He leans down as we walk back inside. "You're in charge of running the household now," he murmurs. "Act like it."

His reprimand burns. It infuriates me that he talks to me like I'm a foolish child, treats me like I'm ignorant, and yet clearly wants me as much as any man wants a woman. I pull away from him, following him into the large kitchen that faces out towards the gardens.

Waiting on us are the staff he wants me to meet. A tall, slender woman with greying hair, wearing a uniform-like outfit of black dress pants, a cream-colored blouse, and a blazer. Next to her is a stouter, but slightly younger woman, with blonde hair wrapped in a tight bun at the back of her head. Behind them are a handful of other staff, men and women, and I wonder if this is all of them or only the ones that Salvatore thought it was necessary for me to meet.

"This is Agatha." He nods to the uniformed woman. "She has handled the household for me for years, and she'll help you now. Frances—" Salvatore looks at the stouter woman. "My cook. And your personal maid will be Leah." He motions to one of the women standing at the back of the room, a girl who looks only a few years older than me with dark hair and eyes, wearing an outfit similar to Agatha's. "The others are my primary staff—in charge of cleaning, landscaping, and otherwise maintaining the house and grounds. They will follow your directions, unless they conflict with mine, in which case Agatha will come to me to discuss."

Resentment instantly spikes in my chest. "So I'm not really in charge."

I can feel the tension in the air immediately, and see the other staff glancing at each other out of the corner of my eye. Some of them clearly didn't expect there to be dissent between Salvatore and me, but when I look at Agatha and Frances, they don't appear surprised. *So, some of them have an idea of what's going on.*

Salvatore ignores my comment. "You can discuss the running of the house with them, Gia. I'll be in my office. I'll find you before dinner."

And with that, he turns and leaves.

I feel a prickle of unease as I turn back to the two women in front of me. I'm not at all prepared for this—if there's one thing Salvatore *is* right about, it's that I didn't learn as much as I probably should have about this sort of thing. But I didn't think—and still don't—that Pyotr would care about that. And I'm not about to admit that Salvatore has a point when it comes to any of this.

"It's a pleasure to meet you, Gia," Agatha says, although I think I can hear a hint of dislike in her voice. "Salvatore has asked me to fill you in on the running of the house, so that you can more easily manage it going forward." She gestures towards the table. "We can sit. Leah, you stay, along with Frances and I. The rest of you should go back to work."

"Shouldn't I be telling them that?" I ask sharply, and Agatha glances at me.

"You can save the sharp tongue for your husband, Mrs. Morelli," she says calmly. "I'm only following the don's instructions. We'll share the duties of running this place, and I'm sure that with my help, you won't feel *overburdened*."

The way she says it stings, as if she clearly thinks I'm a spoiled child. *Everyone thinks that.* Bitterness worms its way through me, because the Bratva *wanted* me. To them, I was a prize. *Pyotr* wanted me. Instead, I'm here, with a husband who refuses to fuck me, and a house full of staff who seem to think I'm an annoyance. Someone to be worked around instead of respected.

"Fine." I sit down, my spine ramrod straight as I look at her evenly. "*Fill me in.*"

The rest of the staff disperse, and the other three women—Agatha, Frances, and Leah—take their seats. "Salvatore likes routine," Agatha says. "Meals are served at the same time every day. Breakfast at seven, lunch at noon, and dinner at six. He takes his meals in the informal dining room, where I expect he'll want you to join him. During the rest of the day, he makes himself scarce. He expects neatness, and the staff is used to that, so I'm sure they would be pleased not to have to pick up after clutter, if that's your way."

I can't help but bristle at that. "I know how to pick up after myself."

"Leah will bring you tea or coffee in the mornings when you wake, at six," Agatha continues, as if I hadn't spoken. "So you can enjoy it in privacy while you get ready."

I realize, as she says it, that Salvatore must not have informed her about the change in plans—that I'm no longer going to have my own room, but share his. "Salvatore said I'll be sleeping with him," I say stiffly. "So she should bring it to our room."

It feels wrong on my tongue to say that. A brief look of disapproval crosses Agatha's face. "He told me yesterday, that as he had married his goddaughter, you would be put in the rooms across the hall from his."

"Things changed." I don't elaborate on *what* changed, because I enjoy seeing this woman squirm. Enjoy seeing her imagine that her precious boss's lusts overtook him, and he ravaged me on our wedding night, with every intent to continue doing it in the future, rather than the truth—which is that we were attacked, and he wants to keep me close for my safety.

Or so he said. I'm not entirely convinced.

"Well." Agatha clears her throat, and I see her exchange a brief glance with Frances. "Then Leah will bring it to you there. She'll handle your laundry, errands, and anything that you need."

"I thought I'd have Claire come here. The maid who took care of me at home." I know arguing is useless, but I can't stop myself from trying. Every plan I had for myself continually seems to be undone.

"This is your home now," Agatha says stiffly, echoing Salvatore. "And I'm following the don's instructions. If you disagree, take it up with him."

I intend to. I take a slow breath. "What else?"

"You are allowed to use the house and grounds as you please, but you are not allowed to leave the estate without the don's permission. All of the security is aware of this. If you wish to make any changes to the house, let me know, and I will see to it."

I clench my hands in my lap, my irritation rising by the second. *So now I'm not allowed to leave. To see my friends.* I want to shout at Agatha, but deep down, I know it's not her fault. It's Salvatore's. And I have every intention of taking it out on him.

Agatha stands up. "You can discuss meals with Frances. Leah, come with me. I'll make sure your things have been delivered, and Leah will arrange them in your room."

I nod, unable to speak. If I say anything, I feel like I won't be able to stop an outburst, and they'll think even less of me than they already do. My throat tightens, frustrated tears burning at the backs of my eyes, but I don't dare cry.

I want to think I was raised to be tougher than this, but the truth is that I wasn't. My father *did* spoil me, but not in the derogatory way that Salvatore likes to say. He didn't prepare me to have to face these kinds of obstacles, the attitudes of disapproving staff and a cold husband, because I wasn't *supposed* to have to deal with any of them.

If Salvatore hadn't interfered, I'd be happily married by now, settling into the home Pyotr and I planned to share.

Frances clears her throat, and I turn my attention back to her. "Salvatore can be particular about meals," she says calmly. "I can give you an idea of his preferences, and you can base the weekly menus on that. He prefers seafood and lamb most days for dinners, occasionally chicken or duck—"

"I don't care." I blurt it out before I can stop myself, pushing my chair back and standing up. I feel like I'm vibrating, like I need to get out of this room before I scream, because I can't stand to hear about Salvatore's *food preferences* as if nothing is wrong. As if any of this is how my life was supposed to go. "Make whatever you want. I don't care about any of it."

I see the look on Frances' face at my outburst. I can see *exactly* what she thinks of me—that I'm stubborn and spoiled, that I don't deserve Salvatore, who all of these people seem to like. But no one seems to give a shit about what *I* like, or want.

"Salvatore is a good man," Frances says, as if echoing my thoughts. "We were—surprised, to hear he married his goddaughter. But he must have had good reason." Everything she *doesn't* say is dripping from her tone—*he should have picked a better wife. Someone who doesn't stamp her foot and argue. Someone who isn't so spoiled.*

Briefly, I can't help but wonder if he might change his mind about the marriage, with so much pushback all around him. It's clear that the heads of his staff—whom he clearly respects—disapprove. That they don't like me, and thought this was a marriage of convenience, not a real marriage. That the idea that it might be more than that disturbs them. Maybe if he sees I'm not the only one who feels that way, he'll give me back.

But I know that's all but impossible now. It would be one thing if I could run away and get to Pyotr before Salvatore actually takes my virginity, or if Pyotr managed to steal me back first. I might be able to convince Pyotr that he would still be the first man to actually be inside of me, to finish in me, the only man who could possibly be the father of my future child. But as far as everyone in *our* world goes—

The marriage has been witnessed. It was public, in front of the other families, vows spoken in front of a priest, the sheets sent to be seen by the head of the Family and the *pakhan*. For us, it's all but impossible to dissolve now. Only my infidelity could do it, and maybe not even then, if the paternity of Salvatore's heir is proven, and it's his.

What it comes down to, simply, is that I'm not willing to give in just yet. I'm not willing to accept that Salvatore is going to be my husband, that this is going to be my life, that all of my wants are ash now, and my only future is what he's chosen for me.

And if that *is* true, I'm going to make him pay for it.

"I mean it," I tell Frances. "Cook whatever you want. Go nuts. Make what you know Salvatore likes. I don't care about any of it."

And then I turn on my heel, and stalk out of the room.

I need to burn off some energy. I feel like a trapped animal, and for the first time in my life, I wish I liked running. But that's never been my exercise of choice.

Instead, I go up to the master suite—I can't bring myself to think of it as *my* bedroom yet—and see Leah unpacking boxes and unzipping garment bags. "I can handle this," I tell her, but she shakes her head.

"It's my job," she says simply, and starts to put away my clothing.

Truthfully, she's right. And if I were home, I wouldn't object to it. I'm used to having most things like this done for me. But I'm tired of standing in place like a doll while everyone moves around me, and insists I do things *their* way.

I snatch a stack of clothing out of her hands. "I'll put these away," I tell her sharply, and she just looks at me for a moment, before nodding and turning back to another box.

I feel a little guilty for snapping at her. It's not her fault any more than it's anyone else's here besides my new *husband*. But he's not here at the moment for me to lash out at him.

I need to burn some of this off. I look for my exercise clothes, grabbing a pair of my favorite leggings, a sports bra, and a tank top, before going into the bathroom to change.

No one has unpacked any of my toiletries yet. Everything in the bathroom is painfully masculine, all of it Salvatore's. His razor, his shaving cream, and brush, and a bottle of his cologne. The room smells like him, and I can't help but think that despite how I feel about him, it's a pleasant smell. Warm and woodsy, and I breathe in before catching myself and shaking my head.

Once upon a time, I liked him well enough, even if I didn't pay very much attention to him. He was my godfather and my father's best friend, a fixture in our lives, but one that I didn't give much more consideration to than any other fixture. Like furniture that's always there, until you forget about it, or a painting you don't notice any longer. But now, he's set himself up to be the central part of my life. The thing around which everything else orbits.

My husband.

I suck in a breath, willing myself to calm down as I change and hurry past Leah to go downstairs. There's a workout room past the library that Salvatore showed me, and I'm looking forward to using it. It's well-appointed, with weights, a boxing bag, mats, and a few exercise machines. One of the walls is entirely a mirror, and I put one of the mats down in front of it, filling a water bottle and then settling in to stretch.

After a few minutes, the physical exertion starts to clear my mind. I focus on it, on the feeling of my muscles, the tension slowly flowing out of them as I go through my familiar stretching routine. When I feel warm and limber, I run through a few core exercises, and then go to where the free weights are racked.

This will help. It's already helping. The burn of my muscles, the repetition, the feeling of being stronger, it all helps. It's been the better part of a week since I've had time to work out, but I sink back into it easily, and the world fades away from me, Salvatore briefly forgotten. I promise myself that I'll make sure to do this regularly—if only so I can escape from my new reality for a little while.

I'm so lost in it that I don't hear the door open at first. I'm back on the mat, working through a Pilates routine with a video pulled up on my cell phone in front of me, when I suddenly look up and see Salvatore standing in the doorway.

"I'm busy." I look away from him, focusing on holding the stretch I'm in, my core tight and my legs scissored in front of me. But suddenly, I feel exposed. I can feel his eyes on me, on my body in the tight spandex, on the shape and flex of my lean muscles under my skin. All of it belongs to *him*, and I'm suddenly painfully aware of it, sweat prickling on my spine as I glance up in the mirror again. "What do you want?"

"You're going to be late for dinner." Salvatore shifts, leaning against the doorjamb. "You don't look as if you're about to be finished. And you'll need to shower and change. I believe I was clear that I expect—"

"I don't care what you *expect*," I snap. I let myself fall out of the position I was in, my concentration broken, and my good mood dissolving by the second. "I've been informed of how sacrosanct *your* routine is, by both you and your house manager and your *cook*, for fuck's sake, but apparently mine doesn't matter?"

Salvatore snorts. "I don't think you have a routine, Gia. Anyone as spoiled as you just does whatever she wants when the mood strikes her. At her own whim."

Anger instantly bubbles up in my chest, and I seethe. "Oh fuck you," I snap. "I'll go upstairs and change when I'm ready. And I'm not done yet."

I turn my attention back to my workout, and I expect him to leave. I hoped I put enough finality in my tone that he'd take the hint for once, and let me alone. But clearly, it wasn't good enough, because when I look up again, he's still watching me in the mirror.

"I want privacy." I look at him, moving my legs back and forth, my body in a V-shape. "You want privacy in your study, I want it in here." My voice comes out more breathless than I'd like, this far into my workout. Strained. The way I sounded in bed on our wedding night, when Salvatore made me come apart, his fingers between my legs. Inside of me.

"It's my house." Salvatore shrugs, his gaze fixed on me in the mirror. And I realize, with rising awareness, that he's having a hard time leaving. He wants to watch me.

Get back at him. Make him want you. Punish him.

I roll over onto my hands and knees, facing the mirror. For the briefest moment, Salvatore's eyes dip, down to the shape of my ass in the tight leggings. Down further, to the cutouts along my legs filled in with black netting. Back up to the mirror, fast enough that I could have missed it if I weren't watching him, too. I arch my back, moving into the next part of my routine, and I see Salvatore tense.

"I thought it was *our* house now." I stretch one long leg out and then another. I see his jaw tighten, and his gaze flick over me again. "So I should get places where I can be alone, if I want."

"I came to remind you about dinner." He shifts his weight, and when I look at him again, I can see the beginning of the shape of his cock in his trousers. I'm turning him on. If I were a betting woman, I'd guess that he wants to leave, but can't bring himself to.

He's not just lying to me about his desires. He's lying to himself, too.

"Well, I'm reminded."

"You're going to be late, Gia. You've been in here long enough."

"How do you know? Maybe I just started."

I see his eyes sweep over me again, taking in the patches of sweat on my clothing, the way it clings tightly to my damp skin. I see him shift again, see his cock thicken. "You didn't," he says tightly. "Stop making everything so difficult, Gia."

"I'm sorry." The tone in my voice implies I'm not sorry at all. "I didn't mean to make it so *hard*."

Salvatore flinches. His eyes meet mine, and he sees the challenge there. The rebellion. He takes a step into the room, and shuts the door behind him, flipping the lock.

My pulse leaps.

He strides across the room quickly, his long legs eating up the space before I can do more than move so that I'm sitting on the mat. He sinks down next to me, his hand suddenly pressed between my breasts as he pushes me down onto my back, looming over me. He's breathing hard, his chest heaving, his eyes gone dark with arousal.

"You're testing me, Gia," he says darkly. "What will it take for you to learn manners? A little bit of gratitude, even?"

"For what?" I glare up at him. "You *ruined* my life."

"No, I didn't." Salvatore meets my eyes, his own growing heated. "I saved you, but you're too—"

"Too what?" I fire back. "Don't say *too much of a child*, you fucking hypocrite, because you're not looking at me like one right now."

Salvatore's breathing quickens, his jaw tight. "You're right," he grinds out. "I'm looking at you like what you are."

"And what's that?" I whisper, feeling that warmth spread over my skin again at the look on his face, the rough desire in his voice.

Salvatore leans down, his hand still pinning me as his mouth moves closer to my lips. "My fucking wife," he growls.

And then his mouth presses hard against mine.

His tongue sweeps over my lower lip, sliding into my mouth when I gasp in shock, tangling with mine. He tastes like spices, with a hint of something sweet, and for a brief moment, my senses are overwhelmed with him—with the taste of his mouth, the heat of his body, and the ruthlessness of the kiss. The one, brief moment where he gives in to the desire he keeps denying he feels, and kisses me like he wants me.

And then he pulls back, his expression cold and hard. His hand stays pressed against my chest as the other slides down my side, his fingers hooking in the waistband of my leggings.

With one swift motion, he yanks them and my panties down to my thighs.

"What are you doing?" I yelp. My refusal to come to terms with the fact that Salvatore is eventually going to take my virginity aside, I do *not* want to lose it on an exercise mat. "You said you didn't want to hurt me when you fucked me! You will if you—"

"I'm not going to fuck you," he says stiffly, pulling my leggings down further, over my knees, down to my calves. "I'm going to teach you a lesson."

I stare up at him like he's lost his mind, while I try to ignore the sudden heat that washes through me the moment he says it. My blood suddenly feels too warm in my veins, my skin tingling, that ache forming between my thighs again. "What the fuck are you talking about—"

"Language, Gia." He keeps me effortlessly pinned with one hand, and for the first time, I realize just how strong he is. I noticed his muscles on our wedding night, when he took his shirt off, but it didn't really sink in. Even this morning, when he grabbed my arms, it wasn't as clear as it is right now.

That heat builds. The ache grows stronger. I feel the dampness between my thighs, a throbbing in my clit as my breath catches. And I know Salvatore sees all of it, and I hate him a little more for it.

"You're a spoiled brat," he says casually. His other hand, the one not pinning me down, touches my left knee. "You need a lesson in obeying your husband. I could spank you, lock you in our room, deny you anything other than time to think about your attitude. But instead, I think I'm going to show you how ridiculous you're being. Acting as if I'm hurting you when all I've done is protect you. When all I did on our wedding night was give you pleasure. And yet you still fight me and act as if you're a prisoner of war."

"You're hurting me," I hiss. "You're keeping me locked up in this house, confined to your estate. I *am* a prisoner, and I don't want you—"

"Don't you?" Salvatore's voice rasps, his gaze darkening. "Open your legs, Gia." He turns, reaching for one of the blocks that I used for my workout, and grabs my shoulder, lifting me up so that he can slide it under my shoulders. I start to try to twist away, but his hand holds me in place, his gaze full of warning. "Accept your lesson, Gia. Don't fight me.'"

I *want* to fight him. I want to thrash and scream and hit him. I want to run. But there's something else, too. A blooming curiosity spreading through me, and the memory of what he did on our wedding night, the desire to know what there is that's *more*. I don't want to let him follow through with whatever he's doing—and I'm also not sure I want him to stop. The ache throbs between my legs, and I look at Salvatore, suddenly frozen.

"Open your legs," he repeats, and nudges my knees apart. "Do as I say, Gia, and you'll learn another lesson in pleasure. Isn't that what you want?"

"Not from you," I hiss, and he laughs darkly.

He pushes my legs open with his arm, no longer waiting for me to obey. His hand slides down my stomach, down to the curls between my thighs, and I gasp as I feel his fingers slide between my folds, spreading them open. "Look," he demands.

"At what?" I hiss, breathless, turning my head away. "At you assaulting me?"

"I'm not doing any such fucking thing," he snarls, losing his composure for a brief second before regaining it. "You're lying when you say you don't want me, Gia. *Look*."

When I refuse, his hand leaves my chest, wrapping in my ponytail. He turns my head to the mirror, keeping my chin tipped up so that I can see my reflection. Half-undressed, my leggings at my ankles, my legs spread. Salvatore's fingers spread the folds of my pussy, displaying me for his view and mine, and for the first time, I see the most intimate part of myself.

He shifts, moving so that he's next to me, his voice in my ear as he holds me open. "Look at yourself, Gia," he murmurs, his voice low and husky. "You're wet, wife. Flushed and pink." His fingers rub along my folds, and I clench my teeth to keep from making a sound. "Your pretty little clit, about to peek out for me. To swell and harden, while I rub it for you. You've been a very bad girl. But this is your lesson—and your punishment."

Salvatore moves then, shifting behind me, moving the block so that suddenly I'm trapped against his chest. His legs move mine apart, holding me, his hand still spreading my pussy as his other moves to stroke my clit. "You're going to watch," he murmurs in my ear. "Watch while I make you come, Gia. See all your body's reactions to what I do to you. And then, lie to me again about whether or not you want what neither of us have chosen."

I start to snap that he *did* choose this, that he *did* steal me at the altar, but I can't find the words. The index finger of his other hand rubs over my clit, and I feel it swell and throb under his touch, more of my arousal wetting his fingers as a rush of desire tightens my stomach and makes me whimper.

I feel the vibration of Salvatore's chuckle at my back. "Good girl," he murmurs, his finger rubbing back and forth. My head starts to fall back against his shoulder, and he stops abruptly, his fingers entirely still on my aching pussy.

"Don't—" I start to say, and then stop myself, sinking my teeth into my lower lip. Salvatore's dark laugh spreads through him again, rumbling against me.

"You're already learning your lesson, wife. Good." He keeps his hands still. "Watch me, Gia. Look in the mirror. I won't let you come until you do. And every time you look away, or close your eyes, I'll stop. I don't care how close you are."

I want to fight him. I *do*. I don't want to obey. But the aching pulse that's taken up residence between my thighs is stronger than my will to resist, at this moment.

I open my eyes, and look in the mirror.

I look lewd. My face is flushed, my hair falling out of my ponytail, half-naked, while Salvatore sits behind me, fully clothed. And between my legs—

I'm a wet mess. The curls of my pubic hair are soaked, Salvatore's fingers spreading my swollen folds wide, my clit visible against his index finger. He has my legs open wide enough that I can see everything, down to my clenching entrance and the tight hole beneath, and I feel my face burn hotter with embarrassment.

"You're going to come for me, wife. And you're going to watch while I do it." Salvatore growls in my ear, and his fingers begin to move again.

He knows the rhythm I like, remembers it clearly from the first night he was in bed with me. His fingertip circles my clit slowly, then faster, up and down, stroking me with merciless precision as he keeps my pussy open for us both to see. I feel the ridge of his cock against my spine, impossibly hard, and I know he must be aching. But he only strokes my clit, rubbing faster, and then slower again, pushing me closer to the edge.

I want to come. That thought has begun to push everything else out of my head, demanding to be heard, for him to give me what I need. I whine before I can help myself, a whimpering moan spilling out of my lips as I start to try to buck against his hand. But his legs are holding mine open, holding them in place, and I can barely move. I can't do anything other than watch, and surrender to the pace he's set.

Salvatore slides the index finger of his other hand down, circling my entrance as he keeps stroking my clit. "Look at yourself," he breathes into my ear. "Look at your tight pussy, wanting to be filled. Wanting my finger." He nudges the tip against me, and I feel myself tighten, as if to pull him inside of me. "That's a good girl. Take it for me."

I feel him slide the finger inside of me, my pussy clenching around him, and I moan. I'm so close, all of the sensations heightened by watching as he touches me, by my embarrassment—lust, shame, and confusion all wrapped up together, and I watch as Salvatore starts to finger me. He slides it in and out, and my embarrassment mingles with fascination as I see how wet his finger is, how I clench around him, the reactions of my body as he pushes me closer to my orgasm.

When he adds a second finger, still stroking my clit slowly, I cry out. My hips push forward as much as I can, and I clench my teeth before I can say anything, before I can beg for his cock. *I can imagine how it would feel. Thick and hot inside of me, filling me up, thrusting hard, harder, fucking me until I come all over him*—the lewd thoughts fill my head like a litany. I gasp, moaning and twisting helplessly, hovering on the very edge of the pleasure I so desperately need.

Behind me, Salvatore is rock-hard. I don't know how he can bear it, if his desire is anything like I feel right now. If he *needs* like I do in this moment. I don't know how he can stand to make me come like this, instead of tossing me back onto the floor and fucking me.

The thought makes me moan, and Salvatore lets out a low groan, his hips shifting slightly, as if his control is fraying, too.

"Can you take a third finger, wife?" he murmurs in my ear. "Will you learn your lesson then, and come on my hand?"

I nod helplessly, desperate. I watch, trembling with tense need, as he slides a third finger to join the other two, stretching me lewdly. I gasp as I see him start to thrust those three fingers; my pussy opened wide, his other finger rolling over my clit. It presses down, rubbing, and Salvatore nips at my ear.

"Come for me, Gia," he groans. "Take your punishment, little wife. Let me teach you a lesson. I'm telling you to come. Come for me—"

His voice reverberates in my ear, the words flowing over me, and then they suddenly stop as I tighten, my entire body going tense as my hips buck upwards, and I cry out. I start to let my head fall back, but he uses his shoulder to stop me, forcing me to watch as he buries all three fingers in my stretched pussy up to the knuckles at the base of his hand, two fingers of his other rubbing my clit wildly. I watch as his hand glistens with arousal, wetting him to the wrist as it spills out of me, my clit slick and swollen, my pussy visibly throbbing as I come hard on his hand. I moan, the sound raising to a shriek as he keeps fingering me, keeps rubbing, his hips hard against my ass as I feel his cock throb against my spine, and I feel sure he's going to come too, that he's going to lose control and come in his boxers while he fucks me with his hand. The thought sends another spasm of pleasure through me, and I whine and twist on his fingers, wanting more. I want his cock. I want to be fucked, want—

Salvatore pulls his hands away, both of them on my knees as he holds my legs open as far as they'll go. "Look at yourself," he snarls in my ear, and I hear anger tangled with lust in his voice. "Look at that wet pussy. You'd come again for me right now if I fucked you. If I took that little clit in my mouth and sucked." His teeth graze against my ear, biting briefly, and I feel him shudder against my back. "Don't fucking act like I'm forcing you, Gia," he growls, and he reaches down, swiping two fingers through my pussy and making me cry out at the brief contact with my oversensitive clit. He presses them to my lips, and when I try to turn my head away, he spreads the wetness over my mouth. "You want to be fucked. And you can tell yourself that you don't want it to be me, but you're lying."

His hand presses against the flat of my belly, holding me against him for a brief second. His cock throbs, and I realize dimly that he's still hard, that he hasn't come yet. And then I feel him shudder again, and he pulls away from me, pushing himself to his feet.

I half topple onto the mat, my body still faintly pulsing with the aftershocks of my orgasm, pleasure making me feel soft and vulnerable. I watch him stride towards the door, not looking back, leaving me there tangled in my clothing.

He slams the door behind himself, and then he's gone.

Salvatore

I *have to get out of here. I have to get away from her.*

The thought beats in my heat in time with my elevated heartbeat as I slam the door of the exercise room, striding down the hall to my study. I yank open the door, bolting inside and shutting it hard behind me, locking it as I lean back.

I try to catch my breath, to steady my thoughts, but I can't. I can feel her heat on my fingers, breathe in her scent still. Wet and soft and tight, so fucking perfect, and she's mine. My wife. Mine to fuck whenever I please. Mine to take, to fill her with my cum, again and again, until she's pregnant with my child. Until—

My cock throbs, my balls tight to the point of pain. I need to come. And if I stayed in that room another moment, it was going to be inside of her.

I hadn't meant for it to go so far. Only to—

Only to what, Salvatore? The words are mocking, in my head. *To teach her a lesson, by fingering her in front of a mirror? What lesson was that supposed to be, exactly? What kind of punishment is making her come so hard all over your hand that she drenched you with it?*

All I'd been able to think, at that moment, was how angry she made me. How furious I was that she acted like I was assaulting her every time I touched her, like she didn't get wet for me last night, like she didn't moan and whimper when I let her feel what it was like to have someone pleasure her.

Like she didn't all but beg me to stay and finish consummating the marriage. To take her virginity. *And now she wants to act like a kidnapped bride.*

I hadn't grasped, until now, just how fucking difficult this marriage is going to be. How hard it's going to be to manage any kind of peace between us. How impossible it feels to control my desire around her. I thought I wouldn't want her, but I do, terribly. I want her with a desire that's rapidly approaching an uncontrollable intensity, and I don't know what to fucking do about it.

Neither my own guilt, nor her infuriating brattiness seems to affect it. If anything, it only seems to make me want her more.

I fumble roughly with my zipper, my hand wrapped around my cock before it's even entirely free. I lift my other hand to my mouth, breathing in her scent, licking the taste of her off of my fingers as I start to stroke. I wanted to eat her pussy, to spread her open and lick her until she came all over my mouth, but I knew if I did, I wouldn't be able to stop. I would have fucked her there, sweaty and disheveled, in front of that mirror, and she was right when she'd said I shouldn't finish the job of taking her virginity there.

But *god*, afterward—

My mind fills with images of her just the way she was as I fingered her, only now she's in my lap, naked and spread open, her back to my chest, kneeling on either side of my thighs as I hold her against me and sit her down on my cock. As I make her watch while I fuck her, my cock splitting her open, making her *mine*. My arm around her waist, sliding her up and down, one hand teasing her clit until she comes for me, drenches me, and admits that she wants this as badly as I do. Until her only thought is of *me*, and not the Bratva animal that thought he could have her.

Possessiveness fills me, a victorious lust at the idea that what they thought they could have is *mine* now instead. My breath comes in short, hard pants, my hand gripping my cock hard as I stroke it feverishly, imagining my hand on Gia's hips, her throat, holding her in place as I surge inside of her and fill her with my cum.

"*Fuck!*" I snarl between gritted teeth as my hand stutters along my length, my cock throbbing as the orgasm hits me, my knees nearly buckling with the force of it. I have just enough time to cup my hand over the tip, the heat spurting against my palm as I shudder with the wracking spasms of pleasure.

Pleasure that would be a thousand times better with her.

I suck in a deep, shaky breath, as I come back to myself. Once again, guilt settles over me, because I've lost control of my desires, my imagination. I've pleasured myself while thinking about things I shouldn't. And unless I manage to control myself, this is only going to get worse.

Or she'll settle in, and get bored of taunting me, and we'll find a routine. That's my hope—that Gia will stop acting out once she comes to terms with what has happened, and we'll learn to live in peace together. But twenty-four hours in, I'm no longer so certain that's a possibility.

Letting out a sharp breath, I go to my desk to find tissues to clean up, tucking myself away. Sharing a room with Gia presents another challenge—I don't want to face her right now, but I also need to change clothes for dinner myself. I open the door to my study, glancing out into the hall.

The door to the workout room is still closed. I head up to the master bedroom, and when I walk inside, I find that Gia isn't there. There's no sign of her yet, except for her things that Leah arranged—the sudden markers of a wife scattered around the room that, up until today, has always been wholly mine.

I find, surprisingly, that I don't mind it. I had wondered how I'd feel, sharing a space with someone when I never have before. I'm not too proud to admit that I can be set in my ways, that I've grown accustomed to a particular way of living, without anyone to interrupt it once I'm home and alone. But Gia has shaken all of that up, and I wondered if a part of me might resent that.

Instead, I look around the room—at the glimpse of her clothing hanging alongside mine, at the sight of her jewelry box sitting on the dresser, her books next to the bed—and feel an odd sense of comfort. Of no longer being quite so alone.

Unfortunately, I've married a woman who feels very much the opposite.

—

I'm already at the table when Gia comes down for dinner. When she steps into the room, my chest briefly tightens at the sight of her, and it's difficult to mask my indrawn breath. She looks beautiful.

I've seen her dressed up for meals before—at dinners with Enzo, at her home when I lived there after his death. But then she was my ward. Now she's my wife, and it's as if I'm looking at her with different eyes. Seeing her this way for the first time.

She's wearing a red dress with a fitted silhouette and scalloped sleeves, the neckline a modest sweetheart. It comes down to her knees, and she's wearing flats with it—there's nothing particularly sexy or seductive about the dress. But on her, it makes my mouth go dry, my cock twitching despite my frantic orgasm only a half hour ago. Her hair is loose, tumbling in soft waves over her shoulders, and I remember the brush of it against my cheek and neck as I made her come.

My pulse is beating hard. I clear my throat, trying to regain my composure. *She would be the perfect mafia wife*, I can't help but think as she sinks down into the chair next to me, *if only she would just behave. If only she could come to terms with how things are now.*

That's what I need to focus on with her. Her behavior. The expectations that come with this marriage. What the future needs to look like, in order for this to work without driving us both mad. Not my desire.

The first course is brought out, a French onion soup with Gruyere cheese melted over the top, and set down in front of us. One of the maids sets a decanter of red wine between us, and Gia reaches for it immediately, filling her glass.

"We need to talk about the expectations for this marriage," I say calmly, glancing at her, and Gia narrows her eyes.

"What? Are you going to tell me I'm not allowed to have wine now? I'm old enough to marry, but not old enough to have a glass with dinner?"

Three seconds in, and she's already testing my patience. "I'm not talking about that, Gia. Andrea came and mentioned that the conversation between the two of you was tense today. That you don't seem pleased with your new role, and she worries there will be too much friction in the house."

Gia raises an eyebrow. "I'm not pleased. I was *forced* into this, remember?" Her mouth thins. "Do you want me to lie?"

"I want you to behave as a proper mafia wife should. I want you to focus on your duties here, to this house, as I've always focused on my duties to your father—and now to his legacy.'"

Gia's expression instantly darkens. "Part of his *legacy*," she snaps, "was to have brokered a peace between the mafia and the Bratva. But you haven't hesitated to tear that down, have you? All so you could have his daughter in your bed. And then—" She smiles tauntingly at me. "You can't even manage to finish that."

"*This*. This is what I'm talking about." I set my spoon down, the soup momentarily forgotten despite how hungry I am. "Your attitude.

Your mouth. Your refusal to believe that those in charge of protecting you are acting to do exactly that. None of this is how a woman of your station, your wealth, your privilege, your *name* should act."

"Except I don't have my father's name any longer." Gia's voice drips acid. "I have yours. And who are the Morellis, anyway? No great mafia house I ever heard of."

My chest tightens, and I can feel the burn of anger behind my ribs. "Now it's the name of a don," I growl. "Because your father left it to me. He trusted me—"

"And what did you do with that trust?" Gia looks like she's on the verge of springing up from the table. "How *dare* you sit there and tell me about my *attitude*? About what *proper* mafia wives should do? You stole me, and then you can't even be a proper mafia *husband*. You tease and lust after me, only to never finish what you've started. One of the duties of a good mafia wife is to provide heirs, isn't it? But I can hardly do that when it's only your fingers that you've ever been able to get inside me."

I clench my teeth hard enough for them to grind together. "This isn't appropriate talk for the dinner table, Gia."

"Oh. Of course not. Because someone other than the two of us is clearly listening. Because it really fucking matters what room we argue in—"

"Language, Gia!"

"Oh, shut the fuck up!" She slams her hands down on the table, the crockery and wine glasses rattling as she starts to stand up. "You're not my fucking father, or my godfather any longer; you've made *certain* of that. So don't tell me how to speak. My *husband* doesn't get to tell me how to speak—"

"Oh, I certainly can." My voice is low, dark and dangerous, more so than I meant for it to be. "I could punish you for your attitude, Gia. For your outbursts. For your unladylike mouth. I just haven't yet, because I'm trying to keep things civil between us."

Gia takes a deep breath, her dark eyes sparking with anger as she looks at me. "I want out of this marriage," she says quietly. "I want to go back to Pyotr."

"That's impossible." I shake my head. "The sheets were sent to the head of the Family, and to the *pakhan*. The proof that your virginity is lost and the marriage consummated has been viewed by those who matter. You are my wife, Gia. You can fight me on this, or you can begin to accept how things are."

She sinks down into her chair, and her face looks paler than before. "So that's it. I'm married to a husband I don't want, doomed to sit around and wait for an old man to figure out how to *actually* take my virginity, because of a spot of blood on a sheet."

I frown at her. "I'm not an old man, Gia. And I think you already know that. I don't think you see me that way at all, to be honest. But you want to get under my skin. That, at least, won't do it."

Her eyes narrow. She can't say I'm lying—I saw the way she looked at me when I took my shirt off on our wedding night, the lust in her eyes this afternoon. She doesn't think of me as a decrepit old man, she only wants to mock me, and my virility seems to be the topic she latches onto first. "So what, then? Don't you want heirs?"

I let out a slow breath. "In time, Gia."

Frustration is written plainly across her face, and I frown at her. "I would have thought you'd be pleased I hadn't insisted on a full consummation yet. Considering how you feel about this marriage in the first place.'"

For the first time since our marriage, Gia gets very quiet. She looks down at her bowl of soup, not bothering to pick up the spoon. When the maid walks back in a moment later, trading out our soups for a Caesar salad with Frances' homemade dressing, she says nothing, only sits back a little for the maid to swap out the dishes.

It alarms me, a little. Gia has never, not once, been at a loss for words since the moment I took Pyotr's place at the altar.

"Gia?" I lower my voice, attempting to be calm. To sound comforting. "What's wrong?"

She swallows hard, taking a slow breath. She reaches for her glass of wine, sipping it for a moment, and then she looks up at me, her face suddenly sad. It startles me—I've seen her furious, and petulant, and demanding, and angry. But I haven't seen her sad for a while now, not since the first months after her father's death. It tugs at something in my chest, to see her that way now.

"I was an only child," she says quietly. "You know that, obviously. I always wanted brothers growing up. Even though I know my father loved my mother, and didn't want to marry again, a small part of me hoped he would. That he'd want an heir badly enough to give me a brother. I would have preferred an older brother," she adds, laughing softly. "I loved that idea, as a child—having an older brother who would protect me and look out for me. But I would have been happy with a younger brother too. Or a few of them." A small, lopsided smile curves one side of Gia's face. "So as I got older, and realized my father was never going to remarry, that desire changed. I started looking forward to being married myself. To having my own sons. I knew I'd be expected to have a nanny—that I'd probably want the help, some of the time. But I imagined that they wouldn't be raised by the nanny like a lot of mafia children are. I'd be their mother, truly. I'd tell them stories, make up adventures with them, and take them on trips. We'd go outside and create elaborate stories and act them out. So—" She shrugs, her face suddenly shuttering as she realizes how much she's said. "You talked about me having children so soon as if it were something I didn't want, Salvatore. But the truth is, I've been looking forward to it."

For a moment, I'm not sure what to say. Gia's stubbornness, her tough exterior, that defiance, and unwillingness to submit to the desires of others—all of that begins to be cast in a slightly different light. I look at her face, carefully smoothed out now as if she's realized she's been too vulnerable, and wonder how much of those personality traits aren't entirely what I thought they were. If her willfulness isn't only on account of her having been spoiled all her life.

Enzo didn't have a son. And I realize, for the first time, that she might have spent her childhood and early youth trying to be both a son and a daughter for her father. That Enzo, in allowing her to make so many of her own decisions, consulting her on things that a daughter typically isn't, might have been treating her as both, as well.

"You know how close I was to your father," I say quietly, resisting the urge to reach out and touch her hand. "I can tell you for certain that he never felt the lack of a son. He never desired more children —more than just you, Gia."

She looks up at me, and I can see the faint glimmer of tears in her eyes. "I imagine there's a lot that you could tell me about my father. Stories from when you were younger."

"There are." I sit back in my chair, looking at her. "Before you were born, we'd go to a cabin he had built in upstate New York, once a year. He loved the quiet. Loved to fish—which isn't a hobby you'd expect from a wealthy, influential mafia don." I can't help but chuckle, remembering it. "I was the one who cleaned and cooked them. Always his right hand, doing the dirty work. But I never minded it. Enzo was too gentle for a lot of what he inherited. I was the bridge between what he couldn't do, and what needed to be done."

Gia frowns at me, and I wonder what she's thinking. I can't read her face. "What about my mother?" she asks quietly.

"She was kind, like he was. They were a good match for each other. They would have been happier if they had been born different people, I think. But they did their best." It's the first time I've ever said that aloud, and I feel a dull pang in my chest. I, for myself, have never wondered what my life would look like if I had been born a different person. I've always accepted my place, my duty, and the life

I was given and looked for the parts of it to be grateful for instead of the difficulties.

Gia looks at me curiously. "Different people? Not mafia?" She bites her lip. "I know wealth didn't seem to matter to him so much. My friends—their fathers, their husbands…their brothers, even, it always seems like it's never enough. Never enough power, or wealth, or influence. But I don't think my father saw it that way. Even the deal with the Bratva—it wasn't about power. It was about trying to stop so much violence."

She gives me an accusing look, and I know what she's thinking—she's voiced her opinion on it enough times already that she doesn't need to say it aloud. I can feel the moment of intimacy between us fraying. Her walls are going back up, that vindictive expression on her face again.

I don't want her to go back on the defensive. But neither do I want to keep sharing stories of the past. It might soften her, bring us closer together—but I don't think that's what I want, either. I care for her—as someone I'm meant to protect, as a responsibility. I don't want it to become more than that. I don't want emotion that goes beyond duty to be involved.

That won't help anything. It will only make it more complicated. Make it harder for me to focus on my duties.

Silence hangs over the table as the maid comes in again, trading out our barely-touched salads for lamb chops and roasted potatoes. I feel a twinge of guilt—Frances has made a point to make one of my favorite meals, and she's going to see I've barely eaten. Both Agatha and Frances have worked for me long enough that they're more like family than staff, and I don't like to disappoint them—especially Frances. She's closer to my own age than that of someone who could be my mother, but there's always been a motherly feeling around her that I've found reassuring.

"What about what happened last night?" Gia says suddenly, looking up at me. "The attack at the hotel. Have you found out anything else about that?"

"It was the Bratva," I say flatly, reaching for my silverware.

Gia lets out a frustrated sigh. "I know that. I mean—*why*? Was it to take me back? Are they going to try again?"

"Don't get your hopes up." I look at her, and she glares back at me. "Don't pretend you aren't hoping they'll raze this place to the ground to come and get you, Gia. But this is a fairytale you've made up in your head. The *pakhan* has no use for you now that you're not a virgin any longer. Pyotr will no longer desire you now that you can't be his alone—"

"You haven't *had* me," she snips. "And he'd believe me if I told him all you've managed to do is stick your withered fingers in me—"

"Gia." I rub a hand over my face. "This isn't—"

"'Appropriate dinner conversation,'" she mocks my tone, narrowing her eyes. "What? Go ahead and tell me how I came on your fingers this afternoon. But make sure to include the part where you were so hard you jerked off in your office afterward."

I wince, and I know she sees it. A moment of weakness that she'll sink her claws into, I'm sure. *She must have heard me, walking past.* Guilt coils in my stomach, cold shame sinking into my blood, but I do my best not to let her see.

"The Bratva won't come here for you, Gia. And whatever their plans are, I'll protect you." I set my fork and knife down, looking at her evenly, doing my best to focus on the part of this that matters. Not her taunts, not my twisted desire, but her safety. "As long as you obey me, you'll be safe. My goal in all of this has only ever been to protect you. And here, no one will be able to get to you."

There's an expected flash of disappointment on her face. Anger quickly follows, and she tosses her head, her eyes still narrowed. "I didn't ask to be protected," she snaps haughtily. "I didn't ask for any of this. And they wouldn't have hurt me last night. All of this *danger* you're prattling about is your own creation, because you wanted me for yourself, and broke a treaty to have me."

"I've already said—"

"You bit off more than you could chew, though, didn't you?" she taunts, pushing her chair back. "You wanted your friend's daughter, but you can't satisfy her now that you have her. Poor Salvatore." Her voice rises, mocking, and something snaps inside of me. My gaze meets hers, level and hard.

"You were certainly satisfied earlier," I remind her coolly, and I see her blanch, her eyes sparking angrily.

"I'm going upstairs," she snaps, tossing her napkin on the table. "I'm afraid I've lost my appetite."

And with that, she spins on her heel, and leaves the room before I can say a word.

Gia

Salvatore doesn't come upstairs for a long time. I suspect he's trying to give me time to cool off, but I'm too angry for that. *It's only been a day*, I think to myself as I lock the bathroom door and draw a hot bath, nearly trembling with anger. One day, and I want to strangle him. I can tell he's not pleased with me either, though he does a better job of restraining his temper.

How am I supposed to endure a lifetime of this? A marriage I don't want, a husband I don't love, the promise of a future with both of those things stolen away from me. Children would make it easier. With children, I would have love. A way to occupy my time, something to focus on. But Salvatore won't even give me that.

No matter how I turn it over in my head as I lie in the bath, I can't come to terms with my situation. I can't be okay with it, as Salvatore seems to expect me to. He seems to think that I should just believe him—that I should accept that he's saved me from a terrible fate I don't understand, and acclimate to my new role as his wife.

He picked the wrong woman if he wants someone biddable. He's made it clear that this marriage can't be dissolved, that the Bratva wouldn't take me back even if he offered, but I don't believe him. I don't believe Pyotr would abandon me so easily. I don't believe that he wouldn't still want me, still love me, if I managed to get back to him. *It's not as if I willingly left him for Salvatore. I was stolen away.*

I close my eyes, trying to drift back to those hours we spent together at my home, sitting in the library by the fire, out in the garden in the warmer weather. Of the things we talked about—his future as the leader of the Bratva, his hope that our fathers' efforts would lead to peace. Of how our children would grow up safer, because I agreed to marry him. He liked that I talked back sometimes, that I would tease him, that I'd let him flirt and touch a little, and then pull away. We were good for each other, I believed. My father believed that, too.

So who does Salvatore think he is, to decide otherwise?

I'm so angry. I don't think I've ever been this angry at anyone or anything—even when my father died, it wasn't anger that I felt, but grief. He was ill—there wasn't anyone to be angry at. It was tragic, but I was *sad* about it, not furious.

Now, I feel like I'm full of rage, churning through me every time I really think about my situation, about what's happened. And every time, it comes back to Salvatore.

He's the one to blame. And I hate myself a little, too, for giving in to his advances. For letting him please me. For not resisting, and refusing to let my body be swayed by his touch, by his breath in my ear, by his all-too-skilled fingers.

I hate him, and deep down, I'm beginning to desire him. I want this to be over, to be free of this situation that I've been forced into, but I don't see a way out.

Not unless Pyotr steals me back. And Salvatore seems to think there's no possible way that can happen.

He wants me to be a quiet, proper mafia wife, fading into the background so that he can go on with his life, virtually unchanged after turning mine upside down. And while I don't have much control over anything else that happens, I can, at the very least, control that.

I'm not going to make this easy on him.

I get out of the bath, drying off, and slipping into a pair of soft sleep shorts and a tank top. Salvatore still isn't in the bedroom, and I get into bed, exhausted from the day and the roller-coaster of emotions. I'm glad he hasn't come upstairs yet—with any luck, I'll be asleep before he does.

I slide under the covers, in a strange bed, a strange room, and I miss home. I close my eyes, pretending that I'm back in my own bedroom. That my future still has the possibility of being everything I had hoped for.

A tear rolls down my cheek, just before I fall asleep.

I wake up with the heavy weight of a male body pressed against my back, one arm across my waist, holding me against a broad, warm chest. I smell Salvatore's woodsy scent, feel the tickle of the scruff on his jaw against the back of my neck, and I go very still.

He must have moved close to me in the middle of the night, while he was sleeping. I don't move a muscle, unsure of whether I want him to move away or not.

I've never been held by anyone like this. Never shared a bed with anyone. I should hate it—should hate having him so close, waking up in his arms, a reminder that I no longer have the right to even sleep alone in my own bed. But—I don't hate it as much as I should.

He feels good against me. Solid and warm, the muscled shape of his body curved around mine, my ass perfectly nestled in the cradle of his hips, my back to his chest. I feel him shift behind me, his cock hardening against the small of my back, and an unexpected jolt of desire sparks along my skin.

I hear him groan quietly in his sleep, his hand splaying over the flat of my belly, and my pulse picks up speed. I can easily imagine him nudging his knee between mine, spreading my legs, angling himself so he could slip into me from behind. I feel myself tighten in anticipation, warmth pooling in my veins, and I arch against him without thinking, pushing the soft curve of my ass against his growing hardness.

What the fuck are you doing? The words echo dimly in the back of my mind, but the rest of my thoughts are taking a different turn. *What if you seduced him? He says you can't go back. That you're stuck. What if, instead, you got what you wanted? Made him give in. Made him give you children. Made him give you something you want instead of only taking, and taking.*

I squirm again, grinding a little against the thick ridge that's now digging into my spine. Salvatore groans again, sleepily, his hand sliding up my ribs, almost to the curve of my breast beneath my tank top. I feel a warm ache between my legs, and I twist, my hand slipping between us to stroke the shape of his cock through the soft pants he wore to bed.

Salvatore's eyes flick open. For a moment, he doesn't react, the only response is his cock twitching against my palm, pushing forward eagerly at my touch. And then he seems to come fully awake, pulling away from me as the hand beneath my breast slides down and grips my waist to keep me from coming closer.

"Enough, Gia," he growls, his voice still rusty with sleep, and sits up near the opposite side of the bed.

My frustration is immediate. "You're really going to keep doing this? Even when I act like I want it?"

Salvatore narrows his eyes at me. "I'm figuring you out more quickly than I think you would like, Gia. For instance, I know exactly what you're doing."

"What's that?" I cross my arms under my chest, and I see his eyes flick to my breasts for a split second before they return to my face. He shakes his head, getting up.

"I'm not arguing with you five minutes after I wake up. Not even that, for god's sake." Salvatore runs a hand through his hair. "I'm going to take a shower."

I clench my teeth, watching him walk to the bathroom. His cock is pushing against the front of his button fly, and I catch a glimpse of the thick shaft through the gap in the fabric. He's huge, and I feel a momentary flicker of fear, but not enough to stop.

If he's going to insist on being my husband, then he's going to act like my fucking husband. I seethe for just a moment, watching as Salvatore disappears into the bathroom, and I hear the hot spray of the shower, before I fling back the blankets and stalk after him.

I throw open the door, ready to continue our fight—and freeze in my tracks.

Salvatore's black sleep pants are hitched down around his sharp hipbones, that deep cut of muscle mouthwateringly visible on either side of his thick, hard cock.

Which is currently in his hand, his fist sliding feverishly along it as he grips the counter with his other hand hard enough to turn his knuckles white.

It takes a moment for my anger to catch up. I've never seen this much of a man before. Salvatore didn't take off more than his shirt on our wedding night. Didn't take off so much as a stitch of clothing yesterday, while he made me watch him finger me. I stare at his cock for a moment, taking in the size of it, the vein throbbing along the top, the swollen head dripping pre-cum as he strokes. My mouth feels dry, that ache pulsing between my legs. I want him. I want him to fuck *me*, and he's in here jerking off.

"What the fuck is wrong with you?" I snap, and Salvatore jerks backward like he's been struck, letting go of his cock abruptly. It juts out between his thighs, and my curiosity is almost unbearable. I want to touch him. I want to *taste* him. I want to find out every forbidden thing that I've fantasized about for so long. "Why won't you enjoy your wife? I was squirming up against you five minutes ago, but instead, you're in here masturbating?" I can hear how angry I am in every word, and I can see in Salvatore's face that he can, too.

His jaw is tight. He reaches down, yanking his pants up over his throbbing erection, and I can see the frustration in his eyes. His hand is damp with his arousal, and he glares at me. "Mafia marriages aren't about desire," he grinds out. "They're about duty. I will get to my *duty* of fucking you and getting an heir when I'm good and damn well ready, Gia. And until then, I'll handle my desire as I see fit. *Leave.*"

It's an order. And I've never been very good at obeying those.

I cross my arms, glaring back at him. "Come back in the bedroom and fuck your wife, then."

"No." Salvatore's teeth grind together. "Get *out*, Gia. You've been spoiled all your life by being given exactly what you wanted, and it would only have hurt you in the end. It's long past time all that changes."

"I'm not leaving." I tip my chin up. "Fine. Go ahead and finish. I'll watch."

The muscle in Salvatore's cheek ticks. "I want my privacy, *wife*."

"Like you gave me mine yesterday?" I glare at him. "Should *I* make *you* come while you watch?" I take a step towards him, my gaze flicking back to his thick erection, and Salvatore closes the distance between us.

For a second, I think he's going to give in. I have a vivid vision of him sitting me on the edge of the counter, bending me over it, pushing me up against the wall. None of those are particularly comfortable places to have sex for the first time, I imagine, but with adrenaline filling my veins, the strange eroticism of our fight thickening the air between us, I'm not sure I care.

But instead, he grabs me by the shoulders, and backs me out of the room. "You are *my* wife now," he grinds out, his gaze dark with frustrated rage. "You will listen to me. You will obey me. And right now, I am *telling* you that you will leave me alone right now. You will get dressed, and go down to breakfast, and I will meet you downstairs. You will *not* argue with me. You will *not* continue to piss me off before I've even had my goddamn coffee, Gia!"

I feel myself starting to tremble, fear trickling through my veins, beginning to replace the desire. Cooling off the heat a little, though not all the way. I look up at him, refusing to show that fear.

"And what are you going to do?" I ask, sickly sweet, and Salvatore glares down at me.

"I'm going to shower. I'm going to jerk off while I do it. And you're going to leave me be until I'm ready to deal with you again."

"And if I follow you in there? What are you going to do about it?" I snip, and Salvatore shakes me hard, once.

"You don't want to find out."

His voice is cold and hard, and the fear is suddenly like ice, skittering down my spine. I suck in a breath, my eyes widening, and Salvatore seems to realize he's gone too far.

He lets go of me, taking a step back. "Just leave me be for a little while, Gia," he manages, his voice tight.

And then he turns sharply, disappearing back into the bathroom, the door locked behind him.

Breakfast is cold and silent. I pick at my oatmeal, studded with dried fruits, sipping at the coffee next to it. Salvatore doesn't say a word until he's finished his eggs and sausage, and then he stands up, putting his phone in my pocket. "I'm leaving for the day," he says brusquely. "Business meetings. Don't bother trying to run, Gia. It's not worth your efforts, and I'll know."

My heart sinks. I can hear the cold finality in his voice, and I know he's not bluffing. He looks at me, and his expression is so hard that I briefly don't recognize him.

"I know you don't believe me," he says calmly. "But the Bratva don't want you back for the reasons you think. Neither does Pyotr. And if you *were* to escape, you would regret it. I promise you that."

He strides towards the door, leaving without a backward glance. And it takes me a moment to realize that he didn't say whether the Bratva would make me regret it—or if he would.

The morning passes in a frustrated haze. I do my best to avoid the staff—Frances still wants answers about what to cook, Agatha wants to fill me in on more of how the household works, and Leah is probably bored out of her mind with nothing that I really need her to do—and I don't want to deal with any of them. I lock myself in the workout room and do Pilates until I'm breathless and sweating, the memory of Salvatore in here with me yesterday still burning in the back of my mind. I go upstairs to the bedroom afterward and make myself come, trying to ease the frustration, and take a shower.

I still have most of the day left. I could settle in somewhere and read, but my focus feels fractured. I keep thinking about how angry Salvatore was this morning, how cold he was when he left. I want him to hurt as much as I do, to be frustrated and miserable with his choice, but it's just now occurring to me that I could put myself in danger that way.

Salvatore says he wants to protect me. That his only goal is my safety. But he's also a man—a dangerous one, at that. My father's enforcer. Once upon a time, a mafia soldier. And he's my husband. According to every tradition that matters in our world, I belong to him. He can do as he pleases with me.

A shiver runs over my skin. It didn't occur to me that I might have cause to fear him. It gives me pause, just for a moment—but I'm still so angry that I'm not entirely sure if I care. A part of me *wants* to make him lash out, just so I can throw it in his face. So I can point out that he forced me to marry him to 'save' me from the supposed Bratva threat, and yet he's the one hurting me.

But he hasn't hurt me yet. Not really. He's just frightened me a little.

I flop back onto the bed after my shower, wearing nothing but my panties, wondering what to do with the rest of my day. It's a warm late spring afternoon, and I'm considering putting on a bikini and going down to the pool when a knock comes at the bedroom door.

"Who is it?" I call out, half-hoping it's Salvatore, come back early. If he walked in and found me like this, it would make it all too easy to torment him further. But on the other hand, I don't think he'd knock.

"It's Leah, ma'am." Her voice is timid. "There was a delivery for you."

That piques my interest. I have no idea who might have sent me something, but a small part of me hopes that it might be a gift from Pyotr. Something to remind me that he hasn't forgotten about me, that he still intends to get me back. To give me hope that Salvatore *isn't* telling me the truth about the Bratva's disregard for me now that I'm no longer a means to a treaty.

Pyotr loves me. I know he does. I know mafia marriages aren't typically made for love, but ours was different. That's why my father arranged it in the first place. He knew it was different, and he wanted that for me. A love like he had, when my mother was alive. What my marriage would have flowered into, if Salvatore hadn't stolen all of that away from me.

"Ma'am?" Leah's voice comes through the door again, and I grab my robe, throwing it on and belting it.

"Come in," I call out, and the doors open a moment later. I catch a glimpse of the curious look on Leah's face as she sees me in my robe in the middle of the afternoon, but my attention is quickly diverted by what she's holding in her arms.

It's a long, black matte box decorated with a wide black ribbon, a narrower box stacked atop it. "This came for you," she says, standing awkwardly in the middle of the room. "Where should I put it?"

"Um—you can set it on the bed." I get up, moving out of her way, and Leah quickly deposits it where I was sitting. "Thanks."

Leah pauses. "Is there anything else you need, ma'am?"

"No. You can just call me Gia," I offer. "'Ma'am' makes me feel very old."

She raises an eyebrow. "Alright," she says simply, and I resist the urge to let out a frustrated huff. At least Claire and I were friendly with each other. But Leah is stiff and formal, clearly unwilling or unable to try to be friendly. I wonder if it's how Salvatore has always run the house—but I've seen that Frances and Agatha are more at ease around him.

Maybe they all just don't like me. The thought irritates me, because I don't want to be here any more than they seem to want me here. It's not *my* choice.

"You can go," I tell her, my curiosity over what might be in the boxes overriding everything else. I'm still hoping it's something from Pyotr, and as soon as Leah leaves and closes the door behind her, I slide the ribbon off of the larger box and open it.

When I lift the lid, I see sheets of silvery tissue paper, a thin cream-colored card atop it. I open the card, and immediately see Salvatore's name in thick script.

My heart sinks a little. *Not something from Pyotr, then.* But I'm still curious, and I read the note, wondering what possessed Salvatore to send me a gift.

I believe our argument this morning got out of hand, Gia. I want to make it up to you. Inside is a gift that I hope you will wear tonight. I'll be home at seven, with plans to take you out to dinner.

–Salvatore

I bite my lip, more than a little confused. He was angry with me this morning, and cold, but he seems to regret it now. He wants to take me out to dinner—for what purpose? To soften me? To make me happier? I don't know what to make of it, but I lift the tissue paper, looking at what's beneath it.

It's a beautiful black silk evening dress. When I lift it out of the box, the silk slithers expensively through my fingers, and I can't help but be impressed by his choice. It's fitted through the waist and hip, splitting mid-thigh and spilling open from there. It has a sweetheart neckline and off-the-shoulder sleeves, and I can tell by looking at it that it's exactly my size. Next to it is a flat velvet box, and my heart flutters despite myself as I reach for it.

I've always loved beautiful things. I can't help it. I love gorgeous dresses and jewelry. I love things that make me feel good—luxurious toiletries, flowers, sweets. I bristle a little, thinking it, because I can only imagine what Salvatore would have to say about that—that I'm spoiled, that I've been indulged too much with things like that in my life. But for whatever reason, he's decided to be the one who indulges me today.

When I open the box, a set of diamond jewelry twinkles up at me. A pair of round diamond studs, surrounded by smaller onyx stones in a halo, and a delicate white-gold bracelet with alternating diamonds and onyx. It's beautiful, glimmering in the light coming in through the balcony doors. I reach excitedly for the other box, sure that it contains shoes to match.

It does. Sleek, black, and high-heeled, with the signature red-bottomed soles. I look at the outfit, and a small flicker of excitement tingles over my skin. The outfit is beautiful—seductive, even, and I wonder if Salvatore is setting it up for tonight to be the night that he finishes consummating our marriage. If he thought about what happened this morning, and has decided that he needs to finish his *duties*.

I press my lips together at the thought, a tangle of confusing emotions battling for supremacy. There's curiosity and a little excitement for what tonight might have in store, resentment at being considered someone's *duty*, and mingled fear and confusion over the possibility of tonight being *the* night.

Do I want this? Do I not? Ultimately, I know it's not up to me to decide. But I'm no longer entirely certain what I feel. I want to go back to Pyotr, but if that's truly not a possibility—

The memory of just Salvatore's hands on me makes me shiver. He's like a different man when he surrenders to his desire, one that makes me wonder what other things he could show me. Teach me. What other pleasures I'm unaware of that he has to offer.

I could fight him on it. I could refuse to put on the dress, refuse to go out tonight, dig in my heels, and remain stubbornly uncooperative with every little thing. But I suspect he wants to talk to me about something over this dinner, and a small part of me is curious as to what it might be.

So, an hour before he said he'd be home, I get ready.

The dress fits perfectly. It slides over my body, clinging in all the right places, the off-shoulder neckline framing my sharp collarbones in a way that I know looks enticing. I style my hair loose, curling it so that it falls down my back and over my shoulders in thick waves, and do my makeup lightly—a thin cat eye and a red lip. The entire effect, paired with the black heels and the diamond and onyx jewelry, is darkly seductive.

When I walk downstairs, precisely at seven, Salvatore is in the entryway waiting for me. He's talking to Agatha, saying something quietly enough that I can't hear it, and when my heels click on the wooden steps, he looks up instantly.

For a brief moment, before he has a chance to control his expression, I see the stunned desire on his face. His gaze sweeps over me, taking it all in, and my pulse leaps in my throat. For that moment, I forget how I feel about all of this, too. The heat in his eyes draws me in, the look of frank appreciation on his face making me feel older, more confident, beautiful. He's seeing me as a different person than the girl he once knew. And it makes me feel *good*.

And then his face smooths, carefully blank again, and the moment passes.

Salvatore clears his throat. "I'm glad you were agreeable to a night out," he says as I reach the bottom of the stairs, offering me his arm. "I thought you might argue, to be honest."

And just like that, I feel the frostiness between us grow again.

"I'm not difficult about everything," I murmur tightly under my breath. "You just feel that way because you *demand* everything."

Salvatore frowns, but he doesn't respond. Instead, he leads me out of the house and down the front steps, to where the car is waiting. The driver opens the door for us and I slide in, my heartbeat picking up pace as I remember the last time I was in Salvatore's car.

Only a few days ago, on my wedding day. I'd been angry and scared and confused, fighting back with everything in me, like a cornered, snarling cat. It hasn't been long enough for me not to immediately feel all of that again, my stomach tightening with the reminder of how different everything was supposed to be.

Salvatore picks up on my mood instantly, as soon as he gets into the car. "If you were going to be cold the entire night, you could have just said no," he says wryly, looking at me from the seat opposite mine. "You didn't have to agree, and then ice me out all night."

"Would you have let me say no?" I lean back against the cool leather seat, resisting the urge to fidget. Instead, I cross my arms beneath my breasts, feeling the silk slide against my forearms. "I wasn't under the impression I got a choice in any of this."

"You have choices, Gia. You can choose how you react to your circumstances. I thought when you came down the stairs, wearing what I picked out for you, that you'd chosen a different tactic for tonight. But it seems I was wrong."

"Where are we going?" I change the subject, unwilling to go back and forth on the subject of how much *choice* I have. "I assume dinner, based on the time."

"Correct." There's a hint of dry humor in Salvatore's voice. "Among my many business ventures, I own a restaurant in Little Italy—one that I think you'll find quite nice. I've directed my staff to close tonight, so that we'll have it to ourselves."

"Giving up a whole evening of profit, just to have dinner with me?" I raise an eyebrow. "I didn't realize I was worth so much to you."

"I think you'll find I have no shortage of wealth," Salvatore says dryly. "But I am looking forward to an evening alone with you, Gia, away from home, and just the two of us. I think we could benefit from a civil discussion over delicious food."

He emphasizes the *civil*, and I don't miss the pointed way he says it. He expects me to *behave*, but I have every intention of saying and doing what I please. It's the only freedom I have left, in this new life that Salvatore has chosen for us.

"We'll see about that," I murmur, looking out of the window at the shadowed treeline, the driver taking us from the outskirts of the city to downtown.

It's only been a few weeks since I was in the city, but with so much having happened, it feels like an eternity. I feel my chest tighten with excitement as the lights come into view, the skyline glittering in the dark as the driver turns into the tunnel and drives through it, out into the traffic-clogged streets.

It takes us another half-hour to get through traffic and to the line of businesses, shops, and restaurants where Salvatore's is located. The car pulls up in front of a tall brick building, and comes to a stop, Salvatore opening the door and holding it for me as I slide out. Warm yellow light spills out from the low windows of the restaurant, and Salvatore offers me his arm once again. Unthinkingly, I take it, suddenly curious. I had expected a more modern, fancier place, but this has a sort of rustic charm that feels enticing even from the outside.

When Salvatore opens the black wooden door and leads me in, I'm immediately struck by the scent of mouth-watering food. Fried garlic, rich olive oil, the fresh scent of tomatoes and basil—I can smell all of it wafting from the kitchen, and I feel my stomach clench with anticipation.

"The chef is excellent," Salvatore says, and I can see from the small half-smile on the edge of his mouth that he noticed my reaction. "This way, Gia."

The interior of the restaurant is beautiful. Worn brick walls, a large fireplace at one side, small black tables with matching chairs, and dark wooden booths with soft-looking black leather seats at the other. Further back, there's an area with tables more spaced out, in view of the kitchen, and Salvatore leads me there.

"This restaurant was a concept that I designed myself," he says casually, as he pulls out a chair for me. "The kind of comfortable, rustic atmosphere that you'd get in a restaurant in Italy, with warm textures and old-fashioned decor, but with the very highest quality food. All imported and prepared by an expert chef." He moves to sit opposite me at the table, and I look for a menu. "The dishes have already been selected—Emil said he wanted to design the menu tonight for us himself."

Another thing chosen for me. I start to bristle, and Salvatore lets out a small sigh. "It's meant to be a pleasant night out for us, Gia. Can you try to see it as that, maybe?"

I press my lips together. "Why?" I give him a challenging look. "Why do you care? You married me—according to you, Pyotr can no longer have me. I'm confined to your house and estate—according to you, the Bratva can't possibly get to me there. Your only goal in all of this was to prevent the Bratva marriage and 'protect' me. So why bother with all of this?" I wave a hand, indicating the restaurant around us, the kitchen where the food is being prepared. "What's the point?"

Salvatore looks at me, and I can see a glimmer of frustration in his eyes, but he appears to try to rein it back in. "Normally, we would have had a honeymoon, Gia. But the circumstances of our marriage have made it too dangerous for us to do anything like that. And beyond that—" He lets out a slow breath, and I see him briefly frown, rubbing a hand over his mouth. "I frightened you this morning," he says simply. "I'm sorry for that. I was frustrated, but it doesn't excuse my handling you roughly, or shouting at you. That's not the way I want to behave as your husband, and it doesn't befit my reasoning for marrying you in the first place—which was to protect you."

It's very close to what I was thinking, after he left this morning. I nod slowly, feeling a little caught off balance by his admission, and his apology. It's touching—more so than I want to admit. I don't want to let him see that he's made me feel something other than hateful anger towards him.

"We're both on edge," I start to say. "But—"

"It doesn't need to be that way." Salvatore sits back as a waiter dressed in all black brings a bottle of red wine and a plate of assorted charcuterie, pouring us each half a glass and then melting away into the background. "We can find a way to live happily, Gia, if—"

"You're wrong." I cut him off abruptly, refusing to allow my walls to lower enough to even consider what he's saying. "You cheated me out of both my chosen husband and my wedding night. You cheated me out of the marriage that *I* wanted. And, as you've pointed out, you cheated me out of a honeymoon. Pyotr and I—" I break off abruptly, because Pyotr and I never actually discussed plans for a honeymoon. But that doesn't matter. I'm sure that he had something planned, some surprise that I would have discovered the next morning, when he whisked me off to whatever destination he had in mind. "I don't even think that was the right call," I add haughtily, reaching for a piece of cheese. "Leaving the country might have been safer, if the Bratva really are such a threat."

I say the last sarcastically, still not believing that Salvatore has any real reason to think that the Bratva wants to harm me, only a desire to make me think that he needed to save me. But instead of replying sharply, Salvatore goes quiet, appearing to think for a moment as he reaches for his wine and dips a piece of bread into the herbed olive oil that the waiter brought.

"Why do you feel that way?" He looks at me curiously. "That it would have been safer to leave the country."

"If this Bratva threat *is* real, then wouldn't it be better to get me as far away from them as possible?" I make sure he can hear the doubt in my voice, that I don't really believe any of this. "They're going to know you took me home. Where I am. And maybe your mansion *is* difficult for them to attack, but that's what they're going to be planning for." I shrug. "But of course, I'm sure you know best." My tone is sickly sweet, but there's not a hint of actual affection in it.

To my surprise, Salvatore still appears to be thinking. "Maybe you're right," he says slowly. "My instinct was to put you behind a high fence and thick walls, with a heavy guard, and simply make it impossible to get to you. But maybe it would be better to take you somewhere else entirely, until I've managed to smooth this over."

Shit. I realize that, inadvertently, I've potentially given Salvatore a reason to take me even further from Pyotr's reach. I wanted to argue with him, but I argued a little *too* well.

He's listening to you, though. I can't help but feel myself soften, just a little. For the first time, Salvatore isn't dismissing my opinion or ignoring it. He seems to actually be taking what I'm thinking into consideration.

If Pyotr really wanted you back, wouldn't he have tried again? Wouldn't he have demanded you back from Salvatore? I bite my lip, wondering if he *has*, and I just don't know about it. I wouldn't be surprised if Salvatore simply didn't tell me.

"Has Pyotr tried to meet with you?" I ask suddenly, as the first course is taken away and the second brought to us—a Caprese salad with thinly sliced circles of mozzarella, fresh tomatoes, and basil arranged artfully on a patterned china plate. "Has he tried to bargain for me back?"

Something almost like sympathy glimmers in Salvatore's expression, and I feel a stab of anger in response. I don't want pity. I don't want him to feel *sorry* for me. He shakes his head slowly. "The communications from the Bratva are threats of violence, Gia. Pyotr is not bargaining for your return. If they want you, it's not for marriage. Pyotr has no intention of taking your hand any longer."

My chest tightens painfully. "I don't believe you." My voice cracks the tiniest bit, and I clench my teeth, hating it. I don't want Salvatore to see my hurt, my weakness. I want him to regret what he did, but I don't want him to see how fragile my heart feels right now. "You wouldn't tell me even if he did. You wouldn't want me to hope that he'll come for me. You want me to believe your lies about him, about the Bratva—"

Salvatore runs a hand through his hair. "Can we go even one meal without this argument, Gia? We're at an impasse. I know the truth—both about the Bratva and why I married you instead of allowing Pyotr to have you. You refuse to believe me, and I truly don't know what proof would change your mind, short of handing you over to them and letting you experience their cruelties first-hand. And that, of course, is not something I'm willing to do. I married you to spare you what your future with them would be."

"What future would that have been?" I spear a bit of the salad delicately, lifting it to my lips and following it with the wine. I watch Salvatore's eyes flick to my mouth, and I resist the urge to moan at the flavor that rolls over my tongue. Rich and salty and sweet all at once, it's some of the best food I've ever tasted. I can't wait to see what the rest of the meal has in store—but I'm not about to let Salvatore know that. I don't want him to know that I'm enjoying any of this.

"I'm not going to go into details, Gia," Salvatore says sharply. "I refuse to sit here, over a dinner that was meant to be a pleasant evening for us both, and regale you with horror stories of the Bratva's cruelty. Of the things your supposed *love* might have done to you. Of the things they would do to you now, if they got their hands on you. The example that they would make of you, to hurt me." His mouth tightens, and I see real anger blaze in his eyes for a moment. It makes my stomach tighten, cold flickering through my veins.

I don't believe him. I don't. All of my feelings about this marriage are predicated on the idea that Salvatore stole me for himself, because he coveted his best friend's daughter. That the Bratva threat is overblown, even a flat-out lie, to cover for what he's done. That without his interference, the marriage treaty would have gone off without a hitch, and I would currently be a blissful bride, loved up in Pyotr's penthouse as we discovered all the secrets of wedded happiness together.

But either Salvatore is the best liar in the world—or he truly believes what he's saying. I might be innocent and a little naive, sheltered by my father, but I'm not stupid. There's no artifice in his face or in his voice. His expression is hard, cold, his voice sharp, his eyes full of anger at the thought of what could happen to me. And it's the possibility that the latter is true—that he really believes I was threatened by the arrangement—that sends ice crackling through my veins.

What if it is true?

The thought is awful. It makes me set my fork down, swallowing hard as I dab my lips with my napkin and try to hide what I'm thinking from Salvatore. If what Salvatore is saying is true—if the Bratva would have hurt me, if they want to hurt me now, if all of this was a ploy—then it shifts my entire world on its axis. If that is all true, then Pyotr never loved me. All of our romantic afternoons together, the whispers and promises and fantasies, were lies. If it's true, then my father was a fool for making the treaty, not a crafty diplomat. And if it's true, then Salvatore really did save me from a terrible future, instead of stealing me away and ruining my life.

I'm not ready to face that. I can't. Just the thought of everything shifting so dramatically makes me shudder, a panicked feeling flooding through me. I'm only just recovering from the grief of losing my father. I can't deal with my world being rocked so thoroughly all over again.

I have to cling to what I've believed all along.

Across from me, Salvatore lets out a slow breath. "I want to shelter you from all of this unpleasantness, Gia," he says finally. "I would like to make it so that you can simply be happy, without fearing the complications of the Bratva or dealing with the knowledge of our current negotiations." He holds up a hand before I can say anything, his eyes narrowing. "Don't say that you can't be happy, on account of all of the nefarious ways I've ruined your life. I've heard that speech enough to have memorized it by now, Gia, so I think we can accept that I've heard you, and understand your position, even if I disagree with it."

He pauses as the server brings the next course—a veal bolognese in an elegant white serving bowl—and spoons it onto a plate for each of us. A new vintage of wine is poured, and Salvatore waits until the server has walked away before he looks at me, reaching for his wine.

"So where does that leave us?" I ask quietly. "You say you understand, but it doesn't change anything. I'm still your wife, and not his. I'm still trapped in your mansion, instead of living in a Bratva penthouse. I'm still—" I start to say *a virgin*, but my cheeks heat a little as I wonder just how true that is. I am in the most technical sense, but after some of the things Salvatore has made me feel—and some of the thoughts I've had—I don't feel very virginal.

Salvatore looks at me for a long moment. He's set his fork down, too, as if the conversation has also ruined his appetite, and I feel a small flicker of guilt. For all of the contention in our brief marriage, it does seem as if he tried to do something nice. Like this dinner really was planned to give us a chance to talk on neutral ground. I think of the dress and jewelry that he sent today, the carefully curated meal, all of which I saw as a more high-handed means of choosing things for me.

Or, alternatively, he's trying to spoil me. To make up for the situation. Designer clothes, jewels, a five-star meal put together by a private chef. That's another way to look at it—a nicer way.

But that might be giving him too much credit. *Don't let it soften you too much,* I warn myself. *It doesn't change what he's done.*

"Where does it leave us," Salvatore repeats the sentence carefully, reaching for his fork as I take a bite of my food. The noodles are butter-soft, the veal rich and perfectly spiced, the sauce full of flavor. It's exquisite, all of it, and I reach for my wine, trying not to let myself soften too much. *This could be a perfect night, if I wanted it to be.* The temptation is there, to accept my circumstances. I don't like being unhappy. I don't *want* to be angry.

"You might be right about a honeymoon," he continues. "Perhaps it would be a good thing, for us to get away. After all, it's not as if I don't have a means of handling things here, even from a distance. It could be good, to put space between you and the Bratva. And perhaps some time alone, elsewhere, could put us on better terms."

My immediate instinct is to lash out, to tell him that we'll never be on 'better terms,' not when he's undone my life so completely. But I wonder, as I twirl another bite of the bolognese around my fork, whether or not that's true.

He listened to me. He could have refused the idea altogether, just because I was the one who proposed it. He could have dismissed it as my being silly and spoiled, wanting a honeymoon for a marriage I've bucked against. But he took me seriously instead. *Maybe it isn't all bad.*

I push the thought away as quickly as it enters my mind. I can't afford to let myself soften towards Salvatore now. Because I only have two options. Either he's telling me the truth, and everything since my father arranged the marriage for me has been a lie—not an intentional one on my father's part, but on Pyotr's—or Salvatore is the one who's lying, to make me feel exactly what I am right now. To make me trust him, believe him, that all of this—tonight, the possibility of a honeymoon, his willingness to consider what I'm saying—is the truth.

It's easier to believe that Salvatore is a selfish man who stole me for his own desires than to believe that my father was tricked by the Bratva, and that all his efforts to do right by me would have only ended up hurting me in the end. So that's what I cling to, pushing the small voice that wonders otherwise to the back of my mind.

Salvatore finishes his food, sitting back in his chair as the server comes to take away the plates. "You're not arguing with me," he points out, and I force myself to smile, to paint that mocking, taunting curve on my lips that I know he's expecting from me right now. I don't want him to see how conflicted I am.

"Why would a girl argue about a honeymoon?" I tilt my head. "I've never been out of the country before. I wouldn't say no to that. Or to a luxury hotel, or five-star meals—"

"I get the idea, Gia," Salvatore says dryly. "I'll plan the trip, then. We'll leave in two days, if you have no objections?" The tone of his voice implies that he expects me to object, on principle, if nothing else, but I don't.

The trip will take me further from Pyotr, it's true—but a part of me *wants* to get away from all of this. From the grief of losing my father, the shock of my altered marriage plans, the loss of what I'd planned for my life. I don't think Salvatore's mind will be changed on this, now that he's agreed—and if I do argue, he'd likely say I'm being contentious on purpose and use it to discredit any argument I make in the future. So, I see no point in trying.

Maybe going somewhere new will help me heal from all of this. And if Pyotr really loves me, I reason, nothing will stop him from getting me back.

If he doesn't, then none of this matters anyway.

"I need to go shopping." I toy with my dessert fork as the server delivers an artfully plated piece of tiramisu, setting it between us. "I'll need some new clothes for the trip. New bikinis. I assume we're going somewhere tropical?"

Salvatore chuckles, a rare moment of humor appearing on his normally stern face. "I think I'd enjoy some sun and heat as well. Early spring here can't exactly be depended on to be comfortably warm."

"When was the last time you took a vacation?" The question comes out before I realize it. I didn't mean to ask him something personal —to sound like I actually give a shit. But as the words slip out, I realize something else.

I am actually curious.

I've known this man my whole life—in the sense that he's always been there, on the fringes of it. My father's best friend, his voice, his right hand. Before my father died, I saw Salvatore often in passing—at dinners where I was excused after the dessert course, before the men really started talking—as he was leaving the house after meetings with my father, at christenings and weddings and funerals, every event my father was ever required to go to that was also appropriate for me to attend. I've spoken to him casually a thousand times over the course of my life—a hello, a goodbye, a *how are you?* But before this, before my father died, he was never anyone of any consequence to me. I never thought of him as a *person*, only as a fixture in my father's life.

Like the bar cabinet in the living room, or a comfortable sofa.

But then my father died, and he became my guardian. And now, he's my husband.

He's no longer a silent fixture. He's a living, breathing, flesh and blood man. A man who is meant to share every intimate facet of my life.

And I truly have no idea who he is.

Salvatore considers my question, as if it's something serious, rather than what could conceivably be considered small talk. "I've never been on a vacation," he says finally, and my head snaps up, my eyes narrowing.

"What do you mean?"

"It's a simple statement." His mouth twitches, a little of that rare humor glimmering through again. If I didn't know better, I'd think I actually amused him.

"I don't like being laughed at," I sniff, dipping the tines of my dessert fork into the creamy, spongy slice of tiramisu on my plate. "Forget I asked."

Salvatore lets out a slow breath. "Your father was not a man who took vacations. Or rather, not in the sense of what you would likely think of one. I told you we went fishing together, in upstate New York, once a year."

I raise an eyebrow, trying not to wrinkle my nose. "That's not a vacation."

Salvatore laughs quietly, and I can feel the tension dissipating between us a little. He takes a bite of his dessert, and I become aware of the crackle of the fireplace on the other side of the room, the warm, low light, the intimacy of the moment. *Look at us,* I think grimly, my gaze fixed on the handsome older man across from me. *Having a conversation like a normal couple. Not a hint of an argument in sight right now.*

"Like I said." He takes another bite. "Not your idea of a vacation. But Enzo was never comfortable going too far from you for long. And he worried about taking you somewhere. He feared something would happen to you." He hesitates, and I wonder what he isn't saying.

If he's thinking of the threat he believes the Bratva poses, what he thinks my father almost unintentionally handed me over to, and not saying it because he doesn't want to fight with me again.

"He thought taking me on a vacation would endanger me?" I frown, reaching for the small glass of port that the server brought. I've had more wine with this dinner than I think I've ever had in my life, and my head feels a little fuzzy. "That doesn't really make sense." I *had* always wondered, though, why we always stayed so close to home. All of my friends have been on tours of Europe with their families, to other places in the States, often going on summer trips to Sicily. But my father never went to any of those Family summits, or took me anywhere at all. I assumed he was a homebody, but I know he could have afforded to take us anywhere he wanted.

Salvatore lets out a slow breath, his brow furrowing as if he's deciding what he wants to say, and how. "There's a lot you don't know about your father, Gia."

I stiffen at that. "I knew my father perfectly well."

"That's not what I'm saying." He holds up his hands, as if to stave off whatever barbed words I might fling at him. "I'm not saying your father was someone totally different, or you never really knew him, or trying to chip at your bond in any way. Alright?"

I feel a small flush on the high points of my cheekbones. *Maybe that was a little out of line.* "Alright," I reply calmly, and I see the slightest flicker of surprise on Salvatore's face, there so quickly that I almost miss it before it's gone.

"I've never been a father—to my knowledge," he adds, a wry twist to his mouth that sends an odd flush of jealousy through me. For some reason, even though I know Salvatore has been in bed with other women—he's forty-something, for god's sake—I don't like hearing it, or thinking about the reality of it. Especially not when he gets me free and clear, without a man ever having done more than briefly touch me before. "But I expect there's things that all fathers try to hide from their children. Things they see as weakness, maybe. I expect if I had a child, I'd want them to see me as strong. Unshakeable. Someone not prone to the weaknesses of other men."

I frown, trying to understand what he's saying as he continues. I never thought of my father as weak. And I certainly don't see anything weak about Salvatore.

"Your father loved your mother very much. It was a rare love match. He was inconsolable when he lost her, although he tried to hide it. And he was so afraid of losing you in some way. He coddled you, sheltered you, because you were all he had left of her. And he was hesitant to take you anywhere, to expose you to any danger. A car accident, a plane crash. An enemy who marked you as a target. A mugging gone wrong. Any of the ordinary dangers of life, and the inordinate ones that come with the life we live. He wanted to keep you as sheltered from it as possible. And that meant keeping you home, where nothing could happen to you."

Salvatore takes a deep breath, and I get the feeling that he's watching my face keenly, looking for my reaction. "I think maybe it's time to change that. The danger is as much at home as anywhere else now. And I think it would do us both good to have a change of scenery."

I can't think of what to say. I feel like I'm still absorbing everything he's just said to me.

"I didn't mean to upset you, Gia," Salvatore says quietly, and I look up, meeting his eyes. He looks surprisingly—concerned, as if he genuinely is worried for me. "I don't want to make you think less of Enzo. I would never want that."

"I don't." I shake my head, finishing my port and setting the glass aside. "I could never think less of him. He was my father, and he was a good one. Maybe that wasn't the right way to handle it, but—I can understand it." I bite my lip. "I can't really imagine what it would be like to love someone that much. I hope I'll do things differently. But I can't fault what he did."

Something crosses Salvatore's face, an emotion I can't read, or maybe one I just don't recognize. He straightens, his expression smoothing, as he sets his cloth napkin on the table.

"As long as you take a considerable amount of security with you, you may go shopping tomorrow in the city," he says, his voice brusque and businesslike once again. All traces of softness and intimacy are gone, the momentary closeness evaporated, and a clear demarcation of space between us once again. "You can have my driver take you. Meet your friends, if you like."

I feel myself bristle at being told what I *can* do, at being given instructions and guidelines. I want to snap back, to tell him that I'll do as I please—but the truth is that I can't. If I refuse his rules, I simply won't be able to go. And that chafes at me, too. It chases away the brief softness I felt towards him, reminding me of the imbalance of power between us. I'm not his equal, or his partner. I'm his duty. His responsibility. I might be his wife in the eyes of God and the law, but he won't treat me as anything other than one more thing to be managed and contained.

"Fine." I drop my napkin on the table, too. "Driver. Security. Whatever you say." The sarcasm is thick in my voice, and I know he hears it. His expression hardens, and he stands up, stiffly coming around to pull out my chair for me as I stand up.

Just like that, I feel the moment of possibility between us fade away, the room around us going cold as I'm snapped back into reality.

Gia

I wake up in the morning to a cold, empty bed. Salvatore is already gone for the day. In the brief amount of time I've shared a room with him, I've noticed a few small things that can only be learned by sharing private space with someone else—that he leaves his watch at the side of the bed, that he hangs his suit for the next day on the front of the wardrobe, his tie coiled neatly on the dresser next to it and his shoes lined up.

All of those items are gone, leaving only the book he was reading last night and his reading glasses atop it, sitting next to the lamp on the bedside table.

I sit up, rubbing sleep out of my eyes. I have a faint headache, undoubtedly from the amount of wine I drank last night. It made me foggy and sleepy on the ride home, and I passed out almost as soon as I got undressed and slid into bed.

Despite the assumptions I'd made about Salvatore's plans for the night when he sent me the beautiful dress, he didn't touch me. Didn't even try. He went into the bathroom and stayed there while I changed into a pair of modest sleep shorts and a tank top, and reemerged in those soft black pants and a t-shirt, as if to prevent any thoughts I might have about his bare chest.

Which is, as I recall, an uncomfortably nice chest.

I shake my head, clearing it. My innocence—or what remains of it, anyway—is still intact, and I don't know how to feel about it. I don't know whether I feel relieved that he hasn't finished the job, hopeful that it will mean Pyotr might still retrieve me, or disappointed that I'm still being denied the most basic part of a marriage—both the potential pleasures of the marriage bed, and the possibility of children.

And, possibly a little offended that he seems to so easily be able to stifle any desire for me, able to sleep next to me without giving in to the urge to touch me when he hasn't even really had me yet.

Is he, though? A memory of yesterday morning flickers back into my mind, of those soft black pants hanging off Salvatore's sharp hipbones as he gripped the edge of the counter with one hand, his other—

I shake my head again, hard. *I am not going to sit here fantasizing about this man.* Especially after last night, when he nearly drew me in, almost made me let down my walls, only to remind me of the absolute control he has over me.

A knock comes at the door. "Gia?" Leah's voice filters in from the other side. "May I come in?"

"Sure." I rub at my face as the doors open, and she walks in, balancing a tray that she sets down on the dresser. There's a covered plate on it, as well as a steaming cup of coffee and a glass of orange juice.

"Don Morelli has already left for the day, so I brought your breakfast up. Do you need anything else?"

I shake my head. "No. Thank you."

When she leaves, I reach for my phone. I sent messages to Angelica, Cristina, and Rosaria last night, to see if they'd want to meet me to shop today. I wondered if they'd be able to on such short notice, especially Angelica, who is married and has her own household to run. But there are texts from all of them, excitedly agreeing to meet me at a coffee shop downtown so that we can come up with a plan of action for the day.

I send a group message, letting them know I'll be there in a few hours, and slide out of bed. I feel a flush of unexpected excitement at the idea of a day of relative freedom—I'll be bogged down with security, true, but at least I'll be away from the estate and with my friends. It feels like a breath of fresh air after how things have been since the wedding.

The wedding. I wince, remembering the fiasco at the altar, the expressions on their faces. I have no idea what they thought then or have thought since. I've been with Salvatore every minute, my phone only returned last night so I could get in touch with them. I still have it, presumably because there's nothing I could really do with it to get myself in trouble. It's not as if I have Pyotr's phone number. Every meeting, every conversation we ever had was pre-arranged by our fathers, set up in a place where we could be watched. We never had a private word with each other.

I push thoughts of Pyotr out of my head, sliding out of bed and looking at the tray Leah left for me. There are scrambled eggs and a homemade cherry-filled croissant under the cover, and I reach for the pastry, taking a bite of it and a sip of the coffee. The room feels very quiet this morning, waking up alone, and I try to imagine living here for the rest of my life.

It doesn't feel like home. It feels like I'm a guest in someone else's room. Salvatore told me I could redecorate—ostensibly because he understood I'd feel this way and for some reason gives a shit—but I don't know what I'd want to do with it. I don't know what I could do to make this place feel like home.

I take another nibble of the pastry and another sip of coffee before I go and get into the shower, putting my hair up atop my head. Afterward, I dry off and spray a little dry shampoo and texture spray through my hair, running my fingers through it, and then go to get dressed. Jeans, a blue silk camisole, a thin grey cashmere cardigan for warmth against the chill outside, and a pair of high-heeled black ankle boots. I hesitate next to my vanity, and then reach for the diamond and onyx studs and bracelet that Salvatore sent me yesterday.

If I really want to be petty, I should never wear them again. I should banish them to a corner of my jewelry box and never look at them, forget they even exist, as if they mean nothing to me.

And they don't, I tell myself as I slip them into my ears, clasping the bracelet. They're just pretty, and I like pretty things. There's nothing deeper to it.

With that thought firmly in my head, I finish my breakfast, and go down to find Salvatore's driver.

By the time we're on our way, I'm thoroughly irritated. *Heavy security*, it seems, means two SUVs of private bodyguards following the town car I'm in, and one in the passenger's seat next to my driver. Unsurprisingly, Salvatore's number is in my phone, and I fire off a message as soon as I'm in the car, annoyance flooding me.

I don't need a private army to go shopping.

This is ridiculous. Even my friends, who are used to this life, will find it ridiculous. Insane, even. They always have one or two bodyguards following them when they go anywhere, but Salvatore has practically sent a company of mercenaries with me, like I'm some princess in danger of assassination.

Of course, that's not far from what he believes.

My phone buzzes, and I look at it, almost surprised he bothered to respond at all.

If you want to leave the house, Gia, this is how you do it. Or I could have a personal shopper deliver items for you to look at?

I resist the urge to throw my phone across the car. He *would* give me an order, and then follow it up with a ridiculous flex to remind me of how much wealth and power he has, that he can provide anything I require without my lifting a finger—even if I *want* to.

It's fine, I text back angrily. ***I guess this is just my life now.***

There's no response—not that I expected one. I let out a sharp sigh, craning my neck to see the SUVs following us. It's not just irritating, it's embarrassing. Proof of Salvatore's obsession, and his insane certainty that my life is in mortal danger.

What if it is? I remember the sound of gunshots in the hallway of the hotel, in my room as I'd crouched in the bathroom, more afraid than I've ever been in my life. I believed it was Pyotr, coming for me. But what if it wasn't?

The possibility flickers through my head again that Salvatore is right. That he has a reason to be so overprotective. But I can't let myself believe it.

I'm not sure I can handle that particular truth.

Angelica, Rosaria, and Cristina are all at the coffee shop when I walk in. The bodyguard who was in the car with me sticks close to my side, taking a seat at the table nearest them. I see four other men with similar builds and attitudes nearby—presumably my friends' security. The two teams that followed me over are no doubt spread out outside the building, making sure there's no one watching us, or waiting for us to head outside.

"Gia!" Rosaria is up first, heading straight for me to give me a hug. "We missed you."

"It's only been a few days." I laugh weakly.

"We don't normally go that long without hearing from you." Angelica chews on her lip. "We were worried. My husband—"

"Just give me a minute, and I'll explain. I'm going to get coffee."

I return a few minutes later with a raspberry mocha, courtesy of the heavy black credit card that Salvatore left next to my phone this morning. I have no doubt that it doesn't have a limit, and I plan to exercise that to the fullest today.

"What happened?" Angelica looks at me, her pretty brow creased as she taps her fingers against the side of her mug of tea. "All of that was—" She bites her lip again, glancing at the other two girls. "I heard my husband on the phone that night. I don't know who he was talking to. One of the other dons, I assume. They're concerned about Salvatore's state of mind, after that."

"What do you mean?" I ask, a little defensively. I'm not sure why, but the idea of the other dons talking about Salvatore behind his back upsets me. It shouldn't—I'm furious with Salvatore. He ruined my wedding and stole me. As far as I can tell, he gave in to selfish desires and betrayed my father. But—it's different if the other dons are talking about it. If they decide he's unfit—

"Well—" Angelica chews on her lip, and I can't help thinking that if she doesn't stop, it's going to bleed and ruin her lipstick. "My husband wouldn't tell me everything. He said it's not really for me to worry about. But he said that Salvatore helped broker that deal with the Russians."

"Of course he did. He was my father's right hand."

"Right." Angelica frowns. "So why would he destroy a deal he helped broker? It doesn't make sense to them."

"He says he thinks my father was wrong to make the deal. That the Bratva would have hurt me and that I would have been in danger with Pyotr." I wince as I say it. Saying it aloud feels like a betrayal of everything I thought Pyotr and I shared, of the future we planned together. I wait for my friends to exclaim that Salvatore is crazy, that my marriage was arranged for a reason, that he was wrong to step in.

But instead, Angelica and the other two exchange another look.

"What?" I press my lips together. "Just say it."

Rosaria lets out a slow breath. "We're all afraid of the Russians. You hear things—" She takes a nervous sip of her coffee, and the cup clatters a little when she sets it back down. "They're dangerous."

"So are we. Or the mafia, anyway," I point out. "But that doesn't stop you from marrying a mafia son."

"Marrying one of them is marrying one of us, though. You just said it," Rosaria points out. "Those marriages might not be for love, but we come from the same backgrounds. If one of us marries a son of a mafia family, we understand each other. What could you possibly have had in common with Pyotr?"

She doesn't say what she's really asking, but I can hear it. *Why would he want to marry you?* It makes me bristle. I know she doesn't mean to hurt me, but it does.

"He wanted me. He was—I thought he was falling in love with me." My voice cracks when I say it despite my best efforts not to, and Cristina automatically puts her hand over mine.

"I think what Rosaria means is that—what was in it for the Bratva? Not just Pyotr. But this was a treaty, you said. An arrangement for more than just what you and Pyotr wanted."

"I mean—" I bite my lip, trying to think. I've never really thought that hard about it. My father arranged the meeting, and I wanted Pyotr. My father wanted to give me what would make me happy. It was always as simple as that in my head. The part of it that was an arrangement took a backseat in my head. I only really started to consider what it meant when it became something to fling in Salvatore's face—first as a means to keep him from postponing the wedding, and then to remind him of his betrayal. "It *was* about what we wanted. My father wanted me to be happy with the man I married. He loved my mother, and he wanted a chance for that for me, too. So he introduced me to Pyotr, thinking we'd be a good match. And when I genuinely liked him, he let us continue courting. And I fell for him." I look down at my cooling latte. "But I've talked about all of this before."

"Right." Rosaria looks at Angelica, and back at me, and I have the distinct feeling that just like the dons have been talking about Salvatore since then, they've been talking about me. I don't like it. "That's what was in it for you. For your father, even, if his primary concern was your happiness." There's the tiniest trace of bitterness in her voice—I know her father has been working on arranging a match for her, and there hasn't been any concern for whether or not she likes the men he's been considering. "But what was in it for the Bratva? Not Pyotr, but his father? And the rest of them?"

"An end to all the fighting." The answer comes automatically, but it doesn't relax the expressions on Angelica or Rosaria's faces. Even Cristina lets out a sigh, as if it doesn't make sense to her.

"It's not like we're experts," Angelica says slowly. "But I've never heard my father or husband or anyone at all even hint that the Bratva have ever really wanted peace. As long as I've known, they *live* for bloodshed. They love violence. Why would they want to broker an end to it?"

"My father always says they're animals." Rosaria shudders. "I didn't want to ruin your happiness, Gia, but I was so worried for you, when you told me you were marrying Pyotr. I couldn't imagine how it would turn out well."

I feel myself getting tense. This isn't how I expected the conversation to go. I thought they would all be horrified at what Salvatore did, hopeful that Pyotr would save me, as invested in the future of my seemingly doomed romance as I have been.

But they seem to see Pyotr and the Bratva as the enemy as much as Salvatore does.

"I'm not saying what Salvatore did was right." Angelica takes another sip of her coffee. "I was shocked. We all were. Like I said, I think the dons are discussing options if this kind of—erratic behavior continues. After all, he only became don because your father didn't leave an heir." She says it matter-of-factly, but once again, I feel a flicker of defensiveness on Salvatore's behalf.

"He was always loyal to my father," I remind her. "Of course, he would inherit, since my father gave my hand to Pyotr and I didn't have a brother."

"I think that's part of it," Cristina says. "I hear things, too—my father talking over dinner and such. Everyone always believed your father would marry you into another Italian family, to pass the title on that way. Not give it to his right hand, and send you to the Bratva." She pauses. "I think they see it as a strange shift in loyalty on his part. It doesn't seem like his decision to make that treaty was discussed outside his own close circle. But again—" She shrugs. "I don't know everything. Or much about it at all, really. And you say it was because he wanted to make you happy."

"He did," I say softly. "And look what happened."

"What *has* happened?" Angelica frowns. "Salvatore threw the Bratva out and took Pyotr's place at the altar, said the vows—we all saw that. But then—the reception was canceled. We all went home. And none of us heard from you after that. We were all genuinely worried."

I'm not sure what to say. Suddenly, I don't know how much I want to tell them. If we were having coffee a few days after my wedding night with Pyotr, I know I'd be excitedly gossiping with them about how it had gone, if it had met my expectations, what exciting new things I'd discovered, and how passionately he'd made love to me. Angelica and I would be comparing notes, and Rosaria and Cristina would be hanging on to our every word, imagining—or dreading—their own wedding nights, but still curious.

But now...

I don't know if I want to tell them about my confusing wedding night, about the pleasure Salvatore gave me, only to abruptly stop as soon as he saw blood on the sheets. I can feel the heat start to crawl up my neck at the thought of telling them about what happened in the exercise room. It feels shameful, wrong somehow, to admit how Salvatore has made me come in the same conversation where I've talked about how much I wanted to marry Pyotr. It feels confusing to admit that even though I hate him nearly all of the time, sometimes I desire him, too. That I both want him to take my virginity, and not, all at the same time.

That the stern, forbidding man who took over as my guardian isn't the same as the muscled, virile man who came to my bed on my wedding night.

I'm not sure that I want to admit that I'm still technically a virgin, days after my wedding, or to explain the complicated situation. But as I look up and see the curious looks on all three of my friends' faces, I don't know if I'm going to get that option.

"I didn't think you'd be this shy about it!" Rosaria exclaims. "After all that time you spent flirting with Pyotr and hoping to sneak kisses on your dates. I thought you'd want to share all the details."

Angelica is looking at me more closely. "He didn't hurt you, did he?" She frowns, her eyes narrowing. I see a glimmer of something sympathetic mingled with the concern on her face, and I remember her recollection of her wedding night. It didn't sound pleasant, that's for sure.

"No." I shake my head. "He didn't hurt me."

"But it wasn't good?" Cristina clicks her tongue sympathetically. "He was so passionate about it at the altar, I thought maybe it would be."

"He—" I lick my lips, feeling embarrassed. I hadn't thought about how this part would feel, confessing this to my friends. "We haven't —yet."

Another look, exchanged among the three of them. I feel my cheeks heat. "He says he didn't marry me because he wants me like—that. He says he did it to protect me from the Bratva, and nothing more."

"So what happened on your wedding night?" Angelica's frown deepens. "He can say he's protecting you all he likes, but if there was no proof of consummation, then—"

Her voice is low, but I glance quickly around the coffee shop, hoping that no one else is listening in. "He was—getting me ready. And saw blood, and said that was all we needed. And then he left."

"And he hasn't touched you since?" Rosaria's voice rises sharply, surprised, and I glare at her.

"Don't shout about it," I hiss, and she winces.

"Sorry."

"No, he hasn't." It's technically a lie—Salvatore has definitely touched me since our wedding night. But not the way Rosaria means.

"But we're shopping for your honeymoon today." There's an ever-present note of optimism in Cristina's voice. "So if he hasn't yet, then we'll just have to find things for you to take with you to tempt him."

"What if I don't want to?" The question comes out before I can stop it. "I didn't ask for this. I didn't want to marry him. I wanted to marry Pyotr." I can hear the note of petulance in my voice, but surely, if anyone can understand being put in a position of being pushed into an unwanted marriage, it's my three friends. That particular Damoclean sword is hanging over Cristina and Rosaria both. It's already happened to Angelica. "Maybe I want him to stay out of my bed."

Angelica bites her lip again. "I know it's difficult," she says finally. "But you might be better off with the marriage consummated. It can't be argued against, then. You'll be safer. There's no risk of anyone finding out the truth."

"If she doesn't want him, though—" Rosaria ventures, and I feel my face flush deeper. I don't want to admit that sometimes I *do* want him. That I'm not as certain of all my feelings as I'd like for them to think.

"I think it's romantic," Cristina says suddenly, and everyone—including me—looks in her direction.

Her expression turns defensive. "What? He thought you were in danger and saved you. He risked a lot to interrupt that wedding. It was daring and romantic and well—" She presses her lips together, looking a little sheepish. "He's handsome. Come on, you all can't argue with me that he is."

I *could* argue, but I have a feeling it would fall flat. Because the truth is that Salvatore is gorgeous. I can't think of many women in the world who could look at him and not want him. He's the definition of rugged, brutal masculinity, a man unafraid to get his hands dirty, but also able to talk his way out of a situation. And I don't want to admit it, but seeing the way Cristina's eyes widen and hearing her voice soften when she talks about my husband that way makes me feel a flicker of jealousy.

My husband. I've never thought of Salvatore that way before with anything but disdain. Maybe he is getting to me. *Maybe all it took was a nice dinner out and the promise of a honeymoon.*

Angelica sets her cup down with an audible *clink*. "Well, either way," she says decisively, "we *are* shopping for your honeymoon. So let's start looking, and Gia can decide how tempting she wants her wardrobe to be."

With our security drifting behind us—and the small army that Salvatore sent with me thankfully blending in with the scenery and making themselves unobtrusive—we head towards the first of several stores. The only thing I really *need* are swimsuits—I have one nondescript red one that I've used for years when laying out at my family mansion's pool—but I'm not going to pass up an opportunity to abuse Salvatore's credit card. I can at least get that much out of the arrangement.

Thankfully, with it being early spring, the designer shops are full of breezy, tropical options. I try on a handful of sundresses, settling on a light yellow chiffon that comes down to just above my knees with a ruffle on one side of the skirt and thin straps, a palm-frond maxi with a low-v neckline and slits up the sides, and a light blue halter sundress. Cristina is of the opinion that the one with the palm-frond print will drive Salvatore crazy, and although I roll my eyes, the thought lingers in my head—the idea of him looking at me across a balcony in the middle of paradise, his gaze sweeping over me as I walk out into his view.

I feel a small flutter in my chest. I don't *want* to care about pleasing him, but a tiny part of me likes the idea.

For new shoes, I buy a pair of high-heeled Louboutin sandals with thin straps, woven espadrilles, and a pair of flat thong sandals for the beach. We browse through a jewelry store where I pick up a few pairs of hoop earrings, a dangly bracelet with diamond teardrops hanging from it like charms, and a matching gold necklace that will drape beautifully down into the neckline of the maxi dress.

We break for lunch at a sushi restaurant after dropping off the bags with my driver, and Angelica runs down the list of items she thinks I still need.

"Definitely some other clothes just for beach days—do you have any idea where he's taking you, exactly?"

I shake my head. "Somewhere tropical. That's all I really know."

"Some cute shorts and tops, maybe. And swimsuits, still. And probably a few *nice* dresses, in case you go out somewhere fancy—" Angelica trails off as I laugh.

"I have plenty of evening dresses and nice dinner dresses. And heels."

"No, what you *have* is an unlimited credit card," Rosaria points out with a grin. "Did he give you a budget?"

I shake my head. If there's one thing I *don't* think Salvatore is concerned with, it's money. I've never heard him mention an allowance or imposing limits on spending. Truthfully, he's avoided the topic of finances with me altogether.

"Then let's go nuts," Rosaria says with a grin. "There's nothing stopping us. After all, you should get *something* out of this arrangement."

It's what I was thinking earlier, so it's hard to argue with. And I don't exactly feel guilty—I hate when Salvatore calls me spoiled, but it's true that I was raised without much in the way of any limitations on getting what I want. The idea of blowing five figures on a shopping day doesn't faze me. And as long as Salvatore isn't going to come down on me for it—and maybe even if he did—I have no problem enjoying today.

I order a bottle of pinot grigio for the table, and the omakase menu for us all. For the next hour, we sit and chat about the kind of meaningless things we used to—theorizing about what tropical destination I might be going to tomorrow, discussing dress options for a charity gala Cristina is expected to attend with her mother next week, cheering up Rosaria with ideas for a bachelorette night if her engagement is finalized. A bachelorette party isn't a customary thing for mafia brides, but I want to reassure Rosaria, who is clearly dreading her marriage. If I have to, I'll convince Salvatore to let them all come over to the mansion for an evening.

I can imagine the look on his face if I suggested that.

When the last bite of sushi is scooped up, and we've polished off a second bottle of wine among the four of us, I pay the tab, and we head out to the next shop. Cristina has a devilish look on her face when we start browsing through the swimsuits, and I understand why when we get to the dressing room and she hands me what she has in her arms.

I mostly picked bikinis that were reasonably modest, as well as a couple of one-pieces with fun cutouts. I hadn't intended on using my swimwear as a means to torment Salvatore. But as I hang them up on the rack in the dressing room and see some of what Cristina has chosen, I can't help but think of what his reaction might be.

After all, my plan *has* been to make him rue the day he stole me at the altar. Either by making him as miserable as I've been—or, alternatively, driving him mad with desire while he continues to try to pretend that there wasn't a lustful thought in his head when he ousted my intended groom from the church.

I pick up one of the bikinis. It's comprised of what could politely be called scraps of black material, held together by delicate gold chains at the hips and breasts. I try to imagine Salvatore trying to conceal his reaction if I walked out to the pool in this, trying to pretend to be unaffected, and I feel a glimmer of cruel delight.

He wants the best of both worlds, in my eyes. He wants to style himself as my honorable protector, but also have me as his wife. He wants to tell himself that he'll come to my bed in due time when it's an absolute necessity, but he also couldn't keep his hands off himself five minutes after waking up next to me.

He wants me, and if I'm going to be forced to get used to the idea that he's going to keep me, then he's going to be forced to confront how he actually feels.

I try on the bikini with the delicate chains, stepping out of the dressing room to let my friends see. Angelica's eyebrows shoot up, and Rosaria giggles. Cristina grins.

"He's going to go crazy when he sees you in that," she says. Rosaria nods, biting her lip.

"You're going to have a wild honeymoon if you wear that." She blushes, obviously thinking about the possibility of her own honeymoon in the future. There's a look of apprehension on her face, but I see a curiosity there, too, that I recognize—because I still have some of that same curiosity.

It's at least half of what's responsible for whatever desire I feel towards Salvatore. At least, that's what I tell myself—that it's mostly curiosity. I repeat it in my head while I try on the rest of the bathing suits, settling on three more besides the black one. There's an emerald green option with a halter top that pushes up my cleavage in an eye-catching way with skimpy bottoms, a tiny white bikini, and a pink balconette style with a small ruffle along the top. It's sexy in an old-school movie star kind of way.

I buy the bikinis, and we stop at a few more shops, picking up some pairs of denim shorts and a handful of cute tops. Cristina insists that we stop in a lingerie store, and I feel an uncomfortable tightening in my stomach as we step inside the warmly vanilla-scented shop.

We're surrounded by lace and silk, velvet and ribbons, nightgowns and corsets and garters and stockings. Everything in this store is designed to seduce, to entice, to make someone desire the person wearing it. And I'm not even sure if I really *want* Salvatore's desire. I'm not sure how I feel about any of this at all. But as I pick up a sheer red nightgown with a ribbon tied at the cleavage, the reality of what we're doing hits me.

I'm going on a honeymoon. To an isolated place, for a length of time, I don't know, to share an intimate space with a man who I don't even know if I like. Who has yet to finish consummating our marriage. There won't be the vast space of the mansion to lose myself in, to avoid him as much as possible until I can't any longer. We'll be *together*. In a place made for romance.

We're either going to kill each other, or—

I swallow hard, trying not to finish that sentence in my head. I look around the shop, feeling suddenly panicked. "I'm going to the bookstore," I tell Cristina. "You can all look around if you want. I just—need a minute."

Cristina starts to protest, but Angelica shoots her a look. "That's fine," she says gently. "Just go take a minute. We'll come find you in a few."

There's no such thing for me as really getting a moment alone, or any kind of space, especially not now. I can feel my bodyguards trailing me, and even though I don't exactly know where the rest of them are, I'm acutely aware that they're there. But I try to pretend anyway that I'm on my own, walking down the chilly sidewalk to the bookstore a block away.

Inside, it smells like tea and paper, and I take a deep breath. I hear the door open and close behind me again, and I know it's my security, but I don't look. I keep walking forward, pretending that I'm by myself. That I can have a moment to collect my thoughts without anyone seeing me.

I head for the romance section. It might seem like an odd choice, considering the fact that my own love life is in such complete shambles, but the truth is that I want to lose myself in someone else's happiness. I scan the spines, looking for a few of the ones I love—usually historical or fantasy romances. I want to be swept away in the story of a woman being swept away by a rogue, or taken away to a vampire's castle, or seduced by an outlaw cowboy. I want something so far removed from my own life that I won't think about it for a while, and I can remember when I still felt hopeful about my future. When I still believed that a love like this was in the cards for me—a willful mafia princess and her bad-boy Bratva prince.

I scan through the titles until I find a few that sound good. I'm at the counter handing over the credit card when the door chimes again, and I see Angelica, Rosaria, and Cristina walking in. Cristina is holding a matte silver bag with the name of the lingerie shop in curling script on the side of it.

"Here." She holds out the bag, and I frown at her, confused. "We picked out a few things for you. Just in case your honeymoon goes —well."

"You didn't need to do that." I bite my lip, taking my books from the cashier. "You didn't need to spend money on me—"

Angelica snorts. "Please. Like we don't all have credit cards with someone else's name on them that we can use pretty much how we want."

I feel a small smile at the corners of my mouth. "Okay," I relent. "That's fair. Thank you."

Bags in hand, we head back to the car. My driver heads to a parking garage where their individual rides are waiting, and we all hug, exchanging goodbyes, and promises from me to take lots of pictures.

The doors close, and I'm left alone in the warm leather interior of the car, my stomach instantly in knots now that I'm alone with no distractions.

Tomorrow, I'm going somewhere far away with Salvatore. Somewhere that I've never been before. I'm excited and scared all at once.

It's making me realize that I haven't had many new experiences in my life. For all that, I was happy with it, right up until six months ago, it was a quiet, sheltered life.

Now I'm going on an adventure. And despite the company I'll be keeping, I can't help but feel a thrill prickle over my skin.

Tomorrow, I'll be somewhere I've never been before. He promised me somewhere warm, and I can't help but fantasize about where we might go—warm sun on my skin and the taste of salt air on my tongue, the smell of fresh tropical air. I can already feel the thrill of adventure, and I don't even know where it will be yet.

Regardless of who it is that I'm going with, this will be the most exciting moment of my life so far.

Gia

Salvatore is nowhere to be seen when I get home. I consider knocking on his office door, but I don't actually want to talk to him; I'm just curious as to whether he's even here. There's an hour until we would usually have dinner, but instead of changing clothes and heading down to the dining room just before seven to see if he's there, I go up to the bedroom instead.

Leah will bring up the rest of my shopping bags, but I grabbed the one with my books. I slip out of my jeans and cardigan, leaving my clothes in a pile on the bed, and go to draw a hot bath.

If Salvatore wants me to come down for dinner, he can come find me. I'm not particularly hungry after the big lunch I had with my friends, and the last thing I want to do right now is sit primly at the dinner table and try to dance around an argument with him.

What I want is to escape. And since I can't do that physically, I do it with one of my books instead.

I sink down into the hot, almond oil-scented water, letting it close over me up to my collarbones, letting out a sigh as the heat sinks into my muscles. I reach for my book, feeling myself relax as I open it. I picked the vampire novel—a story about a reclusive vampire prince who falls in love with an ordinary human woman, instead of marrying a vampire princess. Despite everyone who tries to protect her from him, he sweeps her away anyway.

Romance novels have always been my guilty pleasure. Most of the ideas that I have about what happens in the bedroom come from them—something that Angelica has often pointed out would probably lead to disappointment in the end. But I didn't think that would be the case with Pyotr.

It hasn't been the case with Salvatore, either, that little voice in the back of my head whispers. Aside from the crushing disappointment when he left me alone on our wedding night, every time we've come close to being intimate has been—

Stop it. I try to refocus on the page in front of me. I don't want to think about Salvatore, or his dextrous fingers, or the rasp of his voice in my ear as he urges me towards pleasure. I want to vanish into the pages of my book—or if I'm going to fantasize about anyone, I want it to be Pyotr.

I used to do that, before the wedding, while Pyotr and I were still courting. I'd lie in the bath, or in bed, reading a book and imagining Pyotr in the place of the hero. I'd close my eyes after a particularly good part, and replay it in my head—only I'd be in the place of the heroine, and Pyotr would be the one touching me, kissing me, making all those wild fantasies come true. I didn't even know if I actually wanted to do most of them, in real life. Some sounded better in theory than in reality. But the *fantasy* was always what was so good.

And I'd hoped that at least some of it could be a reality.

I try to think of Pyotr as I read. To imagine him storming the gates of Salvatore's mansion, intent on stealing me away and taking me back for himself. I try to imagine him gently pushing my hair behind my ear, looking down into my eyes, and whispering to me that it doesn't matter to him what's happened since we've been separated. That I'll always be the only one for him. That he would die to have me back in his arms.

But for the first time, it's hard for me to picture Pyotr's face. And as I read, suddenly it's Salvatore that slips into my mind.

Salvatore, shoving his way past startled wedding guests, his face hard and determined as he stormed up to the altar. Salvatore, facing down the Bratva *pakhan* as he put a stop to a marriage that he believed would hurt me.

Salvatore, holding my hand in his rougher one, looking down at me and swearing to protect me, *'til death do us part.*

And when I think hard enough about it, when I remember that moment without the veil of shock turning it to a haze, I don't think I remember seeing desire in his eyes.

What I remember is ferocity. Enough to stand up to an army of Bratva, if he had to, in order to make sure I walked out of that church with him instead.

What if I got this all wrong? I set the book down, closing my eyes. What if Salvatore was the one looking out for me all along?

I swallow hard, past the lump in my throat. This isn't my fantasy. This isn't what I had so carefully played out in my head.

But I'm not entirely sure that matters any longer.

When I'm finished with my bath, I put on soft, comfy clothes, and start packing. I could have Leah do it for me, but I'd rather do it myself and make sure that everything that comes with me is exactly what I want. I pack all of the things I bought with my friends today, as well as some of my other favorite clothes, and my toiletries. I pack my books, a few magazines, and anything else that I think I might need in order to keep busy while we're there. I have no idea what Salvatore's plans are for the trip. For all I know, he might tell me I'm confined to the hotel room for my own safety, and then spend the entire trip handling business elsewhere. It's not outside the realm of possibility.

I keep wondering when he's going to come up to our bedroom. But an hour passes, and another, and another, until I'm done packing and I've gotten sleepy. I crawl into bed with my book, with no sign of Salvatore, as if he's avoiding me. It makes me wonder if he's changed his mind and decided to cancel the trip, and is just avoiding the inevitable fight that will go along with that decision.

I'll find out in the morning, one way or another. So I turn off the light, and go to sleep.

—

"Gia."

Salvatore's voice wakes me. It's morning—the light is filtering through the curtains of the bedroom, and when I glance over at the clock on the nightstand, it says it's eight in the morning. I rub a hand over my face, sitting up sleepily.

"What?"

He frowns. "The private jet leaves in three hours. Leah can take your things downstairs. Go ahead and get dressed, and meet me in the entryway in an hour and a half. She'll bring your breakfast up."

Everything he says is curt, brusque, without any emotion. I sit up fully, pushing my hair behind my ears. "Where were you last night?"

He ignores my question, as if I didn't say anything. "An hour and a half, Gia. Try not to be late.'"

And then he turns on his heel, and strides out of the room.

I watch him go, frowning. There's none of the attempts at softness or intimacy from our dinner together the night before last. He's entirely closed off, and I'm not sure why.

A small suspicion wriggles its way into my head. *What if he was with someone last night?*

It's entirely possible. Mafia husbands aren't known for being faithful. Marriages like my parents' are the exception, not the rule. Most mafia men have mistresses on the side, girlfriends, or women at clubs that they go and visit when they want something exotic. Even as sheltered as I've been all my life, I'm aware of that.

It would be perfectly normal, in terms of what's acceptable in our world, for Salvatore to have someone on the side. In fact, most people—my friends included, most likely—would think I was the strange one for being upset about it. Mafia wives are supposed to accept that their husbands philander, as long as they're discreet and don't get other women pregnant.

I *shouldn't* be upset about it. I should be glad, if anything, that there's a possibility Salvatore is taking care of his needs elsewhere and leaving me alone. Leaving me still technically virginal enough to marry Pyotr, if Pyotr were to come and rescue me.

But the thought of Salvatore with someone else sends an irrational flood of jealousy through me, making my chest tighten and my stomach churn. I think of his hands on another woman, making her moan, his lips at her ear whispering the filthy, encouraging things he whispered to me in the workout room, calling her his *good girl*, and I grit my teeth, wanting to scream.

How dare he be with someone else, when he hasn't even finished the job with me?

I throw back the covers, striding to the closet to get dressed. I don't have any proof of it, but the suspicion worms deeper. He probably wanted to enjoy himself before being trapped for however long on a honeymoon with a wife that he apparently has no intention of fucking. But he doesn't know what's about to hit him. I think of the bikinis I picked out, some of the skimpy clothes, and I'm filled with fresh determination to make his part of this trip as difficult as possible.

I'm going to make it an utter misery for him to keep his hands off of me. I'm going to make sure he has to face exactly what he feels, and think about what he's done.

I throw on a blue and white sundress and a pair of flat sandals, put my hair up in a bun, and add a pair of rose gold and diamond hoop earrings. My luggage is all stacked neatly by the door, and a few minutes later, Leah knocks on the door and walks in with my breakfast tray.

I'm too excited to eat very much. For all my confusion and jealousy over Salvatore—which is also tying my stomach in knots—I'm going on a vacation overseas for the first time in my life, and the anticipation is driving me crazy. I pick at the muffin and yogurt that Leah brought up, sipping my coffee, until it's time to go down and meet Salvatore.

He's waiting in the entryway, as he promised. Unexpectedly, my heart stutters in my chest when I see him. He's talking to his head of security, and he looks different than normal, less buttoned-up. He's wearing dark grey chinos and a white linen shirt with the first few buttons undone, enough to show the soft dark hair on his muscled chest, a thin golden chain lying just below his collarbones. His dark hair looks thick and a little messy, and there's a shadow of dark stubble on his chin.

He looks more rugged than usual, a little dangerous, dark, and deadly. I feel heat bloom in my chest, radiating outwards, my pulse suddenly fluttering in my throat.

I swallow hard, telling myself it doesn't mean anything. But all the same, I brace myself not to let him see. I want to have the upper hand on this trip, not him. And if he knows I'm standing here with my heart racing just because he looks a little more undone than usual, I would be the one at a disadvantage.

The man Salvatore is talking to glances towards the stairs, and Salvatore stops mid-sentence, turning to look at me. For the briefest second, I think I see a look of frank appreciation on his face as his gaze sweeps over me, and then his expression shutters again.

"Right on time," he says evenly. "Perfect. The car is waiting outside."

I follow him out to the waiting SUV. I have no idea how much security is coming with us, but I have a feeling it's a decent bit. Ever since the wedding, I don't think we've gone anywhere without a full team of bodyguards.

My suspicions are confirmed when we get to the hangar. No fewer than twelve men in black cargos and t-shirts with guns on their hips get out of the SUVs that followed us, hanging back as mine and Salvatore's luggage are unpacked from the cars and taken to the plane. I follow Salvatore to the jet, my pulse suddenly fluttering with anticipation.

I've never been on a jet before. Never flown before. It's all new and exciting, and all of my frustrations and suspicions take a backseat as I follow Salvatore up the steps and into the interior of the jet, which smells of leather and lemon-scented cleaner, and the soft scent of flowers.

The interior of the jet is lovely. The seats are all smooth beige leather, with plenty of legroom, and burnished wooden tables between some of them. Along the wood-paneled walls, in intervals, are recessed vases with peonies and roses.

"Are the flowers for me?" I look at Salvatore innocently. I expect him to say no, that the jet is always decorated this way, and then he'll feel bad that I thought it was something more than it is. After all, this is supposed to be our honeymoon. But he just turns and looks at me, his expression still impassive. There's no flicker of emotion on his face, as if he's keeping his walls up just as strongly as I am.

"Of course," he says, startling me. "Normally, the jet is fairly austere. But this is our honeymoon, Gia. It should be a remarkable experience for you. Trust me, there's more to come." He pauses. "I noticed the flowers in your wedding bouquet. I asked the staff to decorate with those."

His tone is stiff, almost formal. But when he lays his broad hand on the small of my back, urging me forward to our seats, his skin feels hot through the thin layer of my dress. My pulse picks up again, and I swallow hard.

I feel more confused than ever.

Salvatore takes me towards the back of the jet, and sinks into one soft leather seat as I sit opposite him. There's a soft grey cashmere throw folded on the seat next to me, and I see, to my surprise, that there's a bottle of champagne chilling in an ice bucket, two flutes waiting for us. Salvatore reaches for the bottle, popping the cork smoothly as I hear the low roar of the jet engines. In my peripheral vision, I can see his security settling in on the other end of the plane, more of them than I initially thought. No one is going to bother us on our honeymoon, that's for sure. I feel sorry for anyone who tries.

"To our time away," he says, pouring champagne into the flutes and handing me one. "You'll love it, Gia."

"Where are we going?" I tuck my legs under me, taking a small sip of the champagne.

"I think it's better as a surprise." Salvatore leans back in his chair. "It won't be all that long before we're there."

I can't read him very well—I don't know him well enough yet. I'm not sure if he's enjoying this being a surprise for me, or if it's just an easy way to avoid having to have a conversation. My suspicions from this morning well up again, and I glance at him, taking another sip of the champagne.

"Where were you last night?" I repeat my question from this morning, and Salvatore lets out a sharp breath.

"Can we enjoy this, Gia? Or do I need to account for where I am at all times with you?"

My heart thuds against my ribs. *Why do I care so much?* I don't really have an answer for that, but suddenly, I want to demand that he tell me what's going on.

"Were you with someone else? Is that why you don't want to tell me?"

Salvatore raises an eyebrow, a small smirk on the corner of his mouth. As if he's amused by the question. "Are you jealous?"

Now I'm getting angry. I press my lips together, glaring at him. "I'm your *wife*. I have the right—"

"You don't, actually." Salvatore finishes his champagne, pouring another glass, this time with the focus usually reserved for actual liquor. As if he needs a drink to continue this conversation. "You're naive, Gia, but I think you're well aware that husbands in our world don't usually need to be accountable to their wives for what they do when they're not home."

"So you weren't home last night."

Salvatore fixes me with one of those long-suffering stares that I'm beginning to become irritatingly accustomed to. "I was," he says finally. "I was in my office, working. Is that enough for you?"

I swallow hard. I could have found out just by knocking on his door, as I'd suspected, but the truth is that I was avoiding him last night, too. "Okay." I finish my champagne and pour myself another glass, too. "You could have just said that from the start."

"And you could have not tried to start a fight." Salvatore reaches for his tablet, raising an eyebrow. "Is there anything else you'd like to argue about, Gia, or can I get some work done until lunch?"

I frown at him, but his attention has already diverted to his tablet. I have a feeling my initial suspicions were correct. He's mollifying me with the honeymoon, making his life easier by taking me far from the Bratva and Pyotr until the situation can be handled, and he'll simply ignore me as much as possible for the duration of our stay wherever it is that we're going.

After all, that's been what he's wanted since the wedding. To stash me somewhere and keep me out of the way so that he can keep going on with his life.

But I wanted a husband. A partner. A lover. That's what I was promised with Pyotr—what Pyotr and I promised each other.

It only deepens my resolve to make Salvatore regret taking that away from me, especially if he has no intention of providing it instead.

That frustration is tempered by excitement, as the jet takes off. I'm on the edge of my seat as we ascend into the air, my heart hammering with nervous enjoyment. I catch Salvatore watching me with what looks like amusement from over the top of his tablet, but even that can't dampen the fun that I'm having.

He comments on it when lunch is served—grilled chicken salads with gorgonzola and a berry vinaigrette, along with more champagne. "You're excited for this, aren't you? I hadn't expected you to be so thrilled about our honeymoon. Or being alone with me for so long."

"That's not why I'm excited." It comes out before I have a chance to think about it, my automatic biting reply, and I'm startled to see what looks like hurt cross his face for a split second. It's so fast that I'm not entirely sure it's really what I saw, but it seemed like it hurt his feelings.

My stomach unexpectedly twists, which brings me up short. I've enjoyed hurting Salvatore's feelings up to this point, tormenting him, and making everything as difficult as possible for him. I had planned to continue that. But I don't feel pleasure or gratification when I see that look on his face.

If anything, I feel a little bit bad.

"I'm sorry," I say quickly. "I just meant that I'm excited about going somewhere new for the first time. And flying. And staying in a hotel. It's all new for me."

"Of course," Salvatore says mildly. "I wouldn't have expected you to be thrilled at just the prospect of time away with me."

His tone is neutral as he says it, but I suspect what I said cut deeper than I realized. And it brings up that doubt again that I felt last night, that feeling that maybe I've gotten this wrong. That maybe what I thought I knew isn't entirely correct.

I curl up under the cashmere blanket as the air-conditioning on the jet makes it a little chilly, putting in my earbuds and reading my book as the hours pass. I think I fall asleep for a little while, because before I know it, I'm woken by the sound of dinner being served—or the first course, at least.

Salvatore has a glass of cognac next to him now, and there's chilled white wine for me. I pour a glass—the champagne has worn off, and I wouldn't mind being a little buzzed for all of this. Any kind of alcohol has an effect on me, since I've only recently started drinking more.

On the table, there's caviar and crostini, as well as thin crackers with delicately folded prosciutto, soft cheese, a tiny jar of fig jam, and slices of salted cantaloupe. I glance up at Salvatore, who is setting his work aside in preparation to eat.

"This is an awfully fancy dinner to have in the air."

"I'm a billionaire, Gia," he says calmly, reaching for a crostini and the tiny spoon to spread caviar onto it. "You know that as well as I do. So nothing is too fancy."

I don't exactly believe him. Not about the billionaire part—I do know that's true. But the casualness with which he says it rings hollow. Salvatore is a man who ordinarily toes the line of austere—I don't believe for a second that it's his usual way to have caviar and expensive champagne on a jet. He told me just a couple of nights ago that he's never taken a vacation outside of fishing trips with my father. This jet didn't even belong to him until six months ago.

I think this is all for me. A display of *something*, although I'm not sure what. His ability to protect me and provide for me, maybe. A reminder that everything my father had, he entrusted to Salvatore after his death—except for me. And now Salvatore has taken it upon himself to have that, too.

The thought makes my throat close up, until I'm not sure I'll be able to eat. My first reaction, every time I'm reminded of that fact, is always anger. But with the doubts that have filtered in, this time, there's another thought, too.

If my father trusted Salvatore so much, enough to give him everything, then should I do the same? Should I trust that Salvatore's reasons were honorable, instead of looking for something illicit in everything he does when it comes to me?

I don't have answers, and the only person in the world I would have trusted unquestioningly to tell me is gone. I only have Salvatore now—and he's either my captor, or my savior. I know which one he wants to paint himself as.

I'm just not sure which one is the truth.

I've never had caviar before. It's salty and rich, as is the prosciutto, which pairs wonderfully with the sweetness of the soft cheese and jam. The entire first course is a study of those salty and sweet flavors, washed down by the cold, crisp white wine, and I focus on enjoying it. I love this kind of thing—good food and the pleasures of luxury. I've never been ashamed of it in the past, and I don't intend to start now.

The rest of the meal is equally delicious. The first course is followed by a Caesar salad, and then by delicately cooked salmon in a buttery lemon-blueberry sauce, with roasted potatoes and vegetables on the side. Dessert is a coconut creme brulee, and by the end of it, I'm stuffed and sleepy all over again.

"I never would have thought that we could have such a fancy meal on a plane," I murmur sleepily, and Salvatore chuckles.

"There's more to come, Gia. Get some rest."

I oblige, retiring to the bedroom at the back of the plane. There's a small shower and bathroom, and I quickly rinse off, brushing my teeth and washing my face before changing into my pajamas and going to lie down in the surprisingly soft and large bed. It feels not all that different from being back in the mansion.

I wondered if Salvatore would join me, eventually. But he doesn't. I fall asleep alone.

When I wake up, I'm still alone. I get up and go through my usual morning routine, opting for a pair of denim shorts and a ruffled, cropped yellow off-the-shoulder shirt from my shopping trip. It shows a sliver of my flat, toned stomach and my long legs, and I decide that it's as good a time as any to show Salvatore what he's missing. I might have felt bad yesterday about hurting his feelings, but I still intend to try and get under his skin.

I want to uncover the truth about this marriage that I've been forced into. I want to know for sure why it is that Salvatore married me. And I don't intend to be relegated to a corner of his mansion while he goes about his life as if he didn't upend mine.

If I have no way out of this, then he's going to be my husband in all the ways that matter, and give me what I want. Or I'm going to drive him insane until he wants nothing more than to give me back.

I walk back to where I sat yesterday, to find Salvatore still there, a cup of coffee and a croissant on the table in front of him. He appears to be working still, as if he never actually stopped last night.

"Do you actually not sleep, and you were just pretending that first night I was in the mansion?" I accuse him as I flop down in the seat opposite. "Because you've only actually slept next to me once."

Salvatore looks up from his tablet. I see the momentary shock on his face as he sees what I'm wearing. I've generally dressed much more modestly around him in the past. For a moment, it's as if he can't gather himself as his gaze travels up my long legs, to the edge of the denim shorts, lingering on the bare skin between the waist and the hem of my top, flicking up to my breasts. His gaze finally meets mine, and he lets out a short breath.

"Maybe I'm a vampire," he says sarcastically, reaching for his coffee. "It would explain my preternaturally good looks at the ripe old age I've reached."

My breath catches a little. Not just because it makes me think of fantasizing about him in the bath the other night, while I read my romance novel, but because I want to laugh. *He* made me want to laugh, but I refuse to give him the satisfaction of knowing that he's made a joke I find funny this early in the morning.

"The flight attendant will bring you breakfast," he says neutrally, looking back at the files in his lap. "We'll be landing soon."

Soon is an understatement. I've barely gotten the cup of coffee and piece of coffee cake that the attendant brings me before the plane starts to descend. I abandon breakfast, instead looking out of the window as I see clear blue-green waters and crystal-white sands scattered with straw-topped buildings and floating piers come into view. I let out a small gasp at the beauty of it, and when I look over at Salvatore, I see that he's smiling.

"Welcome to Tahiti," he says, and my eyes widen.

"That's so far away."

"It is," he agrees. "Very far away, which I believe was part of the point of all of this. To make sure you were as far removed from the threat of the Bratva as possible."

My stomach swoops. All at once, I'm both excited and reminded of how far I am from Pyotr and the possibility of returning to him. I bite my lip, wanting to enjoy this moment, my first time being somewhere new. The plane is descending further, everything coming into clearer view, and I suddenly can't wait to be off of the jet.

Salvatore seems to sense my excitement. He packs up his things, glancing over at me. "We'll be off the jet in no time," he says. "And then you can see where we'll be staying."

He still hasn't said exactly how long that will be. But I'm not sure I care. This place is paradise, and I can't wait to explore it. I hope that Salvatore doesn't have plans to confine me to one of those villas, and then make sure that his security doesn't allow me to leave.

The humidity smacks me in the face the moment we walk off the plane and onto the tarmac, making me glad that I chose the outfit I did—and that most of my clothing is lightweight. Salvatore leads me to a waiting car, and I slide in after him, eager to get to our destination.

He sits across from me, looking at something on his phone. I'm struck all over again by the fact that he's barely touched me since the morning I woke up with him pressed against me, only to be followed by that scene in the bathroom. Not even the sort of affectionate touches that a husband would normally give his wife. His hand on my back as he escorted me onto the jet yesterday was one of the rare moments. He doesn't try to touch my hand or my leg. He barely looks at me.

The car pulls up at the edge of a long pier. The driver opens the door, and Salvatore steps out, waiting for me. I notice he changed clothes at some point—he's wearing a similar pair of chinos, this time dark brown with a tan linen shirt. He has that same ruffled, slightly undone air about him that made my heart flutter on the stairs, and I swallow hard, following him as we step onto the pier.

Our surroundings are so beautiful that they take my breath away. On either side of the pier we're walking down, clear, glass-blue water spreads out as far as the eye can see. Sprinkled further down the beach, I can see buildings—probably bars and restaurants, but the villas are scattered across the water, more of the long piers leading to each one.

One of them is ours.

Salvatore leads me all the way to the front door. He opens it to the scent of coconut and lemon, my sandals smacking against the tile floor as we step inside. Everything is cool and crisp and white, with tall, thin greenery in ceramic potting for contrast. The main room that we step into is bright and airy, with a pale light wood table next to the door—a mosaic dish sitting on it—a large three-pane bay window overlooking the water with a cushy reading nook, and a large sectional couch next to sliding glass doors that open up onto a balcony just above the water. To the left, next to the reading nook, is a doorway that leads to what looks like a small kitchenette. There's no stove—if I had to guess, we have our own personal concierge service here and meals delivered—but there's a refrigerator, a stocked bar cabinet, and a table nook overlooking the water.

The doors ahead of us are open, showing us the rest of the villa. My heart thumps hard in my chest as I see the huge white bed that takes up the center of the bedroom, a vibrantly colored throw blanket folded at the foot of it that matches the smaller pillows stacked against the crisp white ones. There's a pale wooden nightstand with a mosaic-shaded lamp on either side of the bed, a matching dresser and wardrobe, and a woven rug next to the bed stretched over the tile. To my right, glass doors open out to a deck with an infinity pool, the edgeless rim of it seemingly flush with the water surrounding it, although I know it's an optical illusion. There's a set of stairs leading down to the water, for anyone who would rather swim there.

The bathroom is equally luxurious. I walk in to take a look, trying to avoid thoughts of that huge bed and what might happen in it later. There's a glassed-in shower, a huge white soaking tub surrounded by greenery, and the calming scent of eucalyptus hangs in the air. The countertop is smooth granite, with bowl sinks, and a large well-lit mirror above it.

It's luxurious and beautiful, and it's in the middle of paradise. It's everything I could have possibly asked for on my honeymoon.

Salvatore is taking off his watch, setting it next to the bed when I walk back out. "Is it all to your liking?" he asks, and I nod, trying to think of what to say. I don't want to be too effusive, but at the same time, I find that I don't want to hurt his feelings again. Not when he so obviously picked this because he thought I would enjoy it.

"It's perfect," I tell him. "I didn't really have anything specific in mind, other than *warm*—but I couldn't have picked a better spot if I tried."

It looks as if genuine pleasure crosses Salvatore's face. He smiles, and then glances at the bed.

"I didn't sleep well on the plane," he says after a moment. "I think I might take a nap. Feel free to swim, lay out, whatever you like. But don't leave the villa just yet," he adds. "I brought plenty of security along, Gia. So don't think that they won't stop you if you try to go off and explore on your own."

Just like that, my enthusiasm dampens, just a little. I'm afraid he's going to confine me here, and that just makes me all the more worried that that's true. But he said don't leave *just yet*, which makes me hope it won't be a permanent situation for our entire stay here. That he'll loosen up before too long.

Although *loosened up* isn't a phrase I would ever really think of to describe Salvatore.

He slips off his shoes, setting them neatly next to the bed before lying back on it and closing his eyes. He's still fully clothed, and I bite my lip, trying not to look too hard at the muscled v of his chest showing in the open space of his shirt, or think of how it might feel to touch him there.

Instead, I go to the bathroom, and change into one of my bathing suits. I throw a sundress on over it, grab a book, and head out to the deck. The sun is warm and welcoming, the scent of salt and flowers in the air, and I take a deep breath. Despite everything, I feel some of the tension I've been carrying drift away, and I sink into one of the soft lounges on the deck in the sun, opening up my book.

I lie out there for a long time, at one point stripping off my sundress to take a dip in the cool, crystalline pool, and then drying out in the sun again while I read more of my romance novel. At some point, I fall asleep, because I wake to the sky blazing with the vibrant colors of a tropical sunset, and the air cooled off a little.

Inside, I hear Salvatore moving around. I throw my sundress back on, gathering up my book, and pad back into the villa to see him stepping out of the bathroom, freshly showered. He's barefoot, his chinos rolled up at the ankles and his linen shirt half unbuttoned, his dark hair wet against his head. There's that faint shadow of stubble, and my fingertips tingle as I think of what it might feel like to run them over his cheek.

He looks up as I walk inside. "Ah, there you are. I was about to come get you." His gaze flicks over me, taking in the sheer blue swimsuit cover I'm wearing and the outline of the bikini beneath it, and he clears his throat. "Dinner will be delivered soon. They'll set up on the balcony."

"Okay." I swallow hard, trying to ignore the tension that feels as if it's sprung up in the fifteen or so feet of space between us, thick enough to cut with a knife. "I'm going to shower, if I have time."

"Of course." Salvatore glances at me once more, as if I were something that might bite, and walks out onto the deck.

I walk into the bathroom, closing the door behind me; the stone tiles cool on my bare feet. I'm suddenly acutely aware of how alone we are together, in how small of a space, that even here, behind a closed door, he's only a room or so away. There's no sprawling mansion, no staff, no one here but the two of us. It's intimate in a way that I don't know how to handle, because I've never experienced it before.

The shower is wonderful, hot and relaxing, the glass-enclosed space filling with eucalyptus-scented steam. I end up just sitting on the stone tiles of the shower floor for a little while, letting the spray beat against the back of my neck and back, closing my eyes, and breathing in the steam. Outside of the shower is Salvatore, and dinner, and navigating our honeymoon, and all of the things that I don't know how to navigate. In here, there's just me, and the ability to shut it all out for a little while.

Eventually, I get out of the shower, lingering in the bathroom to dry off, and braid my wet hair into two braids, pinning them around the back of my head. I slip into a white sundress with a ruffled v-neckline and thin straps, adding the diamond and onyx jewelry that Salvatore bought me and slipping on a pair of sandals. The villa is utterly quiet except for the sound of the breeze and the lap of waves, and when I walk out to where I can get a view of the balcony, I see that dinner has already been set up.

Salvatore is waiting for me at the table on the deck, overlooking the water and the view beyond. There's a lit candle in the center, champagne and wine chilling in ice buckets next to the table, and a spread of seafood waiting for us for an appetizer. Salvatore is scrolling through something on his phone, but he puts it away immediately and looks up when he hears the balcony door open.

"Dinner is served." He gives me a pleasant smile, motioning for me to join him, and I walk hesitantly towards the table. It's beautiful and romantic, everything I could have asked for, and I feel a little guilty for having even the slightest thought that I might prefer to be here with someone else.

He's trying. I can't describe it as anything else. No one is forcing him to have dinner with me, or to arrange for it to be this nice, or to sit and talk with me at all. He could have added up all of my rebuffs so far, and simply assumed that this was never going to work in any capacity other than the most basic components of a marriage. And as much as I want to cling to my anger, it's difficult when I see that he's clearly trying to meet me at least partway.

"I can't say I picked out all of the courses myself," Salvatore admits as I sit down, pouring us each a glass of white wine. "But I did ask for their recommendations, and I think you'll be quite pleased."

I can't argue with that. The appetizers look delicious—there's a silver dish of cocktail shrimp with a pool of sauce in the center, a tower of oysters with a dish of mignonette and lemon, and a plate of shelled crab with drawn butter, as well as a green salad in front of each of us with small tangerine slices and a light vinaigrette on top. Paired with the crisp, cold white wine, it's all exquisite, and something about the salt air and sitting on the deck with a view of the water only makes it that much more delicious.

Salvatore is quiet for several long minutes, sipping at his wine as he picks at the shrimp and oysters. Finally, he looks up at me, sitting back a little as he twirls his fingers around the long stem of his wine glass. "Assume for a moment, Gia, that our marriage is not dissolvable. That your dreams of being rescued by your former Bratva fiancé and your beliefs about his honor are, as I've said, false. Can you do that for me, for the sake of one conversation?"

I look up at him sharply, a little startled. My immediate instinct is to snap back, but there's something in his tone that stops me. It's not pleading, exactly—I can't imagine that Salvatore is a man who would ever *plead* for anything—but I get a sense that this conversation is one he needs to have. One that he has, perhaps, been waiting for the right moment to press forward with. So I let out a breath, and nod.

"Alright," I say softly.

Salvatore presses his lips together briefly. "Alright, then. What would our future look like, to you? What would you hope for, in a life with me?"

At first, I'm not sure what to say. *Nothing*, is the first word that comes to mind. *I don't want this marriage at all, so how could I want anything?* But I know that's not what he's asking. He's asking if I can picture any kind of future, and, if I had no choice, what would make our marriage palatable for me.

The problem is that I can't think of a good answer. Not when my focus has been on waiting for Pyotr to rescue me.

"I don't know," I say truthfully. "I know that's not what you want to hear. Children? We talked about that before. I've always wanted sons. Daughters too, of course, if that's what I'm given—but I always had so many dreams of raising adventurous sons. There was that part of me that wished I had been born a boy, I suppose, that I could find an outlet for. I wouldn't mind getting my hands dirty, playing sports with them, going outdoors, and making up adventures. Coming up with stories." I shrug. "There are plenty of mafia wives who don't love their husbands, right? I could be happy with a family, I think. As long as I had that."

There's the barest shadow that crosses over Salvatore's face. I'm not sure what it means. I don't know if it's disappointment that I don't want more from *him*, that nothing I've said has anything to do with the relationship between him and me, and everything to do with my relationship to the children we'll have to one day have. Or it could be his ever-present reticence to do what needs to be done to give me children at all.

That last thought makes my stomach tighten, a flare of resentment washing over me. I do my best to push it down, to not start a fight when he's so clearly trying to open up a conversation with me.

"Is that all?" Salvatore asks, his head cocked slightly to one side, and that flicker of resentment rears up again.

"No," I say briefly, picking up a piece of shrimp. "But that's all I can see getting out of this marriage."

That time, I'm sure that I see the shadow that darkens his eyes. "And if you had children, you would put ideas of running back to the Bratva out of your head? Of being whisked away by your fantasy prince?"

There's a hint of condescension in his tone, and I press my lips together, fighting the urge to say something rude back. Instead, I just give him a slight nod.

"If I had children, I can't imagine Pyotr would want me any longer," I say quietly, ignoring the small stab of pain in my chest at the statement. "There's no world where I have a place among the

Bratva after having children with you, Salvatore, and we both know that."

"And you would no longer want to leave?"

"I wouldn't want to leave them." It's the best answer I intend to give him, and I think he knows that. "What about you? Don't you want heirs?"

Salvatore lets out a slow breath. "For a long time, I didn't have reason to think I would need them. I didn't know if Enzo would make me his heir, although it seemed certain that he would have no more children of his own. I thought, before he arranged your Bratva marriage, that he would make whoever he chose as your husband his heir."

I frown, reaching for an oyster and the delicate silver spoon to pour a little of the champagne mignonette over it. "That doesn't really answer my question."

Salvatore hesitates. "I suppose I don't have a good one for you, Gia. In my position, I need an heir. That is unquestionable. At the very least, I need a daughter who can marry well, and allow the family legacy to continue that way. That's how things have always been done."

"And that's all? Just the legacy? That's all that matters to you?" I don't know why it hurts to hear him say that. It's true that it's often all that matters to men in his position. The fact that my father cared about something else was a rare quality. "I suppose I thought since you and my father were so close, you would care about more than that, too."

He frowns. "I wish you wouldn't do that, Gia."

"Do what?" It's my turn to cock my head slightly, looking at him with narrowed eyes. "What is it that you would prefer for me to not do?"

"Use your father and my friendship with him against me."

"Why shouldn't I?" This time the words do come out with more of a bite. "He was *my* father. He made his wishes very plain. If he hadn't died, none of this would be happening, and you *know* that's true. So what makes you think you ever had the right to change any of that?"

Salvatore's jaw tightens, and I can tell that he's upset that we've come back to this. "The fact that he entrusted you to me," he says, as calmly as I think he can manage. "I have no entitlement to you, Gia; I know that. I always have. But your father trusted my judgment all his life. I have to believe that he would trust it in this, too." He sighs. "I don't want to fight over our differing opinions on the Bratva, Gia. It's clear you won't believe me, and you won't be swayed."

He pauses just then, as the rest of our dinner is brought out. The appetizers and salad bowls are cleared away, replaced with a platter that has a branzino sea bass in a pool of herbed olive oil, surrounded by roasted vegetables. There's a bowl of coconut rice and a plate of toasted bread with butter, all of it arranged as a fresh bottle of chilled wine is set in the ice bucket.

Salvatore is silent, cutting the fish and arranging some on both of our plates. "What's done is done, Gia," he says finally. "What I want is for us to find a way forward."

"You still didn't really answer my question." I spoon some of the coconut rice onto my plate. "Do you *want* children?"

He's quiet for a long moment, eating his food in small, precise movements that betray how hard he's thinking. "I rarely thought about it, before this," he says finally, setting his fork down. "My entire life was devoted to your father. It consumed all of my energy. When I did engage in a relationship, it was usually casual, and rarely lasted long. Marriage was not on the table for me, since I didn't have enough of myself to give to a relationship of that depth. And without marriage, I had no desire to have children. So now—"

He goes quiet again, and my heart thumps oddly in my chest. I'm not sure what it is that I want him to say. All of this feels like uncharted territory, a conversation that we don't like each other or know each other well enough to have. Yet, we *are* having it, because we're husband and wife, and these are the things we need to know.

"I should say yes," he says finally. "When I think of having children—a family—I think it's something that would bring me joy. But not in the circumstances of our marriage. And I don't see that those circumstances will change. You were my ward, and now you're my wife. I married you for your own protection, with the intent for us to lead as separate of lives as possible, while you remained under my roof and within the safety of my household. That arrangement is not what I hoped for, when I imagined marriage and children in the past. But it's what has happened. So the necessity of children is just that, Gia. Something to be dealt with when it's necessary."

Just like me. But for once, I can't find the rancor within myself that I usually feel when he says things like that. Instead, all I can think about is part of what he said at the very end.

This arrangement is not what I hoped for.

That goes against everything I've believed since Salvatore claimed me at the altar. That implies that he's telling me the truth, that he didn't marry me for desire or lust, that he *did* believe he had no other choice than to protect me by marrying me. It shakes the foundation of my hatred for him more than anything else has so far.

Because I could hear how much it sounded as if he meant it, when he said that.

"So what now?" I ask tentatively, looking at him as I poke at my food with my fork. He glances up at me, refilling his glass of wine.

"I think that's largely up to you, Gia," Salvatore says quietly. And then he returns to his food, falling into silence.

The meal ends with a fruit pavlova, brought out after the dinner is cleared away. Salvatore doesn't ask me anything else, and I'm not sure what to say. I can feel that his walls have gone back up, whatever vulnerability I might have momentarily gotten from him locked away. And mine have, too.

But I feel as if I've seen a little bit of a different side to him. That last bit of conversation, especially, makes me wonder if I've been too harsh. If I'm beginning to understand him in a way that might change my perception of what's happened between us so far.

Salvatore finishes his dessert in silence, setting down his napkin, and picks up his wine glass as he gets up from the table. He retreats to the other side of the deck, and I can't help but wonder what he's thinking. If he's mulling over what we've talked about. I wonder if he would tell me, if I asked.

If I believe everything he's saying, then I'm not the only one unhappy with our circumstances. And if that's true, and we could meet in the middle somehow—

It won't be what I dreamed of, I thought as I watched him sit on one of the lounge chairs, his pants rolled up around muscled calves as he looked pensively out over the darkened water. *But maybe we could have a decent marriage.*

I bite my lip as I walk back into the villa while the staff comes and clears away the rest of the meal. I get one of my bikinis, the black one with the thin chains, intending to go for a swim. But I also want to see Salvatore's reaction. I was covered up earlier, but now I want to see what he does. I slip the skimpy pieces of fabric on, putting my hair up in a loose bun atop my head and looking critically at myself in the mirror. There's nothing I can see to complain about—I look slender and fit, skin tanned and smooth, and I trace my fingers over the small divots of muscle just beneath my ribs. *Is he really going to be able to hold out much longer?* It feels like we've been playing a game, one that I'm not entirely sure I know what I want the outcome of to be.

He has a book propped on his knees when I walk out, and when he looks up, I see him go very still. His gaze sweeps over me, taking in the scant black bikini, the lines of my body, all the way from my face down to my toes and back up again. He doesn't try to hide it this time, a frank appraisal that makes my skin heat and my stomach twist uncomfortably. *I should be angry at the way he's looking at me,* my mind screams, but I'm not sure that I am.

A part of me, I think, *likes* it. A part of me *wants* his approval, and I think I might hate that part as much as I sometimes hate him.

But that warmth is traveling over my skin, into my blood, down between my legs. I feel myself draw in a breath as his gaze darkens. He doesn't move, and I wait for him to tell me to do something. To take off my clothes, maybe. To strip for him. I picture him laying me back on the lounge chair, burying his face between my thighs, pulling me astride him. All of the forbidden things that I've imagined and haven't yet had, that I wanted from someone else but could still get from him.

His jaw tightens, and he looks away from me, back to his book.

A flare of anger swells in my chest, transmuting that warmth of arousal into something else entirely. My frustration with our conversation earlier, with myself for not being sure of how I feel or what I want, all of my uncertainties and anger and confusion coalesce, driving me to the easiest solution in front of me.

Fighting with him is always the easiest solution, it seems.

"Are you serious?" I snap, glaring at him. I let my own gaze sweep down his body, over the glimpse of his tanned chest in the open v of his white shirt, down to where I can see the thick swelling of his cock straining against the fabric of his pants. He's aroused by me—that's not the problem. The problem is that he doesn't want to admit it.

"You came out here to swim, didn't you?" His voice is flat, inflectionless. "So enjoy yourself, Gia."

I suck in a sharp breath, ready to retort. But he's pointedly ignoring me, and I'm suddenly tired. I'd intended to come out here and taunt him, aggravate him with the skimpy bathing suit and the view of me in it, but I realize that I hoped it might actually turn him on enough to stop fighting his desire instead. And now we're just locked in another standoff, with no glimpse of peace in sight, despite our conversation earlier.

So, instead of snapping back, I just turn away, walking to the edge of the infinity pool, and slip down into the water.

It's pleasantly cool, a little more so than the night air, and I let out a soft sigh as I sink deeper. Salvatore fades from my mind for a moment at the pleasure of the water washing over my skin and the beauty of the night around me. The sky is velvet-dark, studded with more stars than I'm ever able to see at home, even outside the city, and the moon hangs nearly full in the sky, gleaming white. The water laps against the pylons supporting the villa, a soft, rhythmic sound that only adds to the peace of the night. Salvatore says nothing; the only sound from him is the occasional dry brush of paper as he turns the pages of his book.

I turn in the pool, looking at him as I rest my forearms on the edge. He looks younger here, almost boyish in the slightly rumpled, more casual clothes, only the faint greying at his temples and in his stubble betraying the fact that my husband is a man in his early forties. That faint hum of desire stirs in my blood again, and as I look at him, I wonder what would happen if I gave in to this.

Pyotr isn't coming for me. He would have stormed the mansion by now, if he really loved me. If he really wanted me. I can hear the whispers in the back of my head, and it makes me wonder how much of all of this really was fantasy, the way Salvatore stubbornly claims that it is. If I was as naive as Salvatore seems to think I was. If I made up a dream in my head about a man who was never going to live up to it in reality.

If, maybe, Salvatore and I could have some measure of happiness, if we stopped fighting each other. If maybe I should just accept this.

What better place to try than in paradise?

I push myself up out of the pool, dripping water onto the deck. Salvatore looks up at the sound of splashing, and I see the way his face briefly tightens, his eyes sweeping over me again. I know what he's seeing—the black swimsuit clinging wetly to me like a second skin, the water beading off of me, dripping to the stone beneath my feet. He draws in a slow breath, setting down his book, and my heart flips in my chest with something that I can't deny feels like anticipation.

"Gia." He says my name with a rough exasperation, but there's something else in it, too, a scratchy rasp that makes my heart start to race. "Aren't you tired of playing these games?"

"Yes," I say simply, taking a step forward, and I can tell that's not what he expected. His eyes narrow, and he looks at me warily, as if he's waiting for the next barbed comment, the next biting remark.

I walk closer to where he's lying, my pulse beating a rapid pulse in my throat. "So let's stop playing, Salvatore."

He doesn't move. I hold out my hand, and I can see that he's aroused, in every inch of his body. He's tense, wound tight, the thick line of his cock straining against his fly. He's resisting me, but I don't think he has very much resistance left in him.

It gives me a heady sense of power that I've never had before. Suddenly, it feels better than those afternoons with Pyotr, better than my fantasies, better than anything. Salvatore is the most powerful man in New York, a man famous for his discipline and self-control, an austere and terse man.

And I want to break him. I want to make him lose control.

I want to be the thing that shatters him.

"We talked about this," I say quietly. "As recently as earlier tonight. You need an heir, Salvatore. So let's stop playing, and take me to bed."

His gaze flicks to my outstretched hand, back to my face, as if I'm a trap he's resisting stepping into. He sits up slowly, and stands up without taking my hand, his dark eyes fixed on mine.

"I will eventually need an heir," he agrees quietly. "You're right about that."

There's nothing seductive about the words either of us is saying, but the timbre of his voice tells an entirely different story. There's that rasp, that deep, faintly accented hoarseness, that tells me he's fighting desire with everything in him. My pulse flutters in my throat, and I can feel the flush creeping over my skin.

"There's no better place to start than on our honeymoon, right?" It comes out breathier than I intended, and Salvatore's gaze narrows, his eyes flicking briefly from mine down to my lips, and back up again.

I can feel his control fraying. He's standing so close to me that I could reach out and touch him, but I don't. I want *him* to touch *me*, for him to give in to what he wants, to admit that in some part of himself, this was never just about protecting me.

If we're going to be married, we're not supposed to lie to each other. At least, that's the sort of marriage I hoped for. And I'm convinced that Salvatore is lying both to me and to himself, when it comes to this.

His jaw tightens, the small muscle there leaping. "Fine," he says, the word gritted between his teeth. "You're right, Gia. What better place than here?"

My breath catches, my heart flipping in my chest. Anticipation and fear tangle together, tightening my throat as he steps away from me, opening the glass door that leads into the villa. I follow him inside, into the bedroom, nerves fluttering through my stomach. It's not a feeling light or pleasant enough to be called butterflies—moths, maybe. This feels like a monumental choice, like something that I won't be able to come back from, once we do it. Uncertainty grips me as he stops at the foot of my bed, and I feel my hands tremble.

But I don't back down. Some of it is curiosity, some of it is pride, and some of it is a simple desire to stop playing this game. The rest is a perverse desire to make him finish taking what he stole—to follow through on what he started when he claimed me at the altar. It's all mixed up inside of me until I'm something that needs a word stronger than *confused* to describe it, but I'm too stubborn to tell him that I'm not sure of my choice.

"Take it off." Salvatore nods to my bathing suit, as he reaches for his shirt. "Lie on the bed."

I blink, momentarily startled. He's colder than I thought he would be, more like he was on our wedding night. I wanted the man who held me against his chest and wrung pleasure out of me in front of that mirror, not the unfeeling husband who acts as if he's just going through the motions. I hesitate, on the verge of backpedaling.

Salvatore's lips press together. "I thought you were done playing games, Gia."

A flare of resentment washes over me. I tip my chin up defiantly, glaring at him as I hook the fingers of one hand in the thin chain on my hip, the other hand going to undo the one behind my neck. I let the two pieces of the bathing suit drop nearly at the same time, the fabric hitting the hard floor with a wet *slap* as I stare directly at Salvatore, daring him to do something about it.

I see him swallow hard, just before he slides his shirt over his head. I see the flex of muscle in his chest and his arms, the glitter of the thin golden chain he wears against the dark hair on his chest. He drapes the shirt over the foot of the bed, reaching for his belt. "On the bed, Gia."

His voice is still flat, hard, as if he's directing a business meeting instead of getting ready to take his wife's virginity. The contrast in his emotionless voice and the reactions of his body are startling, and it infuriates me. I can see how turned on he is; it's in the tension of his jaw and shoulders, the sharp, quick way he undoes his belt, the sight of the thick, swollen base of his cock as he starts to push his pants down his hips.

"Gia." He repeats my name, a command, and a shiver runs down my spine despite myself. My breath catches, and I toss my head, pulling the tie free that's holding my hair up. I see his gaze darken as my hair falls down in thick, heavy waves around my damp shoulders.

"Should I get on the bed?" I lower my voice, making it softer, huskier. "I'm all wet."

Something dangerous glints in his eyes. "What do you want, Gia? We can stop, if you've changed your mind."

His pants are still clinging to the edge of his hips, that deep cut of muscle and the dark trail of hair that dips into them visible, just the base of his cock showing. It's a challenge, one that I know he's throwing out because it's an escape for him. If I tell him no, he can retreat and continue to tell himself that this isn't what he really wants. That taking my virginity, *fucking* me, is an uncomfortable duty that he'll get around to eventually.

Fuck that. He doesn't get to treat me that way. Not when he's undone my whole life in order to put his own ring on my finger.

I walk to the bed, biting my lip at the sensation of the cool sheets against my damp, flushed skin. Salvatore pushes his pants the rest of the way down, letting them hit the floor, and I swallow hard as his cock springs free, the tip slapping against the hard muscle of his abdomen, leaving a faint damp gleam against his skin. I lie back against the pillows as he strides towards me, following me onto the bed as he kneels next to me.

His hand slips between my thighs, pushing my legs open as he moves between them. This close, I feel another small tremor of fear at the size of his cock, rock-hard and visibly throbbing, milky fluid pearling at the tip. He reaches up, wrapping one hand around himself and squeezing as he parts my legs. I feel a flood of hot arousal as I watch him catch that drop of pre-cum with his thumb, spreading it down his shaft as he groans low in his throat.

I lean up, reaching out to touch him. I want to feel the soft hair on his chest, scratch my nails down the ridges of his abs, feel that hot, straining flesh under my palm. But Salvatore pushes me back, his hand catching mine and moving it to one side.

"Hands at your sides, Gia."

I frown up at him. "What if I want to touch you?"

He strokes himself once more, letting go of his cock as he exhales, his breath hissing between his teeth. "This is about consummating our marriage, Gia, not pleasure. We've been over this before. *Lie back.*"

His voice is a low growl, and I see his cock throb again, more pre-cum dripping down his shaft as he leans forward on his knees. His hand slides up my inner thigh, sending another flush of heat through me, and I gasp softly.

I try to reach for him again, and his grip on my wrist is rougher this time as he pushes my hand away, pinning it firmly to the mattress for a moment before letting go.

"I'm going to prepare you, like I did last time," he says roughly as his hand skims up my thigh. "So I don't hurt you when I'm inside of you.'

The words are cold, clinical. But the heat that floods through me is neither of those things, anticipation curling deep in my belly at the thought of his fingers on me, his tongue. "How are you going to *prepare* me?" I whisper, arching my hips upwards, my eyes widening. I see his jaw tighten, his cock twitch against his abdomen, and I know I'm getting to him. The pleasure I get from that is almost as strong as what I remember from how his hands felt on me last time. "Will you use your mouth?"

Salvatore's breath hitches, just for a second. His lips press together, and he lets out a slow breath. "Don't make this difficult, Gia," he murmurs, nudging my legs further apart as his fingers stroke over the soft folds between them, and I see the pulse of his cock as his thumb parts me, pressing against my clit.

I moan, arching upwards at his touch. One brush of the pad of his thumb against me, and I know I want more than just this. I want to find out what all of it is like.

And if he doesn't give it to me, he's going to find out the meaning of *difficult*.

Salvatore

I'm hanging on by a thread.

I've never known sexual frustration like what Gia makes me feel. Every inch of my body feels wound tight, muscles rigid with the effort of holding back, my cock hard to the point of pain. I want to tell myself that it's just deprivation, but I've gone longer than this most recent dry spell without sex before, and been fine.

It's *her*. It's been her since I took off her wedding dress one button at a time. Since I saw her undress in our suite the night of our wedding, and found that the stubborn, willful, fiery woman I married was nothing like the girl I thought I walked to the altar.

The desire I feel for her feels like a living thing, churning through my veins, burning me up. I bite back a groan when I slide my fingers between her thighs, feeling her slick heat against the pad of my thumb, her body instantly responding to the touch.

If she's so responsive to just that, what would it be like to pleasure her the way I want to?

I want her desperately, and it's only getting worse. We're in this bed now because she's right about one thing—I *will* need an heir, and if the tension between us stays the way it has been for all of this vacation, I'm going to lose my mind. I wondered from the moment she walked out of the bathroom on the private jet in those shorts and little yellow blouse if I'd made a mistake. Here, I can't put distance between us the way I can at the mansion. There's not enough space to cool down when she winds me up.

The last thing I should have done was take her to a tropical destination. I should have taken her to fucking Antarctica, where she'd be buried under five layers of clothing. Instead, she's in this huge, white-sheeted bed, damp and gorgeous, the scents of salt and lemon and chlorine filling the room, writhing under my touch as I rub my thumb against her clit.

Just take her virginity and get it over with, I growl at myself. If I can control my own fucking lust, I can make it about the duty that it's meant to be, and not my own pleasure. I run through all my justifications in my head—that I married her to protect her, and as long as she's still technically a virgin, she could still be stolen back. That a don needs an heir, and it's her job as my wife to provide that. That if I get this over with, and give her what she's demanding, she'll let it go.

She will have won. That's what really matters to her in this scenario, I tell myself, struggling to keep my thoughts from blurring. She's squirming against my hand, panting, and my cock throbs, hard enough to nearly bring tears to my eyes. I need to be inside of her more than I need to breathe.

Give her what she wants. Then this will be over, and we'll be able to have the physically distant marriage that I planned for—perfunctory sex to get her pregnant, and nothing else.

The thought of sex with this woman being reduced to *perfunctory* makes my body rebel in every part of me. But I'm stronger than my own desires. I'm not an animal to be ruled by my lust.

Gia was my ward. Now she's my wife. This is just another part of keeping her safe—by making her mine.

I refocus, looking down at her breathless, arching body on the white sheets. I need to make her come first, in order not to hurt her. It's not ego—I know if I don't give her at least one orgasm, she won't be able to take me. But touching her, feeling her slick heat against my fingers, hearing her whimper as I rub my thumb over her clit again and nudge two fingers against her tight entrance, makes keeping the rein on my lust nearly impossible.

She's the most beautiful thing I've ever seen. The most beautiful woman I've ever had in my bed. And I shouldn't—I *can't*—fuck her the way I want to.

Gia tosses her head against the pillows, grinding against my hand as she lets out a frustrated gasp. "Aren't you tired of just using your fingers?" she moans, twisting her hips. "Don't you want to do something else to me, *Salvatore?*"

The way she breathes my name drives me insane. There are so many fucking things I want to do to her. I want to taste her, to bury my face between her thighs and teach her how good a tongue on her clit can feel, fuck her with my fingers while I suck her into my mouth and make her come all over my face. Just the thought makes my cock throb dangerously, pre-cum spilling down the shaft as I clench my teeth against a moan. I refuse to let her see that she's getting to me. If she does, she'll take full advantage; I know that much.

I can't do it. If I let myself give in even that much, I'll fuck her the way I so desperately want to, instead of keeping this brief. I don't need to taste her to make her come. For the necessary part of this, all I need is my fingers. And I need to stick to what's *necessary*, and nothing more.

I slip two fingers into her, feeling the hot, velvet tightness of her pussy squeeze around them, and the sound of Gia's moan makes me feel dizzy with need. Every drop of blood in my body seems to have concentrated in my erection. I didn't know I could be this hard.

"Salvatore—" She moans my name again, writhing against my hand. "Please—"

Her head has fallen back against the pillows, her breasts heaving, her hips arching as she chases the release I'm promising her. I sink my fingers deeper, feeling her helpless whimper of pleasure in my bones, and I grit my teeth.

I could show her things that the young, inexperienced man she was promised to couldn't have. I think she's starting to realize that—to be curious about it, at the very least—and I can't help but think that it might have been better for us both if she hadn't.

I want desperately to show her all of those things. But every time I come close to giving in, every time I let myself want her, the guilt settles back over me, tangling with my lust until I feel like I'm drowning in both. I hear her taunts in my head, telling me that my desires made me break my promises to her father, mocking me with my betrayal.

I believe, to the depths of myself, that I married her for the right reasons. That I threw Pyotr out of that church and made her my wife because I have a duty to keep her safe, because I want her protected. But if I let myself give in to my own desires, it won't just be about that anymore.

Then, she'll be right. I will have betrayed everything that I stood for, by taking what wasn't meant to be mine for myself.

I have to do this—to *make* her mine, so she can't be hurt by those who would use her against me. But I don't have to take so much pleasure in it.

Gia gasps again, letting out another frustrated whimper as I circle my thumb over her clit, curling my fingers inside of her. The desire to taste her is almost painful, it's so strong, but I focus on bringing her to her climax, ignoring the throb of my cock and the slick heat that begs for me to pleasure her in every way I know how.

"Come for me, *dolce*," I murmur, thrusting my fingers. "I know you want it. Come for me, my good girl."

She lets out a strangled, broken moan, shuddering against my hand as I feel her let go. She pulses around my fingers, her hands scrabbling at the sheets as she bucks and writhes, coming hard on my hand as her perfect mouth drops open and she cries out.

"Oh god—*god*—" she tosses her head, arching her hips into my hand, and I suck in a breath at the feeling of her velvet pussy squeezing again. I need her heat around my cock, *need* to feel her squeeze me like that.

It's been a long fucking time, and it takes everything in me not to shove her legs apart and bury myself to the hilt in an instant.

I withdraw my fingers slowly from her, suppressing a groan as I feel her clench again, like she doesn't want to lose the feeling of some part of me inside of her. "Spread your legs wider," I tell her roughly, wrapping my hand around my cock and giving myself one firm stroke. I want her arousal on my cock, want to feel it slick against my straining skin, and I allow myself that one small concession to my raging lust.

Her eyes flash, dark and heated in her beautifully flushed face, and I can see from the way her stomach tightens and her hands flinch against the sheets that my commands turn her on. She wants to pretend they don't, that she hates being told what to do. She'll fight me every step of the way, but her glistening, swollen pussy and her parted lips, her glossy eyes, and heaving chest tell a different story.

Slowly, she opens her thighs wider, without saying a word. The concession startles me and sends another jolt of lust racing through my veins, because it tells me just how turned on she is. She wants my cock so badly she's speechless, and my head spins, everything in me screaming to fuck her the way I imagined in my office days ago with my hand wrapped around myself.

My fantasies are running wild. Spread open for me like this, I can see every inch of her soaked pussy, her swollen clit peeking out from between her flushed folds, her tight entrance waiting for me. The urge to bury my face there and lick her to another orgasm is almost uncontrollable, but instead, I move closer, one hand on her thigh, the other wrapped around my cock as I angle myself against her entrance.

I suck in a hissing breath between my teeth as I feel her slick heat against my oversensitive cockhead. It's been months since I was inside a woman, and the recollection of just how good it feels makes my nerves tingle with a raw pleasure that sends another jolt through my aching cock, my own arousal adding to the slickness between Gia's thighs. She moans as I rub myself against her, clenching my teeth to suppress my own groans as I prepare to push inside of her.

I want more. I want everything. I want to rub the tip of my cock over her clit and watch her come on it as if she's using me like a toy. I want to eat her out and kiss her, so she tastes herself on my tongue. I want to fuck her mouth, her pussy, her ass, to claim every part of her body until she's learned how it feels to come while I fill every hole she has. A torrent of filthy, lustful thoughts fogs my mind, enough to make my cock throb dangerously and my balls tighten with the need to come.

I'm so close it hurts. And all I need to do is come inside her to finish this. So I clench my teeth, banishing every wanton fantasy of how I want to ravish her, and instead brace myself with one hand on the headboard as I guide my cock into her with the other.

The resistance is instant. Gia lets out a sharp breath as my swollen cockhead starts to breach her, her eyes screwing tightly shut with what must be pain. I go very still, the protective instinct that I have towards her overriding all the demands of my body to keep pushing further into her tight heat.

"Are you alright?" My voice comes out tight, raspy, and Gia nods, her eyes still closed.

"You're—so—big—" she breathes, the words a little shaky, and I feel the rumble of a laugh deep in my chest.

"That kind of flattery will send me over the edge before I'm even inside of you," I growl softly, feeling another jolt of sensation ripple down my spine as she tightens reflexively, rubbing against the very tip of my cock. "Relax, Gia. It will hurt less if you relax."

"I'm trying," she breathes. "You could make me come again—"

I swallow hard. I know what she's trying to talk me into doing. She wants to know what my mouth feels like, and I feel a small pang of guilt for denying it to her. *I married her, after all—doesn't she deserve all the pleasure she could feel within a marriage?* But I know if I do—if I let myself taste her, if I find out what it's like for her to come on my tongue, we'll never get out of this bed. I'll keep her here for a week, unable to control myself any longer, and our marriage will be everything I've been trying so hard to keep it from becoming.

Instead, I let go of my cock, keeping the tip pressed against her as I slide my fingers over her swollen clit. She gasps, arching into my touch immediately, rubbing against me in a way that makes my head spin with pleasure. I've had a decent amount of sex in my life, but I can't recall it ever having felt this good, and I'm not even inside of her yet.

Truthfully, I can't remember *anything* having ever felt this good.

I feel her pushing against me as I rub my fingers in tight, quick circles over her, the sound of her moans and the feeling of her writhing against me on the verge of driving me mad. Her hips buck upwards into the sensation, and I feel myself slip into her, my tip sinking into the clenching velvet heat as Gia cries out in a mixture of pain and pleasure.

"Good girl," I manage to gasp as another inch of my cock slides into her. "That's it. You're taking it so well."

She moans again at the praise, and I can feel her fluttering around me, her muscles tightening on the verge of another climax. She's so responsive that it makes me feel half-insane with desire, with wanting to find out all of the other ways I could make her respond to me.

"Salvatore—" She gasps out my name, and I can tell she's so lost in pleasure that she's forgotten to be angry with me. She's forgotten everything except how good my fingers feel, how good it feels for me to fill her up, better than she expected. "Please—"

I know what she wants. She wants everything she was promised, everything that she fantasized about for her wedding night. She wants passion and romance, pleasure and a night filled with her every desire being sated. But I can't give her that.

Not without feeling as if I'm losing what scraps of my own honor I have left in the bargain.

I rub my fingers over her clit, almost roughly, driving her to the edge as I push forward, sinking into her to the hilt. The pleasure of it makes my teeth grind together, my back bowing as I feel her soft folds press against the base of my cock, my balls tight and painful as I rock deeper into her. She tightens around me, moaning helplessly as I push her over the edge with one more quick flick of my fingers. As her sounds of pleasure fill the air, I let my own climax follow hers.

I want to hold back. I want more than one stroke inside of her, more than just these brief seconds of feeling her exquisite pussy clenching around the sensitive length of my cock. But like so much else with her, I can't allow it. If I'm ready to come now—and *god*, I've been ready to come since she took her clothes off—then that's all that's needed to consummate our vows entirely.

I can't stop the groan that escapes me, a ragged sound of pleasure that slips through my clenched teeth as I shudder above her, my cock throbbing and my vision blurring as I fill her with my cum. She gasps, trembling underneath me as I allow myself one more thrust, my hand clenching in the pillow next to her head as I spurt inside of her, the sensation of it stronger than anything I've ever felt in my life. I've never come like this before. I couldn't have ever imagined it could feel this good.

"*Fuck*—" I breathe aloud before I can stop myself, rocking my hips against her, chasing the last jolts of sensation as I spill my remaining cum inside of her. Gia is moaning softly, her eyes open now as she looks up at me, and I feel like I can't catch my breath. My chest feels tight, my cock still raging hard, and I don't want to slide out of her. I want to stay here in the perfect, tight clutch of her forever.

Instead, I separate us with one swift movement, clenching my teeth against the sensation as I pull out of her and roll onto my back. My cock remains stubbornly hard, pressed to my abdomen and glistening with her arousal and my cum. Gia blinks at me, frozen completely still for a brief second.

"Is—is that it?" Her voice is a high squeak, disappointment plain in it, and inexplicable anger surges through me. Not so much at her as at myself—for not finding some other way to keep her safe, for getting us into this position in the first place, for being entirely unable to satisfy either of us. Her clear dissatisfaction pricks at my ego, especially when I know beyond a shadow of a doubt that I could show her pleasure beyond her wildest dreams. I could make her come in ways she never imagined, satisfy her more than she ever thought possible.

And I'm not satisfied, either. Sinking myself into her as a matter of duty and then allowing myself to come moments later isn't what I want in bed. My stubborn erection is proof enough of that.

"I made you come twice," I mutter. "I thought you'd be happy with that."

Gia's mouth drops open. She lets out a sudden, shocked whimper, and then, to my surprise, bursts into tears.

It startles me so much that I don't know what to do at first. And before I can roll over and reach for her, before I can figure out what kind of comfort she might need, she grabs the sheet and wraps it around herself, yanking it off of the bed as she jumps out of it.

And then, as I stare after her, she flees the bedroom and runs out to the deck in tears.

Gia

I'm not entirely sure why I'm crying. Maybe it's the roller-coaster of hormones and emotions from *finally* losing my virginity. Maybe it's the shock of the actual act lasting less than a minute. Maybe it's the disappointment of realizing that even this isn't going to be what I want. Even if I convince Salvatore to take me to bed, he isn't going to crack and give that to me.

I'm not ever going to have the marriage I dreamed of.

Another sob escapes me, my hand covering my mouth as my shoulders shake, and I sink down onto the lounge chair with the sheet wadded around me. *It's over. It's all over.* It doesn't matter if Pyotr comes for me now. It doesn't matter if he wants to rescue me, if he still cares about me, or if Salvatore is right, and he never really gave a shit at all.

I'm no longer a virgin. I can't argue that Salvatore's cock hasn't been inside of me, that I'm still a virgin on a technicality, that if Pyotr stole me back, he would still be the only man to have ever fucked me, the only man who could be the father of my children.

Salvatore was inside of me. He *came* inside of me. I'm his wife now, in every way that matters in our world.

And all the other ways—all the other things that I dreamed of in a marriage, they only matter to me.

This is all I get. I'd gambled that if I could convince him to go to bed with me, if I could break that much of his control, he'd snap and show me everything I dreamed of. He'd crumble under the barrage of my taunts, and his ego would get the better of him. I thought he'd *need* to be the man who made me scream for him in bed, who taught me everything he could do to me.

But Salvatore is stronger than that. And for the first time, I think I actually believe that he didn't marry me out of lust. He married me out of a belief—misdirected or not—that he was keeping me safe. And somehow, that's actually worse.

I will never get what I wanted. I'll never have a husband who loves me, who desires me, who gives me passion and romance, and all the fantasies I once had. The best I can hope for is a family. And even then, Salvatore has as much as said that he doesn't see himself as a part of that family. Not with me.

Because he can't let himself feel about me the way a husband should feel about his wife. And truthfully—it's not fair to either of us.

But he dug his own grave, and now I have to lie in it with him.

I cover my face with my hands, sobs spilling out of me. I never expected losing my virginity to feel like this. I feel robbed, just like I did that first night—robbed of a passionate wedding night, robbed of the marriage I planned for, robbed of love and hope and sex and everything that I thought I was getting out of the marriage my father arranged for me.

And Salvatore can't even try to give me what he took for himself. I can't believe any longer that he took me out of lust, because if he had, he should have been ravishing me every night. If he had, he shouldn't have been able to control himself while I lay there in our bed, naked and moaning for him.

He acts like it's a chore, and now I actually believe that it is one for him. It hurts more than ever, knowing that I'm nothing but a burden. A duty. I could hate him for lusting after me, for stealing me—but this just makes me feel crushed. Hopeless. This is something I can't fix. Something that won't be made better by anything I can think of.

Emotions wash over me like a tide as I sit there and cry. Anger and hurt tangle up in knots in my stomach, and I regret ever trying to understand him. All I wanted was pleasure and affection, and he can't give me either of those things. All he can give me are attempts to spoil me, and vague tries at meeting me halfway in conversation.

Nothing that I actually want.

I hear the door open, but I refuse to look up. Even when Salvatore says my name, I keep my gaze firmly fixed on the deck, wiping at my swollen eyes.

"Gia." He repeats my name, his tone more tired than anything else. I let myself look up just enough to see that he's put on a pair of sweatpants and a t-shirt, as if covering himself will help at all. As if anything could help now. "What's going on?"

I shake my head, rubbing my hands over my face again. "You wouldn't understand."

"Try me." There's a tense note to Salvatore's voice. "We're sharing a house right now, Gia. When we go home, we'll continue to share a bedroom. Even the mansion isn't big enough for all of this, if you're sobbing this way. Tell me what's wrong."

"I feel—" I don't even know how to begin to explain how I feel. I don't know if I want to. But the idea of bottling it up and refusing to say anything at all feels equally terrible. "I feel unwanted. Heartbroken. Disappointed. Angry—" I bite my lip. "You took everything I wanted from me. And you won't give any of it back. I can't even have a good sex life with my husband. I can't find out what it's like to *really* be a wife, when it comes to that. All I get is—" I wave my hand towards the bedroom. "I might not know *everything*, and a lot of it might come from books, but I know it's supposed to be better than that!"

I look up defiantly then, glaring at him. "I know that much, at least," I repeat stubbornly, and Salvatore lets out a sigh.

"Any desire I might feel for you is wrong, Gia. You were my goddaughter. You were entrusted to me. I married you to make good on that trust, on that responsibility, not to have you for my own selfish desires. If I *want* you, if I let myself do the things to you that you're asking for, if I *truly* treat you like a wife in every way—that's taking advantage of that trust. I'm supposed to look after you, not—"

"Not fuck me?" I can hear the bitterness in my own voice, so I know he can.

"You're right that we have a duty to make an heir," Salvatore continues, as if I haven't even spoken. "With any luck, you'll be pregnant from tonight, and I won't need to touch you again. You'll have the child you want, and I'll have the heir I need."

Every word feels like a slap in my face. I push myself up to my feet, all my tears forgotten in the rush of anger that I feel at how easily he's dismissing *my* wants, *my* needs. "So that's it? You decide to marry me, you decide where I live, you decide when I get to have sex, you decide how much pleasure I get out of it, *you decide, you decide!*" I shout it into his face. "And what are you going to do? Go out and fuck whoever you please when you get horny, so you can pretend like you're some honorable man for not going to bed with your *wife*? Just because once upon a time you had an entirely different role in my life? Don't fling that godfather shit in my face either—that's nothing but a title. But you should understand that, since you seem really fucking stuck on making sure that *husband* is just a title, too!"

"Gia—" There's a warning note in Salvatore's voice, but I ignore it. I'm in no mood for a lecture, in no mood to be told to calm down.

"You're not more honorable for cheating on your wife instead of fucking her, just because you feel guilty that you want me!" I fling the sheet to the deck, letting it pool around my feet as I stand there naked in front of him, under the moonlight, as bare as I was earlier underneath *him*. "*That's* your definition of a good man? One who is unfaithful?"

"For fuck's sake, Gia!" Salvatore grabs my arm, a little more roughly than usual, and pulls me back into the villa. "Stop it! You're letting your emotions get the better of you, instead of thinking. You're acting like a child."

"Well, you married an eighteen-year-old, so what the fuck did you expect?" I shout it at him, trembling with rage, not even caring any longer that I'm naked and he's clothed. His face is flushed with anger, and I can see his pulse beating hard in his throat.

"I never said I was going to cheat on you." His voice is deep and rough, nearly as angry as mine, but I don't care. I do my best to ignore the shiver that runs down my spine at the sound of it, at the dark look in his eyes. "I never said anything about that at all."

"So, what? You're going to be celibate for the rest of your life?"

The moment I fling the question in his face, I can see that he hasn't thought through the consequences of marrying a woman that he can't bring himself to fuck. I see the flicker of uncertainty, the knowledge that the rest of his life is a long time to go with a cold bed. I know then and there that a faithful husband is yet another thing that's going to be stolen from me.

"I'll add that to the list," I grind out between my teeth. "A marriage I didn't want. A husband who won't fuck me the way I deserve. A house I didn't ask to live in that I'm not allowed to leave when I please. A child oh-so-begrudgingly given to me, eventually, that you don't want to be a father to, because *I'm* its mother. And now an unfaithful husband, on top of that."

"You really think Pyotr would have been faithful to you?" Salvatore's voice rises, his own anger spilling over. "You think he wasn't out there getting his cock wet every night he pleased while you were engaged? That he'd have kept his pants zipped up unless it was you he was fucking? You're more goddamn naive than I knew, if you really believe that, Gia. And as for the rest—" He shakes his head angrily. "Pyotr wasn't going to dote on your children. He wasn't going to play the adoring husband. He was going to use you and lock you away and make your life a living hell, while pretending that he was keeping up the agreement he made with your father. And you can believe me or not, but for god's sake, *stop* pretending that I've robbed you of some fucking fairytale!"

He's shouting so loudly the glass door next to us vibrates. I see the cords standing out in his throat, his teeth clenched, so much anger balled up in him that he's holding back.

"We're both in this, Gia. I kept your life from being a hell you couldn't have come back from. I don't care anymore if you believe me. You're my wife now, whether you like it or not. And I'll decide what my goddamned honor means to me."

"I *don't* like it," I hiss, and Salvatore scoffs, shaking his head.

"Fine." He turns on his heel, stalking back towards the bed.

I stand there, on the other side of the room, watching him go. A part of me wants to go sleep on the couch, just to be away from him, but the other part resents the idea that he can not only ice me out of our marriage but also keep me from sleeping in a bed. So instead, I snatch my sleep shorts and a t-shirt out of the dresser, throw them on, and crawl into bed as far away from him as I can manage.

It's not difficult. The bed is huge—we're not touching unless we want to.

And right now, the last thing I want is to touch him.

In the morning when I wake up, Salvatore is already gone. The sheets and blankets are tugged up on his side of the bed, smoothed over as if he wanted to erase any trace of where he was the night before. I sit up blearily, wondering if he's still somewhere in the villa, but I don't hear any sounds that indicate there's anyone else here. Even the security has made themselves scarce since we got here. However, how they've managed to stay so invisible, I have no idea. Whatever Salvatore pays them, he should probably pay them more.

My head is pounding from crying last night, and I'm sore. Salvatore tried to be gentle, I'll give him that much, but I was always going to be sore the morning after no matter what.

With the memory comes a sinking feeling of dread, a reminder of how we left things. My marriage is set in stone now, a divorce nearly impossible, and all possibility of my former engagement coming to pass vanished. But nothing is better between Salvatore and I. If anything, it's worse.

I shove the blankets back, swinging my legs over the edge of the bed, and see a note left for me on the nightstand. Next to it is a heavy black credit card.

Gia,

I'll be gone on business most of the day, probably until dinnertime. You're free to explore, so long as you take plenty of security with you and don't try to evade them. The credit card is for you to use as you please.

–Salvatore

. . .

That feeling of dread eases, just a little. It's still there in the back of my mind, that feeling of being trapped with no way out, but at least I'm not trapped *in* this villa for the entirety of our "honeymoon," with only Salvatore for company when he comes back. I can get out and get some fresh air and explore, and that at least feels like a reprieve.

The day is mine, and the thought of being able to do whatever I please with it is enough to lift my spirits a little more. I call the number for our personal concierge for breakfast, and then, while I wait on that, I take two aspirin for my pounding head and sink into a hot bath, adding a generous pour of lavender vanilla Epsom salts from a vial sitting on the gold tray that's perched atop the bathroom counter with a variety of expensive toiletries. The heat instantly soothes the tenderness between my thighs and my aching muscles from last night. I pile my hair up on my head to keep it out of the water, sinking deep into the tub and closing my eyes.

When the water starts to cool off, I pry myself out of it, drying off and putting on my emerald-green bikini with the palm-frond print maxi dress and a pair of woven espadrilles. I pull my hair up in a high, fluffy ponytail, adding hoops and a dangly bracelet, and rub sunscreen over all of my exposed skin before I go back out into the bedroom and find my breakfast waiting for me.

It's practically a buffet. There's coffee, coconut-flavored and plain creamer, orange juice, and water, along with a plate of scrambled eggs, blueberry maple sausage, smoked salmon, and a stack of fluffy pancakes with strawberry syrup and butter. It's more food than I could ever eat in a single meal, and I pick at it, taking a few bites of each thing while I sip my coffee. The smoked salmon and eggs, in particular, are delicious, and I end up putting more of that onto a single plate and carrying it out to the deck to nibble at while I finish the coffee.

The morning is beautiful. This is absolutely a tiny slice of paradise, with the crystal-blue water stretching out in every direction and the white-sugar sand beach visible like a thin strip in the distance. I glance out at the other villas scattered along the water, wondering about the other people staying there. Other honeymooners, maybe, happier ones than Salvatore and I. Or couples here on their anniversaries, girlfriends on a trip for a bachelorette, a girls' weekend away. I can't help but wonder if anyone else here feels the same way I do, the same way that Salvatore claims he does. If anyone else is here trying to save a marriage, or get pregnant after trying for a long time, or on a honeymoon they'd rather be sharing with someone else. Surely, even here in such a blissful place, we can't be the only ones struggling.

The sun is warm and bright, the morning just this side of a little too hot, but after being in the rainy, cold spring weather at home, I don't mind. A part of me is tempted to just sit on the deck in the sun with a book, but I don't want to squander the opportunity to wander *almost* on my own. So I finish up my breakfast and coffee, and pack up a straw beach tote with a towel, my book, sunscreen, and a few other things I might need for the day. But as I walk out of the front door and onto the pier leading to the beach, I'm immediately stopped by a tall, bulky man in cargos and a black t-shirt.

"Salvatore said I could leave for the day." It comes out automatically, and I can hear the defensiveness in my voice. "He said—"

"I know what he said." The man speaking to me looks vaguely familiar—I think his name is Vince. I know Salvatore's primary security enforcer, Josef, is always with him, so it's definitely not that guy. They all start to blur together for me—men in the same outfits, with the same buzz-cuts and stern expressions on their faces. "I'm just letting you know that I and several of my men will be accompanying you, Mrs. Morelli."

"I figured as much." I shade my eyes with my hand, glaring up at him in irritation. I knew he and some of the other guards would be coming along, but I didn't want to be reminded of it. "Can I go, then? Or do I need to wait for you to collect them?"

"No, ma'am. We'll be right behind you."

He steps out of the way, and I let out a sharp breath, my excitement somewhat dimmed by his attitude. But he can't completely kill my mood, and I still have the whole day stretching out in front of me.

I do my best to ignore the fact that I know I have an entourage, walking at my own pace as I head down the pier and out to the sandy beach just beyond it. I pull up a guide on my phone, eagerly looking for what I want to fill my day with.

There's a local open-air market, and I head there first, the sound of the waves fading into the distance as I head away from the beach. I'm sweating a little by the time I get there, but I don't mind. Ironically, this is the first time I've ever had this much freedom. My father, for all that I know, he loved me very much and kept me very sheltered. I was allowed to go out with my friends into the city—with the same kind of security that Salvatore insists on—but he never would have allowed anything like this. Like Salvatore said, the reason I've never been away from home before is because my father worried about the possible consequences of straying very far.

It feels blissful being out like this. The chatter and noise of the open-air market sounds like its own kind of music, filling the air with the sounds of happy people out shopping and haggling and just enjoying the morning. I walk past stand after stand of bags and jewelry, scarves and home goods, and further down, stands selling various types of food. I get a bowl of sliced fruit sprinkled with chili-lime salt and a cup of lemonade, perching on a nearby bench to eat it while I watch the people passing by. I know somewhere nearby, that Vince and his security are watching me, but I do my best to ignore it. If I try hard enough, I can almost pretend I'm entirely alone.

When I finish the fruit and lemonade, I circle back to some of the stands I passed earlier, ready to put Salvatore's credit card to work. I buy a gorgeous handwoven silk sarong that will look perfect with my bikinis, and a gorgeous pearl bracelet. The bracelet is a string of pearls in different shades—light blue, purple, and near-black—interspersed with tiny diamonds and aquamarines. I slip it onto my wrist, and then, just for fun, I buy a pair of matching earrings—black pearls with a small aquamarine stud at the top of each one.

I tuck the sarong into my tote, and head out of the market, back towards the beach. The sun is hotter now, beating down on me, and I can feel a light sweat trickling down the back of my neck by the time I reach the sand. Even as much as I work out, walking in the hot sun takes more out of me than I would have expected, and by the time I walk down the beach, I'm ready to stretch out on a blanket and relax for a little while.

The crashing sound of the waves against the sand is soothing. I shake out my huge beach towel and spread it out, getting out my book and slipping my dress off so that I can get some sun. I look around as I pour sunscreen into my hand, looking for Vince or any of his men, but they've made themselves scarce in the way they so often do.

A small part of me likes the idea of them watching me strip out of my dress, my taut, toned body on display in the skimpy emerald green bikini, the halter top pushing up my breasts. Salvatore might not have an appreciation for the view, but I bet some of his men do. I wonder how often they've watched me since we got here, while I took a dip in the pool or laid out under the sun, or if they're watching now while I rub sunscreen over my cleavage and down the flat expanse of my stomach, wishing they could touch me and knowing they can't.

I shouldn't fantasize about men other than my husband. I know that. That's *definitely* not what a good mafia wife does. But I'm angry with Salvatore, feeling robbed and neglected, and I can't help seeking what little pleasure I can find elsewhere.

Like, for example, imagining that even if my husband doesn't want me, surely one or more of the men set to keep watch over me do.

The thought makes me linger a little while I apply the sunscreen, slowly sliding my hands over my long legs, pushing up the edges of my bikini bottoms to smooth it over the curves of my ass, making sure to thoroughly coat my breasts and rub it in. When every inch of me is well-protected, I roll onto my stomach on the towel, opening my book and letting every other thought drift away.

Eventually, it gets too hot, and I tuck my book away and wander down to the water's edge. I've never swam at a beach before, only in pools, and I wade in carefully, keeping an eye out for sharp shells or jellyfish. I can only imagine Salvatore's reaction if I came back injured in some way—it would give him the perfect excuse to not allow me out again.

That's the last thing I want.

The water is cold, and I let out a little yelp as it laps at my calves, slowly wading deeper. I make it all the way to my hips, pausing as I try to get used to the chill, running my hands through the lapping small waves.

It feels good, all of it. The relative freedom, compared to what I've had before, the hot sun and the cold water, the smell of salt, and the taste of the fruit and lemonade that I had in the market still lingering on my tongue. For a brief second, I consider the wild idea of trying to disappear here, of running away from Salvatore and my marriage and my responsibilities as his wife. Of the kind of freedom that only those not born to this life can ever expect to truly have.

I know some people—a lot of them, actually—would laugh at me for thinking that way. Hate me, even, because I never have to worry about money or a roof over my head or enough food to eat. Yet, at this moment, I so desperately want to run. I know I'm privileged enough to have a lot of things that others don't.

But what I don't have is my own life. My own agency. And sometimes, I think there are so many things I'd be willing to give up in order to experience what that's like.

I walk out further into the water, welcoming the chill that pebbles my skin, the shock of the water in comparison to the hot sun. When it's nearly up to my breasts, I take a deep breath and dive underneath it, forcing myself to open my eyes after a moment.

The salt stings my eyes, but it's worth it. Under the water, everything is crystal clear, from the sand to the small fish that I can see swimming around. I let myself sink down a little, watching the way the sun's rays cut through the water to shimmer on the sea floor.

It would never work. I want to dream of the possibility of running away, of disappearing here, but I know better than that. Even if I went to the nearest ATM, withdrew every cent that it would allow me from the credit card, and threw it in the trash before trying to slip away, Salvatore would find me. His men would find me. And then he'd make sure I never had the opportunity to run again. Not in any explicitly cruel way, I don't think—he'd just ensure that I couldn't leave the mansion. My every need would be provided for, but within a gilded cage, the bars locked tight to make sure I could only sing from behind them.

My life was set from the day I was born. I can only make do with the cards I was dealt, not draw a new hand.

I push myself up to the glittering surface, sucking in a deep breath of air. Further down the beach, I see a glimpse of my security, probably making sure I didn't try to drown myself or get swept out to sea.

Just to make them worry a little, I dive back under the water, blowing out my air so I sink to the bottom. I run my fingers through the grains of sand, picking up tiny shells, sticking my hand out to try to touch one of the small fish that swims away too quickly before my fingers can brush against it. It's beautiful down here, and I promise myself that I'll come back if I get another chance to wander out on my own.

When I surface again, this time, I start to walk back to the shore. I go back to my towel, stretching out until I dry off again under the hot sun. By the time all the water has evaporated off of my skin, I'm a little too warm, and starting to get hungry. I don't want to go back to the villa yet, so instead, I slip my book back into my bag and shake out my towel, reaching for my dress.

And then, on second thought, I wrap the silk sarong around my waist instead, slipping my feet back into my sandals and tucking my folded dress away. I'm sure Salvatore would have a fit if he saw his wife walking around in public in a bikini top and sarong, but I don't care. The same jealous rebelliousness that led me to linger while I put on sunscreen in hopes of flustering my security guards makes me like the idea of the attention I might get going back into town dressed like this. And it's not like it's abnormal—plenty of tourists walk around in their swimsuits. I saw several earlier, while I was in the market.

I wait for someone to put a stop to my fun, for Vince to come and tell me to cover up or something like that, but no one does. My feet are starting to hurt, but I'm in no hurry to return to the villa. Instead, I head towards where I saw a string of restaurants and bars, further down the beach.

One of the first ones I see is open air, with a long bar towards the back and tables scattered throughout it. It's fairly busy, but I see room at the bar, and I feel a small thrill go through me at the idea of going and sitting at a bar alone and ordering a drink. It's something I've never done before, and, truthfully, never really thought I would do. But today, no one is going to stop me.

I can hear the faint sound of music playing over the speakers as I walk in, a backdrop to the hum of conversation filling the space. And then I walk towards the bar—and I see the man standing behind it.

He's gorgeous. Tall, with dirty blond hair that gives him a surfer look, medium length in a shaggy cut. He's wearing a tank top with the sides cut out, revealing deep cuts of muscle along his abdomen every time he moves, and leather armbands on his wrists. There's a thong necklace with what looks like a pirate coin hanging from his neck, and I catch a glimpse of shorts as he ducks around the other side of the bar to grab a bucket of ice.

When I get closer, I can see that he has bright blue eyes, as full of mischief and laughter as his smile appears to be. And as soon as he catches sight of me, I see him stop in the middle of reaching for a glass.

"Hey, there." He grins at me as I approach the bar and slide onto one of the stools. His gaze flicks down to my bikini top briefly, before trailing back up to my face. He's not ashamed of checking me out, and I can't really imagine why he would be—there are probably plenty of gorgeous women who make their way through this bar, and plenty of them probably end up in his bed. He definitely looks like the kind of man who would never be lonely for very long.

He also looks to be around my age. As he pushes a menu towards me, his eyes don't leave mine for a second. "See anything you like?" he asks with that same glimmering smile, and I'm not so naive that I don't know a flirtation when I hear it. I haven't even had a chance to look at the menu yet.

"I don't know. I haven't had a chance to look around." I flash him a smile, and his deepens.

"Well, feel free to look all you like." He winks at me, leaning on the bar, his hands tapping against the wood as if he can't stay still for long. I notice he has an engraved silver band on his index finger. "Do you know what you want to drink?"

"I—" I hesitate. I've only ever drank wine and champagne, and I want to try something new. "Something tropical? Surprise me."

"My favorite two words to hear." He grins at me, moving a little further down the bar. "You're going to love what I have for you."

I bet I would. I bite my lip, watching his long-fingered, dexterous hands as he muddles fruit in a glass, pouring shots of liquor and coconut water. It baffles me to imagine that there are so many people in this world for whom this is a normal occurrence—going to a bar, ordering a drink, flirting with a hot bartender. Going home with one, even. What feels daring and exciting to me is a normal Friday night for someone else. Jealousy floods me at the thought. Not because I desperately want to hook up with this bartender, but because I wish I had the *option* to. I wish I had the option to choose anything about how my nights will go—my days, too.

"Here you go." He pushes a glass towards me, filled with a fruity pink and yellow concoction. "If you don't love it, I'll make you something else. On the house."

I reach for it, taking a tentative sip. It's sweet and fruity, with the barest bite of liquor under all the fruit and sugar. I have a feeling I'd have a hard time walking back to the villa if I drank more than one of these. "It's really good."

"I knew you'd like it." He flashes me another of those perfect smiles. "I'm Blake. You on vacation?"

No, I'm on my honeymoon. Instead, I nod. "Gia," I introduce myself, taking another sip of the drink. His gaze flicks over me again with clear appreciation, taking in my breasts in the bikini top, my small waist, the silk sarong clinging to my hips. But I can hardly blame him—I haven't stopped looking at his abs since I walked up to the bar.

"That's a pretty name. Your first time here?"

I nod again. "I haven't really traveled much." That's a truth I can tell him without giving too much away.

"You picked a hell of a spot for your first time." He drums his fingers against the wood of the bar again. "Have you been surfing yet?"

I shake my head. "I don't know if I'm that adventurous."

"I teach lessons three days a week. I'll be out on the beach tomorrow. You should try coming out later at night, too. A lot of the bars go wild—live music, dancing…it's a great time." He has a keen interest in his gaze that tells me he's thinking of doing those things with me. My heart leaps a little at the thought, if only just because of how pissed off it would make Salvatore. But that's not exactly a risk I can take.

Not to mention, he won't let me out of his sight once he gets back to the villa.

"I'm not here alone. I don't know what plans there are for the evenings." I don't say that I'm *with* someone, exactly, and I'm not sure why I'm dancing around it. It's not like it can change anything, or as if something could happen between Blake and me. But I have a feeling he might stop flirting if he knew I was married, and I like the feeling of being flirted with, of being wanted. I'm not ready for it to be over so soon.

I wrap my left hand into a fist in my lap, slipping off my ring. I don't want him to see it. I know I can't get away with anything, but this feels like getting back at Salvatore, just a little. A small victory.

I drop the ring into my tote. "Those surfing lessons sound like they could be fun, though."

"You should come and find out." That smile is still on his face, and I don't really know much about men or flirting, but it looks genuine to me.

Genuine enough to get us both in trouble, if I were to let it go too far. But this is just flirting, and that can't hurt anyone. Especially not when I feel sure that my husband is going to spend our marriage doing far more than just *flirting* with whoever catches his eye.

He didn't say he intended to be unfaithful last night, but he also didn't deny it. I saw the look in his eyes, the one that said he hadn't considered whether or not celibacy was something he could commit to, if he was committed to not sleeping with me unless absolutely necessary.

Just the memory makes me grit my teeth. Salvatore acts like it's a chore to take me to bed, like he's defiling us both in some terrible way, and it feels good to be looked at differently. To see this sexy bartender eyeing me purely because he can, with no moral qualms about it or feelings of guilt that he likes what he sees.

Salvatore isn't the man I chose, but if he's insistent on being my husband, he should at least be able to do that.

I scan the menu to try and distract myself while sipping at the drink Blake made me, finally settling on sweet potato and corn tacos with a cream of coconut drizzle on them. When he offers me a second drink, I take him up on it, even though I know it's probably not the best idea. But I don't really care. I have no idea how many more days like this one I'll be allowed, on my own with only my stealthy security for company, and I want to make the most of this one.

It feels like the closest thing to a really good day that I've had in a long time.

It's not until I push Salvatore's credit card across the bar to pay for my meal and drinks that I remember his name is on it. Blake's going to figure out pretty quickly that I'm here with a man. And even though I don't have any plans to do more than flirt, I feel a flicker of disappointment at the thought that I won't be able to come back and have this feeling again.

But when he brings the card back, I don't see any change in his expression. He pushes it and the receipt back towards me, that mischievous smile still on his face.

"You should think about checking out the surfing tomorrow. I'll even give you one free lesson on the house." He winks, and I feel a flutter in my chest.

This is a bad idea, and I know it. But I tell myself that a little flirtation never hurt anyone. That if Salvatore is so uninterested in treating me as his *real* wife, that it shouldn't matter what else I do, so long as I don't cross certain lines.

I know I'm rationalizing. But I return Blake's smile, slipping the card back into my tote. "Maybe I'll stop by."

"I hope you do." He looks at me for a moment longer, before grabbing the dishes and disappearing into the back room to the left of the bar.

I slide down from the barstool, feeling a little tipsy. It's time to head back to the villa, and I take a moment to steady myself before I start to walk. I feel warm and slightly sunburnt despite all the sunscreen, full of good food, the taste of the sweet, tropical drink still lingering on my tongue and the feeling of it buzzing in my head. I feel a little like I'm floating, and I realize that I'm spontaneously smiling for the first time in days.

That is, until Vince appears seemingly out of nowhere at my elbow. "You might not realize it," he says quietly, his voice pitched so that only he and I can hear what he's saying. "But Salvatore is a dangerous man. He's not one you want to cross."

He falls back then, without another word, melting back into the stealthy obscurity that he and the rest of his men have maintained.

I know the warning for what it is. He saw me flirting with Blake, maybe even saw me take my ring off, and is letting me know that there could be consequences to my actions. It annoys me more than anything else—I know that already. Of course, I do.

It's not as if I were planning to let anything happen between us, I think irritably as I walk back, fumbling in my tote bag for the ring to slip it back onto my finger. *I'm just having a little fun. God forbid* I get to have fun.

Salvatore isn't back yet when I walk into the villa. Someone has been by to clean, and it smells of lemon spray and clean floors, everything neat and polished. I set my things down in the bedroom, stripping off my clothes and going to take a long shower, washing the salt and sand off. I linger until I hear the faint sound of the door shutting from the front room of the villa, before I finally get out and braid my wet hair again, slipping into a different sundress.

"Gia?" I hear Salvatore call my name from the bedroom. "They'll be serving dinner soon."

"I'll be right out!" My stomach knots at the thought of sitting down at the table with him for dinner after last night. I can't tell from his tone how he's feeling—if he's still angry, or if he's planning on pretending as if none of it ever happened—and it makes me anxious.

This doesn't feel like a honeymoon. But then again, I'm not sure why I expected that it would.

When I emerge out onto the deck, Salvatore is sitting at the table already, wearing what I've come to think of as his vacation uniform—chinos rolled at the ankles and a linen shirt with the first few buttons open. There's a similar setup to last night waiting for me—a bottle of wine with a glass already poured for me, a platter of baked oysters, and a plate of sashimi, along with a clear soup. I sit down, smoothing my napkin over my lap, and glance up at him as I put some of the sashimi on my plate.

"How was your day?" I ask neutrally, not sure if I really want to know, but asking all the same. It's the only topic of conversation I can think of that doesn't lead us back to the same old argument.

"I was about to ask you the same." Salvatore takes a sip of his wine, reaching for one of the oysters. "Vince tells me that there were no issues."

Oh, thank fuck. I'd been a little afraid that Vince might tattle on me, that he might tell Salvatore about my excursion to the bar and what he saw—or what he thought he saw. Although I suppose if he had, Salvatore wouldn't have been nearly so calm when I came out to dinner.

"It was fine." I shrug, as if nothing out of the ordinary happened. As if today hadn't been one of the best days of my life. I don't want to give Salvatore a chance to give himself the credit for it, to pat himself on the back and say that he's the reason because he brought me here, and allowed me the freedom to explore. That he's doing a fine job as a husband because of it. "I went to the market and did a little shopping, and went to the beach. I had lunch and came back home. It was a beautiful day out. I think I might go back to the beach tomorrow morning, if you're planning on being occupied with work again." I watch his face cautiously for some sign that he might object, but he just nods.

"That sounds acceptable, so long as you don't try to evade your security."

"I didn't try today," I mutter irritably, reaching for another piece of fish. "I'm not a child, Salvatore. I understand that they're there to keep me safe." I might not like it, but I *do* understand. Here, the danger of something happening to Salvatore or me is low, but it still exists. It's possible that someone could figure out who we are, or that we could have been followed by someone who wishes us harm. Not even just the supposed threat of the Bratva. A man like Salvatore has other enemies, and by extension, they're my enemies, too.

"All the same, Gia, it bears reminding." He scoops another of the oysters out of its shell, looking out over the water as he reaches for his wine glass. "You're reasonably safe here, but it's still my job to make sure you stay that way."

"Of course." I give him a faux-sweet smile, reaching for my wine. "You'll protect me physically, just not my emotions."

Salvatore gives me a warning look. "I tried to speak with Igor today. I wanted to find some way to come to terms with him, something he would accept as a different means of brokering peace. As I think you can expect, he wasn't overly receptive. I didn't actually manage to speak with him, only one of his brigadiers."

"Why are you telling me this?" I wait for his answer, as the first course of our dinner is taken away and replaced with a spread of fish tacos and various accoutrements to sprinkle over them. "It's not as if you want my opinion on any of it."

Salvatore sighs. "I thought it might help you to understand that Igor is angry. You're *not* safe at home, and it was a good idea to bring you here. It's also worth noting that they're not without the resources to find where we've gone, although I don't think we'll be followed."

"Of course, he's angry. You stole his son's wife." I reach for one of the thin corn tortillas, beginning to pile flaky fish, pico, a lime crema, and crumbly cheese onto it. "He's not going to say *thank you*."

"We're not going to debate the semantics of that again." Salvatore begins to fix a taco of his own, but I can't help but notice that there isn't all that much enthusiasm to it. He barely touched the first course, either. He doesn't seem to have much appetite—almost as if he's preoccupied or worried.

Why do I care? I'm preoccupied and upset, too, and he seems determined to avoid any discussion of my emotions tonight. I look down at my food, frustrated at him dismissing me so easily.

"Are you going to be gone every day of our honeymoon?" I ask innocently, leaning down to take a bite of my taco.

Salvatore raises an eyebrow. "I would have thought you'd be glad to not have to deal with my company. I don't seem to improve your mood."

There's a hint of something in his voice that stops me for a moment. It's similar to the moment on the jet when it seemed as if it had hurt his feelings to realize that I was excited about our destination, not about spending time with him. As if a part of him wants me to want him around.

I can't resist poking at him. "There are things we could do that I'm sure would improve my mood."

Salvatore narrows his eyes at me. "We've been over this, Gia. It's entirely possible that you're already pregnant from last night, and if so—"

"What if I'm not?" I interrupt him. That sharp, hot resentment rises up in me again, bitterness that he's intent on depriving me of an essential part of our marriage, that he finds it so repugnant.

"Then we'll try again next month." He says it with a finality that feels like a slap.

I sit back, slowly absorbing that. *His intent is only to sleep with me once a month?* I'm well aware that he's always framed it as a chore, but that feels somehow even worse. I can see him timing it to when I might be most likely to get pregnant, perfunctorily fucking me, and then leaving me cold for the other twenty-nine days. It's so clinical that it makes me feel physically ill.

"You can't be serious."

Salvatore blinks slowly, as if reining in his own impatience with me. "I'm entirely serious, Gia. And I have no intention of last night happening again, while on this vacation. You convinced me of the need for an heir. So we've started that process."

I stare at him. "You make it sound like a—like a fucking passport application or something! For fuck's sake, you know it probably takes more than once, right?" I can feel my cheeks heating. "This is ridiculous—"

"I'm in no hurry." Salvatore leans back, his expression impassive. "It's been a long day, Gia. While you were out gallivanting on the beach, I was dealing with stressful matters back home. I'd like some peace at the end of my day. We are in paradise, after all. I'd like to be able to enjoy the calm."

I'm nearly trembling with anger. He makes me sound like a fishwife, like a shrieking harpy that won't give him a moment's peace, and all I want is for my husband to treat me like a wife. For him to *want* me.

"Don't you even care how it makes me feel?" I hate how my voice trembles, but I hate the feelings coursing through me just as much. I feel small and unwanted and trapped, confused as to how the man who married me could find it so awful to sleep with me. He claims it's about honor, that it has nothing to do with desire or a lack thereof, but I don't know what to believe any longer.

Salvatore narrows his eyes at me. "I'm well aware of how it makes you feel, Gia. You've told me at length."

Except I haven't. Not the most vulnerable parts of it, not the parts that right now are making me feel as if I'm going to burst into tears. And I don't feel like I can sit at the table with him for a moment longer.

"Excuse me," I blurt out, tossing my napkin onto the table with my unfinished dinner. I grab my wine glass, getting up quickly, and heading towards the door that leads back inside the villa, and a part of me wants Salvatore to call after me. A part of me wants him to tell me to come back, that we'll talk things out.

But he doesn't. I slip inside, glancing back once through the glass door, and I see him still sitting pensively at the table, looking out over the water.

I go to the living room with my wine, curling up on the couch and pressing my forehead into the back of it. There's silence in the villa for a long time, except for the staff coming in and out to swap out the courses and clear away dinner. They don't acknowledge me, and I sit there until I hear Salvatore come in from the deck, and the sounds of the shower turning on a few minutes later.

Once I hear the water, I go into the bedroom and change into one of my bikinis, slipping back out to the deck. The moon is high over the water, shining on the glassy surface of the pool, and I watch it break apart as I slip into it. All traces of dinner are cleared away, the deck empty and clean, and I set my wine glass on the edge of the pool as I swim. I half-expect Salvatore to come out after a while, but he doesn't.

I'm tired after a long day, but I'm not ready to face sleeping next to him yet. I stay in the water for a long time, thinking about Pyotr, Salvatore, and my father, about all the ways I thought my life would go, and trying to imagine what might happen now.

It all feels uncertain, uncharted, but not in a good way. Not in a way I can anticipate. I just don't know what will happen.

I don't even know if I'll be able to be happy.

I felt lonely after my father died, the first time in my life that I ever felt it. I thought that feeling would pass after I married Pyotr, that my life would be full again, that I'd have someone at my side to chase the loneliness away.

But now, I'm lonelier than ever. And to hear Salvatore tell it, I never would have had what I thought was possible with Pyotr and me.

Apparently, I was always going to feel this way.

Eventually, I go back inside and change into something to sleep in, after rinsing the chlorine off. Salvatore is already in bed, and I realize when I sit down on the edge of the mattress that he's already asleep, snoring lightly. Somehow, that only makes the ache in my chest worse—that he went about his night as if I weren't even here.

I slip under the covers and close my eyes, wishing that I could hope tomorrow will be better.

But it feels like it's just going to be more of the same.

Gia

In the morning, I once again wake up alone. The sheets and blanket on Salvatore's side of the bed are once again tucked up neatly and smoothed over. I frown, wondering how he once again managed to get up and leave without disturbing me at all. I typically sleep well, but either he's actually being careful not to wake me—which seems like more concern than he actually feels—or the sun and relaxation of vacation has me sleeping more deeply than usual.

I sit up, glancing to see if he's left another note for me, but there's nothing. I didn't take the card out of my bag yesterday, and I hope that it's still there. If he retrieved it, I won't be able to go out today.

Pushing back the covers, I stretch and swing my legs out of bed. *I'll have a quick breakfast,* I decide, *and then go see about those surfing lessons.* I have no idea if I'll like it or not, but it seems like fun. At the very least, the flirtation with Blake will be, especially after Salvatore's attitude last night.

I pad to the bathroom, pushing the door open with the intent to take a quick shower—and freeze as I see Salvatore standing at the counter, not unlike that first morning that I walked in on him in our bathroom at home.

He's shirtless, his soft sleep pants pushed down below his hips, low enough to show the deep cuts of muscle in his abdomen that carve down to the thick tuft of his pubic hair, his hipbones standing out in sharp relief, the swell of his ass just visible. His eyes are closed and his jaw set, his forearm flexed as his hand grips his swollen, lubed cock, sliding swiftly up and down the hard, straining length.

"What the hell?" I burst out before I can think better of it, staring at him. "What the fuck are you doing?"

Salvatore's eyes fly open. His hand goes still, clenched around his cock, and I see frustrated anger glimmer in his eyes. "For fuck's sake, Gia," he snaps. "Do you ever knock?"

It's hard for me to tear my gaze away from his cock. *That's been inside of me. It felt—*

It felt like it *could* have been good. If he'd slowed down, if he'd given me a chance to really feel it, if he hadn't rushed to the finish because he wanted it over with. I bite my lip, and I don't miss the way Salvatore's gaze briefly flicks to my mouth.

God, he really is handsome. He looks like he's been carved from stone, all chiseled muscle and tanned olive skin, that dark chest hair inviting me to run my fingers over it.

"Gia." He growls my name in a way that makes a shiver run down my spine. "Get. Out."

Defiance rears its head, and I shut the door behind me, crossing my arms over my chest as I start to move toward him instead. "No."

Salvatore's eyes widen. He lets go of his cock abruptly, as if he's only just remembered he was still holding it. "Gia—"

"Go on." I motion to his stiff cock. "Since you can't be bothered to fuck your wife. Let me see how you take care of it yourself."

Salvatore lets out a shuddering breath, and I see his cock throb visibly. His hand flexes. "Gia—"

"Good. You remember my name, at least." I move to one side as he starts to try to go around me, blocking him. "What, you don't want to finish? Or maybe you want me to take care of it for you." I reach out, as if to touch his cock, and Salvatore smacks my hand away. As he does, his own hand grazes his stiff length, and he lets out a hissing breath. His fingers wrap around it as if on instinct, and his jaw clenches.

I reach down impulsively, dragging my tank top over my head. I'm not wearing anything under it, and I see the muscle in Salvatore's jaw leap as his gaze flicks down to my bare breasts. A shiver of desire tingles over my skin, my nipples hardening, and I see his hand tighten around his cock.

"You don't want my hand, either?" I take a step closer, and he steps back, towards the counter. "Do you want my mouth? I could get on my knees for you, if you want. Wrap my lips around it, run my tongue all over you—" My voice lowers as I speak, teasing, husky, and Salvatore's gaze darkens. His hand moves, almost as if he doesn't mean for it to, stroking down his length as his palm rubs over the swollen head, and I see his hips jerk.

"A good mafia wife doesn't know about any of those things until her husband teaches her," Salvatore murmurs. His voice has lowered, too, thickening, his accent deeper as his hand convulses around his cock. I'm getting to him, and we both know it. I feel a delicious curl of anticipation in my stomach—tormenting him might be *better* than sex. It's better than the sex we had the other night, although maybe not as good as some of the other things we've done—

"You're supposed to be innocent." Salvatore's hand slides along his length again, his gaze flicking to my breasts and back up. "A virgin bride shouldn't even know what to do with her husband's cock."

"Well, I guess you'll just have to make do with your *spoiled* bride." I reach up, plucking at my nipples with my fingers, and Salvatore's lips press together, his hand sliding up and down his length again. I see pre-cum pearling at the tip, dripping over his fingers, and I lick my lips. "You're going to make a mess," I pout, blinking innocently at him. "Do you want me to lick it up?"

"For fuck's sake, Gia—" Salvatore closes his eyes, his hand moving faster. His expression is taut, tortured, as if he wants to stop and can't. "You are fucking spoiled," he growls, his eyes opening again, his palm sliding down to rub over his tip again. "Just not in the way you mean. You're a little brat." The word comes out on a thick snarl, his voice catching in his throat. "You want to make me feel bad for what I've done. Nothing makes me feel worse than this." He narrows his eyes at me, still stroking. "Looking at you, and wanting to touch you. I'm so fucking hard it hurts, from sleeping next to you all night. And I can't even fucking get off in peace. I should punish you." His voice lowers. "Maybe then you'd learn to behave the way a wife should."

"How is a wife supposed to behave?" I taunt, raising an eyebrow. "Isn't a good wife supposed to make her husband feel *good*? Take his cock when he needs to come? Isn't she supposed to pleasure him however he wants?" I hook my fingers in the edge of my shorts, shoving them down my hips along with my panties, and I hear Salvatore's groan as he watches them fall to the floor. "You could bend me over the sink right now. You're *so* hard. I'd feel so good to you, wouldn't I? It'd feel so good to bury yourself in me while you come—"

Salvatore lets out a pained sound, and I see his other hand flex, as if he wants to reach for me. He steps back, his hand still clenched around his cock, and I circle around him to the bathroom counter, pushing myself up onto the edge of it. I remember his reaction the first morning I woke up in his bed, when I teased him, and I spread my legs, letting him see every inch of me. I don't know if it's him I want or if it's just the sudden power that I feel that turns me on, but I can feel the heat between my thighs, the slick, dampness of my arousal.

"If you're so guilty," I murmur, spreading my legs wider still, "then stop jerking off. Stop right now."

Salvatore swallows convulsively, his throat tightening as his gaze dips between my thighs. I see his hand stutter on his cock, see the way it throbs in his fist, but he doesn't stop. He keeps stroking, and I can see the effort that it takes for him to look away from the view of my pussy, open and wet for him.

"You can't stop," I mock him, reaching down between my thighs. I'm so wet it startles even me, as I spread my folds open, making sure he can see exactly what he's missing. "You can't stop, and you can't fuck me, so what kind of man are you, Salvatore? One who can't control himself but can't fuck his wife?"

I rub my finger over my clit, leaning back with my other hand braced on the counter, and Salvatore groans. The look on his face is pained, his hand squeezing his throbbing cock. "Come fuck your wife," I purr, rolling my finger over my clit again. "I'm so wet. Don't you want me all over your cock? Don't you want to come in me?"

Salvatore snarls, and before I can take a breath, he crosses the space between us to stand between my legs. For one moment, my heart pounds as I think he's going to thrust into me, that he's finally going to break. But instead, he keeps stroking, his other hand coming up to grip my chin as he glares into my eyes.

"You are the bane of my existence," he hisses, his voice choked with lust. "You are a *constant* torment. You drive me insane, Gia, and all I have *ever* done is try to protect you. You are a spoiled, ungrateful woman. I *continue* to protect you, and all you do is try to hurt us both. To *break* me—" His voice breaks on a moan as his hips thrust into his fist. "You test *everything* I believe in, and to you, it's just a game."

"And you've stolen everything from me!" I try to wrench free of his grip, but he's holding me tight, keeping me there staring into his face as he jerks off an inch from my skin. I can feel the heat wafting off of him, see every clenched muscle in his body. And I can't seem to stop, either. My fingers are still rubbing frantically over my clit, my own body winding tight, the emotion and lust rising higher by the second as Salvatore leans in. "You took everything, and you won't give anything back."

"I won't allow you to destroy everything I've devoted my life to, Gia," he growls. "You can try all you like, but I can control my own lusts."

"Interesting you would say that," I gasp, arching into my hand as I feel my orgasm approaching, "when you're about to come all over me."

Salvatore's eyes squeeze shut, a groan tearing from his lips as his entire body goes rigid. I look down just in time to see his cock swell in his fist, throbbing as cum spurts from the tip, splashing over my belly and up to my breasts as his hips jerk rhythmically. He moans like an animal in pain, his hand on my chin tightening as he fucks into his fist, another spurt of hot cum coating my breasts and triggering my own orgasm.

"Oh, *fuck!*" I gasp aloud, my back arching as the sensation crashes over me, my hand gripping the counter to hold myself steady as I moan aloud. It feels incredibly good, better than I would have thought, the feeling of the liquid heat splashing over my skin, combined with the sound of Salvatore's near-feral groan and the forbidden tension of it all heightening my climax to something that feels as if it rips free of my body. I keep rubbing my fingers over my clit, wanting to draw it out, to make it last. I feel Salvatore's hand drop away from my face, hear his panting breaths, and open my eyes to see him turning his back, looking away from me as he tugs his pants up around his hips.

"It's unfortunate there's only one shower in here," he growls, his voice low and irritated. "But even though it'll make me late, I'll be a gentleman and let you go first, Gia."

And then he turns and stalks out of the bathroom, closing the door hard behind him.

A half-hour later, I emerge to find the bedroom empty. I lingered in the shower longer than I probably should have—not out of a desire to make him even more late, but just to get my thoughts in order. I feel more confused and frustrated than ever.

I thought I'd feel more of a sense of satisfaction from "winning" that particular fight. I *did* win, I think—Salvatore might not have given in and fucked me, but he certainly did something he didn't mean to do. He wanted to force me to leave while he took care of business himself, alone. I forced him to face up to his fantasies, to look me in the eye while he gave himself the relief he so clearly needed. Not to mention, he lost control enough to come *on* me, something I'm sure he thought he was too good to do.

But I don't feel satisfied, or happy, or in control. If anything, I just feel tired, as if the fighting is starting to wear on me, too. As if the entire situation is beginning to wear me down.

If Salvatore is telling the truth, and Pyotr really would have been awful to me, then I would have been in a bad situation no matter what. Maybe a worse one than this, if he's to be believed. But no matter what, if that's true, I would have left that altar facing an unhappy future. It feels almost soul-crushing to believe, to feel that my future was doomed regardless.

An emotionally unavailable husband who pretends he doesn't want me to salve his own conscience, or a violent one. Neither are options I wanted, and neither is what I expected to get. It's a hard thing, to think that I'm stuck between the past possibility of a cruel marriage, or my present situation of a marriage that's cold and contentious by turns.

I catch a glimpse of Salvatore sitting out on the deck, what looks like a breakfast spread arranged next to one of the lounge chairs. The glass door leading out to the deck is open, letting the warm tropical breeze in, and I see Salvatore look up as I walk through the bedroom.

He stands, and I flinch, knowing he's going to come and talk to me. I don't have any idea what to say.

"Gia." His voice is flat and neutral. Courteous, even, as he walks into the bedroom. "Are you finished in there?" He nods towards the bathroom.

I touch my wet hair self-consciously. "Um—yes. I was just going to let my hair air-dry." The strangeness of the conversation strikes me instantly, discussing something so innocuous with a man who, moments ago, was grasping my chin in his fingers while he jerked off naked between my legs. It's like he's an entirely different person now, outside the grip of the lust he's trying to suppress. It makes me wonder what he'd be like if he just let himself feel what he wants to feel.

"There's still breakfast outside." Salvatore gestures towards the deck. "I'm finished, feel free. The coffee should still be hot."

"Thanks." I bite my lip, unsure of what to say, but he doesn't really give me a chance to say anything else. Instead, he strides to the bathroom, closing the door firmly behind him. I think I hear it lock.

I go out to the deck, where an array of breakfast foods very similar to what was brought to me yesterday is laid out. I pour myself a cup of coffee and pick at some scrambled eggs, looking out towards the sandy beach beyond the rippling water. It seems like I'm going to have another day to myself, and the anticipation of that is enough to suppress the confused feelings tangling up in my chest.

Except—

I let myself imagine, just for a moment, what it would be like if Salvatore and I were behaving like a real couple on this "honeymoon." I try to imagine him out here having breakfast with me, walking down to the beach together, strolling through the market. I imagine him buying me something because it caught his eye and made him think of me, sharing lunch and a drink in the open-air bar, splashing each other in the water. It's hard to envision Salvatore enjoying himself so much.

Maybe that's part of his problem. He's been so focused on duty his whole life, he doesn't know how to enjoy himself. Honestly, I wouldn't be surprised if he felt that way about sex, too. If it's always just been a means to an end for him, rather than something done in pursuit of hedonistic pleasure, and so he can't fathom letting himself lose that much control.

I *want* to know what it feels like to lose myself in that kind of pleasure, to give myself completely over to my partner in bed. I want to discover all the things I've only ever read about or imagined, and I want to do them with someone who *wants* me. I don't want to have to be half in and half out of my head the entire time, wondering what's going through my husband's mind while he works up the initiative to fuck me.

This isn't fair. And at least Salvatore had a choice in the matter, even if he wants to act like he didn't.

The door opens a little wider, and I turn to see Salvatore standing there, his wet, dark hair swept back, wearing his more relaxed "vacation" clothes. "I'll be back this evening, Gia. Feel free to do whatever you like, as long as you have your security."

"Okay." I bite my lip, wondering why I feel the urge to ask the next question that slips out. I don't really care, do I? "Why are you going somewhere to work? Can't you just work here at the villa? It's not like you need to meet anyone in person—"

Salvatore frowns. For a brief second, I think he's going to tell me it's none of my business. But then he lifts one shoulder in a careless half-shrug. "Staff comes in and out of the villa during the day to clean and such. I rented a space where I can have privacy for meetings and work. There's silence, a beautiful view, and I'll be left alone."

"So this isn't a vacation for you." I look at him curiously. "Did you ever intend on relaxing on this trip? Or was that all just made up to make me think that's how it was going to go?"

He gives me an odd look. "Why do you care? It's not as if you want to spend time with me."

That makes me pause. The truth is, I don't really know why I care, or why I asked. I don't have an answer for him. Salvatore seems to realize that, because after a few beats of silence, he shrugs and turns away. "Enjoy your day, Gia," he says flatly. "I'll see you for dinner this evening."

I watch him leave, hearing the sound of the front door shutting behind him. And once he's gone, all that there's left for me to do is finish my breakfast and head down to the beach.

―

At this point, checking out Blake's surfing lessons is just a distraction. I slather on sunscreen, put on shorts and a patterned, fluttery crop top over my bathing suit, and start the trek toward the stretch of sand just beyond the bar where I met him yesterday. True to his word, I see a shack-like wooden stand with surfboards propped up against it, a small crowd made up of mostly women, and Blake standing behind the low wooden counter, shirtless and wearing only a pair of board shorts.

I try not to feel a flutter of jealousy at the idea that I'm far from the only woman he's flirted with into coming down here, and that he's clearly not hurting for attention—that I'm just one more in a sea of pretty, tanned, eager women waiting for him to look at them with those big blue eyes.

But the moment I approach the counter, his gaze immediately locks onto mine, and his mouth spreads into another of those wide, genuine smiles that I was the recipient of yesterday.

"Gia." He steps away from the blonde talking to him, and walks towards where I'm standing, his gaze flitting over me with frank appreciation before he looks back up at my face. "I'm so glad you came. I wasn't sure you would, actually."

I want to ask him why that is, but I'm pretty sure I already know—he can't have missed the name on the credit card I used yesterday. "I've never tried anything like this before. But it sounds like fun."

"It's a blast." Blake grins. "Come on, I'll get you signed up, and then we'll all troop down to the water and get started."

He hands me a piece of paper—just a waiver in case of injury and some basic information about myself. I fill it out quickly, hesitating only a moment over the spot for my name. I end up writing my maiden name, *Gia D'Amelio*, instead of my married one. It's a tiny rebellion, but it feels like taking a small bit of my own agency back. I prefer the name my father gave me to the one that Salvatore did.

I leave my tote bag and sandals at the shack, curling my toes into the warm sand as I wait with the other women for directions. I can't help but wonder what Vince and the rest of my security are thinking about this. I feel a small curl of unease in my stomach, wondering if Vince might call Salvatore and tell him. *But I'm not doing anything wrong*, I remind myself. I'm taking a surfing lesson—there's nothing wrong with that. Just because the instructor happens to be handsome and flirtatious doesn't mean that I'm committing some kind of sin.

"Okay, Alice, you first." Blake motions to the blonde as we get down to the water's edge, and she walks over to where a surfboard is waiting in the sand. I feel another of those tiny flickers of jealousy that he didn't pick me first, but I quickly quell it. It'll be my turn soon enough.

"Have you done this before?" A tall, thin, dark-haired girl to my left turns towards me. "I'm Michelle, by the way," she adds.

I shake my head. "No, this is my first time. Oh—Gia. I'm Gia."

"Nice to meet you." She glances back towards the water. "I've been here for a week. This is my third lesson. Blake's a really good teacher—very patient. Which is great, because I'm far from a talented surfer." She laughs self-consciously.

"I've only been here a couple of days. I went out exploring yesterday—I met Blake at that bar." I gesture up the beach. "He told me I should come check this out."

"I'm glad you did! It's always nice to make new friends. Here, let me introduce you."

She nudges me towards three other girls who are standing and talking in a small circle, and I'm quickly introduced to Melanie, Bethany, and Victoria. The entire foursome has similarly perfectly fit, toned figures, all of them exuding careless wealth and the kind of sleek gloss that only comes from having lived that way their whole lives. It only takes me a few minutes to find out that they're here on a bachelorette week away, and Victoria holds up her left hand. There's a gigantic oval-shaped diamond on it, and she waves it so that the sun glints off of it, sending out a prism of rainbows.

"That's gorgeous." I'm glad I slipped my band off and left it in my tote again. If anyone looked closely enough, they might notice the thin tan line on my left ring finger, but I doubt any of them will.

"He picked it out himself." Victoria grins. "After I left a bunch of magazine photos in very conspicuous places, obviously. I might have *accidentally* forwarded him an email about ring styles I liked, too."

I bite my lip, thinking of what ring I might have liked to have. I hadn't ever really considered it. Pyotr hadn't given me a ring at our engagement, telling me instead that it was his family's tradition to gift an heirloom ring at the altar. And Salvatore had just pushed a gold band onto my finger. I hadn't even had a chance to think of whether I liked an engagement ring I'd been given or not.

Now, I probably never will. I can't imagine Salvatore going out of his way to buy me a ring, especially when he doesn't have to. As far as he's concerned, he's done everything he has to do in order to protect me. There's no reason to go further than that.

"Where are you from?" Michelle asks. "I live in Boston. Victoria and Melanie co-own a clothing store in San Francisco, and Bethany owns a chain of restaurants in Seattle. You can imagine we don't manage to get together very often, so this vacation has been really nice."

"I'm from New York." I bite my lip. Thankfully, she hasn't asked what *I* do—I have no idea how I would actually answer that question. I never put much thought into why the only friends I've had—the only friends that my friends have—are the daughters of other mafia families. But now it occurs to me why that is. Who else could understand us, and our way of life that doesn't entirely fit into the twenty-first century? I can't tell any of these women, as nice and eager for friendship as they seem, that I'm the daughter of a mafia don, that my marriage was arranged, that I'm here on my honeymoon, and my husband is my godfather, who upended my planned wedding at the altar because he claims to have been afraid for my life.

I can only imagine what the looks on their faces would be.

"What brought you here?" Their curiosity seems genuine, and I feel bad having to skate around the truth. But I can't really give it, and I don't want to talk about Salvatore, especially not with strangers.

Right now, all I want to do is escape from my reality, and that's what I came down here to do. Not be reminded of it.

"Oh, just—you know." I raise one shoulder in what I hope looks like a casual shrug. "Just needed to get away."

That, at least, is true—even if it's probably not the reasons that they'll assume.

"I hear that!" Michelle laughs, only to turn and glance towards Blake as he calls her name for her turn. "Okay, wish me luck."

I watch as she strides down towards the surfboard. Alice doesn't appear to have done too well—her hair is half out of its ponytail and plastered around her face. Michelle, on the other hand, seems to be keeping her balance fairly well for all her claims that she was bad at it.

While we wait, I end up learning a little more about my new friends. Victoria and Melanie both went through fashion school, intending to open up a boutique clothing store. Victoria's fiancé is a hedge fund manager in San Francisco. Bethany has aspirations of opening a new restaurant in Los Angeles in a few years. They're all clearly from wealthy families—they all grew up together in Boston, where apparently Michelle stayed and became a lawyer, but they've all gone on to inherit their trust funds and have their own aspirations and careers. Victoria is the only one who's engaged, although Melanie thinks her boyfriend is going to propose any day.

It reminds me that I don't have aspirations like that—or rather, I can't. My life has always been set. I can't have my own career, business, or plans. My life was always going to revolve around the husband that was chosen for me and my place in the mafia world. It makes my stomach sink when it hits me that even if I had married Pyotr, even if he wasn't what Salvatore claims, that would still have been my life.

I believed that it would make it better that Pyotr seemed to see me as an equal. That I'd be his partner in running the Bratva, not just someone left on the sidelines. But being here, seeing the full lives that these women have in vivid color, I wonder if even that would have been enough. Or, if one day, I would have wished for more.

I hadn't realized how much I was missing. And I don't know if it makes it better or worse that I'm experiencing a small part of it now.

Michelle and her friends must have signed up as a group, because Blake calls their names one after another, before bringing them all down to the surfboards together for a final group lesson. I spread my towel out on the sand as they all go to meet him and watch, nervous for my turn. I don't want to embarrass myself.

Finally, Blake calls my name. Michelle grabs my arm as I pass, flashing me a smile. "Meet us up at the bar when you're done," she says. "We can all get drinks and lunch. We're going to go do some shopping first."

"Okay." I return the smile, nodding. "That sounds great."

Blake is waiting for me when I make my way down the sand, his blond hair plastered to his skull and darkened from getting wet. The sun is glinting off of his damp abs, and I try not to look too hard. I'm sure he's used to women ogling him all of the time, but I'm not supposed to.

It cuts both ways, though. I left my shorts and crop top on my towel before coming down to meet him, and I can tell from the way he looks at my skimpy bikini that he likes what he sees. *All that Pilates paid off*, I think wryly, as I wait for instructions. I might have plenty of insecurities, especially when it comes to my own husband, but at least I know I can hold my own against all the other gorgeous women on this beach.

"Alright," he says enthusiastically, as if he never gets tired of trying to give awkward women lessons on how to use a surfboard. "We're gonna push it out into the water, just up to like hip-deep, and then you sit on it. Just try to get your balance at first, okay?"

I feel my cheeks flush when he says *sit on it*. I can think of things I'd like to sit on, and I'm glad my better sense keeps me from saying it aloud. I don't want him to think of me as just another married woman who's flirting with him because she's lonely or bored. A part of me just wants him to *like* me. It feels like that, as much as anything, is what's missing from my life. A man who not only finds me attractive, but genuinely likes me.

Blake pushes the board out into the water, and I follow, shivering a little when the chilly water hits my bare legs. He moves around to stand next to me, and I nearly flinch when his bare hand touches my back. "Alright. Can you get up on it?"

I nod, hoping that the sun is a good enough explanation for how hot my face is. Blake's hand stays on my back, steadying me as I try to climb up on the surfboard as gracefully as possible, and I have another small flash of fear as I wonder if any of my security can see what's going on in enough detail to see Blake touching me. I can only imagine how Salvatore might feel about that.

And what would their opinion be if they saw someone else touching him? Probably nothing, and that thought pisses me off enough that I stop worrying about it.

Once I'm astride the surfboard, Blake grabs his and jumps onto it. "Alright. We're just gonna paddle around a little to start. Get used to feeling it under you, how it moves, get your balance. Okay?"

I nod speechlessly. *I'm already way off-balance.* I hadn't realized how sexual learning to surf could sound. Or maybe it's just me, and my mind's in the gutter because of all the unresolved tension in my marriage.

"There you go," Blake praises, as we move the surfboards through the crystal water. "You're getting the hang of it. Now, let's try getting up on your knees, and balancing that way."

Oh, for fuck's sake.

Everything about his expression as he says it, is completely guileless. But I don't miss the way his gaze is fixed on me as I carefully rearrange myself on the board, getting onto my knees. I can't help but wonder if he's imagining this in a different scenario, a scenario that then leaps into *my* mind, and I feel myself blushing deeper than I imagined possible.

"Are you alright?" Blake raises an eyebrow. "You look flushed. If the sun is too much—"

"No, I'm fine," I reassure him, almost a little *too* quickly. "What now?"

The rest of the lesson, at least, requires enough focus that I'm able to stop thinking about him *quite* so much. Eventually, I get to a standing position on the board, and Blake praises me effusively, which only makes me feel that much more flushed and uncertain around him.

"I rarely see anyone able to make it all the way up on their first lesson!" he exclaims, grinning. "You must have *great* core strength."

"It's the Pilates," I mumble, still red-faced and looking out towards the breaking waves to see if any of them are heading our way. "Should I stay up—"

"Yes! There's a small wave coming this way; see if you can ride it to shore." Blake gestures, moving his own board out of the way to give me a clear line to stay on mine and take the wave back to the beach.

"I don't know—"

"You can do it!" His enthusiasm, truthfully, is enough to make me believe it. He'd be a great coach. I eye the small wave again, trying to hold my center of balance—and then I feel momentarily as if I'm floating as the wave catches the board, sending me towards the beach and the small cluster of other women waiting there.

For a second, I think I'm going to fall. And then I find my balance again, and manage to stay upright all the way until my board skids onto the sand, stumbling off of it as I try to get a new kind of balance once more.

My crush on the instructor aside, it was *fun*, I realize. The kind of fun I've rarely had—the kind I've been discovering since I got here. I'm glad, suddenly, that we have at least the rest of the week here, if not longer. I want more of this.

"I told you that you could do it!" Blake comes up behind me, his hand touching my waist as he grins at me, his skin once again glistening from the water. This time, I don't think I can pretend that the touch is normal, or that he does this with everyone. In the water, it could be construed as help, but I didn't see him touching any of the other women when they finished their lessons.

"I'm impressed with myself." I manage a small, shaky laugh. "It was a lot of fun."

"You should come back. You'll keep improving." Blake's hand is still brushing against my skin, and I feel a warm tingle spreading out from where his fingers are lying against the curve of my waist. I think if I leaned in and kissed him, impulsively, he wouldn't hate it. He'd laugh, and probably kiss me back. And then he'd ask me to meet him later.

It would be careless, and fun, and mean nothing, I realize. And I wish I could do something reckless that meant nothing. I've never been able to do anything like that.

I take a step back, putting distance between us before I can make a mistake. "I need to meet my friends. Thanks for the lesson."

"Anytime. And I mean that." Blake grins. "I'll be at the bar when I'm done with lessons for the day."

"We're going to have lunch there. So maybe I'll see you."

"I hope so." He winks, that smile still on his face, and goes back down to where the boards—and the other women—are waiting.

I swallow hard. The smart thing to do would be to go back to the villa. But I want to have lunch with my newfound friends, and I want to have a drink in the sun, and I want to flirt with Blake a little more, and hold onto this feeling. So I move my towel a little further down the beach, stretching out in the sun until I've dried off enough to get dressed again, and then I gather up my things to meet the other four women.

They're not there yet when I get up to the bar, and neither is Blake. I get a table this time, ordering a water and looking over the menu while I wait. The day is beautiful, just this side of hot, but the breeze that moves through the open-air bar helps mitigate it enough that it's pleasant. Besides, after months of New York winter, I'd rather be too hot than cold.

About twenty minutes later, I see Michelle and her three friends walking up to the bar. I wave in their direction, and they immediately make a beeline toward me, setting their bags from the market down by the chairs.

"How was the lesson?" Michelle grins at me, waving at the waiter to come over. "I saw the way you were looking at Blake. Hard to focus with an instructor that hot, isn't it?"

I can immediately feel myself blush again, and I feel a flicker of panic. If this woman, who's known me for less than an hour, picked that up, I'm worried about what Vince might have thought—especially after his warning yesterday.

But I haven't done anything wrong. Nothing that Salvatore can legitimately be angry about. If Vince wants to tattle on me for looking, I'll be sure to let Salvatore know how I feel about that.

"He said I actually did really well. I managed to stand up and ride a small wave in."

Melanie whistles. "I don't think *any* of us did that well! But we were all too busy staring at him to pay attention, I think."

Bethany laughs. "There's *so* many surfers on the West Coast. The three of us see them all the time." She motions to herself, Melanie, and Victoria. "But honestly? He's really up there in the top ten hottest ones I've seen. And this whole *I don't care, island life* vibe that he has is really hot, too. A lot of the guys out there pretend to be carefree and the type to just ignore rules or whatever, but they actually want to make it to the top and eventually be rich. Everyone out there just wants to get noticed, one way or another."

"It's so true." Victoria lets out a little sigh. "I'm so glad we made that *no social media* rule for this trip. It's been so nice *not* worrying about posting every little thing." She glances at me. "It's so exhausting, you know?"

I bite my lip. "I actually don't have any social media," I admit. "I never have."

Michelle lets out a surprised sound. "Well, lucky you. To be fair, I ignore mine most of the time. Being a lawyer means every post on the Internet is a minefield. Wrong person gets ahold of it, twists my words around—there goes being a judge, or any kind of political career. But there's still that pressure to post every latte and aesthetic breakfast I have, you know?" She laughs. "Or I guess you don't."

"It sounds stressful." Privately, I think it actually sounds kind of fun—the idea of showing off a carefully artistic, curated view of my life to others. But I'm sure it sounds appealing only because I've never had a chance to actually do it. I'd probably be exhausted if it was an expectation, the way it seems to be for them.

"It can be." Bethany pulls out a menu, looking it over as she sips at her water. "But I try to just stick to the parts of it I like. Food influencing can be a lot of fun. It's Victoria and Melanie that really have to do all that daily nonsense to keep their brand going."

"Hey." Michelle taps me on the arm. "Blake made it back."

I look up, and see him walking in, a tank top and cargo shorts on now, his blond hair still damp and shaggy around his face. I feel a flutter of something that could be anticipation or apprehension, I'm not sure which.

He looks over, scanning the bar as if looking for something—or someone—and stops as soon as he sees me. I feel that flutter again, and see Victoria's knowing grin.

"Go talk to him." She smirks at me. "He likes you. He kept looking at you this morning, even with everyone there paying attention to him."

"Oh shit," Melanie murmurs. "He's coming over here."

Blake walks directly to our table, stopping at the edge of it. "Hey there, ladies. Gia." He smiles at me, and I can't miss the way my name is the only one he says. "Can I get you all something to drink? Gia, I can make you what you had yesterday, unless you want to try something new."

I don't think I'm imagining the undercurrent in his voice, the insinuation there. His hand is resting on the back of my chair, and I'm very aware of how close he is.

"What you made me yesterday is fine," I manage, swallowing hard, and I can see the expressions on the others' faces.

"Oh my god," Melanie whispers once Blake takes the rest of their drink orders and heads back to the bar. "He's *really* into you. You should see if he wants to meet up. Maybe after he gets off of work—"

She wiggles her eyebrows suggestively, and I blush.

"It's just fun to flirt." I shake my head. "It's not going anywhere."

"Why *not?*" Victoria laughs. "If I wasn't engaged—"

Because I'm married. It's the obvious answer, but it's one I can't give—to them, especially. It'll open up an entire line of questioning that I'm not prepared to fill them in on, and that I don't want them to know the answers to. I don't want to explain my life and its strange ins and outs to them. I want to be this version of myself, the one who isn't tied to the mafia, who can have an innocent flirtation, who has an entire life that I could make up on the spot if I felt like it.

I shrug instead. "I just don't know if I want to do all of that on my vacation. But who knows?"

Who knows? The question lingers as Blake brings our drinks, hanging around to talk a few minutes more before returning to the bar, and the girls tease me a little bit before turning to other topics of conversation. *Could I let it go further?* I'm not sure how—I can't leave the villa without security. I can only imagine the hell that Salvatore would rain down if I tried to sneak off and evade them…especially if something bad happened as a result.

Especially if he found out it was over another man.

But I can't help but let the fantasy go a little further. If what Salvatore has given me is all my marriage is ever going to be, then why shouldn't I think about having fun elsewhere? If my marriage bed is going to be cold, then why shouldn't I find pleasure where I can? That's what mafia husbands do all the time, after all, and no one stops them. It feels wholly unfair that I'm held to different standards just because I'm a woman.

We order lunch—a platter of different tacos—and sit and chat, ordering a second round of drinks. Each time, Blake brings our drinks personally, standing by my chair while he hands them out. Michelle makes sure to point that out, and I try to brush it off. But it makes me feel shivery, anticipatory, even though I know I can't act out what I'm thinking.

I can't add as much to the conversation as I'd like—I can tell that the other women know I'm being cagey. "You must have one of those jobs where you get in trouble just for talking about it," Victoria says teasingly, and I just smile, letting them believe that. It's easier than the truth, or saying that I just don't *want* to talk about it. But I like hearing about *their* lives—about the high-powered rat race of being a lawyer that Michelle is so happy to get away from for a week, looking through Bethany's Instagram profile as she shows me some of the dishes she's created, or hearing about Victoria's plans for her wedding. In the space of a couple hours, over fruity drinks and tacos, I hear about an entire world that I know I'll think about in the future, wondering how their lives are going.

Of course, it all comes up short when they want to exchange phone numbers, promising to get in touch when we're all back in the States. I tell them I forgot my phone back at the villa, but write theirs down, promising to text once I'm back. Of course, I'm not going to—and that realization makes me more than a little sad. I probably won't ever see or talk to these women again once I go back to New York.

"You should go talk to him," Melanie urges, as we pay our checks and they prepare to head back to their villa. "I *know* there's something there. He's been looking over at you the whole time we've been here."

I linger for just a moment after they leave, considering going up to the bar to talk to Blake. He's busy taking orders, the bar packed, but I know he'd take a minute if I went up there. But what would I say?

I need to go back. It's starting to get late in the afternoon, and by the time I get back to the villa, shower, and change, it will be dinnertime. And the more time I spend talking to Blake, the more chances there are that Vince will think something is amiss, and tell Salvatore about it.

So instead, I grab my tote, and start the walk back to the villa.

It's the same as yesterday when I return. The sky is beginning to turn the brilliant colors of the tropical sunset, but Salvatore isn't back yet. The villa smells fresh and clean, everything organized, quiet except for the lap of the water outside. I can't help but think, as I set my things down and go to get in the shower, that it's strange how easily people adapt. I've been here all of two days, but I've already started to form a routine.

By the time I get out of the shower and change, Salvatore still isn't back. I'm surprised to feel a flicker of worry, and I reach for my phone, hesitating. He's never told me *not* to text or call him, but I can't help but wonder how he'll feel about my checking up on him. Still—it feels strange that it's dark out, only a few minutes away from the staff starting to bring dinner, and he's still not here.

Letting out a sharp breath, I walk out onto the deck, sinking into one of the lounge chairs and quickly typing out a message.

Hey. I'm not trying to nag or anything, but you're not back yet, and I'm a little worried. Are you alright?

There's no immediate response. As the minutes tick by, I frown, wondering if I should go get Vince and ask him to check in with Salvatore's security. I've never really thought of what I should do in this scenario. But just as I'm about to get up, my phone buzzes.

I'm surprised you worried about me. I was just briefly held up. I'll be back soon.

I purse my lips, glaring down at the message. I can almost *hear* the sarcasm in Salvatore's voice as he says it, and it's more than a little irritating. But before I can give in to the urge to say anything back, the door opens, and one of the staff starts to bring out dinner.

"Mr. Morelli is running late," I tell her quickly, as she starts to set up the ice bucket for the wine, and puts a glass dish of shrimp cocktail on the table. "If you can hold anything hot, he should be here soon."

"Of course, Mrs. Morelli." The woman smiles at me, and then hurries back out. I wince, getting up to go to the table. Hearing myself referred to as *Mrs. Morelli* is always strange. I don't like it. But then again, I haven't liked very much about my circumstances since my wedding day.

It's another fifteen minutes before I see Salvatore's shadow moving through the bedroom. I've already finished a glass of wine and nibbled my way through half the shrimp cocktail. I see his raised eyebrow when he steps out onto the deck and sees the decimated appetizer.

"What?" I ask defensively. "You didn't say anything about waiting to eat."

"I would never," he assures me, his tone amused. He walks over to join me, sitting down and immediately reaching for the bottle of wine. "Far be it from me to deny my wife food if she's hungry."

"Well, at least that's one thing you won't deny me." The words come out sharp and biting, before I can even think twice about them, and from the way Salvatore pauses with the wine bottle halfway to his glass, they sting more than I realized they would.

He lets out a slow breath, pouring himself a full glass of the chilled white wine before setting it back into the bucket, and glancing over towards the door. He doesn't say anything until the woman bringing our salads drops them off and scurries away, and then he turns his tired gaze on me.

"I know fighting with me is your favorite pastime, Gia." His voice is laced with exhaustion, and I feel another surprising flicker of worry.

"But could we take a night off from it? I don't have the energy to fight with you tonight."

I don't care what he has going on, I tell myself—but for once, I can't convince myself that it's entirely true. Looking at his slightly drawn expression and tired eyes, I find myself wanting to know what's bothering him. "Alright," I say slowly, and I don't miss the slight raise of one eyebrow, as if he's surprised that I've given in. "Did something happen?"

Salvatore draws in a slow breath, pausing as he looks at me almost warily, as if he's deciding whether or not to discuss it with me. "There was an attack at the mansion," he says finally. "A test, I think, to see what our defenses were like. And possibly, whether or not you and I were there. Igor still refuses to speak with me, but I am still trying to open communication with him, especially after this."

"You don't want to just retaliate?" I frown. "Isn't that how you would normally respond?"

"In the past, perhaps yes." Salvatore takes another sip of his wine, visibly uninterested in his food. I find myself suddenly worrying about that, too. "I would have urged your father to take stronger action, in a situation like this. But I find myself wanting to negotiate for a more peaceful solution, in the hopes of still achieving some of what your father set out to do." He looks at me warily. "I would still like to achieve that peace that he worked for, and honor his wishes. Just without endangering you in the process."

I hesitate, looking at him uncertainly. I can hear the tension in his voice, see the stress in his expression, in the way he's holding himself. He doesn't look like a man on vacation. He looks like a man overwhelmed.

"Maybe you should try to relax a little while we're here," I venture, picking at my own salad. "This is supposed to be our honeymoon, after all. Maybe take a little break—"

Salvatore lets out a sharp, exasperated breath. "How do you suggest I do that, when the danger is so imminent? When the men I've left behind in New York, the men who work for me, for the mafia, for *our* family, are now in danger from the Bratva? When I need to consider whether or not Igor will try to find us, once he finds out we've left? Or take into consideration how long we need to stay, and how to try to come to an agreement before we return, so that I'm not delivering you directly back into that same danger?"

He shakes his head. "None of this needs to be laid on you, Gia. It's my responsibility to protect you, not burden you with my worries and concerns. But since you're asking—I don't think you realize the pressure there is on me, to make sure not only you, but countless others are as protected as I can manage. The responsibility of having so many who rely on me—for their employment, for their futures, for their safety. The men who work for me do so knowing the danger, to themselves and their families—but they trust me to mitigate that danger as much as I'm able. Not every don takes that responsibility seriously, but I do."

The sincerity in his voice brings me up short. For the first time, before I respond, I think—really *think*, about what it is that he's saying. What he's trying to tell me, to impart by saying that much. It's more than he's said before, in these conversations.

"You could talk to me about these things," I venture slowly. "We're married. That's what a husband and wife should do, right? Talk about their problems with each other? Lean on each other?"

Salvatore presses his lips together thinly. "I don't think we have that kind of marriage, Gia."

He says it curtly, as if it closes the topic, but I'm not so certain that it does. I look at him across the table, and I feel a flicker of understanding that I didn't have before. Not regarding the state of our marital intimacy—just thinking about that still makes me angry and resentful. But the rest of it—the tension that's always simmering just below the surface, his restraint, the way he always seems distracted by things outside of what's going on between us—I think

I understand that a little better. And I feel a burgeoning respect, too, that I didn't have before.

Regardless of the problems in our relationship, it's clear that he takes his duties as don seriously. As seriously as my father did—perhaps even more so, because it was his job then to oversee those duties, just as it is now, only with added pressure. Now, the decisions are his and his alone.

I can see how sincere he is. How worried. And it reframes all of this once again, making me doubt everything I've believed. The man sitting in front of me isn't a man who would upend the security of the family for his own lust. He's not a man who knows how to *give in* to those lusts. He doesn't even seem to want to admit that he has them.

"It could be different." I bite my lip, wondering what's possessing me to reach out to him like this. To try to bridge this gap between us. What's the point, when it always ends in fighting?

But no matter how much I tell myself that I don't care about him, that I *want* him to hurt, the idea of revenge for what he's done just doesn't feel the same any longer. Not when I see this look on his face, and feel that he's punishing himself enough. Not when I'm beginning to believe that his desire to protect me is genuine—that it really is what drove all of this.

I feel a flicker of guilt, too, for my flirtation with Blake. While I've been ogling a bartender and teasing myself with fantasies about what I could enjoy if I weren't married, Salvatore has been worrying about me, about his home, about his men still in New York. About the Bratva. It makes me feel like the spoiled girl he's accused me of being in the past, and I don't like it.

"Gia." Salvatore lets out a sigh, and I realize with a cold, sinking pit in my stomach that this isn't going to work. We're two different people, and he doesn't want me to reach out to him. He wants me to stay where I am, obeying him but not standing next to him. "This isn't necessary. You don't need to pretend to care. I've been handling all of this for years; I can continue to handle it now."

His dismissal should make me angry. It usually does. But instead, I just feel a wave of disappointment, followed by the sting of rejection.

He doesn't want my affection, or my desire, or my love. He simply wants to know he's done his duty. He wants me safe, and nothing more.

But *I* want more than that from the man I'm going to spend the rest of my life with. And I don't know how we're ever going to get across the chasm that divides us.

Salvatore

I make sure to get up well before Gia, as soon as the sunlight coming in through the gauzy curtains wakes me. I don't want a repeat of yesterday morning, or a difficult conversation before I leave for the day.

I want peace, but it's clear that with my marriage, any chance of that has been well and truly shattered.

It's only been a short time since I stood at that altar and coerced that *I do* out of her, but it feels like a lifetime. I knew it would be a struggle for her to adapt, that her strong personality and willfulness would make this difficult at first—but I hadn't imagined how much *I* would struggle. How hard this would be on me.

I had no idea how much I would want her. I hadn't imagined I could desire her the way a husband should desire his wife, or how differently I would see her once she was in that role.

I also hadn't imagined that I would begin to truly care for her. Not just as a ward, or as my responsibility—but as a woman. As my wife.

There are aspects about her that make me wish that there was a way to make this genuinely work between us. She's smart, and brave, and tougher than I realized. Not everyone would take the opportunity to explore a new place on their own—or as much as security would allow them to—but Gia didn't hesitate to go out and enjoy the island. I can tell that if she would give up her stubborn refusal to think badly of the Bratva, she would understand the risk they pose. She might even have useful ideas on how to handle the situation.

And, despite the headache that it gives me, she hasn't backed down in the face of our marriage, no matter how much she dislikes it. Her willfulness and attitude drive me to the brink of madness at times, but I have to admit that I prefer it over someone who would cry endlessly, or lock themselves away in a room and pout. She's not shy about showing her displeasure, but she's also tough and defiant in the face of what she considers to be adversity. She's not a wilting flower, or someone who crumbles under pressure.

I'm beginning to see how rash I was in my decision-making, when it came to this union. I still believe that there was no other choice, that marrying her was the only way to protect her from the Bratva and their cruelty. But I understand how that decision not only upended my life, but hers as well.

I look at her as I dress, feeling a pang in my chest. She looks fragile when she sleeps in a way that she never does when she's awake, her face soft and young, her dark hair tumbling around it. Awake, it's hard to believe that she would need protecting from anything or anyone, but like this, the urge to keep her safe wells up in me until it's nearly overwhelming.

It could be different. Her words from last night come back to me, haunting me. She's right, of course. It could be different. I just don't see how.

The gulf between us is too vast. Not just in age and experience, but in what we want. She wants a fantasy of a husband, a passionate, intense lover who puts her on a pedestal, and I've never let an encounter with anyone go beyond a night or two. Sex, for me, has always been about fulfilling a need, like eating a meal or drinking water. I've always kept my baser desires on a tight rein. And what I feel for her—

I'm afraid to let myself indulge it. It feels wrong, especially when it comes to her. I'm supposed to protect her, not ravish her. Shelter her, not bare her to me, and make her expose all the softest and most vulnerable parts of herself. And truth be told—I'm not sure that I want her to see mine, either. That kind of passion cuts both ways, I expect, and I've never let a woman see me laid bare. Gia, with her ability to cut to the bone even now, could tear me apart in ways I can't imagine if I let myself be vulnerable with her.

When it comes to the other part of a marriage, the idea of partnership—I know how to work for someone, and how to manage my own affairs, but working *with* someone is not my strong suit. I can follow authority, as I did with her father, but sharing it is another matter. And all of that, aside from my commitment to Enzo and his legacy, is why marriage was never on the table for me before this.

I've never been the marrying kind, until I was pushed into this as surely as she was. And now all we've accomplished so far, besides her tentative safety, is making both of us miserable.

Guilt floods me as I look at her once more, while I gather up my things. The ache of desire that I feel for her is a constant, and the guilt that I feel because of it is overwhelming. I *shouldn't* want her. I shouldn't feel the things for her that I do. I shouldn't want to go back to bed, to pull the blankets back, to strip us both bare so I can touch every inch of her flawless skin with mine.

The heavy ache in my groin is another constant, but I ignore it, focusing on the guilt. I gave in yesterday—what red-blooded man wouldn't, after seeing her since we arrived, for two nights, wet and half-naked in the bikinis she brought along undoubtedly to torment me? And all that resulted from that was Gia catching me, and escalating things in a way that satisfied neither of us and only made me feel worse.

How long can I endure this? That question plagues me as I leave the villa, heading to the space that I've rented to work at while we're here. Breakfast is waiting for me as requested—an egg and bacon sandwich on a croissant with coffee—and I sit heavily down in my chair, picking at it while I open my laptop and try not to think about how long a lifetime of this will undoubtedly be.

But the question worms its way back in, over and over, as the morning crawls by. Gia confronted me about being unfaithful, which she clearly expects from me, and I didn't know what answer to give her. I have no *desire* to be unfaithful to my wife, but I'm also not certain that one quick, perfunctory fuck every month—or not at all, once I have a son with her—will always be enough for me. I certainly don't think celibacy is something I can manage, although I've never sought out company before on a constant basis. But at the same time, I recognize how unfair that is to her—on both sides of the question—just as surely as I recognize that the idea of anyone else touching her makes me feel half-mad with rage.

But the thought of touching her outside of sheer necessity makes me feel as if I'm being swallowed up by guilt for the things I want. It's an impossible problem, and one that I don't know how to resolve.

I have a meeting with Josef over a video call, discussing reinforcements and how best to proceed with Igor. It's hard for me to focus as we talk, my thoughts constantly drifting back to Gia. This morning, after I got up, I found one of her romance novels next to the bath. I flicked through it for just a minute, startled at what I read on the pages. It made a little more sense, then, how she knows as much as she does about what she *thinks* I want in the bedroom—and imagining doing those things to her nearly drove me to lock the door and wrap my hand around my cock again, just to ease the arousal. Some of it, I could so easily imagine—and some of it made me feel filthy, for reading it and knowing that it would turn me on to do those things with her, when they should horrify me.

Frustrated, I get up when the meeting is over, intending to go for a walk in the afternoon sunshine—maybe get some lunch instead of having it delivered to me. My conversation with Gia from the night before replays in my head, and I can't help but wonder if I was too abrupt in cutting off her bid to close that gap between us. If, maybe, it would have been better to entertain her attempt, and encourage her to open up to me.

I can't be the lover she wants me to be. I'm not even sure that I can be the sort of husband that would make her happy. But maybe things could be less contentious between us. Last night was the first inkling I've had from her that she's willing to try to achieve that. I'm sure that my curt response caused her to throw up her walls again. But there's the possibility that I could soften the blow from last night.

I know her well enough to know that she likes pretty things—luxurious things. I know she likes jewelry. Despite the contention between us, she's worn the set I gave her for our evening out more than once. There's a small jewelry shop that I've passed twice now on my way to my workspace, and I head there as I leave, just to take a look.

A small bell chimes as I walk in, and I can smell watch oil and the scent of some kind of potpourri, along with floor wax. My shoes click on the gleaming hardwood floor as I walk in, and I immediately see a middle-aged woman with her black hair up in a high bun come out from the back, a welcoming smile on her face.

"Is there anything I can help you find?" She walks up to the glass counter. "We have all sorts of jewelry. Are you looking for anything specific?"

"Just looking around. I'll know what I want when I see it, I think." I return her smile, pleasantly, and she nods.

"Well, just call for me if you want to see something closer up. I'll be in the back."

There are several displays of engagement rings and wedding sets—unsurprising, since I imagine there are plenty of people who come here for a proposal or to get married. It occurs to me that Gia doesn't have an engagement ring, but it feels disingenuous to get one for her, considering that I didn't ask, and she has no way out now. I don't know what she would want, either, and picking something out she disliked would have the opposite effect of what I'm trying for.

I browse a selection of necklaces, and then look a little further down, at a case displaying bracelets on plastic wrist mannequins. Most of them are diamond, a few turquoise, but one catches my eye.

"Can I see this closer?" I call out, and the woman appears immediately, bustling toward the case where I'm standing.

"Of course." She unlocks the glass case, reaching for the bracelet I point out and laying it out on a velvet pad. "Here you are."

It's lovely. Delicate and feminine—a tennis bracelet style comprised of pink garnets and small pearls interspersed between each other. I can picture it on Gia's delicate wrist easily, and I have a feeling that she'll love it.

"I'll take it," I tell the woman decisively, reaching for my credit card.

"Of course. We have matching earrings, too." She carries the bracelet to the register, dipping into a different case to pull the earrings out to show me. They're dainty flowers, the petals comprised of matching pink garnets, with a pearl in the center of each. "I'm sure your wife would love these. Or whoever it is that you're purchasing them for." She gives me a sly smile, and I raise an eyebrow.

"I'll take them as well." I ignore the comment, pushing my card towards her. I'm sure there are plenty of men who bring mistresses here, but that's not my style, and it's also none of this woman's business.

I actually can't recall ever having bought a woman a gift before, other than those first gifts I bought Gia. As I wait for the woman to wrap them up, I find myself hoping that Gia will like them. I thank her as she hands them over, tucking the small boxes into my pocket, and look at my phone to see where she is. The location sharing on the phones isn't because I want to keep track of her so much as to ensure that if anything ever were to happen, I'd have a better chance of getting to her quickly, if she managed to keep ahold of her phone. It makes me feel more secure, knowing I have at least some chance of knowing where she is and that she's safe, although I'm sure Gia might have other opinions about it if she knew.

The map on my phone shows that she's at a bar and restaurant about a mile away—probably having lunch. I tuck my phone back into my pocket and pick up my pace, and I find that I'm looking forward to the idea of surprising her at lunch. The thought of sitting down for an impromptu meal with her and giving her the gift lifts my spirits, and makes me wonder all over again if maybe she was right. Maybe we do have a chance, if we try. Even if we can't come to an agreement just yet on the physical aspects of our relationship, maybe there's the possibility of a friendship between us. With time, and carefully growing that friendship, maybe there can even be some measure of a partnership between us.

For the first time since I interrupted the wedding, I feel a flicker of hope for the future, rather than just resignation. There are a vast amount of issues to conquer between Gia and me, but I consider that we can, perhaps, tackle them one at a time. If she continues to feel the way she did last night, when she was willing to talk with me rather than fighting, I feel as if it's possible.

I round the corner towards the restaurant, looking forward to seeing her. And then I do—and I stop in my tracks.

Gia—*my wife*—is sitting at the bar. That in and of itself wouldn't be cause for alarm—except for the fact that the bartender, a handsome younger blond man, is leaning towards her. His hand is on her arm, his thumb brushing the soft inner skin of her wrist. And I feel a surge of anger, so sharp and primal that it doesn't begin to compare to anything I've ever felt before.

I've never been an overly violent man. In my younger days, I enjoyed my enforcement duties a little more than I should have, from time to time. I liked the feeling of being tough, of bringing down Bratva, of ensuring that the mafia territory was protected. But I grew out of that quickly enough—and I never felt anything close to what I'm feeling now.

I want to rip his hand off of her arm, and break every bone in it. I want to snap his fingers while he begs for mercy, for daring to touch her. And then—

Slowly, I move closer, wanting to hear the conversation. And what I overhear makes my blood boil even hotter.

"—I didn't see you at the surfing lesson this morning." The bartender's hand doesn't leave her arm, and Gia doesn't pull away. "I didn't run you off, did I? Maybe I came on a little strong yesterday, but—"

"It's complicated." Gia's voice is soft, almost breathy. There's none of the sharp anger that I'm used to, the cutting edge. Her eyes are wide, looking at him with an expression that makes me seethe.

"I get it." His hand slides down, wrapping around her fingers, and I clench my jaw tight. "I saw the name on the credit card. You're not here with girlfriends, are you?"

"Blake—" Gia bites her lip, and it takes everything in me to wait a moment to approach, to let myself find out where this is going. I'm seeing red, my hands clenching into fists, on the verge of exploding into a rage more violent than anything I've ever felt.

While I was working to lessen the Bratva threat, this is what she's been doing. While I've been buying her jewelry, she's been sitting here flirting with another man. My teeth grind together, the anger in me a living, palpable thing.

"Come back tonight," he urges, still holding her hand. "Sneak out after he's asleep, or whatever. We'll go dancing and have a good time. You can't be enjoying your vacation with him, not if you're here, flirting with me."

"Is that what this is?" Gia gives him a small smile, still biting her lower lip, and I can't contain myself any longer.

"It certainly looks like that's what it is," I growl as I stride forward, nearly knocking over a barstool.

Gia jumps, snatching her hand back from Blake's. Her eyes go wide, her cheeks instantly flushed, and I can see the guilty look in her eyes. "Salvatore, it's not—"

"Don't bother." I reach out, my hand gripping her upper arm as I pull her up off of the stool. "We'll talk when we get back to the villa."

"Salvatore—"

"Hey, man. Maybe take your hands off of her—" Blake starts to speak, only to blanch, flinching backward as I turn towards him with a vicious expression on my face.

"Listen carefully, son," I growl, narrowing my eyes at him. "You're only in one piece because I have more important things to do than take you apart joint by joint for touching *my wife*. But there's a hell of a lot of security around here, even though you won't have noticed them, and they all do my bidding. If I tell them to, they'll mince you into so many pieces even your dental records won't be enough to tell who you are. Do you understand me?"

The boy looks so pale, I think for a minute that he actually might pass out. "Yes. Yes, I—"

I snort. "See this, Gia? One threat, and he's practically on his knees begging. *This* is what you prefer?"

"No, I—" She swallows hard, looking fearfully at Blake and then back at me. "It was just a flirtation, Salvatore. It didn't mean anything. Just harmless fun."

I know she's frightened because she's not snapping at me, not arguing, not yelling, and demanding I take my fucking hands off of her. I want to feel bad that I'm scaring her, but I can't, because I know that she's not afraid for herself. She's afraid for *him*, and that makes me even more furious.

"We'll talk about it in private." I pull her away from the stool, towards the door. "And you, *Blake*—I suggest not sleeping too soundly for a while."

He stammers something that I don't hear, because I'm already hauling Gia towards the door. Unsurprisingly, the moment I get her outside, she tries to wrench free of my grasp.

"What the hell do you think you're doing?" she hisses, trying to pull away. "You can't just come grab me and take me wherever you want —*ow*! You're hurting me. And how the hell did you know where I was, anyway?"

I whirl her to face me, both of my hands on her upper arms. "You're lucky I don't have Vince kill that bartender on sight," I snap, glaring down at her. "Not another word until we're back."

For once, she actually listens. Her mouth is set in a hard line, her eyes snapping fire, but she follows me as I keep my hand wrapped around her wrist, taking her back to the villa. She doesn't say a word until we're inside, and I've marched her all the way to the bedroom, closing the door hard behind us.

The moment I let go, she yanks her hand away, crossing her arms over her chest as she backs up.

"You're overreacting." She tilts her chin up, giving me a haughty, arrogant look that just pisses me off that much more.

"I'm not." I stalk towards her, the anger still burning in my chest as I back her towards the bed. "You're *mine*, Gia. *Mine*, and no one else looks at or touches what's mine? Do you understand?" I reach for her again, holding her in place as I stare down at her gorgeous, defiant face. "I'll lock you up in a room if I have to, if this is how you're going to behave."

The words pour out, sharp and angry, and they might startle me if I could think past my anger. I've never been a man given to rages. I've never been possessive of anyone or anything. But just the sight of that boy's hands on Gia made me murderous. It made me want to do unforgivable things. And right now, having her here, in our bedroom, I want to do far worse than that.

I want to remind her who her husband is. I want to drive every other thought of any other man out of her head, until she's so wholly mine that nothing and no one can take her from me. I want to devastate her, *ruin* her for anyone else. And the worst part of it is that I think deep down, she wants it, too.

I think a part of her didn't want him at all. She just wanted to push me to this.

And my control is so very, very close to snapping.

"I don't belong to you," Gia hisses, trying once again to wrench away from me. Her hair has tumbled down out of the loose bun it was in, falling around her face, and she looks painfully beautiful like this. "You can't treat me like this, Salvatore—"

"I can do what I want." I push her back, until her legs hit the edge of the bed, and I feel her tremble—with fear or anticipation, I'm not sure which. My cock twitches, thickening against my leg as I hold her there, and desire mingles with the anger until I feel like I'm going mad with it. No one has ever made me feel this way before, as if every repressed desire and emotion I've ever felt is surging to the surface all at once, on the verge of drowning us both.

"No, you can't!" She twists in my grasp again. "I won't stand for it, Salvatore! You can treat me as an equal, fuck me like a wife, or leave me alone to my own devices. But you can't have it all! You can't ignore me, leave me cold and push me away, and expect me to just take it—"

"And you think your Bratva husband would have treated you as an equal?" I nearly snarl the words, and I feel her stiffen, but I don't care. We're too far gone for me to stop, her flirtation with another man, the spark that's lit the fuse, about to go off.

"Yes!" She cries out. "Yes, I thought that. And now I'll never know, because you—"

"So what do you want?" I let go of her with one hand, grabbing the romance novel off of her nightstand that I saw this morning. "This? Is this what you want? The kind of thing written in here?"

"Salvatore—"

"Is this what you fantasized about when you were engaged to Pyotr? Do you picture him, while you read this?"

"I—"

Before she can say another word, I toss the book back onto the nightstand, spinning her around to face the bed. I grab both of her wrists, pulling them behind her back as I grip them in one hand, fumbling for my belt buckle with the other. "Alright, Gia," I growl, yanking my belt free. "If you want to behave like a slut, I'll give you what you want. If you want a man who acts like a Bratva husband, I can give you that, too. Since you crave it so much, you can go ahead and fucking have it."

She's shaking now, her lips parted and her eyes wide, but I can't tell if it's fear or arousal that's driving her. The possibility of the latter stiffens my cock until it aches, until it's straining against my fly as I push her face-down onto the bed. I toss the belt onto the bed next to her, grabbing the skirt of her dress in my fist and shoving it up to her waist.

"Salvatore, what are you—" She gasps the words, and I curl my fingers into the side of her bikini bottoms, yanking them down her thighs and letting the damp fabric hit the floor with a soft *thud*.

"Punishing my wife." I push her dress up higher, so that I'm holding it out of the way with the same hand gripping her wrists. "Teaching you a lesson, Gia. I should have done this the first time you talked back to me. I should have taught you what happens to spoiled brats. But better late than never," I add, reaching for my belt and folding the leather, gripping it by the buckle and the end in my other hand. "If you take your punishment well, Gia, I'll stop at ten."

"Salvatore—" She gasps my name, twisting against my hold on her wrists. "Please—"

"Please, what?" I mock. My cock throbs as she says it, the sound of her gasping, *please,* doing things to me that I didn't know were possible. "'Please, stop?' Or 'please, keep going.' This is what you fantasize about, isn't it?"

"I—" She swallows hard, letting out a whimper as I drag the leather belt over the firm, tanned curve of her ass.

She's perfect. She's so goddamned perfect it hurts. My cock is aching, every muscle in my body wound tight, all of me demanding that I take this further. I've never spanked a woman, never done anything like this before, but just the thought of it has me so hard that I can feel the pre-cum dripping from my tip, soaking my boxers and my shaft as I grit my teeth against the throbbing, driving need to be inside of her.

But first, I want to see her ass red while she begs me to forgive her.

"Ten strokes with the belt." I drag it over her ass again, down to her thighs. "To remind you what happens to unfaithful wives."

"What happens to unfaithful husbands?" Gia snaps, some of her defiance returning as she twists her head to look at me. "What do *I* get to do to *you* in this scenario?"

"I don't know." I lift the belt, looking down at her. "But I haven't been, so we'll cross that bridge if we get there."

And then I bring the belt down across her ass with a *crack* of leather against flesh.

She cries out, and my cock lurches, straining to be free. The red stripe against her ass is perfect, and I resist the urge to let go of her so that I can run my other hand across it. I bring it down again, across the other side, and Gia yelps again.

"Please!"

"Please, what?" I growl, bringing the belt down twice more in quick succession. "That's not the word I want to hear from you, Gia."

"What, then?" She gasps as I spank her a fourth time. "What do you want?"

I want you to beg my forgiveness for ever looking at another man. I want you down on your knees as an apology, worshiping my fucking cock until I let you have my cum, and swallow down every drop as a thank you for my forgiveness. I want—

My balls tighten at the thought, lust rippling down my spine and tightening my muscles until I'm afraid for a moment that I'm going to lose control of my orgasm at the picture of her on her knees, whispering how sorry she is around my cock stuffed in her mouth.

I've never imagined such filthy things before. Never wanted to defile a woman so badly, *especially* her. But my control is fraying, the guilt no longer enough to stop me, and I don't know what happens next.

Gia lets out a muffled sob as I bring the belt down again, her perfect skin crisscrossed with red now. "It hurts—"

"It's a punishment. It's supposed to." I spank her again, twice more, bringing the count to seven. "Take it like a good girl who knows she's done wrong, Gia."

As I say it, my cock throbs—only to hear her soft, almost imperceptible moan, enough to make me freeze for a split second.

I had wondered if it might turn her on. As I nudge my foot between her ankles, pushing her legs apart, I see the telltale gleam of her arousal on her soft, puffy lips, swollen with desire and dripping wet for me.

My erection hardens to the point of pain. I grit my teeth, bringing the belt down again twice more, my hand tightening around her wrists. Gia lets out another sobbing moan, and I bite back the growl that nearly erupts from me as I bring the belt down once more, hard across her ass.

Her back arches, her legs spreading wider as she cries out, and I can't tell if it's pain or pleasure any longer. Her folds part as she does, showing me the wet, glistening pink of her hot, tight opening, and my head pounds. I can hear the blood roaring in my ears, and I feel almost dizzy with lust.

I can't stand it any longer. I toss the belt aside, my hand still gripping her wrist, and tear open the front of my pants. I hear a button *clink* against the floor, but I don't care. I don't care about anything except being inside of her, can't think about anything beyond how badly I need to fuck her, how badly I need to come.

I moan as my hand closes around my hard length, the skin taut and beyond sensitive as I free my aching cock, the tip slick with my arousal. I push the swollen head against her drenched entrance, the heat tearing another pained groan free of my lips—and then I thrust into her, hard and fast, giving us both what we want.

What I can't stop myself from taking any longer.

Gia

The feeling of Salvatore thrusting into me takes my breath away.

It *all* takes my breath away. My body feels wound tight, confused, pain and pleasure all mixed together, the ache between my thighs spreading through me until all I want is for him to fuck me harder, until we both come.

I'm furious at him—and for the first time, there's no question in my mind about whether or not I want him. His possessiveness and jealousy made me angrier than I've been since the day he disrupted my wedding and took me for himself—and also turned me on more than I thought was possible.

For once, he stopped thinking. He stopped fighting how he felt, and just *acted*. And as angry as I am at him for manhandling me, for telling me what to do, for *punishing* me—I'm also painfully aroused.

I've touched myself more than once, imagining just that. Spankings, being tied up, forced down to my knees, ordered to do all sorts of things that a good mafia daughter shouldn't know about. But I never knew how good it could feel in reality. How that burning pain could turn into something else, a hot ache that left me dripping, hollow, desperate to be filled.

And now Salvatore is doing just that.

He draws himself out to the tip, thrusting shallowly at the entrance, and then drives himself into me again to the hilt. It's almost too much, his cock almost too big, but the pleasure of it filling me, hot and thick and impossibly hard, drives the pleasure so high that the pain only enhances it.

"Is this what you want?" he growls, his hand tight around my wrists as he thrusts again, grinding against me as he fills me completely. "You want to be fucked like this, Gia? Held down while I use you? Is this going to make you come?"

"Yes," I gasp helplessly, beyond argument, beyond shame. He hasn't touched my clit, but I can feel my orgasm building, his thick length rubbing every sensitive inch of me inside, sending waves of unimaginable pleasure through me. He slams into me again, his hand on the back of my neck, pinning me to the bed as he fucks me hard. "Please—please don't stop—"

"Oh, *fuck*—" Salvatore groans, his jaw tight as I twist my head to look back at him, his chest heaving. "God, you're so fucking tight. So fucking good. You fit my cock so perfectly, *fuck*—"

He's lost control at last. I'd wondered what it would be like, what he would do if he snapped, and it's everything I could have imagined. He looks like a god fucking me, all taut muscles beneath his clothes, his linen shirt clinging to his damp skin, his pants ripped open and hanging off of his sharp hipbones as he thrusts into me again and again. I catch a glimpse of his swollen, glistening cock as he draws out of me again, and my legs spread wider without thinking about it, my back arching to take more of him.

"Greedy girl," Salvatore growls, his hands holding me down. "You want more of my cock, don't you? You want it harder, you little *troia*?"

The filthy word, growled in his deep voice, his accent thick and rough, pushes me over the edge. I moan helplessly, the sound rising in a desperate whine as I buck against his hands, the orgasm crashing over me in waves. I feel myself clench around him, pulling him deeper, hear his desperate groan as I arch into his thrusting cock, wanting more, wanting him to fuck me, to come in me, to fill me up. I don't even realize that I'm moaning those words aloud until Salvatore lets out a sudden string of curses in Italian, his voice a rasping growl as he thrusts into me to the hilt, his body pinning me to the bed. I feel his cock stiffen and throb inside of me, feel the hot flood of his cum as his mouth presses against my shoulder, his hips jerking rhythmically against me as he comes hard on the heels of my own violent orgasm.

For a brief moment, neither of us move. I lay there trembling, the aftershocks still rippling over my skin, and I find myself hoping that he'll stay hard, that he'll keep fucking me, that he'll make me come again.

But instead, he recoils from me, letting go of me abruptly as he pulls free. I moan as his cock slips out of me, feeling empty, the hot dampness of his cum leaking onto my thighs as Salvatore yanks his pants back up around his hips, breathing hard.

And then, before I can get up or even say anything at all, he storms out of the room, slamming the door behind me as he leaves me there, a disheveled mess on our bed.

―

When he comes back, it's dark out. I've since showered and changed, and I'm sitting out on the deck when he returns, watching the glassy surface of the pool while I sit on one of the lounges. I hear the glass door open and hear his footsteps approaching, but I don't look up at him.

"Gia―"

"Stop lying to yourself." I don't look at him at first. I've had hours to think about what I want to say. I take a deep breath, finally turning to face him, and as I look up at him, his expression is unreadable. I can't imagine what it is that he's thinking.

"You want me," I say quietly. "You're lying to us both if you keep pretending that you don't. And I don't want any part of that. So you need to either admit it, or find a way to dissolve our marriage. Either way, I don't want any more of your lies."

Salvatore doesn't flinch. His expression doesn't change. "You're mine," he says quietly. "I won't give you up."

I take a deep breath. For once, I don't feel angry. I don't feel as if I'm simmering on the edge of either an outburst or a breakdown. I don't feel sure of the way forward, either—but I feel calm. Calmer than I have in a long time.

Slowly, I stand up to face him, my arms crossed under my breasts. "You remember what we said the other night about playing games?"

Salvatore doesn't respond, his face still implacable.

"I'm done with them," I tell him quietly. "I'm done with this back and forth, with you insisting you don't want me, hurting my feelings, making me feel unwanted and alone, all in the name of *protecting* me —only for you to then swoop in, drag me back here, and fuck me like *that*? What I *wanted*, only not because you were so furious you couldn't control yourself, but because you admitted that you wanted me. So here's what *I've* decided."

I tip my chin up, meeting his eyes, steeling myself not to flinch. "I won't accept less than a husband who treats me as an equal, and gives me what I need." My voice softens, ever so slightly. "You were my first kiss, you know. You've been my first *everything*. Pyotr might have shown me what it meant to *feel* desire, but he didn't show me how to act on any of it. You've done all of that. Maybe I was deluded into thinking that Pyotr would have given me what I wanted—maybe not. Maybe you're right, and I was wrong. But either way—that's what I was promised. Passion, desire, an equal place at my husband's side. And I won't settle for less."

Salvatore's eyebrows rise as I speak, and I see a flicker of something in his face that I don't think I've ever seen before. He looks almost—impressed. As if he's surprised to see me calmly standing up for myself—but that he likes it, too.

He lets out a slow breath, moving to one side as he sinks down onto the lounge chair. "I don't know what I'm prepared to give you, Gia. I lost control earlier. I'm not proud of it. I'm ashamed of myself for becoming so angry, for handling you that way, for letting my lust overcome me. You deserved your punishment—and you have yet to apologize for your behavior," he adds, his eyes narrowing. "But I shouldn't have lost control."

"The way you touched me—that was what I wanted the other night. Not that strange, cold way you fucked me." I bite my lip. "I wanted *you*. I wanted you to want *me*, and—"

"The problem isn't wanting you," Salvatore says quietly. "The problem is that I shouldn't."

"And why not?" I demand. "I'm yours now; you've made that clear. You've taken my virginity; there's no going back to Pyotr for me. I'm not your daughter, Salvatore. There's no blood between us, only a promise made by you to protect me if need be. You've done that, in the only way you said you thought that you could. I'm a *woman*. I'm not a child. I'm your *wife*. The only thing you've done wrong is not treating me like your wife. I'm not some object you can just put behind glass to keep it safe, and never touch! I'm a person. And if you want to protect me, to take care of me—you have to think of me as the woman you married."

I see the way he tenses when I say that I'm his, the indrawn breath. I see that he wants me, even now. All he has to do is let himself accept it.

"I can appreciate you standing up for yourself like this, Gia," Salvatore says finally, his hands clenched between his knees. "But I don't know what I can give you. What is it that you want?" He looks up at me, his gaze dark and unreadable. "What do you want from *me*?"

A dozen responses run through my head, from sweet to sharp, soft to biting. But I let out a slow breath, and sink down onto the chair next to him. Not touching, not quite—but next to each other.

"To start," I say quietly, "you can behave like a real husband, on our honeymoon."

Salvatore raises an eyebrow. "What do you mean by that?"

I smile, just the tiniest bit. "I want to spend the day together tomorrow," I clarify. "You and I, on our honeymoon. No work. No talking about New York, or danger, or what you're dealing with there. For one day, we're on vacation together. And we'll see how that goes."

Salvatore doesn't smile, but I think I see the corners of his mouth twitch. He reaches down, the side of his hand brushing against the side of mine. The slightest touch, but one of the rare occasions that he's touched me casually of his own volition.

"Alright," he says slowly. "One day of vacation. Just the two of us."

Salvatore

In the morning, I wake to see Gia still asleep next to me. My first thought is that I need to shower and dress so that I can be gone for work before she wakes up—and then I remember that I promised to spend the day with her.

I don't regret the promise. It just feels odd. I'm not someone who has often taken days off, for anything. Other than that annual trip with her father that I mentioned, I've always had a tendency to use my 'days off' to still do work at home. And when I have taken time in the past to relax, more often than not, it's at home, at least in the last ten years or so. I haven't been the type to spend my time off out at a bar or a club in a long time.

So the thought of spending a day doing leisure activities seems, oddly, a little daunting. I'm not sure if I want to mention that to her or not, and I mull over it as I shower, taking my time this morning since I have nowhere that I need to be immediately. It makes me realize, as I think about it, that it's come to matter to me what she thinks of me. That it worries me that, if I tell her I have no idea how to plan a day at the beach for us, she'll think I'm boring.

She already wishes you hadn't married her, I think grimly as I rinse out my hair, breathing in the eucalyptus-scented steam in an effort to calm myself. *It's not as if you can make things worse.*

That, ironically enough, is the nudge I need to just talk to her. I finish my shower, putting on a pair of khaki shorts and a linen button-down with the sleeves rolled up, and go to wake her. I hesitate for a moment at the edge of the bed, looking down at her peaceful, sleeping face. I haven't been the one to wake her in all the time we've been together so far. In fact, I can't recall ever having done what's in my head just now. I feel as if I'm outside my body, watching myself as I lean down to brush her hair out of her face with one finger and kiss her lightly on the forehead.

It feels sweet. Intimate. Things that have never been a part of my life. Something in my chest cramps with a feeling that approaches panic, but I push it back down. I'm going to have to face these things, if I want a possibility of a future with her. I have to figure out how to allow myself to feel the things that I've closed myself off from my whole life.

Gia makes a small humming sound under her breath as I pull back, sleepily shifting in bed. I have that same urge that I felt the last time I looked at her like this, the desire to simply rejoin her in bed and keep her there—and I'm flooded with the same guilt, too.

But that's not what today is about. Today is meant to be about getting to know each other, feeling out what life together might be like if Gia could accept that there's no going back on our marriage, and if I could give her what she needs. And I realize, as I reach down to gently urge her awake, that I'm afraid of either outcome.

If there's no possibility of us finding a mutual middle ground, then the future ahead of us is one of mutual unhappiness instead. We'll find other things in life to give us happiness, I'm sure—Gia has already said that she sees our future children as a source of that for her. But there will be no happiness, no satisfaction from our marriage.

But if we do find a way—

I don't know how to make a wife happy. How to be a good husband. I'm confident that I'm a man capable of intimidating others when necessary, of exercising diplomacy when need be, of handling sensitive business dealings, and managing dangerous situations. None of that helps me when it comes to knowing how to make Gia happy, how to be the kind of husband she seeks, how to give her the intimacy she craves. And I feel as if I'm going to disappoint her, no matter what.

She makes another of those soft sounds as I gently nudge her awake, her eyes fluttering open. "Salvatore?" She sounds briefly confused, as if she, too, forgot that there was a reason I wouldn't have already left, and then a small smile curves the corners of her mouth. "You didn't go to work."

I feel an odd pang in my chest. "You thought I would, after what we agreed to last night?"

Gia pushes herself up, sitting back against the pillows, and I have to resist the urge to reach out and touch her hair again. It looks thick and soft, falling in heavy dark waves around her face, and I want to feel it slide through my fingers. "I thought something might come up," she admits.

It's a careful way, I know, of saying that she thought I would find an excuse to back out of it. It hurts a little that she would think so, but at the same time, I can understand it. Our marriage hasn't exactly been amicable so far.

"Do you want me to leave?" I smile a little as I say it, trying for a joke. I want to lighten the mood between us, to start this day off right.

The smallest of smiles curves the edge of her lips. "Would you?" she asks, and I raise an eyebrow, moving a little closer.

"No." The word comes out huskier than I mean it to, her proximity affecting me even now. "You asked for a day with me, Gia. And I do want to give you what you want when I can."

Her eyes widen a little, and I think I see that flicker of hope there, reflected in her, too.

"I'll call for breakfast," I tell her, taking a step back. "We can sit on the deck, have something to eat, and plan our day. What do you say to that?"

Gia bites her lip, but she nods. "Alright. That sounds nice."

Breakfast is delivered, and Gia goes to shower and dress while we wait. When she comes out of the shower, I glimpse her through the glass door, her towel dropping to the floor as she reaches for the bikini that she laid out on the bed.

My body instantly reacts, every muscle tightening and my cock immediately swelling against my thigh. She's so fucking perfect, every inch of her—from the lithe, taut muscles of her back to her narrow waist, and the heart-shaped curve of her ass. From this angle, I can just see the slight curve of her breast, and something about that drives me even more wild than seeing her breasts entirely bare. My palms itch with the urge to feel that soft shape against them, my cock suddenly stiff and throbbing, and I reach down, pushing the heel of my hand against it in an effort to subdue my erection.

I can't help but wonder if she's doing this on purpose—if she made sure to leave her clothes out in the bedroom in hopes that I'd see this little show she's putting on for me. I let out a sharp, frustrated breath, squeezing the edge of the lounge chair's cushion to keep myself from getting up and going to her.

It's only made all the more difficult when she bends over to step into her bikini bottoms, her ass perfectly angled to give me a glimpse of her soft folds. I'm absolutely sure, in that moment, that she did it on purpose to torment me.

She stands up, hooking her bikini top behind her back, just as the staff member with our breakfast tray walks in. I'm so focused on Gia that I nearly jump with surprise at the sight of another person, breakfast totally forgotten in my fixation on my gorgeous, naked wife.

You need to start thinking of me as your wife. Her words float back to me as the guilt over ogling her begins to take root, and I do my best to push it away, to take into account what she said. There's a part of me that knows she's right. She's young, and that will pose its own challenges in our relationship, but she isn't a child. And she doesn't deserve to be treated as less than the woman she is, just because I feel guilt over my choices.

"You look like you're thinking particularly hard about something," Gia teases as she walks out, waiting for breakfast to be set out on the table before taking her seat. She raises an eyebrow. "Aren't you going to come join me?"

She did do it on purpose. There's no question of that, when her mouth is curved in that small smirk, her gaze flicking down to my lap as she waits for me to get up from the lounge chair and come join her at the table. If I stand up right now, there'll be no missing the thick outline of my cock in my shorts.

It doesn't help that she didn't put a sundress on yet over her bikini. She picked the emerald green one, as if she figured out that I liked that one the best out of all of them. The color is perfect against her tanned, olive skin and dark hair, and just looking at her makes me ache.

Gia reaches over to pour orange juice and champagne into a flute glass as if nothing is amiss, putting scrambled eggs, smoked salmon, and a scone onto her plate. She glances up at me once more, that small smile still flickering at the corners of her mouth. I grit my teeth, forcing myself to stop thinking about the throbbing between my legs as I push myself to my feet and walk over to join her.

She doesn't say anything, but I don't miss the way her gaze flicks down to the front of my shorts ever so briefly, before returning to her food. "So what do you want to do today??" she asks innocently as I sit down, reaching for her mimosa.

I can think of one thing right now. I press my lips together. I have no intention of saying anything even close to that. For one, I don't know if I'm ready to go back on my insistence that our marriage bed will remain cold, other than for the purpose of having children. I'm not sure if I'm ready to allow the kind of lust that I felt for Gia yesterday to be an acceptable feeling to have about my wife, or if I'm ready to let myself feel that kind of desire entirely, instead of when I can no longer keep it on a leash. And for another, that's not what Gia asked for last night, when she talked about today.

"I'm afraid planning vacation days isn't my strong suit," I say wryly, reaching for the orange juice. "But I'm open to ideas." I pour a little into my glass, adding champagne.

"What about all of this?" Gia motions to the villa around us, and I laugh.

"Well, one of the perks of our lifestyle is that whatever needs to be done, there's always someone who can be hired to do it. My assistant, and a very good travel agent put together a portfolio of ideas and sent them over to me, and I approved what I thought you would enjoy—the villa, the room service, all of that. I told them to spare no expense," I add. "I wanted this to be an unforgettable experience for you, Gia, regardless of the reasoning behind why we left. I told them to make certain to book the best of everything that was available."

Gia gives me an odd half-smile. "That was sweet," she says softly. "Anything you planned yourself would have meant a lot, though, you know. All of this is beautiful, and stunning, and I've definitely never experienced anything like it. But I want us both to put some thought into today."

"You first." I return her smile. "And we can bounce ideas off of each other. How about that?" I can see that she's full of them, and I truthfully didn't plan to do much more than enjoy the villa itself at night, and work.

"You did say you'd never really been on a vacation before," Gia admits, shaking her head. She leans forward, pursing her lips as she scoops up a bite of salmon and eggs with her fork. "Well, I was thinking we could walk around the market first. I went there on my first day here, and it's a lot of fun. A lot of unique vendors, fun foods, that kind of thing. And then we could go down to the beach, lay out for a little while, go for a swim. When we're ready for lunch, we can go to one of the beachside restaurants—a different one," she adds quickly, when she sees my gaze darken at the memory of the bar I found her at yesterday. "Have lunch and a drink, maybe walk through some of the shops. And then, after dinner, we could go back out to one of the bars. Supposedly, there's live music and dancing. That could be fun. It's been a while since I went out dancing," she adds. "Not since the last gala I went to with my father, and that feels like it was ages ago. And those parties are all so stuffy, anyway. I feel like this would be different. More relaxed."

I feel another vague flare of panic. Dancing at a beachside bar sounds so far out of the realm of something I would do that I can't even quite picture it. But I see Gia's eyes light up as she describes her ideas, and I find myself not wanting to disappoint her. In fact, I find myself wanting to go along with her ideas, just to see if it would be as much fun as she seems to feel that it would. "I can't think of anything to add. But everything you've suggested sounds like all of the best things we could get up to here. I'm fine with that."

Gia's smile broadens, just a little, and I feel something flip in my chest. I like making her smile, I realize. I like making her happy. And despite what happened yesterday, I find myself willing to look past it, if there's the possibility of fixing how we got there in the first place.

"I'm going to go finish getting dressed," Gia says, when she's done with her breakfast and mimosa. "Give me maybe twenty minutes?"

"You can have as long as you need," I assure her. "If it's a day off, then there's no rush, right?"

Gia laughs. "Now you're getting the idea. And put on some swim shorts," she adds. "We're going to the beach, remember?"

Her laugh tugs at something in my chest. It's bright and happy, a sound I can't really recall having heard from her since we've been married, and certainly never directed towards me. It makes me want to hear it again, to do something else that pulls that sound from her. It makes *me* feel happy, in a way that I can't remember having felt in a long time.

"Alright," I concede. "I did bring a pair, although it's been a long time since I've used them."

"There's a pool at the mansion," Gia points out. "An indoor, heated one, too, for the winter months."

"That doesn't mean I've ever used it." It occurs to me as I say it how much I really don't ever take advantage of the luxuries that my life offers me—or take all that much pleasure in the ones that I do indulge in. I eat the finest foods available and dress in tailored, bespoke clothing, with the best liquor I could ask for delivered to my mansion. Every indulgence or form of entertainment I might want is available to me, but I don't enjoy it the way I should. I've been so focused on work, on serving Enzo for so much of my life, that I've taken for granted the things around me that enhance my life so much.

In that way, I realize, my marriage to Gia could be good for me. She clearly has no intention of giving up on the things that she enjoys about life and, given the opportunity, will indulge in any new experience offered to her.

It's one of the things that makes me feel sometimes dangerously close to feeling more for her than I planned, or than I feel I should.

I grab a pair of swim shorts, going into the bathroom to change while Gia pulls one of her sundresses out of the wardrobe. It's odd—I've been physically intimate with her, been *inside* of her, the first man to ever do so…and yet, I feel uncomfortable undressing in front of her. Doing so casually feels like a greater level of intimacy, even though it's a perfectly natural thing to do in front of my wife.

When I come back out, Gia has a white sundress on, a pretty lightweight thing made out of a gauzy material with a halter neck and a lacy hem. I hesitate, remembering the gifts I bought her yesterday. When I'd seen her at the bar with Blake, I'd had half a mind to throw them in the damn ocean, after what she did. A part of me doesn't think she deserves gifts after flirting with another man.

And part of me accepts that regardless of whether or not her behavior was acceptable, it was because of the circumstances of our relationship. Circumstances that I've created.

I can, at least, accept that holding grudges won't help us move forward.

I walk over to the chair that the pair of pants I wore yesterday are draped over. The cleaning staff hasn't been here yet since yesterday afternoon, so no one has cleaned up the dirty clothes, thank goodness. The boxes are still in the pocket, and I slip them out, turning to Gia.

"I have something for you." I sink down on the edge of the bed, holding out the two small boxes to her.

She blinks at me, startled. "You bought me something?"

I nod. "I went out at lunch yesterday to find a gift for you." I take a deep breath, trying to think of how to explain how I felt yesterday, before everything blew apart. "I know I'm not making you happy, Gia. But gifts seem to make you happy, and so I—"

The look on her face makes me break off abruptly. "I'm not saying you're spoiled," I add quickly. "I'm saying I know that you like pretty things, and when I gave you those onyx earrings to wear with your dress for dinner, I noticed you wore them a few more times. So I thought—" I let out a sharp breath. "These are for you."

Gingerly, Gia takes the boxes out of my hands. She sets the smaller one on the dresser, lifting the top off of the longer one first. When she sees the bracelet nestled inside, I see her eyes go wide.

"Oh," she says softly. "It's beautiful."

"You think so?" I let out a sigh of relief. "I don't really know how to pick these things. I've never shopped for a woman other than you."

Gia looks up at me, a small frown on her lips. "No? You've never bought anyone else gifts?"

I shake my head, feeling vaguely uncomfortable with the line of questioning. I hadn't really expected to talk to Gia about any other women. "I had an assistant send flowers in the past," I say finally. "But I've never been with anyone long enough to think about getting them anything fancier than that."

Gia nods, as if she's not entirely sure what to say. But she reaches down, gently taking the bracelet out of the box. "Here." She holds out her wrist. "Put it on me?"

I feel her shiver, ever so slightly, when I touch her skin. Her wrist feels delicate, almost fragile in my fingers, and I'm struck with that urge to protect her all over again. She's stronger than she looks, I know that, but she feels so breakable like this. It makes me want to hold her close, to promise her that I'll protect her from any harm.

But I've promised her that already, and it hasn't been enough. It's not what she needs, not really. Or maybe it's what she needs—but it's not what she wants. What she wants from a husband—from me —is much more complex and harder to give than something as simple as protection.

Gently, I clasp the bracelet around her wrist. She glances at the other box and reaches for it, smiling when she sees the earrings.

"These are beautiful, too," she says softly. "You definitely know my taste in jewelry."

"I guessed," I admit. "I'm not entirely sure what your taste is, yet. But if I keep buying you gifts, I'll learn."

Gia laughs. "I like the sound of that. Are you ready to go?"

She's not wearing any makeup, her hair loose, the dress floating just above her knees. She slips on a pair of flat leather sandals, and glances back at me. She looks astonishingly beautiful like this, naturally lovely. To me, she looks even more beautiful than she did on her wedding day, in a gown of lace and silk with her hair and makeup perfectly done.

I take a breath. "Let's go."

It's hard to turn the part of my mind off that's always attuned to what needs to be done—to calls that need to be made, meetings that need to be arranged, business that needs to be handled, and bribes that need to be meted out, warnings that need to be delivered. There's more to this life than sitting behind a desk with a glass of cognac while my men handle things. After decades of this, I'm so accustomed to it that forcing those thoughts out of my head feels unnatural. But I put my phone on silent as per Gia's request, shoving it into my pocket and following her out of the villa with our security in tow.

The day is beautiful. Warm—just this side of hot, actually—the sun shimmering off of the water and a faint breeze carrying the scent of salt and easing the sharp sting of the sun. Gia leads the way, taking me to the open-air market that she said she visited on her first day. It's bustling with tourists, and I feel my muscles tense at first, looking around for signs of danger, and to make sure that the security is watching us. I catch a glimpse of Vince melting into the crowd, and I try to relax, but it's difficult.

And then, I nearly jump as I feel Gia's fingers slip through mine. I glance over at her, and see her looking up at me with a wry smile on her face.

"It's fine," she says gently. "We're not in any danger here, Salvatore. I've been out every day since we came here, and I haven't had any trouble at all. Has Vince told you there was any trouble that I didn't know about?"

I shake my head. "No. He said all's been well, every day so far."

"Then try to relax." She squeezes my hand lightly. "Please."

The last thing that I expected was for Gia to hold my hand of her own volition. The feeling of her fingers curling around mine is good, and I do feel myself relaxing, just a little. It surprises me, how much such a small touch can do. I've touched this woman in ways more intimate than any other man ever has, and yet, I've so rarely touched her in the small ways that feel somehow more intimate than fucking. Maybe it's that I've had sex with plenty of women, but I've rarely held anyone's hand, or touched the small of their back as I guided them into a room, or laid a hand on their thigh. Touch for the sake of lust, to slake desire—that I've had my fill of in my life. But soft, sweet intimacy is something that I can't recall the last time I partook in.

I fold my hand a little more firmly around hers, and follow her further into the market.

Gia is clearly delighted by all of it. We stop at a hat seller's stand, where she looks through a variety of wide-brimmed beach hats before settling on a white straw one to match her dress, with a blue chiffon ribbon wrapped around it. She sets it on her head, tilting her face up to look at me. "What do you think?"

"You look adorable," I tell her frankly, and she wrinkles her nose at me.

"I don't want to be *adorable*."

"What else should I call it?" I reach up, tipping the brim of the hat up so I can dip my head beneath it, and without thinking, I rest one hand on her waist, pulling her closer. I lean in, and brush my mouth against hers.

I feel her gasp. I feel the instant she leans into me, her hands coming up to press against my chest, but she's not pushing me away. For the first time, there's no resistance from her. Nothing other than her soft lips parting under mine, her tongue flicking out hesitantly to meet mine. She tastes sweet, a little sharp, like the mimosa she drank this morning, and my head spins with a sudden, desperate need for her. I nearly slant my mouth over hers, deepening the kiss, until I feel someone bump into me, and I remember where we are.

My arm goes around Gia's waist as I break the kiss, steadying us both as the crowd moves past, and I straighten as I look down at her. Her cheeks are flushed, her chest heaving slightly, and her eyes are wide.

She looks as if she's a little in shock.

"That's the first time you've kissed me since the wedding," Gia whispers.

That can't be true. I run back the list of our encounters through my head—the fraught wedding night, the moment when I lost my control in the workout room, the night she convinced me to take her virginity entirely, her catching me in the bathroom, yesterday afternoon when I lost control with her. And I realize, with something approaching shame, that she's right.

I haven't kissed her since we stood at the altar, on our wedding day.

In some deep, hard-to-reach part of myself, I think I knew it would change things. That kissing her again would mean something. And it did. At that moment, I wasn't thinking about whether I should or not, about whether kissing her was something I ought to be allowed, about whether it fit into the set of boundaries that I built for myself around our marriage.

I saw her face, her smile under the brim of that ridiculous hat, her nose wrinkling with annoyance at my choice of words, and her eyes narrowing, and I wanted to kiss her. It had been so simple, and I hadn't thought about it at all.

"Do you want me to kiss you again?" I murmur, still holding her close. The crowd is flowing around us, and I hear a few murmurs of annoyance, but I couldn't care less.

"Maybe later," Gia breathes, and I see her throat tighten a little as she swallows. "I want the rest of our day. And if you kiss me again, I think we might end up back at the villa."

She isn't wrong. I pull back, letting her lead me through the crowd, my head still spinning with what just happened. I'm lost in my thoughts until Gia pulls me abruptly back to the present, waving a hand at me as she stops in front of a stall.

"I got this the first day we were here," she says. "You'll love it."

I nod numbly, handing her my card and letting her buy whatever it is that she wants. We end up at a picnic table with two small bowls of fruit, covered in a sprinkling of lime juice and chili seasoning, and a large cup of lemonade.

"It's sweet and spicy and a little sour with the lemonade. Try it," Gia urges. "It's so good. I could eat this every day."

I reach down, taking a bite. The flavors explode over my tongue, and she's right. It *is* delicious, different from what I normally eat, but nonetheless incredible. "You're right," I tell her, taking another bite and reaching for the lemonade. "I should ask Frances to learn how to make this."

"Oh, that's a good idea!" Gia exclaims, taking the cup out of my hand. "That would be amazing."

Something tugs in my chest at that, a realization that it's the first domestic thing we've ever talked about happily. It's a small thing that shouldn't mean all that much, but in our circumstances, it feels like it means everything.

We linger a little bit longer in the market, before tossing away the cup and bowls and heading to the beach. I can't help but think that actually being out on the beach isn't all that appealing—it's sandy, and the light wind that's sprung up means it takes us a few minutes to get the blanket that we brought spread out and held down. Even so, there are still grains of sand on it. I feel strongly that I'd prefer looking at the water from our pool deck. But Gia is clearly excited about the beach, and I promised her that today would be whatever she wanted it to be.

When she starts to reapply her sunscreen, I mind being out here less.

I can't help but look as she rubs it over the curves of her breasts, down her sides, over the long stretch of her legs. I find myself curling my fingers into my palms, aching to rub my hands over her body the same way, to be the one smoothing the lotion over her skin. The thought of the security out here the last few days, watching her while she does this, sends that simmering burn of jealousy through my veins, and I have to grit my teeth against it.

Gia turns to me a second later, a smile on her lips. "Put some on my back?" she asks, and I'm all too happy to acquiesce.

We lay out in the sun for a little while, both of us with books that we brought along. I have to admit, once I get past the irritation of the occasional burst of sand blowing onto the towel and sticking to my skin, it's nice to be out this close to the water. The crash of the waves is closer here, and the sound of the seabirds darting up and down the beach, and there's a different feeling to it than lying out on the deck. Still, I know for sure which I prefer.

"I'm going to get in the water," Gia says after a little while. "Come with me?"

I raise an eyebrow. "I already have sand sticking to me. Now we're going in the salt water?"

Gia rolls her eyes playfully. "That'll wash the sand off. A win/win. Come on—we can go get lunch after this."

I frown at her, but the pleading look that she gives me is hard to ignore, and I sigh, standing up as I reach to strip off my shirt. "Alright, then."

The look on her face when I toss my shirt down to the blanket makes me forget all my complaints about the sand. Her gaze sweeps over me, lingering on my chest and upper arms, a heated look in her eyes that immediately makes me think that going into the cold water might be a *good* idea.

It startles me, seeing the desire on her face as she looks at me. It never occurred to me, when I made the impulsive decision to marry her in order to keep her out of the Bratva's clutches, that she might come to want me. I assumed that when I upended all her plans for her future, she would resent me indefinitely. That even if we found a way to make peace on that subject, she would never want me the way she clearly wanted her Bratva fiance.

And I was so sure that I could—and *should*—never want her that I hadn't even considered what might happen if she did.

Now, as I see her look at me with the sort of desire that I never imagined seeing in her face, it hits me that she's *right*. That I've been unfair to her, to steal her away from the marriage she planned for and condemn her to a cold, passionless union for the sake of keeping her protected. It *was* for her own good, and certainly not a fate worse than being trapped with the Bratva—but I thought it would be enough just to protect her.

I didn't think past that one goal.

But if we make this more—

I feel that sense of panic writhing in my gut again as I follow Gia down to the water's edge. I've been around long enough to know what comes of this. To know what could happen if I let myself explore these feelings that she rouses in me. One day of letting my guard down, and I can already see things in her that could make me fall for her. So what happens after that?

I'm afraid of what happens if I let myself love her. It's not just the lingering guilt I feel over my own desire, that nagging reminder that she was entrusted to me to protect, not to take to my bed. I also fear that if I let myself fall for her, I won't be able to do just that—protect her.

Enzo's love for his daughter, his desire to make her happy at all costs, nearly led to her being fed to the wolves. If I allow myself to love Gia—albeit in a different way—will love blind me similarly?

I was raised to believe that feelings are for men without the responsibilities and power that I have. I often thought, as I spent my life working for Enzo, that without my clear-headedness, he might have made many more mistakes than he did because of the innate kindness he had. I gave up the chance for a family to focus on serving Enzo, to make it my life's work. To prevent myself from ever having anything else that could distract me.

But today, I can feel something changing. I find myself wanting to be softer with Gia. To give her what she so clearly wants.

And I can't help but wonder if I have a responsibility to make her happy, since I claimed her on her wedding day, and insisted that she be my wife.

"Are you coming?" Gia's voice cuts through my thoughts, bright and a little high-pitched from the cold as she dashes into the water. I follow her, sucking in a breath at the chill as the water laps at my calves.

"Is this not insanely cold to you?" I shiver, walking a little deeper, wincing as the cold water grazes my upper thighs, and then higher. "It's still spring, you know, even here."

"It feels good to me." Gia dives under the water, and for a moment, I feel a flash of fear as I see her disappear. She resurfaces a moment later, and I let out a breath that I hadn't realized I was holding.

It strikes me how deeply protective I am of her, in ways that I don't think even I fully realized. It's just water, just a tropical beach—but the instant she went under, a dozen different scenarios flooded my mind of ways that something could have happened to her. I know that's not normal. That if I stifle her like that, she'll never love me.

Today has given me a glimpse of what life could be like, if Gia and I were happy together. I'm afraid to want it. Afraid to hope for something that I wrote off a long time ago, that could hurt me if it goes wrong. And there are so very many ways that it could go wrong. Even normal marriages, without the stresses of our strange lives, without the difference in our ages, with more in common than we have, go wrong all the time.

Our marriage is nearly impossible to dissolve. But I know that if Gia and I were happy for a while, only to lose that happiness and for our marriage to go back to the way it was before, it would be even worse than how things are now.

Gia disappears under the water again, and then springs up an inch away from me, emerging like some kind of dark-haired mermaid. Water is dripping down her tanned skin, and she's close enough to touch. I feel my body tighten in response to how close she is, every part of me aching to reach out for her, to pull her close and kiss her under the bright sun, standing here in the crystal blue water.

Why not? The question burns into my mind, challenging everything I've thought up to this point. She's my wife. Why not kiss her here, on our honeymoon, in this beautiful, romantic place? She hasn't moved away, and I can feel her waiting for something. For me to make a decision—a choice, maybe.

I reach for her, my hand dipping beneath the cold water to touch the smooth, bare skin of her waist. It feels warm against my fingers, and I pull her closer, all of my awareness narrowing down to this. To her. I've never felt anything like it before. I've never felt anything so intensely.

Gia tips her head back, looking up at me as I pull her against me. She feels soft and warm, her skin wet against mine, and it makes my head spin with desire. Her eyes widen, her lips parting on a soft breath as she feels us touch, and I reach up with my other hand to slide my palm against her cheek.

Her eyes flutter closed. I feel her lean into my touch—a sign of trust. And not so long ago—yesterday, even—I would have said that the only way I could repay that trust was to deny her. But now, I've started to think that it might be something different.

That maybe it's more than trust. It's a willingness to give me another chance. To see if I might do things differently.

I slide my fingers into her wet hair, feeling it glide over my skin. My thumb brushes under the edge of her chin, tilting it up, bringing her mouth towards mine. And when I press my lips to hers, it feels as if the whole world shifts around me.

It feels as if everything is different. Brighter. The heat of the sun beating down on us, the cold of the water lapping at my legs, the feeling of her hands sliding up my chest, around my neck, holding me as she arches into me and her lips part under mine. The call of birds, the smell of salt—it all forms a moment that I know I'll remember, regardless of what happens next, of what comes after this. I cling to it, because I'm not sure there's ever been a moment that I want to remember more.

My fingers curl around the back of her head, my other hand sliding to the small of her back, holding her against me as her lips part and my tongue slides into her mouth. She tastes sweet and salty all at once, like the ocean water, and I hear myself groan as I deepen the kiss, wanting her in a way that goes beyond lust. I can feel my body responding to her, all the signs of arousal springing to life that I'm so very familiar with, but this feels like something more than that. It's not like any kiss I've had before.

"We could go back to the villa," Gia whispers breathlessly against my lips, when I finally break the kiss. We're still standing very close to one another, touching, her hands linked around the back of my neck. "If you're hungry—" Her eyes twinkle with mischief, and I narrow mine at her.

"I promised you lunch. An entire day out, I believe, was the promise you exacted from me last night. I'm not going to go back on it now."

I lace my fingers through hers as her hands drop to her sides, pulling her in for one more light kiss. "We'll end up back at the villa soon enough."

Gia pouts a little, but I can tell she's pleased that I still want to spend the rest of the promised day with her. We go out to lunch, to a different restaurant with fresh seafood and some of the best tacos I've ever eaten, and drink margaritas sitting out on the deck. Afterwards, we walk through the shops as I promised her before, and Gia ends up buying a long, silky yellow dress and a woven leather belt to go with it, and a pair of dangling shell earrings. She tucks her packages into her tote, and as the sun starts to set, we begin the walk back to the villa.

Gia goes to shower when we get back, and I know she's wondering if I'm going to join her. It seems like the obvious thing, after that kiss earlier in the water. But I hang back, waiting. I see the flicker of disappointment in her eyes, and I know what she's thinking—that I'm reconsidering my apparent change of heart now that we're back here. But that's not it at all.

Tonight, I think things might be different between us. And I want to do that right, if that's where the night is going.

If I'm going to try to give her everything, I want to begin exactly as I would have done it from the start.

Gia

I feel a flutter of anxiety in my stomach as I shower, rinsing off the sand and salt and sunscreen from our day out. It was a good day. A *perfect* day, even, considering what I had expected—which wasn't much. I wouldn't let myself expect very much at all. I'd half thought that Salvatore would come up with some excuse to get out of it, some reason why work took precedence, and that he'd lecture me on the importance of keeping me safe before leaving me to my own devices again.

But he didn't do that at all. Instead, he gave me exactly what I asked for. Everything—and more, really, when I think about that kiss.

Our first kiss since our wedding day.

Just remembering the kiss in the market, and then again in the water, sends shivers over my skin despite the heat of the shower. It was so different from the way he kissed me on our wedding day that I can't begin to compare the two. It was—

It was the way I'd always dreamed of being kissed.

But then we got back, and he didn't follow me into the shower. If anything, it felt like maybe things were going to go back to the way they were before.

I don't want that. Not after getting a glimmer of what they could possibly be. Of what we could have, if Salvatore doesn't close himself off from me again.

The day isn't over yet, I remind myself, as I get out of the shower and dry off, braiding my wet hair before slipping into the canary yellow silk dress that I bought earlier. It has thin straps and is scooped at the neckline, the excess fabric forming soft, draping folds at my cleavage. It clings to me perfectly, slit up either side to my thighs, and it's perfect for dancing if I can convince Salvatore to go out and do that with me tonight.

I slip on the shell earrings, and go out to join him.

"My turn?" Salvatore smiles at me as he stands from where he was sitting on one of the lounge chairs. "I called and asked them to bring us a light dinner tonight. After all, you did say that you still wanted to go out dancing."

Instantly, my mood brightens. "I wondered if you'd still want to do that."

"Why not? You said you wanted to, and today was all about making you happy." The smile is still lingering on his mouth, and I have the urge to step forward and kiss him. But I want him to be the one to make the moves for a little while longer. I want to find out how far he'll let his boundaries go.

"I'm looking forward to it." I see the way his gaze slides over me before he goes to leave, taking in the new dress.

"You look beautiful," Salvatore says softly, lingering for just a moment. And then he disappears back into the villa, to go get ready for the evening.

My heart is fluttering in my chest, and I press my hand over it as I sink down onto the lounge chair. Everything feels like it's changing very quickly, like all the things I wanted are on the precipice of happening. I'm afraid to hope for it, afraid to think that there's a chance at happiness for us. I was so sure, not that long ago, that happiness with Salvatore was an impossibility.

But I'm seeing another side to him. A willingness to try to meet me in the middle. A lighter side to him, too—a possibility that he could be someone willing to let loose and have fun. Maybe he just needed someone to pry that out of him, to encourage him to do exactly that. A reason to relax. Maybe no one ever gave him a reason to before.

I have some idea of how much my father relied on him. It occurs to me how much pressure that must have been—how much it still must be, after his death, with his entire empire resting on Salvatore's shoulders now. And I feel a prick of guilt for accusing him of betraying my father.

If what Salvatore has told me is true about the Bratva, then he's done exactly the opposite. I still don't know which is true. But I find myself wanting to give Salvatore a chance after today. I find myself looking forward to the rest of the night.

Dinner is delivered while Salvatore is still in the shower—salads and shrimp cocktail, with a platter of chilled oysters and white wine. I pour myself a glass while I wait for him to come out, and when I hear the glass door slide open, I feel a fizz of anticipation in my veins.

Tonight is going to be different. I feel sure that it is.

Salvatore is dressed in the clothes I've started to become used to seeing on him. My gaze keeps sliding back to the open v of his shirt, my fingers tingling with the desire to run them over his chest. I imagine hooking my finger in the thin gold chain around his neck, tugging him closer for a kiss, feeling his hard body press against mine. I bite my lip against the sound that threatens to slip out, and Salvatore looks up at me, one eyebrow raised.

"Are you alright, *dolce*?"

Sweet. The sound of the endearment startles me. It's not something I'm used to with him. But I don't mind it. I like the sound of it, actually, when he says it like that—without irritation, his voice softer than I'm used to. As if he's enjoying the conversation.

"I'm fine. Just thinking."

"About what?" Salvatore takes a bite of his salad, looking at me with what appears to be genuine curiosity. But I'm not about to tell him what was actually going through my head just now.

I've been rejected by him too many times to put myself out there again like that just yet. I want him to pursue me a while longer, before I do. It's not even playing games at this point, I don't think. It's just self-preservation.

But it is an opportunity to talk to him about the rest of what's been on my mind, as the day has unwound so pleasantly.

"I enjoyed today," I say slowly, picking up a piece of shrimp and dipping it into the metal tin of cocktail sauce.

"I did, too. It's not over yet." Salvatore still has that curious look on his face. "Unless you want it to be?"

"No. That's not what I meant. I just—" I let out a slow breath, taking a bite to give myself a minute to think, and washing it down with the crisp white wine. I taste hints of pineapple in it, and I make a mental note of the label, to see if we can get it back home.

Home. It's the first time I've thought of Salvatore's mansion in that way. I could try to tell myself that I was simply thinking of New York in general, which has always been my home, but I know deep down that's not true. I was thinking of where we'll go, when our honeymoon is over.

I'm not sure if it makes me fearful or gives me hope, that I thought of it that way.

"My father wanted me to have a husband who was a good match for me," I say slowly. "He believed that was Pyotr."

I see Salvatore's shoulders tense, in preparation for retrodding old ground. But I have a different idea about that conversation this time.

"You want to continue serving my father's legacy," I continue, meeting Salvatore's gaze. "To do right by me and what he left behind. What if you could do that by being a good husband to *me*? By being the kind of husband that I expected Pyotr would be?"

There's a glint in Salvatore's eyes that tells me I'm treading dangerous ground. After what happened yesterday and the day we've had today, I can't imagine he likes hearing me describe how fervently I'd anticipated marrying another man. But at the same time, I want him to understand what I wanted. What I thought I would get out of marriage.

"And what kind of husband is that?" he asks tautly. It's clear from the tone of his voice that depending on how this conversation goes, the rest of our night could fall apart. But I have to hope that we can find a way to talk to each other. That we can learn to communicate like a husband and wife should.

"I know I can be stubborn, and willful. My father knew it, too. He thought that Pyotr would be the kind of husband who would appreciate those qualities in me, rather than being intimidated by them and trying to snuff them out, as so many mafia sons would. He thought that Pyotr would appreciate my rebellious nature, and that, at the same time, he might tame me a little. That we could smooth each other's rough edges. He thought that Pyotr, being about my age, would be able to understand me better than someone older that he might have given my hand to." I see Salvatore flinch at that, but it has to be said. It was part of the conversations my father and I had. "And he thought that Pyotr would see me as an equal. The mafia princess wed to the Bratva prince. A fairytale for our families. We would lead the Bratva together." I trail off, biting my lip. I have some idea of what Salvatore must think of all of this. "Pyotr and I talked, too. I thought he would be—"

"I know what you thought he would be." Salvatore cuts me off, rubbing a hand over his chin. "Forgive me, Gia, but I don't want to hear another soliloquy about how passionate of a marriage you expected to have with your virile Bratva groom." The bridge of his nose wrinkles, and I shove down a brief flare of irritation. I already know firsthand what Salvatore's innate possessiveness can turn into, and that flare of irritation starts to shift into a different kind of heat. If his reaction to thinking about Pyotr makes him realize that he does want me, I reason, all the better.

"Your father and I disagreed on the match from the jump," he says. "I always thought that whatever front Igor and Pyotr were putting on to convince him of the match, it was exactly that. He didn't trust Igor, exactly, and he never thought that Igor was a good man. But as he was blinded with love for you, he believed that Igor was the same for his son. Your father firmly believed that Pyotr was genuine in his feelings and desire for you, and that Igor would treat you well and uphold the agreements to please his son. Just as he wanted to please you."

"But you didn't believe that." I bite my lip. This *is* ground we've already covered, but the conversation feels different this time. For the first time, I'm willing to listen to what Salvatore has to say, and not only because all chance of my being reclaimed by Pyotr is gone. Salvatore has shown me enough of himself that I'm no longer certain of what I once believed. And if Salvatore didn't claim me for lust, then it must have been for another reason.

"I believe Pyotr wanted you, as any man offered both the treasure that you are and the inheritance that came with you would—"

"But not you," I interrupt. "You didn't want me?"

"I never thought of you that way," Salvatore says quietly. "Not until you were already my wife, and I needed to. And I found—" He pauses, and I wait for him to continue. But the silence stretches out longer than it should, as if he's having a hard time saying what's on his mind.

"What?" I murmur, and he looks up at me, his eyes suddenly dark with unexpected emotion. And, I think—desire, too.

"I found that I wanted you." His gaze holds mine at last, and I feel the tension in the air suddenly snap taut, making my skin prickle. "I found that I wanted you more than I thought I ever could. More than I knew I *should*. And I fought it with everything in me, because you were never supposed to be mine, Gia. I was supposed to protect you, and then give you to another man. But—"

He hesitates, letting out a slow breath. "I didn't take you for desire, Gia. I married you because I believed, to the depths of my soul, that Pyotr would only hurt you. Emotionally for certain, and possibly physically as well. When I met with him and his father before the wedding, and suggested that we postpone for the sake of your grief—"

I look at the expression on Salvatore's face, and understanding dawns on me. "He wasn't understanding."

"He was—crude, in the way he spoke about you. He and his father both. Whatever he showed you, Gia, it wasn't the truth. He would never have seen you as his equal. I have never known a Bratva man to treat a woman as such, but perhaps there's someone out there who would. I can't speak for every man. But I can speak to what I saw in Pyotr, and he was not who you and your father believed him to be, Gia." Salvatore breathes out sharply. "If you believe anything I've told you, Gia, I want it to be this. I would never have denied you your wedding and gone against your father's wishes for any other reason other than that I believed you were truly in danger. That your heart and your spirit would both have been broken by him. And I couldn't allow that to happen."

"Why?" I ask softly, and some part of me tenses as I wait for his answer, wondering if he'll say aloud what I can barely imagine him saying at all.

"Because you were entrusted to me," he says instead, and I feel an unexpected stab of disappointment.

I bite my lip, sitting back as I look out over the water for a moment. So much has changed for me in such a short time. And more could change, still, depending on what happens between Salvatore and me.

"If all that is true," I say quietly, turning to look at him, "then it's up to you to give me all of that instead. You married me. It's up to you to fulfill those expectations. That's how you honor my father's wishes, Salvatore. You become the husband that he intended for me to have."

I expect a retort, for him to insist that he was never meant to be that, that he can only give me so much. But instead, he studies me calmly for a long moment, as if he's really considering what I've said. "Do you really think that's possible, Gia?"

Something in my heart lifts at the question. It feels as if, at long last, we're truly having a conversation. Not an argument. We might not fix this in the end, but this is a start. A beginning that gives me hope.

"There's only one way to find out," I say softly. "And we have to try, don't we? If not—"

"Then what?" There's no rancor in Salvatore's voice, only curiosity.

"I don't want to be miserable all my life. I'm not above trying to leave if you can't—or won't—give me what I want."

A small line appears between Salvatore's brows, but he doesn't flinch. "Tell me what it is that you want, then, Gia."

We're leaning towards each other now, the food forgotten, the only sound besides our voices and our breaths, the slap of the water against the deck, and the rustling of the breeze. The night is turning cool, and I think of the rest of it still to come, of the possibility of happiness in the hours ahead of us.

"I want to be happy with someone," I whisper, letting my dreams unfurl as I think about it, all of my wishes that I thought I might have to give up spilling off of the tip of my tongue. "I want a husband who looks at me with desire. I want someone who teaches me all the things a husband should. I want to learn everything there is about love, both physical and emotional."

Slowly, as I speak, Salvatore's hand moves towards mine. His fingertips brush against my hand, grazing over my skin, and I draw in a breath slowly. "I want children," I whisper, and I see his eyes darken. I know what he's thinking at that moment—not about the end result, but how we get there. "Sons, especially. I want to raise a family, and have joy all around me. It was always just my father and I, and we were happy. But I want a big family. I want to know what that's like. And I want a husband who will be side by side with me in that, sharing in that same joy."

I see Salvatore's throat tighten as he swallows. "It's a lot to ask in our world," he murmurs. "Very few mafia marriages are like that."

"I know. But it's what my father and mother wanted. It's what they didn't get to have. And it's what he wanted for me. It's what I was promised. So if I can have it—"

Salvatore's fingers curl around my hand, his thumb brushing over my knuckles. "I thought about a family, from time to time," he says quietly. "I always dismissed it. My life was serving your father. I didn't have time to woo a woman properly. I didn't have time to give any relationship the attention it required."

"Why didn't you ask my father to arrange one? He could have." Not a marriage with someone like me—but there are plenty of women who could have been candidates. Widows, women from lesser families, others who would have been pleased to marry Enzo D'Amelio's right hand, especially with Salvatore's wealth and influence.

Salvatore pauses for a moment. "I don't know," he says truthfully. "I didn't think about it, if I'm being honest. But I think, now that the question is posed—if I was going to marry and have a family, I didn't want it to be an arrangement. I wanted—" He hesitates, and I can feel him tense, almost as if he's afraid of the answer. "I suppose, Gia, that I wanted what you want. A marriage made of love, and a family that I shared in fully. And since I didn't think that was possible, I put it out of my head."

I stare at him for a long moment, struggling to understand. "Then why has this been such a problem, the whole time?"

He pulls back, frowning, as if unsure why I don't understand. "Because I was never supposed to be allowed that with *you*, Gia. Enzo's daughter, my goddaughter, the woman entrusted to my *protection*. I stole you at the altar on impulse, because I couldn't let that animal have you. I went to you on our wedding night sick at the idea of what your father would think, if he knew I was going to bed his daughter. I felt ashamed that I wanted you. At the desire that you aroused in me. Everything I felt for you was wrong, from that night on."

But even as he says it, his hand doesn't leave mine.

"It wasn't wrong," I say softly. "I'm your wife. It can't possibly be wrong for you to want me."

Salvatore doesn't speak for a long moment. "It feels like a temptation, what you're asking of me. To want you. To let our relationship grow naturally. To have children with you." His voice rasps on the last word, and I can see the desire in his eyes, hear the ache in his voice.

"We could have that. We could try."

For a moment, I'm not sure how he's going to respond. And then he stands up, slowly, his hand still wrapped around mine. I can see the tension in his muscles, his carefully controlled movements, as if there's something leashed in him. "I promised you dancing," he says, tugging me up out of my seat. "So let's go out, Gia. And see where the night takes us."

I'd half-expected him to take me straight to bed. A part of me is faintly disappointed that he's still able to keep his desire leashed enough to go out for the evening instead. But more than anything else, I'm pleased that he's keeping his promise to me. And I can feel a slow curl of anticipation building in my stomach, promising something else—that the slow burn of desire throughout the evening will pay off far more than the immediacy of passion now.

Salvatore goes to find Vince as we walk back into the villa, and I slip on a pair of sandal heels. Before I know it, we're leaving the villa with security trailing us, the first time I've left it at night. The air is cooler than before, with the tang of salt still hanging in it, and a soft breeze blowing my hair around my face as Salvatore takes my hand, and we walk down the pier.

I can hear music as we get closer to the bars and restaurants in the distance. Down on the beach, I can see the faint flickers of bonfires. The stars are glittering overhead, more than I can ever see at home, even as far out as we are from the city. The sky is a vast, velvet expanse, studded with diamonds, and I tip my head back to take it all in, feeling the tension drain fully from me. For the first time, I feel the spark of hope that everything might be alright. It's too soon to think that, maybe, but I want to feel it. I don't want to dread my future any longer.

We walk to one of the open-air bars—unsurprisingly, not the one where I met Blake—and Salvatore orders us drinks. He brings me mine, a pina colada, and I make a soft sound of pleasure when I take a sip.

His eyes darken slightly at that, and he lifts his own glass to his lips, his other hand coming down to wrap around mine again. "What are you drinking?" I ask curiously, glancing at his, and he looks over at me.

"Rum and cola. I don't drink rum often, but this seemed like a good occasion for it." Salvatore breathes in slowly, as if savoring the ocean air. Behind us, a guitarist is playing soft music. "There's music up here. Or down on the beach, if you'd rather go down there."

I look over at him in surprise. I hadn't expected him to offer that. Getting Salvatore out at a casual beachside bar at night seemed like a startling enough feat, let alone convincing him to dance. I didn't think he'd even consider going down to the beach, with the bonfires and the people milling about in the dark.

But I know for sure which option I'd like to pick.

My fingers tighten a little around his. "Let's go down to the beach."

Salvatore nods, tossing back the rest of his drink, and goes to order us another round before we head down.

We walk down to the beach, the breeze growing a little stronger and the crash of the waves a little louder as we do. I can hear the sound of the music drifting up, and I kick off my heels at the top of the beach, letting go of Salvatore's hand to pick them up. He raises an eyebrow, but he does the same, setting his drink down briefly to roll up the hem of his chinos above his ankles.

My heart starts to beat faster as we walk down together towards the bonfire. This feels thrilling, exciting, the kind of thing I've never done before. The walls of the mansion back in New York feel a million miles away, and I feel free, as if I could lift off the ground and fly away. I had thought that when I had that feeling before, it was not only because I was away from home, but also because I was away from Salvatore. But now he's here with me, joining in, and I still feel that way.

We stop a little ways away from the crowd of people around the bonfire, Salvatore sipping at his drink as he surveys them. I see him glance this way and that, undoubtedly keeping an eye out to make sure Vince and our security are still nearby, but other than that, he looks remarkably relaxed. More so than I've ever seen him.

When he finishes the drink, he sets the glass in the sand, glancing over at me. I see a small smile at the corners of his mouth in the flickering firelight.

"I believe I owe you a dance, since there was no wedding reception." He holds out a hand. "Can I collect on that now?"

My heart trips a little in my chest. "Yes," I say softly. "I think you can."

The music has picked up, and there are other couples dancing in the sand now, too. Salvatore leads me a little closer to the fire, close enough that I can start to make out the faces of the other people around us and feel the warmth of it, and his arm slides around my waist. He brings me closer, the chiseled lines of his face outlined in the firelight, and it takes my breath away to see how handsome he is.

Out here, so far from home, out of his tailored suits and with his expression relaxed as he holds me in his arms, he seems like a different man from the forbidding, stern underboss that I've known all my life. This is, I realize, the version of him that doesn't belong to the mafia.

It's the version that could belong to *me*.

Salvatore draws me closer, his hand on the small of my back, the other wrapped around mine as we start to dance. Out here in the sand, there are no quick steps or fancy moves, but I think I like this better. The two of us, swaying together with the soft sound of the guitars and the crash of the waves as our rhythm, the slow intimacy of our bodies moving against one another, a promise of what might come later.

My breath catches in my throat, and I lean forward, laying my head against his shoulder as I sway with him. I feel him tense, ever so slightly for a moment before he relaxes again, and then it's my turn to flinch with surprise as he presses a kiss against my hair. We're testing each other out, I realize, nudging at the boundaries with these small expressions of affection. And I want more.

I lean up, turning my face so my lips brush against his collarbone in the open neckline of his shirt. My free hand is wrapped around him, pressed to the back of his shoulder, and I feel his indrawn breath at the touch of my lips. His skin is warm against my mouth, tasting faintly of salt, and I let my tongue graze against the sharp line of bone, sucking lightly.

Salvatore tenses, his hand flexing against the small of my back, pulling me into him. I let out a small gasp as I feel the hard line of his cock pressing into my thigh, and he looks down at me, the two of us still moving together to the music. "Careful, *tesoro*," he murmurs, and I'm suddenly very aware of the heat of his hand through the thin silk of my dress, the quickening beat of his heart against my cheek. "You'll make it difficult for me to walk back."

My heart flips, heat blooming through me as I lean into him, my breasts brushing against his chest as I look up at his face. "Maybe I like teasing you."

I feel the low rumble as he groans. "*Tesoro*," he murmurs, his fingers stroking the silk of my dress along my spine. "You've been teasing me since the night I walked into that hotel room on our wedding night." His hands tighten, holding me against him. "Torturing me, even."

"I thought you didn't want me," I breathe, still looking up into his dark gaze. I feel as if everything else around us has vanished, and it's only us on this beach, moving to the strains of music coming from nowhere as the firelight flickers over Salvatore's features. "I thought you resented me."

"The position I was put in, perhaps, from time to time." Salvatore lets go of my hand, reaching down to run his fingers along the side of my jaw. "I wished your father had listened to me from the beginning."

"And now?" I whisper, almost afraid of the answer.

Salvatore's arm slides fully around my waist, his fingers splaying possessively over my hip as he holds me close, and I know what he's going to say before he even opens his mouth.

"Now," he murmurs, his thumb brushing over my lower lip. "Now I'm glad he didn't listen. Because if you'd married a mafia son, I would have allowed it. And then, Gia, you would never have been mine."

He leans down, his mouth crushing against mine in a kiss that's harder and more possessive than any he's given me before, his hand on my hip holding me tight. His tongue sweeps over my lower lip, urging me to part them, and I do, gasping as I feel his tongue slide against mine. I taste the spice of his drink on his mouth, and I hear myself moan, my hips arching into his as my hands slide up to clutch at his shoulders, my head falling back. *This* is how I've dreamed of being kissed, as Salvatore's mouth devours mine, not out of duty or anger or unleashed lust at last, but *passion*. Because he's finally, finally allowed himself to give in to what he wants.

"Take me back to the villa," I whisper against his mouth when he finally starts to draw back, my heart pounding in my chest. I feel hot and shivery all over, my skin too tight for my body, and I can feel the iron bar of Salvatore's cock against my thigh, his muscles wound tight with need. "Please, Salvatore. I want you."

He nods, his forehead brushing against mine as his lips graze over the tip of my nose. "I want you," he murmurs, and desire floods through me at the admission, my knees weakening with it.

Finally, is all I can think as he steps away from me, his fingers linked with mine as we start to walk back up to the beach. *Finally, I get to find out what this will be like.*

I can hardly contain the anticipation thrumming through me as we start to walk back to the villa. I feel like I'm in a haze, my mind already there, already in our room, imagining what might happen. It feels like it takes forever before my heels hit the wood of the pier, and Salvatore leads us down the long walkway into the cool, lemon-scented interior of our home away from home.

We walk into the bedroom, and anticipatory nerves flood through me as Salvatore closes the door, going to the one that leads out to the balcony. I watch as he opens it, my hands trembling, feeling like it's the first night all over again. I'm not a virgin any longer, but it's never been like *this* before—purposeful, intentional, with the promise of pleasure instead of mixed signals and unmet expectations. *This* is what the first night should have been all along.

"The sound of the water is nice," Salvatore explains, when he sees me glance towards the open door. "And the breeze."

I blink at him, unsure of why he's talking about water and breezes when we're minutes away from being naked together—and then I realize, as I see the twitch of his mouth and the briefly uncertain look in his eyes, that he's *nervous*. Salvatore Morelli, don of one of the most powerful mafia families in New York, a man twenty-something years my senior, is *nervous*.

It gives me a sudden confidence that I didn't have before.

I walk towards him, my heels clicking against the floor. I see him tense, eyeing me almost warily, as if he's unsure what will happen next. I kick off my shoes, curling my toes against the cool surface, and press a palm against his chest. I feel his indrawn breath as my palm presses against his warm skin, the soft rub of the dark hair on his chest against my fingers, the quickening of his heartbeat.

I feel like I should say something, but my throat feels tight, as if I can't get words out no matter what I do. So instead, I lean up, and press my mouth against his.

For a brief moment, Salvatore doesn't react, as if being back in this room has brought back all of his doubts and reservations. And for a moment, I almost want to pull away, all the hurt and resentment from the early days of our marriage threatening to return, whispering that nothing is going to change.

But he's trying. And in order for this to work, we *both* have to try.

So I let my tongue flick out, grazing it over his lower lip, my other hand coming up to press against his jaw. I feel the scratch of his stubble and the hard lines of his face, and I feel him breathing against me, his body wound tight.

His hand comes up, brushing against my wrist, and for a moment, I think he's going to pull my hand away. And then, just as I feel disappointment start to replace the desire flooding through me, his hands drop to my hips, and he pulls me hard against him.

He groans, his fingers digging into my flesh through the thin silk of my dress as his mouth opens against mine, his tongue sliding into my mouth. I can feel every hard line of his body against my softness, melding into me, his cock so hard I can imagine I feel it throbbing through the layers of our clothes.

I reach down, fumbling with the buttons of his linen shirt, gasping against his lips as he reaches up to tangle a hand in my hair. The kiss is turning desperate, the need that I can feel surging through him as intense as the day he dragged me back here from the bar, but without any of the anger. This is Salvatore finally letting go, finally dropping his control and giving in to what he wants, and it's dizzying.

It feels as if he could consume me.

I yank the last button free, his shirt falling open as I run my hands over the hard planes of his chest, down to the thick, ridged muscles of his abdomen. He moans against my lips as my fingers drop to his belt buckle, and I break the kiss abruptly, a smile curving my mouth as I look at his handsome, taut face, his eyes dark with need.

And then I drop to my knees in front of him, yanking his belt open as I drag his zipper down.

Salvatore makes a choked sound. "Gia, you don't have to—" His eyes are wide, almost shocked, as if he both never expected me to do this and is seeing a fantasy come true right in front of his eyes. "Get up, Gia."

"You want me to, don't you?" My voice lowers, husky, as I slip my fingers into his boxers. He doesn't need to answer, I can *feel* how much he wants it the moment my hand brushes against his hard, straining cock, the flesh like hot velvet draped over iron. I wrap my fist around him, freeing him, and the moment I see his cock so close to my lips, I let out a gasping moan.

He's *huge*. I knew how big he was, but like this, it's almost a little unsettling. I'm not sure how I'll fit him all in my mouth. But I look up at him, eyes wide as I run my hand up the length of his shaft, and the look of arousal on his face is something very close to pain.

"You like this," I whisper, pressing my thumb against the underside of the tip, feeling the damp pre-cum against my fingers. "Me on my knees, looking up at you while I suck your cock. You want this, don't you, Salvatore?"

He jerks at the sound of my name on his lips, his cock throbbing in my fist, and I lean forward, my lips close enough for my breath to ghost over the tip. I pause, waiting, and I know that he knows what I'm waiting for him to say.

His hand slides into my hair, fingers twining in it, hard enough to hold my head in place, but not hard enough to hurt. "Yes," he rasps, the admission tearing from him as his hips push forward, pressing the swollen head against my mouth. "I want you to suck my cock just like this, Gia."

A smile spreads over my lips, and I part them, wrapping them around the tip of him as my tongue flicks out to lick the soft flesh beneath.

The sound that Salvatore makes is half-pleasure, half-pain, his eyes dark with lust as he looks down at me. Standing above me, he looks like a god, his tanned body cut as if chiseled from stone, his forearm flexing where his hand is wrapped in my hair, his shirt hanging open and his pants hanging off his hips, his thick cock just barely in my mouth. Arousal throbs through me, and I tighten my mouth around him, licking away the pre-cum and humming a soft sound of pleasure at the taste of him.

I've wanted to do this for a long time. I've wanted to know what it's like. And now that I do, I'm not sure I can get enough.

Salvatore gasps, his breaths coming hard and fast as I start to slide my lips down the length, and when I press my free hand against his thigh, I can feel that the muscles are flexed as hard as a rock. His fingers brush against my scalp, tugging ever so slightly at my hair, and I taste another flood of pre-cum over my tongue as I let him sink deeper, the head pressing at the back of my throat.

"Oh *god*," Salvatore groans, his voice choked. "*Fuck, dolce—*"

His hips move despite himself, pushing his cock into my throat, and I momentarily feel as if I can't breathe. I try to swallow around it, my throat flexing around the swollen head, and Salvatore jerks backward as if I slapped him, suddenly pulling free of my mouth.

The sight of him standing there, panting with his cock glistening from my mouth and visibly throbbing with his arousal, is enough to make me want to push my own hand between my legs and take care of the ache building there. I know if I touched myself right now, I'd be dripping wet.

"I can't—" Salvatore rasps, and he shudders, shaking himself as he reaches for me and pulls me up to my feet. "I'm going to come in your mouth if you do that again, *tesoro*," he murmurs, pulling me close as he tips my chin up with one hand and reaches for the skirt of my dress with the other. "And that's not where I want to come."

He crushes his mouth against mine as he slides my dress up, his other hand falling to my hip and yanking my panties down at the same time that he pulls my dress over my head. I'm not wearing a bra, and as both fall to the floor, I look at him, entirely bare in front of him from head to toe.

Salvatore groans, shrugging off his shirt as his hands grasp my hips, backing me towards the bed. "I'm going to return the favor, *tesoro*," he rasps. "And then I'm going to keep you in this bed until there's no doubt that you're going to be pregnant by the time we get home."

Arousal jolts through me, and I moan as he spills me back into the bed, the rest of his clothing completing the trail that marks our pathway here as he follows me onto the mattress. He looks down at me, his cock so hard that it's pressing against his abs, and his hands skim down the sides of my ribs as he devours me greedily with his eyes.

"I remember you asking me to make you come with my mouth, *dolce*," he murmurs, his hand pressing against my inner thigh, spreading me open. "I think it's time you found out what that's like, don't you?"

My head falls back on a moan as I feel him spread my legs wider, feel his weight moving down the bed as he goes to lie down between my thighs. "Yes," I gasp, my chest tight with anticipation. "Please."

I moan as I feel his fingers slide up my folds, and I hear the low sound he makes in his throat before he's even parted me.

"*God*, you're so wet, *tesoro*," Salvatore groans. "And all for me."

I nod, unable to say anything, to make any other sound except a helpless whimper as I feel him spread me apart, his thumb sliding up through my wetness to rub against my clit.

It feels like electricity, jolting over my nerves. I cry out at his touch, gasping, my hips arching up desperately as he slides two fingers into me smoothly, rolling his thumb over my most sensitive spot until I feel like I'm going to come before he's even barely begun. I can't imagine anything feeling better, that there could be *more* than this.

And then he leans in, and his tongue replaces the pad of his thumb.

My vision narrows, the room swirling around me until I squeeze my eyes tight, my entire body shuddering with ripples of pleasure as he slides the firm, wet heat of his tongue over my clit. I hear myself crying out, my legs splaying open as I arch upwards again and again, grinding shamelessly on his mouth as I ride his tongue to a climax. I'm not even sure when the orgasm begins, if I'm actually coming, or if the pleasure is that intense, but it doesn't seem to end. It rolls over me in ceaseless waves as his tongue laps at my clit, his fingers working inside of me, and my hands fist in the sheets as I cry out his name.

And then I feel his fingers curl inside of me as he adds a third, a sudden weight building deep in my abdomen and unfurling, and I scream as the orgasm hits me.

Everything blurs. I feel his hand on my hip and his tongue lashing at my sensitive flesh, fluttering, licking, the strokes of his fingers inside of me as he keeps going through my climax, the pleasure so intense that it's almost unbearable. I want him to stop, because it's too much, and I don't want him to stop, because it could never be enough. I never want to leave this bed. I never knew it could be this good, and I want to do this forever. I'm writhing under him, riding his tongue as I buck against his face, and I'm still shuddering with pleasure when I hear him murmur my name.

"Gia."

I open my eyes to see him leaning over me, one hand against the pillow next to my head now, the other on my hip. I feel his knee between my legs, his cock laying heavy and hot against my stomach as he waits for me to come to my senses, his face taut with need.

"Salvatore," I whisper his name, and his expression contorts, his hand flexing on my hip. It shifts, moving between us, and I moan softly.

"I need to be inside you," he whispers, his voice choked with desire. "Are you ready for that, *tesoro*? Do you want my cock in you?"

I nod breathlessly, hooking my ankles around him, winding myself around his body as I spread my legs for him. "Please," I choke out, tipping my chin up to look at him, and Salvatore groans as he angles the thick head of his cock against my entrance.

I'm soaking wet, soft, and open from the orgasms, and he's still an impossibly tight fit as he begins to push into me. He sucks in a sharp breath the moment his swollen tip slips inside, gritting his teeth, his eyes closing as his muscles tense and he shudders.

"Are you okay?" I whisper, his reaction bringing a sudden clarity through the fog of pleasure, and Salvatore nods.

"You feel so good, *tesoro*," he breathes, his hand fisting in the pillow next to my head. "I could come right now, you feel so fucking good. So wet and tight, wrapped around me—" He groans, his hips twitching, pushing him deeper, and I moan in response at the feeling of him filling me up, arching upwards for more. "*God, I need to come—*"

He leans forward, his mouth crushing against mine as he kisses me hard, and I taste myself on his lips as his hips snap forward. He sinks into me to the hilt, the taut flesh of his pelvis rubbing against my oversensitive clit, and I moan into the kiss as I writhe under him. He holds himself very still for a moment, his head turning to break the kiss and bury his face in the crook of my neck and shoulder as he breathes me in, his mouth moving over my skin.

"I need to fuck you," he groans. "I can't wait any longer—"

I reach up, wrapping my arms around him, my fingers curling into the hard muscles of his shoulders. "Then don't," I whisper, and I feel him shudder against me.

He pulls back, looking down at me as he starts to slide back, every inch of his cock rubbing against my sensitive nerves. The look on his face is something close to awe as his gaze trails down the length of my body, all the way to where his cock is buried inside of me, and I see his eyes darken as he takes in the sight. His hands slide up my thighs, unwrapping my legs from his as he pushes them back, holding my knees nearly to my chest as he looks down at where we're joined.

"You're mine, *tesoro*," he rasps, his hips beginning to move as he pushes into me again. "*My wife. My* treasure. *Mine.*"

"Yes," I whisper, my voice breaking on another jolt of pleasure as he sinks into me, and starts to slide out again, all the way to the tip as he rubs himself inside of me, small strokes back and forth. "I'm yours, Salvatore. All yours."

He groans, yanking my legs up over his shoulders before surging forward, his lips claiming mine again. All pretense of trying to go slow vanishes, his hips thrusting against me in a hard, ceaseless rhythm as his mouth claims mine, each jolt of his body against mine pushing me closer to another orgasm. "Come for me again," he groans against my lips, rolling his hips against me so he rubs against my clit, his cock buried deeply inside of me. "Come one more time, *tesoro*, and I'll give you what you want. I'll fill you up with my cum, *dolce*."

That alone tips me over the edge. He rocks against me once more, pushing himself deeper, his tongue tangling with mine as I feel him throbbing inside of me. I know he's so close to the edge, and I moan into the kiss, my nails biting into his shoulders as I arch into him and let myself go flying over the precipice of pleasure once more.

I feel myself tighten around him, rippling down the length of his cock as I come, crying out his name against his mouth. My back arches, and I gasp, moaning with a sound that's almost a sob as the pleasure tears through me, ripping me apart at the seams. It feels like nothing I ever imagined. I never thought anything could feel as good as this, as I come hard on Salvatore's cock, his mouth against my ear, whispering soft words in Italian as I cling to him through my orgasm.

The moment the waves of pleasure start to ebb, he pulls back, his gaze fixed between us as he pulls out of me. I nearly protest, wanting him to come inside, but I watch as he grabs my ankles in one hand, pushing my legs back as he fists his cock in hard, urgent strokes with the tip pressed against my pulsing entrance.

"Oh god, Gia—" he moans my name, hips twitching, and then his jaw tightens, his hand flexing as his entire body goes taut. "Oh *fuck*—"

I feel the first hot spurt of his cum against my swollen, sensitive pussy. I look down to see the second spurt splash hotly over my clit, and my body jerks at the sensation, another sharp wave of pleasure bursting over me as he pushes himself roughly inside of me. He pushes his cum into me along with his cock, his hips thrusting hard as he sinks into me all the way, the heat of his cum filling me as I feel his cock spasming. His head tips back as he thrusts, his hand hard around my ankles, his muscles flexing as he groans my name aloud.

It feels so fucking good. Salvatore shudders, moaning once more as he rocks against me, his eyes finally opening as he looks down at my trembling, flushed body underneath his.

"*Fuck*," he breathes, his voice a hoarse rasp. "That was—"

I nod speechlessly, still shaking and breathless from the aftershocks. He reaches down as he lets go of my ankles, letting my legs drop and fall open on either side of him. I moan with startled, surprised pleasure as he sweeps two fingers over my clit, gathering the cum clinging to my skin. And then, I watch as his cock slides free, and he presses his thumb down on my clit as he pushes his two fingers inside of me, getting every last drop of his cum inside along with them.

Salvatore leans in, his tongue sweeping over my lips as he claims my mouth in one more hard searing kiss, his thumb working my clit as he fucks his cum into me with his fingers, sliding them free only to gather up whatever is left on my pussy and push it deeper still. "Come for me again, *tesoro*," he demands. "Make sure you take all of my cum."

I gasp against his mouth, so exhausted I can hardly move, but my body effortlessly obeys his commands. I feel myself clench around his fingers, my oversensitive clit throbbing under his touch, and I come once more for him, moaning his name as he leans into me, the warm weight of his body enveloping me.

"Good girl," Salvatore murmurs against my lips, and I whimper, clenching around him once more as he slips his fingers free. He chuckles softly, rolling to one side as he tugs the blankets down, his arm going around me to pull me into the curve of his body. He's warm, and the feeling of his arms around me makes me feel safe for the first time in so long.

I never, in my wildest dreams, imagined Salvatore Morelli *snuggling* me. But he holds me against his chest, tucking the blankets in around us, and I feel my eyes growing heavy with sleep. I feel wrung out from pleasure, warm and comfortable, and in that moment, I feel sure that I never want to leave this bed.

I feel hopeful, I think, as my eyes start to drift shut. I like the side of Salvatore that I saw today. I enjoyed our entire day together, and I enjoyed what happened after, too. *If every day could be like this*, I think, *I could be happy.*

It's the last thought I have before I fall asleep on his chest.

Gia

In the morning, I wake up with my head on Salvatore's chest, his arm underneath me, and the soft sound of his snoring near my ear. We're still both naked, my leg flung over his and our bodies pressed closely together, and I'm briefly startled before I remember everything that happened yesterday—and last night.

I feel Salvatore stir next to me—from the fact that he's gotten up before me most mornings without waking me, I'm pretty sure he's a much lighter sleeper than I am. I start to move away a little to give him his space, but his arm tightens around my shoulders, pulling me closer.

"I've never woken up with anyone like this before," he murmurs next to my ear, his breath ruffling my hair. "In my arms—" his lips brush against my ear, teeth gently grazing the lobe, and I feel a rush of relief, as if I've let out a breath I didn't realize I was holding.

I hadn't realized, until just now, how worried I was that he would wake up and regret everything about yesterday. That he'd put all his walls back up, and we'd go back to the way things were before. That yesterday would have been a fluke.

But from the way his mouth is moving down the side of my neck, Salvatore definitely doesn't want to go back to the way things were before last night.

A jolt of guilt hits me as I remember how we ended up here in the first place. I squirm away from him long enough to sit up, tugging the sheet up above my breasts, and Salvatore gives me a curious look. There's a wariness in his eyes that I recognize, and I wonder if he's thinking the same thing that I was—wondering if yesterday was just a one-time thing, and we'd go back to fighting each other today.

But I don't want that, and I don't think he does either.

"I'm sorry," I say abruptly, and Salvatore tenses, sitting up further. The white sheet pools around his hips, instantly dragging my gaze downwards, and I can see the shape of his cock beneath it, clearly also eager to pick up where we left off last night.

Salvatore clears his throat, and my gaze shoots back up to his face, my cheeks heating. "What are you sorry for, *dolce?*" he asks gently.

"For making you jealous," I whisper. "That's all that was with the bartender. I was upset, and hurt, and I wanted to make you jealous. It never meant anything."

Salvatore chuckles mirthlessly, a low, dark sound deep in his throat. "Well, you succeeded," he says dryly. "Although maybe not the way you wanted."

My blush deepens, remembering the way he bent me over the bed, the astonishing pleasure of it despite the unexpected violence. I swallow hard. "Well—if that happened again...I'd rather it not be because you're *really* angry with me."

Salvatore's eyes narrow, and I see his mouth twitch a little at the corners. "You want it to happen again, *dolce?*"

My face feels like it's going to burst into flames at that. "Maybe," I mumble. "But that's not the point. The point is—"

"That you're sorry. Yes, *tesoro*, I know." Salvatore's hand reaches for mine, tugging it down away from the sheet, although I keep it clutched to my chest with the other one. "But it is good to hear you say it." He pauses. "Did yesterday make you happy?"

I nod. "It did. It was—it was exactly what I wanted. What I hoped for. I don't—" I bite my lip, feeling a flood of nervousness slide through me. "I don't want to go back to the way it was before. Fighting with each other, and—"

"I don't want that either." Salvatore's fingers link through mine, both of our hands resting on the sheet between us. "I can admit that I was wrong to dismiss the idea that you should be my wife in more than just name. I shouldn't have expected you to be satisfied with that, just because of my own hang-ups." He looks over at me, and with the tension gone, the set of his shoulders, and the lines of his face relaxed, he looks younger. Happier. Extraordinarily handsome, sitting in the middle of the white-sheeted bed, his tan skin and dark hair offset by it, the sun coming in through the window and spilling over us both. I feel a shiver of desire ripple down my spine, looking at him.

At my *husband*. The word no longer makes me feel a tangle of panic, fury, and resentment. Instead, I feel cautiously hopeful about it all.

"I don't see why every day can't be like yesterday," I say softly. "If we both try. If I try to understand the weight of the responsibilities on you, and you try to understand how much of an adjustment all this is for me, and we work on living our lives together—" I bite my lip. "I know every day can't be sitting by the beach, drinking margaritas and getting a tan. But—"

"It's a shame," Salvatore reflects with a laugh. "This vacation thing is beginning to grow on me."

"We should do it more often, then." I swing a leg over him on impulse, settling into his lap, and I feel his sharply indrawn breath as I fling the sheet away and loop my arms around his neck. "Once the Bratva threat is taken care of."

Salvatore's eyes widen, and he looks down at me. A moment before I said that, his hands were on my waist, drifting downwards with a clear intent to make good on my vulnerable position in his lap. But now he goes very still. "So you believe me?" he asks quietly, and I nod.

"I thought you forced me to marry you because you wanted me for yourself," I whisper. "The same thing Igor accused you of. But everything that's happened since then tells me that can't be true. It doesn't make sense. Why fight it so hard, if you married me for lust? Why care at all if I believe you about the Bratva, if you just wanted to make me yours and already have what you want? Why not make certain Pyotr couldn't take me back the very first night? The only answer is that you were telling the truth. And I just didn't want to hear it," I admit softly, biting my lip. "I'm sorry for that, too."

Salvatore reaches up, his fingers sliding along my jaw, tipping my mouth up towards his. "I'm glad to hear it, *dolce*," he murmurs. "But there is one thing that I need to make clear."

"What's that?" I whisper, and his brows draw together, his expression dark as he reaches down to grasp my hips.

"I'd like to never hear you say that boy's name again. But especially, *never* while you're in my bed. And I *never* want to hear it, or any other man's name, while you're naked and in my lap. Do you understand me, Gia?"

His voice is rough, but there's the smallest bit of humor in it. I nod, feeling desire lick down my spine as his fingers dig into my hips, lifting me up enough for me to feel his hard cock brush between my legs. "Yes," I whisper.

"Good girl." He lowers me onto the tip of his cock, letting me adjust to him before sliding me down the length of it, groaning as he fills me, and I settle atop him. "Now, I think it's time I remind you of who your husband is."

And with that, he leans back against the pillows, his hips thrusting sharply up into me as I gasp, my hands falling to his chest. "And I think it's time I taught my pretty bride how to ride her husband's cock."

―

A half-hour later, we're still in bed, this time sweaty and tangled in the sheets. Salvatore turns towards me, a satisfied smirk on his handsome face. "You did well," he murmurs, running one finger down my thigh. "Although I'm not averse to practicing more, if you want to perfect your technique."

I roll my eyes teasingly. "Of course you're not."

"You enjoyed yourself too, from the sounds you made." His fingers dip between my thighs, teasing me a little, pushing inside of me as if to make certain none of his release escapes. I'm too wrung out to come again, but it feels good, and the thought of him making certain that he gets me pregnant turns me on. It's a turn-on for both of us, and I'm looking forward to taking advantage of it every chance I get.

After a few minutes, I sit up, looking out at the deck. "It's time for brunch by now," I laugh, glancing back at him. "I'm hungry. Can you order breakfast while I shower?"

Salvatore nods. He says nothing for a moment, and I feel a small twist of anxiety in my stomach, thinking about him leaving for the day. Our newfound happiness still feels tenuous, and I'm not ready to break the spell yet.

"I want you to stay here," I say softly, turning to look back at him. "Stay and enjoy the day with me. Not just today, either. I want us to enjoy the rest of our honeymoon together. I don't want to be on vacation by myself. This is our time to get to know each other, away from the threats, away from the stresses of daily life. We should take advantage of it."

I hadn't meant to say so much, but I couldn't stop once I started. It makes sense to me. But I see the hesitation on Salvatore's face, and I can't help instantly jumping to the conclusion that he's not willing to give me more than a day of his time.

"You asked what you could do to make me happy." I wrap my arms around myself, looking at him uncertainly. "We said we'd try, Salvatore. *I* said I'd try. But just because we had a good day together yesterday, and this—" I wave my hand at the bed between us. "That doesn't mean everything is completely fine now. And our marriage working, *me* continuing to try to make it work with you—it depends on whether or not I'm happy. I don't want to be bound by the laws of a mafia marriage that says I can't leave. If I'm miserable—I'm not going to stay."

I see the shock on his face—and the instant resistance to that statement, too, that possessive look that I now know very well glinting in his eyes. I didn't intend to threaten him or give him an ultimatum, but I'm terrified that one good day is going to make him think that it's all fine now, and he won't keep trying. That he'll get complacent that quickly, and I'll be miserable again.

Salvatore sits up, moving behind me, his hands skimming up the backs of my arms. "You're mine, Gia." He leans forward, murmuring it in my ear. "I promise you, there's nowhere you could go that I wouldn't find you."

I twist around, looking up at his handsome face. Even like this, dark and possessive, he's gorgeous to look at. Maybe even more so. "You could try," I whisper, a hint of that old mocking, taunting note in my voice. "I'd make it hard for you."

"Oh, *dolce*." His hands skim up my arms again, settling on my shoulders and holding me in place. "Trust me, you make it hard for me every day."

His lips graze my ear, and I shudder, the double entendre mixed with the touch of his mouth against my skin, making me melt. But I pull away before I can give in, slipping away from his hands.

"I mean it, Salvatore," I whisper, my voice breathier than I mean for it to be. "I won't stay if I don't want to."

He reaches out, grasping my chin lightly in his fingers. "Oh, I know, *tesoro*. And I mean it, too."

He leans down, pressing a soft kiss against my mouth. "I won't let you get away. No matter what you do."

For a brief moment, I consider falling back into bed with him. But I need a moment to collect myself, a minute alone. "As interesting as it is that you're ready to go again at your ripe old age," I tease him, pulling away from the kiss. "I need a shower. And I'm hungry."

Salvatore chuckles, kissing me once more before releasing me. "One of these days, *dolce*, I'm going to tie you to a bed and show you just how many times I can be ready for you.'

"Is that a threat?" I slip off of the bed, seeing the way his gaze drags down the length of my naked body.

"A promise," Salvatore assures me. "Go shower, Gia. Brunch will be here when you're done."

He keeps that last promise. There's food waiting when I emerge onto the deck after my shower. Salvatore is on a lounge chair with his laptop, skimming through a document while picking at bites of fruit off of a plate. I look at it, and then at him.

Salvatore sets it aside for a moment, glancing over at me. "A compromise, *dolce*," he says, sitting up a little. "You want me here with you, enjoying our honeymoon. But I can't abandon everything happening back in New York. The Bratva threat won't find us here, but it also won't be ignored. And I wasn't exactly prepared to leave on as short of notice as we needed to. So." He gestures to the laptop. "I'll stay here with you, at the villa. We'll enjoy as many hours of peace and relaxation as we can. Go out to eat, when you like. Maybe even go dancing again."

He smiles at me, continuing before I can say anything at all. "Is that an acceptable compromise, *tesoro*?"

Truthfully, I hadn't expected him to give in so easily. I'm not sure that I thought he would give in at all. But here he is, meeting me halfway, trying to give me what I've said I need to be happy without completely deferring to everything I say. It makes me respect him more, to know that he can create those boundaries without just blowing me off. And this *is* a good compromise.

I nod slowly. "I think that's fine. I don't—" I hesitate, trying to think of what, exactly, I want to say. "I don't expect you to dote on me every second, Salvatore. I'm not *that* spoiled. I just think that while we have this time, we should make the most of it."

"And I agree." He nudges the laptop aside, standing up and stepping towards me, his hands resting on my waist as he pulls me closer. "I don't think you're spoiled, Gia. Not really. I think you've *been* spoiled in certain aspects, but the times I've said that, it was to get under your skin. Just as I imagine, a great many of the things you've said to me have been to get under mine. I want to spend this time with you. But I have to do certain things to make sure that we can go home safely, at the end of it."

"I know." I lean up, kissing him lightly. "And that's fine with me."

He releases me, going back to the lounge chair, and I walk over to where brunch is spread out on the table to fill a plate for myself. The sun is bright in the blue sky, the day gorgeous, and suddenly it feels as if our honeymoon isn't going to be long enough, instead of the expanse of time I'd been half-excited for, half-dreading.

Salvatore is a man of his word. We spend the day outside, him working while I lie in the sun, read, and drift inside to take a short nap after lunch. He wakes me when the sun is starting to go down, so we can change and go to dinner, and when we come back to the villa, he tumbles me back into bed again, stripping off every inch of my clothing slowly in a repeat of last night.

"We have at least a week more, here," he tells me in the morning, when we finally pry ourselves out of bed. "Josef says there's still been attempts from the Bratva to get close to the mansion. I'm trying to work out a deal with Igor, but it's slow-moving."

"He's talked to you?" I sit up, looking over at Salvatore. My feelings about the situation are dramatically different now—I'm loving every second of being ensconced in this tropical paradise with this new version of my husband, but I also want us to be able to go home eventually. And if the Bratva are no longer a threat, we'll be able to do that. We'll be able to find out if what we have here will translate just as well to being back home, in Salvatore's mansion, in our old lives.

I wonder if he worries about that at all. If the isolation and sun and sand have gotten to us, and once we go back to reality, we won't be able to make this work the way we have here.

"Briefly." Salvatore runs a hand through his messy hair. "I think he's beginning to realize that he's at a disadvantage. We can fight each other, but more bloodshed isn't good on either side. He wouldn't have even considered a truce with your father otherwise, though I'm not altogether sure he ever meant to keep it. If I can make a different one, though—"

"A different truce?" I frown. "How so?"

Salvatore hesitates, and he sees the instant reaction to that on my face. "I'm not trying to keep you out of my business, Gia," he soothes. "But we haven't really gotten to details yet. It will have nothing to do with you, I promise you that. When I know more, I'll tell you."

"You will?" I look at him doubtfully, and he sighs.

"I know you want to be treated as an equal, Gia," he says quietly. "I know you want a partnership, not to be pushed to the side and told only what you need to know. I want to give you that, as much as I can. But I need time to adjust to a different way of doing things, too. And there isn't anything concrete enough to be worth talking about yet. When there is, I promise I'll tell you."

"Alright," I relent, sliding back into his arms. And when he kisses me, I can feel that he's sincere.

Every day that passes, over the next week, makes me feel that sincerity more and more. It solidifies the feeling that I have that we have a chance to make this work. Salvatore has meetings, taken over the phone in the main room of the villa, and spends a good bit of time on his tablet or his laptop, going over work. But we venture out, too, going to the market again, trying a few more of the restaurants we haven't been to, and even going out dancing again one night when one of the bars has live music. We relax, and we swim, and we talk, and we spend hours in bed. In the soft expanse of those crisp white sheets, he teaches me a myriad of things, so many of which I've tried to imagine, and some that I didn't know were possible. Salvatore, unleashed from his guilt, is a far better lover than I would have ever thought. And everything he gives me, I try to give back as much as I can, learning what he likes along the way.

We're good together. For a week, I'm happier than I can remember being in a very, very long time. And all too soon, it comes to a halt.

I come out of the shower to a romantic scene on the deck, candles scattered around, champagne waiting for me and a glass already poured, and the first course waiting for us at the table. I look at Salvatore, a little surprised.

"Is tonight something special? More special than just our honeymoon?"

Salvatore gestures to the other seat. "Sit down, Gia."

I feel a flicker of anxiety, but I do as he asks, immediately reaching for my champagne. "Is something wrong?"

"Depends on how you look at it." He lets out a breath. "We're going home."

My fingers tighten around the stem, and I stop, the glass halfway to my mouth before I lower it again. "When?" My voice trembles more than I thought it would. This place has begun to feel like a haven, and I'm suddenly not ready to go.

"Tomorrow." Salvatore looks at me, and I can see a hint of regret in his eyes, too. "I've come to an agreement with Igor."

"What is it?" I narrow my eyes at him. "You promised you'd tell me."

"I did." He reaches for his own champagne, taking a long sip. "A different marriage has been arranged for Pyotr. Bella, your first cousin, will marry him. It's not Enzo D'Amelio's daughter, but since she's no longer available—" he looks at me pointedly, "—Igor was convinced of both the wisdom of maintaining the treaty, and of the suitableness of the offered bride."

I stare at Salvatore, my mind spinning. I'm suddenly so full of different emotions that I don't know what to do with them all.

My first thought is that if Pyotr has agreed to marry someone else, he must really have never cared that much for me. It was never *me* that he wanted, but my status, my name, the usefulness of marrying a mafia don's daughter to make a treaty with us. It never had anything to do with me at all.

But then again, I think I knew that when he didn't kick in the door of my hotel suite the very first night, to carry me away and take me back with him. After all, Salvatore stood up and objected at my wedding in order to make me his, because it mattered to him that I not go with Pyotr. If Pyotr had loved me, he would have done something equally drastic to get me back.

Still, such a clear realization of the truth feels like a punch in the stomach. It feels, for a moment, like I can't quite breathe, and tears sting my eyes. But after how things have changed between Salvatore and me, the last thing I want is for him to see me crying over another man.

So I blink them back, quickly, and focus on the other part of it that concerns me.

"If everything you've said is true, then you thought the Bratva would harm me." I frown at him. "So what about Bella's safety? Isn't she in danger?"

"Part of the agreement is that mafia security will go with her into her new marriage. She'll have bodyguards of her own choosing, not Pyotr's. Igor is aware of my distrust. There have been measures put into place, to retaliate if he harms her."

And you couldn't have done that for me? The question is on the tip of my tongue, but I don't ask it. For one thing, I know Salvatore's decision was an impulse, an inability to let the wedding continue without stepping in. And beyond that, I no longer wish it had gone differently. I know the truth about Pyotr now, and I know Salvatore did save me, not only from unhappiness, but from feeling the same bitter sense of disappointment and betrayal that I just did—only within a marriage shackled to the same man making me feel those things, rather than on the other side of it.

"So that's it?" I frown, feeling somehow unsettled about all of this. "Pyotr marries Bella, Igor is satisfied, and everything is smoothed over? The Bratva are pacified, and we can all go home?"

Salvatore chuckles. "That's a simplistic way of looking at it, but essentially, yes."

"And Bella agreed to this?" The idea shocks me now, after how my feelings about the Bratva have changed, but I know it shouldn't. Not all that long ago, I was eager to run into Pyotr's arms, and angry that I'd been snatched away. He's handsome and charming when he has reason to be, and I can see how Bella might have been caught up in it, just as I was.

I feel a wave of guilt. But I also know that this is how things almost always are, in our world. Marriages are arranged for alliances, for expediency, not for love. I was always lucky in that my father wanted me to have love. Most women aren't. And I won't be able to just stop that practice.

"Yes." Salvatore eyes me, as if he's expecting some pushback. "Her father is going to be rewarded generously. Money, as well as an elevated rank among my men. And Bella herself seems amenable to the match. She wouldn't have expected to marry someone like Pyotr, among the mafia. It's a leap up for her. So long as her safety is ensured, she and her family are happy to go along."

I let out a slow breath, still unsure how to feel about it all. Salvatore gives me a sympathetic look, and I can see that he can tell I'm struggling.

"This is how things are, *tesoro*," he says quietly. "It's how they've always been. You know that as well as I do. I don't have the power to change them so thoroughly that I don't have to make these sorts of compromises. But I can do my best to make it a good bargain for our side."

"What if we have a daughter one day?" I look at him cautiously. "Will she be expected to marry whomever she's told? Or will you let her marry for love, the way my father wanted me to? Will you give her a choice, so she can have the same chance at happiness that we're getting?"

Salvatore nods. "I can't make it all like this, for everyone. I can't tell every family what to do. Bella's father would have married her off to someone, and the choice wouldn't have been hers. But I can make *our* family do things differently." He looks at me intently, his expression utterly serious. "If we have a daughter, Gia, I promise you that she'll have a choice. I'll make certain that she has a chance for love, not just an arrangement."

"Okay." I feel a little better, knowing that. All of this still makes me feel on edge and uncomfortable. But there's nothing I can do. Salvatore is right that our world isn't going to change overnight, and probably not at all. But this is a step in the right direction for our family, at least.

Salvatore smiles at me. "I know you're reluctant to leave. Honestly —" He looks around, drawing in a deep breath. "I am, too. But tomorrow, we'll go home. And we'll start a new life together, Gia." He lifts his champagne flute, tilting it towards me.

It feels frightening. More unknown even than the time right after our marriage, because now I have hope. And it's harder to have something to lose.

But I tap the edge of my glass against his, and I let myself continue to hope. "To a new life together," I echo, and take a sip of the champagne.

The bubbles fizz against my tongue, sweet and sharp, and I draw in a deep breath of the salt air.

Tomorrow, everything will change again. And I have to hope that there will still be happiness for me, at the end of it all.

Salvatore

I can feel Gia's apprehension when we board the jet to leave Tahiti the next morning. We're both tired—we didn't sleep until late, spending the hours after dinner luxuriating in each other's company for our last night on our honeymoon.

Now that I've allowed myself to want her, it's hard to keep my hands off of her. Our nighttime swim in the pool turned into skinny dipping—and far more—before I took her back to bed, both of us staying up nearly until sunrise, unwilling to let the pleasures of the night come to an end. But eventually, we both fell asleep.

Letting myself feel what I do for Gia has been a revelation. I've never enjoyed someone else's company as much as I've found that I enjoy hers, now that we're not constantly fighting. She's remarkably funny, when her wit isn't being used as a weapon against me, and her optimism is infectious. Over the last week, I've felt myself loosening up, learning to relax for the first time in my life, and whereas before, I couldn't wait to get back to New York and my work, now I'm disappointed to leave Tahiti. I could use another week of sun and salt and spending every day wrapped up in my new wife.

But it's time to go home, and solidify our future. And for all the apprehension over how the new treaty with the Bratva might play out, there's a hope in both of us that we didn't have before.

This time, Gia sits next to me on the jet, curled against me while I scroll through documents on my tablet, and she reads. When we get tired, we go back to the bedroom together, and her slow teasing as she takes her clothes off quickly turns into me checking off another item on the list of things to do with my new wife—making her come with my tongue at 35,000 feet before I fuck her until we're both exhausted.

It's late at night when we get home, late enough that all either of us have the energy to do is get back to the mansion, and go to bed. Gia falls asleep in the town car on the way back, and although I should be thinking about what I need to do to finalize the deal with Igor, my attention keeps drifting to her.

She looks beautiful, sweet and innocent in her sleep, and I fight off a pang of guilt that I thought I'd entirely conquered in Tahiti. But now that we're nearly back home, I keep remembering how I felt before that, before she got under my skin and convinced me that everything I was so sure of about her was wrong. It's hard not to slip into who I was before. But I made her a promise, and just like the one that I made to protect her, I intend to keep this one as well.

Once we're back at the mansion, I walk with her up to our bedroom, where she sleepily tumbles into bed, pulling the covers up under her chin as she rolls over. I want to join her, but I have things that I need to check on first—one of which being that I need to check in with Josef about the situation with the Bratva.

He's waiting downstairs for me, as I requested. He nods as I walk down the hall to meet him, unlocking the door to my office and gesturing for him to follow me inside.

"Are there any recent threats?" I ask, without preamble, and he shakes his head.

"Since you and Igor came to an agreement, nothing. Everything indicates that they've backed off. None of my men have seen anyone scouting around, and we haven't received any communications or heard anything over the tapped channels that suggests they're being sent in to try to scope out the grounds, or look for ways to get in."

"I want security heightened, still. Back to what it was right after the wedding, and eyes on Gia at all times. We have a month until the wedding that solidifies all of this—that's plenty of time for them to change their minds or get other ideas in their heads. Understood?"

Josef nods. "Understood, boss. No one will get near her; I promise you that."

I believe him. Josef is exceptional at his job, and there's no one I'd rather have looking out for Gia. But still, I can't entirely feel safe until I know for certain that the deal is finished and done. And the only thing that will solidify that is this new treaty that's been arranged.

I feel for Bella. I know very well that I'm sending her to marry the man that I wouldn't allow Gia to be wed to, and I'm not insensible to the fact that it's my lack of emotional attachment to Bella that allows that to happen. But I've done all I can to ensure Bella's safety within the marriage, and I can't change our entire world overnight. I can only be sure that I can make it better for Gia and our family.

Letting out a long breath, I tell Josef goodnight, and head upstairs to join Gia. More than anything else right now, I need a good night's sleep.

I don't see Gia again until the next evening. I had to leave early in the morning to handle work, before she was awake, and I don't get back home until dinnertime. She's not in our bedroom when I go up to change, and to my surprise, I find her already in the dining room when I walk in, the table set for us with candles burning in the center and a decanter of red wine waiting.

She stands as I walk into the room, and my heart flips in my chest. She looks utterly gorgeous in a cherry-red skirt with a fluted hem and a sleeveless cream-colored silk blouse, her long dark hair falling thick and silky around her shoulders. She smiles as I walk in, and my heart slams into my ribs again, as I realize that this is the first time I've ever walked into this room and had her look at me this way.

It makes me want to sit her on the edge of the table and have my dessert first, instead of dinner.

"What's all this?" I tease her lightly as she walks towards me, resting her hands on my chest as she leans up to kiss me. "And what did you do with my stubborn, willful wife?"

Gia wrinkles her nose at me. "I wanted to do something nice for you. But I can always take it back if you keep that up."

"I wouldn't dream of it." I kiss her again, before going to sit down. "What did you do?"

"I planned a dinner for you. Frances tried to tell me what foods you liked and what your preferences were for weekly menus, when I first moved in. And, of course, I told her I didn't care," Gia admits sheepishly. "I wanted to make it up to you."

"I didn't know anything about that." No one told me, probably because none of the staff wanted to interject themselves in my marital troubles—understandably. But I'm curious to see what Gia has come up with.

"I know. But I still wanted to do it." Gia motions to the decanter of wine as she sits down. "Frances suggested your favorites, and what to pair it with, and I picked one. I never really paid attention to all of that, but I'm willing to learn, so I can handle those dinner parties and such that you were talking about."

She gives me a hesitant look, and I smile reassuringly at her. I know she's thinking about all of the times that I told her that her education as a mafia wife was lacking, and I feel bad about that now, knowing her better. But her willingness to make an effort all the same touches me, and I reach out, squeezing her hand lightly.

"I'm afraid being a husband isn't something I have experience with. But we'll figure it out together."

I can feel Gia relax into my touch, and I reach for the wine, pouring us each a glass. "What else did you do today?"

Gia smiles hesitantly, glancing over as one of the staff brings in the first course—a Caesar salad with Frances' homemade dressing. "You said I could redecorate if I wanted. I started looking into some options for the informal living room and our bedroom, to start. Something to make them a little lighter and airier. The living room, for example, has those high ceilings and big windows, but the colors make it seem dark and small—"

I'm listening to her as well as I can, but the way she so casually says *our bedroom* catches me, making it hard for me to focus on anything else. A week ago, I know she wouldn't have said it so easily. She likely wouldn't have said it at all. And the way hearing it makes me feel—as if my heart is lighter and the future seems open and full of possibility—makes me willing to do anything necessary to ensure that Gia remains happy.

That she remains happy with *me*.

"You can do whatever you want," I assure her. "Spend whatever you like on decorating, re-do the mansion to your heart's content. I paid a decorator for it all the first time around, and I don't have any attachment to any rooms outside of my office. The rest of it is free for you to do whatever you please."

"There's a small room across the hall from ours." Gia bites her lip. "I know there's no solid reason to yet, but I want to turn it into a nursery."

My heart flips in my chest again, a mixture of tenderness and desire flooding me at her eagerness to prepare for the family we'll have together—a family that I'm now anticipating, instead of dreading.

"I like the sound of that, *tesoro*," I murmur, picking up my fork. "And I'm looking forward to seeing what you do with it."

"What about you?" Gia looks at me, taking a bite of her salad. "Is everything still going ahead with the Bratva?"

I can hear the note of worry in her voice—likely the same worry that concerns me, that the deal will fall through in some way or Igor will change his mind. But I want to reassure her, and I nod, choosing not to share my own worries.

"The wedding is in a month. A date's been set, and Bella is making her plans already. We'll attend, to show good faith," I add. It's a detail that I'd been waiting to tell her, since I've been unsure how it would make her feel. "I know it might be strange, seeing him again, and under those circumstances." I can't bring myself to say Pyotr's name aloud to her. "But you and I need to be a united front—the don and his wife, there to see the agreement through."

Gia swallows hard, but she nods. "I understand," she says softly. "I'm your wife now, Salvatore. I know what that means. It won't be an easy day, but I'll get through it."

"We'll get through it together."

The rest of the dinner is perfect—Gia really did make sure that it catered to all of my preferences. The second course is a rich tomato cream bisque, followed by delicately cooked lamb chops and roasted potatoes. When the staff comes to clear away the dishes for the main course, I finish the last of my wine, then stand up and reach for Gia's hand.

She frowns at me. "There's still dessert—"

"Oh, I know there is." I raise an eyebrow at her. "And I intend to have it upstairs."

Her cheeks flush instantly as she catches my meaning, and then her gaze drops, her teeth sinking into her lower lip. "Maybe not tonight," she says softly, and my stomach clenches at her refusal.

Gently, I reach down, skimming my fingers along the side of her jaw as I tip her chin up so that she's looking at me. "Why not, *tesoro*?" I ask softly. "I'll never force it, you should know that. But why the sudden change?"

Her blush deepens. "It's—you know." She winces. "That time of the month."

There's a hint of sadness in her voice, and I can guess why easily enough—it means she didn't get pregnant on our honeymoon. But there's an opportunity here that I'm not about to miss.

I told her in Tahiti that I only intended to go to bed with her when absolutely necessary, and for as long as it took for us to have a child together. Having sex with her tonight won't get her pregnant, but it will do something else—it will prove to her that she's all I want, children or not. That she means more to me now than just my duty.

"That doesn't matter to me." I reach for her, tugging her up out of her chair and into my arms. "Come upstairs with me, *tesoro*."

"But—"

I take her hand, leading her out of the kitchen and to the stairs before she has a chance to protest any further. We go all the way up to our room, and I lead her inside, straight to the huge en-suite bathroom, where I reach over and flip the taps on the huge bathtub, so that it starts to fill with hot water.

"You can always say no," I murmur, sliding my hands down her arms as I pull her close, leaning in to kiss her. "But I promise there will never again be a day when I don't want you, *dolce*. No matter when it is."

She gasps softly when I press my lips to hers, my hands dropping to her waist. I wait for her to protest again as I start to tug it up out of her skirt, but she doesn't, her back arching as my tongue slides along her lower lip.

"I'm sorry I'm not pregnant," she whispers, when I break the kiss to slip her shirt over her head. "I was hoping that the honeymoon—"

"There's no need for apologies, *tesoro*." I toss the silk shirt down to the tiles, reaching for the clasp of her bra as I brush my mouth over hers again. "We'll get there in time. And until then, I'm more than happy to practice with you—and not stop until we have what we both want."

I feel her smile against my lips, her hands reaching for the buttons of my shirt as her bra joins hers on the floor. I reach for her breasts, filling them with my hands, cupping them, and lightly squeezing.

"Careful," Gia whispers. "They're sore."

"Oh, I intend to touch you as carefully as you need, *tesoro*." I sweep my thumbs over her nipples, feeling them tighten under my touch. "So carefully, you'll be begging for more before I give it to you."

Gia whimpers at that, craning her neck as I slide my lips down her throat, and I hear her soft gasp as I slide my hands over her breasts again, around to her back. I trail my fingers down her spine, reveling in the silky softness of her skin as I drag them down to the zipper of her skirt, tugging it and her panties down in one swift motion as she lets out a soft moan.

I cup her full ass with my hands, squeezing, my cock stiffening as I think of the moment when I'll take her there eventually, when I'll make every part of her mine. But for tonight, I know what I want.

Gia takes a step back, breathing hard. "Can you turn around for a second?" she asks, blushing. "I have some things I need to take care of, before—"

She motions to the bath, and I nod, turning around to give her her privacy. I use the moment to finish taking off the rest of my clothing, leaving it in a pile next to hers as I test the water to make sure it's not too hot, and add a generous pour of bath oil to it. The fragrant scent of almonds and vanilla fills the air, the water shimmering with the silky oil atop it. I hear Gia clear her throat softly from behind me.

I don't think I've ever seen anyone as astonishingly gorgeous as she is. Seeing her naked, every time, takes my breath away. And from the way her gaze slides over me, her lips parting as she takes in every inch, she feels the same way.

"Your bath is ready." I motion to the water, and she raises an eyebrow, her eyes dropping to my erection and lingering there. I'm rock-hard, my cock nearly pressed to my abs and already leaking pre-cum, and it's obvious how much I want her.

"Are you going to join me?" she asks softly.

"Do you want me to?"

Gia steps forward, her breasts brushing against my chest, and reaches down, her fingers encircling my stiff length as she strokes me once, from base to tip, tugging a sharp breath from my lips. "What do you think?" she murmurs.

And then she releases me, turning and stepping into the hot bath, letting out a soft moan as she sinks down into the water.

I follow her as if tugged by a magnet, sinking down into the water behind her and pulling her against me as I lean back against the tub. Gia relaxes against me without hesitation, reaching up to pile her long hair atop her head and wind a hair tie around it. Her head sinks back against my shoulder, and I shift, adjusting my cock so that it lies against her back.

She wiggles a little, and I suck in a breath. "Isn't that uncomfortable?" she asks teasingly, and I can't help lifting my hips, pressing my erection against her spine.

"A bit," I murmur into her ear, reaching to run my hands over her breasts again. "But I'll be inside of you soon enough, *dolce*. First, though, I want to make you come for me."

Her soft whimper sends a shock of arousal through me. I run my palm down her flat stomach, a possessive desire filling me and making my cock throb as I imagine it round and swollen under my hand instead. She's *mine*, my wife, and soon enough, she'll be tied to me in every way imaginable, irrefutably mine for all our lives.

She arches up into my touch the moment my fingers graze over her sensitive clit, the warm water heightening everything as I rub my fingertips over her. She's more responsive to me than anyone I've ever touched, and my own arousal is nearly unbearable as I start to stroke her, my entire body aching with the need to be inside of her. I flutter my fingers over her clit as she gasps, making the water ripple against her as I urge her toward her orgasm. As I press my mouth against her throat and lick my way down to her collarbone, she writhes against me, making my cock throb with a desperate need to come.

I've never had trouble holding onto my orgasm before her, but Gia makes me feel as if it takes everything in me not to spill my cum just from the feeling of her against me. She turns me on more than I thought possible, and I rock my hips against her, eager to feel her come against my fingers so I can sink myself into her. I *need* to feel her, tight and wet and hot, wrapped around my cock.

She gasps again, her thighs opening wider as I rub her clit, and I hook my legs over hers, pinning them in place as I start to make small, tight circles with my fingertips. She bucks upwards into my touch, gasping, and I smile against her skin, nipping at the delicate skin of her throat with my teeth as I push her closer to the edge.

"Come for me, *tesoro*," I whisper. "Come for me like a good girl, and I'll give you my cock."

Gia moans, a high, throaty sound as her body obeys my command instantly, her every muscle flexing tight as her hands scrabble against the sides of my thighs, her hips writhing as she comes hard. My cock aches at the sounds she's making, her high-pitched cries sending a jolt of pleasure down my length with every one, and the moment I feel her start to relax against me, I grab her hips, spinning her around in the water so that she's straddling me. I grab my cock in my fist, angling it between us, and drag her down onto me as my eyes roll back in my head at the relief of feeling myself sink into her heat.

"*God, dolce*," I groan, fingers digging into her flesh as I start to slide her up and down on my cock. "Every time I'm inside of you, I think I've died and gone to heaven."

"You're close to it, aren't you?" Gia teases, nipping at my ear as she rolls her hips. "What's your next birthday?"

I turn my head, biting her neck lightly and then catching her mouth with mine, my teeth grazing her lower lip as I sweep my tongue into her mouth at the same moment that I thrust up hard into her. "Remember what I said about tying you to the bed, *tesoro*?" I murmur against her lips, moving her up and down my shaft again as I feel myself tense with the urge to come. "I can punish you all night for your teasing, and still fuck you again in the morning."

"Prove it." She runs her tongue up my ear, and I groan, throbbing as I push myself into her to the hilt. "You won't."

"Oh, I will." I kiss her again, hard, holding her down against my lap as I rock back and forth, luxuriating in the feeling of being so deeply inside of her. "When you least expect it, *tesoro*, I'll take a day and make you beg for me until you're hoarse with it. And then I'll coat your throat with my cum, before I fill you up with it until you're dripping."

Gia gasps, a ragged moan escaping her as she clenches around my cock, and I know I'm seconds from coming. I rock my hips again, grinding her clit against me as I thrust into her with small, shallow movements, wanting to feel her pussy squeeze the cum from my cock. She's close, too, and I capture her mouth with mine once more, sucking on her lower lip as I grind our bodies together, the lap of the water between us adding to the sensation.

It reminds me of fucking her in the pool, at our villa in Tahiti, except this time we're *home*. Together, in *our* bedroom, for the first time. I'm suddenly glad, as she whimpers against my lips and I feel her muscles tense, that *this* is our first time here, after things had changed between us. I'm glad that every time we'll ever be together in this place will be like this, with these new feelings alive between us, with desire and passion and tenderness, instead of what there was before.

I wrap my arms around her, one hand sliding around the back of her head, holding her mouth to mine as the other grasps her hip. I thrust up into her once more, our bodies glued together, and I feel the moment that she tumbles over the edge as she cries out against my mouth, her pussy squeezing my cock as she comes hard on my length.

I can't hold back a second longer. I wrap my arm around her waist, holding her hard against me as I groan her name, the sound swallowed up in the kiss as my cock throbs. I spill my cum inside of her, a flood of it with every excruciatingly pleasurable ripple of her around me. We move together, in a slow, rocking motion as the orgasms course through us both, and Gia moans against my lips as she clings to me, gasping as she feels me throb inside of her once more.

My fingers slide into her hair, and I kiss her once more, feeling the last of my orgasm spill inside of her as she tightens around me one more time, sinking into my chest as the hot water settles around us.

We don't move for a long time. Gia lies there against me, her head on my shoulder, my softening cock still buried inside of her, her legs wrapped around me, and my arms around her. I don't want to let her go, and she seems to have no desire to move.

I have the urge to tell her how I feel, to put a voice to it, to say the three words that I know she'll want to hear from me sooner rather than later. But I can't bring myself to say it just yet. Every time they try to emerge, I feel my throat close up, keeping them from slipping onto my tongue and all the reasons why I shouldn't say it yet filling my head.

I'm falling for her. I've already fallen. I know it, and yet I can't tell her just yet. Not with the treaty still not finalized, not until I know for sure that I can protect her forever, exactly the way I promised.

I need to focus on the danger ahead, and keeping us both safe through that, on making certain I honor Enzo's wishes by seeing the treaty through. And then I'll focus on the other way that I can ensure I honor all that he wanted—by being the husband that Gia needs.

I'll tell her after the wedding, I promise myself, running my fingers down her spine and basking in the small moan that slips from her lips. I'll tell her then, when everything is safe, and the alliance is finalized, when I can feel certain that nothing can separate her from me.

When I can feel safe letting go completely with her, baring myself in full.

I hold her closer, wanting to keep her there forever. And all I can hear in my head is one word, repeated over and over, a steady echo of the feeling thrumming through my veins.

Mine.

And I'm never going to let anyone take her from me.

Gia

One month later

I feel jittery and restless, waiting for Salvatore to come home from his last meeting. We're heading into the city tonight for the wedding tomorrow, and I'm ready for all of this to be over with.

With every day that's passed over the last month, my fears that things will go back to the way they were before our honeymoon between Salvatore and me have dimmed. Nothing has changed. He's been caring and protective without smothering me, keeping me informed about the Bratva and the upcoming wedding, and he's given me everything I could possibly want in bed. The house has been mine to decorate freely, and his wealth mine to spend however I please in that endeavor. It's kept my mind occupied over the past month, keeping me from thinking too hard about the upcoming wedding and the possibility that something could still go wrong, and Salvatore has kept me occupied the remainder of the time.

I no longer worry about him wanting me. But I do wonder whether he'll ever be able to tell me that he loves me—or how long it will take. The words have been on the tip of my tongue for a while now, but I don't want to be the one to say them first. I want him to give that to me, and I'm willing to wait for it. I can feel him holding back, and I'm hoping that it's all this mess with the Bratva that's keeping him from telling me how he feels. That when it's over, he'll tell me what I want so badly to hear.

With a sigh, I set my suitcase on the bed, pausing for a second as a wave of dizziness followed by nausea washes over me. I put one hand on the foot of the bed, taking a deep, slow breath, and I'm so focused on not throwing up that I don't hear Salvatore walk into the room.

"Are you alright, *tesoro*?"

I jump, letting out a small squeak, and turn to face him. "Yes," I tell him quickly. "Just feeling a little under the weather, that's all. It's probably stress."

Salvatore doesn't ask me what I could possibly be stressed about—he doesn't need to. He knows as well as I do that I'm not looking forward to going to my former fiancé's wedding—the fiancé that was thrown out of the church before Salvatore dragged me in front of the altar himself. I'm no longer angry at him over that. Still, it doesn't change the circumstances of how we began, and it doesn't make seeing Pyotr again any easier.

"The stress will be over this time tomorrow, *tesoro*," he murmurs, kissing the top of my head lightly. "In the meantime, I'm going to call Leah and have her come up and help you pack. You can tell her what you want to bring."

"I'm fine—" I start to protest, but Salvatore shakes his head, gently pressing a finger to my lips.

"Don't argue, Gia," he murmurs. "In fact, I'm going to tell Leah to draw you a bath, and you can relax while she packs. I want you well-rested before this."

I can hear the protective note in his voice, a tone I've gotten used to hearing, and I don't argue. It's strange, sometimes, how that dynamic has changed between us. I no longer want to fight him tooth and nail on everything, because I trust now that he means well, even when his protective instincts grate a little against my desire for independence. I know he wants to take care of me and keep me safe, and because I trust him now, that fills me with warmth instead of making me want to fly into a rage.

"Alright," I agree, and I see his eyebrow go up.

"Maybe you are feeling ill," he teases, even though it's been a while now since I've fought him on every little thing. But he enjoys reminding me that once upon a time, I did, if only because I think he enjoys getting a bit of a rise out of me.

I narrow my eyes at him, about to fling a retort back, only for another wave of dizziness to hit me. I weave on my feet a little, briefly wondering if I can somehow leverage this to get out of going to the wedding entirely, but I know that's not fair. Salvatore needs me there, to put on a united front for the Bratva deal, and I want to support him. If his duty is to protect me as my husband, then that's mine, as his wife.

"Gia." There's a faint note of worry in his voice as he guides me to the bed, picking up the phone to call Leah. "Just sit down for a minute."

Ten minutes later, I'm neck-deep in a hot, steaming bath that smells like rich vanilla oil, while Leah follows a list that I dictated to her for packing. I feel a flicker of guilt that she's handling all of it, but Salvatore *does* pay her for that, and the bath is helping. The dizziness has mostly worn off, replaced with a tiredness that makes me wish I could just go to bed instead of us driving into the city tonight.

By the time I get out, I find that Salvatore had dinner sent up to the room, a covered tray waiting for me. My bags are packed and set neatly by the door, and Salvatore is nowhere to be seen—probably downstairs in his office finalizing details for the trip. I feel a faint glow of intimacy at how used to each other's routines we've become, and I sit down on the bed to eat what I can, feeling especially cared for by that gesture.

I know how Salvatore feels about me. I'm just looking forward to him feeling as if he can say it.

The nausea returns after I eat—necessitating asking Leah to bring me up a ginger ale—and I opt for black leggings and a long dove-grey silk tunic-style shirt with ankle boots, instead of something sexier for the drive. I'd had visions of wearing a short skirt and getting up to all kinds of fun with Salvatore in the back of the car, but just now, I don't feel like I'm capable of anything more than a nap.

Salvatore notices, when I come downstairs. He's waiting in the foyer, our bags already taken out to the car, and he immediately loops his arm through mine when I reach his side. "You look a little pale," he says concernedly. "We'll check into our hotel as soon as we get to the city, and you can get a good night's sleep. You look like you need it."

"Flattery will get you everywhere," I tell him dryly as he leads me out to the car, but I know he's worried about me. I feel sure that it's just stress, until we get into the car and I look for a champagne flute to pour myself a glass.

"Are you sure you should drink that?" Salvatore frowns, his brow creasing. "What if you're pregnant?"

I pause, my hand halfway to the glass, a sudden burst of excitement jolting through me. I hadn't thought about it, despite the fact that Salvatore and I have been having enough sex over the past month to get me pregnant three times over—probably because I *have* been so distracted that I'd put it to the back of my head. But now the possibility seems sudden and immediate, and I look at him, a hopeful expression on my face.

"You think so?"

"Well, if not, then I guess I really am going to have to keep you tied to that bed," Salvatore says wryly, pulling his phone out. He starts to type out a message, and I look at him curiously.

"What are you doing?"

He glances up at me. "Texting my assistant. There'll be a pregnancy test waiting for you at the hotel room when we get there."

I blink at him, a sudden, soft warmth filling me. I can hear the hope in his voice, too—a hope that I once wondered if I'd ever hear, and hearing it now gives me faith that eventually, I'll hear the rest of what he feels for me, too.

I find myself hoping that once we get to the hotel and I take the test, it will be positive. *This is exactly what we need before tomorrow*, I think to myself as I lean back against the seat, feeling exhausted all over again. *Something to look forward to, together, when this is all over.*

I'm woken some time later by the feeling of Salvatore lifting me out of the car and into his arms, cradling me against his chest. I blink my eyes open to see the shape of the hotel ahead of us, rising up in a stately white shape against the dark skyline, and I look up at him. "You don't need to do all of this—" I mumble sleepily, and Salvatore shakes his head.

"Shh," he murmurs, kissing the top of my head lightly. "I want to take care of you, Gia. And our unborn child. So you're going to let me do just that."

It's the closest he's ever come to telling me how he feels. I soak in the words, half wondering if I'm dreaming as I lay my head against his shoulder, sinking back into sleep all over again.

I don't get a chance to take the test until I wake up the next morning. I slept so hard that I barely registered Salvatore taking me up to our room, or putting me in the huge king-sized bed that took up a good portion of the suite. I feel a little guilty for wasting the chance to enjoy the bed together, but appreciative that he let me sleep.

He's still asleep when I wake up, and I slide carefully out of bed, heading to the bathroom. The pregnancy test is sitting out on the counter, and my heart flips in my chest as I pick up the box.

I'm nervous to take it. Not because I don't want it to be positive, but because I want it to be positive so badly. Salvatore has said that he's not in any hurry, and that he's happy to have me to himself for as long as it takes, and I feel the same way. But I'm ready to start a family with him. I've been ready to have my own family since I was old enough to start thinking about marriage.

My fingers shake a little as I slip one of the tests out of the box. It's easy enough to take. Minutes later, I'm standing at the counter, watching the little window as I wait for the result. And when it shows up, the word *pregnant* clearly written there, I cover my mouth with my hands to muffle my yelp of excitement.

I grab the test, rush back out into the bedroom, and jump onto the bed. Salvatore groans, rolling onto his back as his eyes flutter open, and he blinks several times as he peers up at me.

"What's going on—what are you waving at me, *tesoro*?"

His voice is deep, raspy with sleep, and in any other circumstances, I'd be quick to slide back into bed with him and bask in all the deliciously dirty things that voice can whisper in my ear. But right now, my thoughts are entirely consumed with one thing.

"Look," I whisper, pushing the test closer to his face. "I'm pregnant."

Salvatore comes fully awake in an instant, sitting up abruptly as he reaches for it. I don't realize I'm holding my breath until the moment his face lights up, his gaze meeting mine with such absolute elation that I realize just how afraid I was that he wouldn't be happy.

"*Tesoro.* Gia." He breathes my name, dropping the test on the nightstand as he pulls me close, his hand sliding into my hair as he kisses me. "How are you? How do you feel?"

"I'm fine," I laugh, breaking the kiss and pulling back. "I don't feel sick this morning, actually. Maybe I have evening sickness instead."

"Whatever sickness you have, I'll make sure you're taken care of." He throws the blankets back, sliding out of bed and tugging on a shirt. "I'll call room service now, and get them to bring breakfast up. Coffee—decaf, of course—"

I can already see his mind spinning, thinking of how I need to be protected, doted on, for the length of this just-realized pregnancy. And I know he's showing me how much he cares for me, that he loves me, in ways that words can't measure up to.

But still, I can't help but feel a little disappointed that he didn't say the words. I'd hoped he would, when I told him the news, that this would be the thing that pulled it out of him.

It makes me fear that things aren't as fixed as I thought they were. That there are still things between us that need to be repaired—or maybe that can't be. That maybe Salvatore can't let his walls down completely after building them so high for so many years.

But as I watch my husband bustle around the room, calling downstairs for my breakfast and intent on making sure I'm pampered within an inch of my life, I tell myself to stay optimistic.

Things have been different between us ever since Tahiti. Today, every obstacle to our happiness will be removed. And by tonight, there will be nothing left but us.

I have to hope that's all he will need.

I might not have morning sickness, but I underestimated just how tired even early pregnancy would make me. After breakfast, I end up napping again until lunch, and then eat with Salvatore downstairs while he goes over some paperwork on his tablet. I can feel his agitation from across the table, and I know he's trying to keep himself busy until the wedding. I do the same, nestling in an armchair with a book after lunch, until it's time to get ready.

About three o'clock, I get into the shower, taking my time. Salvatore waits for me to finish—I've found that he likes his space in the shower—and then swaps places with me while I dry and style my hair, curling it in long, bouncy pieces before pinning them up on my head on a twisted chignon that makes me look put-together and elegant. My dress for the wedding is a soft sage green silk, with off-the-shoulder sleeves and a scooped neckline, the slits on either side coming up modestly to just above my knees. It's a beautiful dress, meant to make me look every bit the wife of the don, while not drawing too much attention. I slip it on, and I'm just finished putting on my strappy nude high heels when Salvatore walks out of the bathroom in his suit, a box in his hand.

I look up at him, surprised. I'd brought the onyx and diamond jewelry he gave me as my first gift from him—I hadn't expected anything else. The box is small, and my heart stutters in my chest for a moment, wondering if he's going to give me a ring. I'm still just wearing the plain, thin gold band that he slipped on my finger at our wedding, and there's never been any discussion of getting me anything else.

"I wanted to surprise you with this," Salvatore says, holding out the box. "But I think the news today makes them even more meaningful."

I feel a slight drop in my stomach, a momentary disappointment that it's not a ring, but it's almost immediately overshadowed by how happy he is that we're having a baby. I reach for the box, opening it, and gasp softly when I see the long, sapphire drop earrings, a diamond stud at the top, and a teardrop at the very bottom framing them.

"They're gorgeous," I whisper, immediately slipping them free to put them on. "Thank you."

Salvatore puts a hand on my waist, drawing me in to kiss him. "Not as beautiful as you, *tesoro*." His hand on my waist tightens as my lips press against his, and I feel the tension thrumming through him, wound tight. We're both on edge, and I can't help but wonder if we really have to go to the reception, or if our presence at the ceremony is enough. I don't want to spend all night watching my former fiancé enjoy his wedding reception—I'd rather come back to the hotel and enjoy this gorgeous suite with my husband.

Salvatore checks his watch as I look in the mirror, admiring the earrings. "We should go. The driver will be here in a minute." There's a hint of regret in his voice, and I know he doesn't want to go any more than I do. But we don't really have a choice.

There are certain duties that are required of a don, and his wife, and this is one of those—our personal feelings about it aside.

Salvatore threads his fingers through mine as we walk down the stairs, his hand holding mine a little more tightly than usual. My heart beats a little faster, anxious at his possessiveness and a little excited by it, too. It's a welcome distraction from my tangled thoughts about the ceremony we're about to sit through, which is raising a multitude of emotions that I don't want to think about.

It's impossible not to, though, as we slip into the car. I remember my hopes for my wedding day. I remember how I felt when I was on the verge of walking down the aisle to Pyotr—and how I felt only minutes later, when Salvatore upended my whole world. Now I'm grateful for the choice he made, happy for our life together and all the future promises it holds. However, I can still remember the blind rage I felt that day, and how awful things were shortly after. I remember how I felt about Pyotr, and what I believed he felt for me. I don't love him any longer, but I still feel the sting of finding out that he never loved me, and I know it will take some time for that to fade.

I'm happier than I ever thought I could be. But with Salvatore's feelings for me still unspoken, I can't help but have moments where it's hard to completely trust in it. And I can't help but be unsure about how I'll feel when I see Pyotr, for the first time since I was snatched away from him at the altar.

As if Salvatore can sense my thoughts, his hand moves from mine to my thigh, resting heavily against it. I can feel the heat of his palm through the thin silk, and my breath quickens, my pulse beating faster in my throat.

"What are you thinking about, *wife*?" he murmurs, the pointed emphasis on the word telling me exactly what *he's* thinking.

"Just—getting through the wedding." The words stick in my throat a little as I say them, not least of which because of the look on his face when I turn to glance at my husband.

There's a dark, possessive heat in his eyes. His hand slides down my thigh, his fingers dipping beneath the slit in my skirt, pushing the silk up my leg. "What about the wedding?"

I can feel the tension rippling off of him, hot as pavement in the summer. Salvatore's jaw tightens, and I know he's thinking about me seeing Pyotr twenty minutes from now, about how I used to feel about him, about everything that's happened since then. His fingertips graze the inside of my leg, and I gasp.

"Answer me." Salvatore's hand slides higher, and my breath catches in my throat.

I can't answer. I don't want to tell him that I'm remembering how I felt on *my* wedding day, sorting through all the complicated feelings then and since, looking forward to the closure that today will give. I don't want to talk about this at all. I just want this part to be over.

Salvatore moves closer, sliding smoothly across the leather seat until he's pressed against me. His hand slides up my thigh, to the very edge of it, and I swallow hard.

He reaches up, pressing his palm to my cheek, and turns my head so my face is pressed against the seat, and I'm looking straight at him. His touch is gentle but firm, and I feel the fingertips of his other hand slip between my thighs, sliding over the smooth fabric of my panties.

"I'll give you something to think about, then," he murmurs, his lips an inch from mine. "You can think about this, while we're in this car. You can think about it in the church, while I sit next to you with my hand on your leg. All the way until you walk out of there with me, because you're *my* wife, Gia."

As he says it, his fingers slip under the edge of my panties, delving between my soft folds. I'm already wet, and I gasp, my mouth an inch from his as his fingers slip easily into me, curling inside of my pussy as I clench around him, his thumb pressing against my clit.

His other hand holds my cheek, keeping me facing him, his fingertip brushing my lower lip as he starts to work his fingers inside of me with excruciating slowness.

"I'm going to keep you on the edge, *tesoro*, just like this," he whispers, the words ghosting over my mouth. "All the way until we pull up in front of St. Patrick's. And then you'll come for me, and we'll walk in with the scent of you still on my fingertips, and you still pulsing with the orgasm I give you when you see him again for the first time."

His hand tightens on my face, and his fingers press deeper inside of me, making me moan and gasp. "Understand, *tesoro*?"

I nod breathlessly, unable to speak. I already feel close to the edge, the sensation of his fingers in me and the driver just on the other side of the divider, along with his husky voice murmuring those words to me, sending me to the very brink of an orgasm. I don't know how I'll follow his instructions, how I'll keep from coming, but as it turns out, I don't have to worry.

He keeps me on the edge, all the way there, just as he promised. His fingers move in small strokes, keeping me close, until he feels me start to tremble, and then he goes torturously still, literally holding me in the palm of his hand as I quiver around him. Until we feel the car start to slow, and Salvatore suddenly starts to thrust his fingers hard, his thumb moving rapidly over my clit as he leans in to whisper in my ear.

"Come for me, Gia. My good little wife."

The orgasm breaks over me like a wave. My mouth opens on a cry of pleasure, only for the sound to be swallowed up as Salvatore kisses me hard, his tongue sweeping possessively into my mouth as I come on his fingers.

When he slips his hand free from my skirt, tugging it down neatly with his other hand, I'm flushed and shaking. The car rolls to a stop, and I put my hands to my cheeks, willing my heartbeat and breathing to return to normal. I see Salvatore adjust himself, pressing down on his obvious erection with the heel of his hand, and I have the sudden urge to lean over, unzip his suit trousers and take him in my mouth until he floods my tongue with his cum.

Instead, I stare at him as he waits a beat, and then another, before taking a deep breath and opening his door as if nothing out of the ordinary happened at all.

He walks around as I try to compose myself, opening my door, and holding out his hand to help me to the curb. His eyes meet mine, as calm as if I didn't just come all over the hand he's holding out to me seconds ago, and my heart flutters in my chest.

"You're mine, Gia," he whispers in my ear as I slip out of the car, and I turn towards him, my lips an inch from his.

"Always," I whisper back.

I feel him relax, just a little. And I feel a new confidence that we can get through this day, so long as we're together.

He needed a little reassurance. And I will, too, I'm sure, before the day is over.

Salvatore links my arm through his as we walk to the church. I should be embarrassed, knowing what we just did, but I can't help liking it more than I should. I *liked* his possessiveness, his driving need to make sure I remembered who I was married to before I see the man who was originally meant to claim my hand. I would rather this than the Salvatore who was consumed by guilt every time he touched me, a thousand times over.

The guests are all beginning to arrive, and we meld into the crowd, moving to the bride's side of the room and finding a place in one of the pews. My stomach tightens as I see Pyotr standing at the altar, wearing a crisp, bespoke suit, his gaze sweeping over the room. He looks exactly as I remember him, but my heart doesn't flutter the way it once did when I would see him. I remember what I once thought we were to each other, the days we spent together, and all the once-bright moments of our courtship, but it feels like it happened to someone else.

Like it's all just a distant dream now.

Even the sting of betrayal is lessened, with Salvatore next to me, his hand on my leg possessively just as he'd said, reminding me of who I'm married to—and what he just did to me. My cheeks heat a little, but the blush is all for him. And from the way he's looking at me when I glance his way, he knows it.

I glance around the church, trying to distract myself. It's wreathed in white and pink roses, decked out for a wedding, and as the last of the guests settle into the pews and the priest steps up to the altar, the music changes. We all turn to face the double doors at the back of the room, craning for a glimpse of the bride.

Bella looks beautiful. She's standing behind her two bridesmaids as the door opens, and I get a good view of her dress as they start to walk down the aisle ahead of her. Her dark brown hair is elegantly pinned up, her eyes downcast on the pink and white bouquet she's holding, so I can't tell if she seems happy or not. Her dress is a beautiful, fitted confection of lace and satin, the bodice off-the-shoulder and long-sleeved, lace all the way down to the full satin skirt that swishes over the narrow aisle carpet as she walks. She keeps her eyes fixed on the flowers, all the way to the altar, when her father pauses in preparation to give her hand to Pyotr.

My breath catches in my throat as the priest steps up, and I hear the same words that sealed my fate, barely two months ago.

If anyone has any objection to why these two should be wed…

No one says a word. I let out a slow breath, preparing myself for the rest of the ceremony, my thoughts already dashing ahead to the moment when I can go back to the hotel with Salvatore, and all of this will be in the past.

I hear the doors of the church shut, the heavy *thud* of the wood echoing through the room. And then, on the heels of that sound, the loud *click* of an ancient lock.

I twist around, just as Salvatore grabs my hand, my stomach dropping. Ten black-garbed, armed Bratva men coalesce in front of the door, just as more of them spill out from the back of the church, surrounding the altar.

Salvatore pulls me to my feet, as the guests start to surge out of the pews, panic filling the room. I hear Bella scream, hear the shouts, hear Salvatore speaking to me as our security tries to fight their way to us, but it's all such chaos that I feel like I'm drowning. I can't hear anything over the pounding of my heart in my ears, think of anything but the terror I see in Bella's eyes and the smugness in Pyotr's, as his gaze finally meets mine. He looks past her, and directly at me, and I *know*.

I know why Igor agreed to this in the first place.

They were planning this all along.

Gunshots erupt, and I scream. A heavy hand closes on my other arm, yanking me backward. For a moment, I'm caught between that hand and Salvatore, dragged in two different directions before my captor yanks me free, pulling me backward.

"Salvatore!" I shriek his name, and he turns, but a wave of guests and security, both mafia and Bratva, have already poured into the space I left, separating us. I scream for him again, and I hear him shout my name, but I'm being dragged back, heavy arms around me as I kick and punch and shriek, twisting to see who it is that's grabbed me.

A Bratva guard. He could be anyone. His face is set, expressionless, and four more men close around us as I'm pulled back into the shadows of the church, towards a back door that someone is unlocking to let us out. I kick again, twisting, trying to get enough purchase on the floor with my feet to get out of his grip, but he lifts me like a sack of potatoes—like I weigh nothing—and hauls me bodily out of the back door towards a waiting, running car.

I scream again, over and over, until my throat is hoarse, but no one comes. I feel my dress rip as he shoves me into the car, and I nearly fall face-first into the lap of another guard, who laughs and grabs me roughly.

"You make a lot of noise, *devochka*," he growls. "Time to do something about that."

I try to fling myself back, away from his grasp, but the door is closed, and the car is moving, and he boxes me in against the door in an instant. Panicking, I fumble for the handle to open it, preferring spilling out into the street from a moving car to being trapped in here with him. But it's locked, and there's nowhere to go.

"Good try, *devochka*," he says, grinning toothily. "But there's nowhere for you to run now."

I see the glint of a needle in his hand, and feel a prick in the side of my neck. He pulls away, sinking back into his side of the car, and I realize why a moment later as the world begins to spin around me.

I've been drugged. I'm about to pass out. And I have no idea where I'll be when I wake up.

Salvatore.

His face, his name, are the last things that go through my head before the world goes dark.

I crumple onto the leather seat of the car, insensible.

Gia

I have no idea how much time passes before I wake up.

When I do, it's dark out. I'm in a bed, and it takes me a moment to blink away the sticky sensation from my eyes and crawl up through the fog in my head to realize I'm in a hotel room.

Not my hotel room. A strange one, smaller and *much* less luxurious. The duvet feels scratchy under my legs, my silk skirt tangled around my knees, and my arms ache as badly as my head does. It takes me a second to realize why—that my hands are cuffed above my head to the headboard, keeping me in place.

I'm a prisoner. A *Bratva* prisoner.

Fear lances through me, hot and sharp—not just for myself, but for my baby. I've known I was pregnant for less than a day, and already I'm afraid that it might be taken from me.

We should have known. But I can't be angry with Salvatore. He wanted to believe that he could fix all of this. That he could protect me and still honor my father's wishes. That he could make a deal with the Bratva that would make up for stealing me from Pyotr at the altar.

That he could smooth everything over.

He was wrong, and my heart breaks thinking about what must be happening to him now, how frantic he must be.

If he's even alive.

I squeeze my eyes shut. I won't think that. I won't. If I do, I'll fall apart at the seams.

The door to the room opens, and my eyes fly open. For a moment, I think my heart is going to stop in my chest.

Pyotr is standing there, still in his suit from the wedding, and I feel a surge of nausea. Bile rises hotly in the back of my throat, and I try to sit up despite how my hands are cuffed to the bed, feeling far too vulnerable in my current position.

He looks at me appraisingly, a small, satisfied smile on his mouth, and fear follows the sick sensation in my stomach. "It took longer than expected, but there you are, Gia. In a bed, waiting for me, just as you were meant to be."

"Fuck you." I spit it out without thinking, seething with sudden anger, but he just laughs.

"That was the plan. Marry you, fuck you, get you pregnant, and then stash you somewhere until I wanted to have a little fun with you again. You were so gullible that it made it easy. You fell in love with me *so* hard, didn't you, little Gia?" Pyotr clicks his tongue, making a *tsk*ing sound as he walks toward the bed, and I stiffen, trying to scramble backward as far as I can.

"But your godfather got in the way of all of that. A shame, really. Your father put so much work into that treaty, just for one man that he trusted to blow it to bits at the last minute." Pyotr shakes his head. "I really was looking forward to our wedding night. But it doesn't have to be a total loss."

"Salvatore was saving me from *you*," I hiss, pulling my legs up under me. I want to be as small as possible, as far away from Pyotr as I can possibly be. My mind still feels a little foggy from the drugs, but one thing is crystal clear—Pyotr wants to hurt me. And I won't let him if I can manage it.

"Not much of a savior, is he?" Pyotr glances around the room, his mouth quirking up on one side as if all of this is funny to him. "But this is just a temporary measure, Gia. Just to make sure you didn't get away from me again. My men were needed elsewhere, and I had to make sure you didn't run from me, or do something foolish like jumping off a balcony or finding a razor blade in the shower. Now that I'm here, we can talk, and then I'll take those off of you." He nods to the handcuffs, and I glare at him.

"There's nothing to talk about."

"Of course there is." Pyotr sits on the edge of the bed, reaching over to touch my knee, and I flinch away from him instinctively. "Our future, for one thing."

"We don't have a future." I swallow hard, looking away from him, feeling as if I have emotional whiplash from how quickly everything has changed. Every part of me is aching for Salvatore. I miss him, and I'm terrified that something has happened to him, terrified for him and for myself, and sick with longing to go back to this morning, when we were happier than we've ever been.

"Of course we do." Pyotr smiles at me, his hand caressing my knee until I feel sick all over again. "We can still have everything we once talked about, Gia. All those conversations in the library and the garden, you remember those, don't you?" He squeezes my knee, his fingers curling underneath it to pull my leg out from underneath me, his broad palm skimming down my calf. I try to pull free of his touch, but his hand tightens, his eyes narrowing. "You do remember, don't you?"

There's no point in lying. I nod silently.

"Good." His smile returns. "Not marriage, of course. I can't give you that any longer. Your godfather ruined you for that, so you can thank him. Unless, of course, you want to try to convince me that he's left you a virgin this whole time?"

I shake my head quickly. It's hard to believe that once, that was what I hoped for. Now, I don't want there to be a shred of doubt in Pyotr's mind that Salvatore has had me in every way he can think of. I don't want Pyotr to keep touching me, or to try to test the veracity of it if I were to try to say otherwise.

Pyotr shudders. "That's what I thought. I could see his sick lust for you from a mile off," he adds, as if he's sharing a secret with me. "He tried to call off our wedding, and then when he failed at that, he ruined it. I'm sorry for that, Gia. I can't marry you now—you're ruined, and I can't have a bride who isn't a virgin." His hand slides up my knee, towards my inner thigh, and I go rigid, my heart beating frantically. "But you can still be my mistress."

He says it as if I should be grateful for the offer, as if he's *giving* me something, instead of it being a threat. It makes me feel sick all over again, seeing for the first time clearly how narcissistic he is, how cruel, how *right* Salvatore was about everything. That this man would steal me back, drug me, hurt me, chain me to a bed—and then offer me a place as his *mistress* as if he were doing me a fucking favor.

"No, thank you," I manage to choke out. "I want to go home. Whatever there was between us, Pyotr—you're right, it can't happen now. Not after I've been married to someone else."

The smile vanishes from his face. His hand grips my thigh, hard enough to hurt, and I bite my lip to keep from crying out. I don't want to give him the satisfaction. "I wanted to give you the chance to accept of your own free will," he grinds out between his teeth, all good humor gone from his face and voice. "To prove that you loved me, Gia. But I see now you were as much of a liar as your godfather."

No, I want to shout. *You want me to give in because it makes you feel powerful.* He wants me to cry and beg, to promise him that I wanted him all along, to choose him even though he's chained me to a bed in order to get me to do so, because it makes him feel good to do it this way. To prove that I can't be stolen from him.

But everything that matters *has* been stolen, and given to someone else. And he'll never get it back from me.

"Where's Bella?" I ask, fear stabbing through me at the thought of my cousin. "What happened to her?"

"She's being kept in another room. I'll likely still marry her. She's useful, and I can blackmail her father that way." Pyotr shrugs. "But I don't care for her. It's you I wanted, Gia." His hand rubs over my thigh again, and I fight back another rush of nausea. "I'll let you sleep a little longer, and then come back. Maybe the next time you wake up, you'll have had a change of heart."

He starts to stand up, pulling his phone out of his pocket, and fear turns to panic at the thought of him having me drugged again. "Pyotr—no. Don't let them drug me." My voice *is* pleading now, and I hate it, but this is about more than me. My baby matters more than my pride.

Pyotr turns sharply back to me, his eyes narrowing. "Why, Gia?" There's a sudden, dangerous edge to his voice, and my heart beats harder, fear making it hard to think.

It could make it worse to tell him. Or maybe there's some small part of him that will balk at hurting a child. Maybe he won't want to, if only to use it as blackmail against Salvatore.

"I'm pregnant." My voice is small, shaking, all of my defiance gone. I want to fight, but I'm so scared. Everything that I never knew I needed to fear is happening, and I wish I had believed Salvatore sooner. I wish I had never said yes to Pyotr in the first place.

I wish I were home.

Pyotr's eyes go dark with anger, and I feel myself starting to tremble. My arms are numb, but the rest of me is shaking as I stare at him, terrified of what happens next.

He crosses the room to me in two quick strides, the back of his hand striking me across the face before I even realize what's happening. My head snaps to one side, and I taste blood on my lip.

"*Whore*," he snarls. "You can forget what I offered you, *shlyukha*. I don't want that used cunt of yours."

His fingers grab my chin, yanking my head back around to face him. "But someone else will. I'll sell you both, you *and* the baby. Traffic you like the mafia slut you are. How does that sound, *suka*?"

I don't know what he's calling me, but I can hear the venom in his voice, and I know it's nothing good. He jerks his hand away from my face, hatred in his eyes, and shouts something in Russian. A moment later, the door opens, and a bulky man with a small black leather case in his hand steps in.

Fear jolts through me, but I tilt my chin up despite it, glaring at Pyotr. "Salvatore will come for me," I tell him, forcing defiance into my voice. "He won't let you do this."

Pyotr chuckles, but there's no mirth in it. "Salvatore is dead," he says flatly. "Your future is mine now, *suka*. And I decide what happens to you."

My heart drops, that nausea welling up all over again as Pyotr walks past the man without a backward glance. The man unzips the case, taking out a syringe, and tears burn behind my eyes.

I won't believe it. I won't. Pyotr can say Salvatore is dead all he likes, but that doesn't mean he's telling the truth.

I have to believe that there's still hope. That if Salvatore would interrupt my wedding to storm the altar and take me for his own, there's nothing that can stand between him and saving me again.

I close my eyes and grit my teeth as the needle touches my skin, holding tight to that—to the only shred of hope that I and my baby have left.

That Salvatore will come for us, before it's too late.

Salvatore

The moment Gia is dragged away from me, I feel something snap inside.

Her hand slips out of mine, and I turn to see a black-garbed Bratva man yanking her back, dragging her towards the flood of Bratva goons pouring in from the left side of the church. My immediate instinct is to go after her, and I spin, reaching for her as I try to dart after the man taking her away from me.

But the crowd separates us, and all I can do is hear her scream.

My hand goes automatically to where I'd have a gun, if I were carrying a weapon. But I'm not. This was supposed to be a wedding, and I'm unarmed. I can see my security, but they're fighting their way through the crowd, guests panicking in an effort to get out of the church.

It's utter madness. A woman is on the floor, her arm broken after someone stepped on her in an effort to get out. I hear children crying, the screams of other guests. And over it all, I still hear Gia.

Gunshots ring through the church, and a body drops inches away from me—one of the Bratva. On pure instinct, I grab his gun, my head pounding and adrenaline flooding me, and I charge in the direction where Gia was taken. One of the Bratva tries to cut me off, and I pull the trigger.

He drops, blood pouring from the bullet hole in his throat.

It feels like everything is moving in slow motion around me. My finger compresses the trigger, again and again, pushing my way through the Bratva that tries to stop me. My ears are ringing, my nose burning with the acrid scent of the gun. I hear Josef shouting for me as I stare at the open door they dragged Gia through, and spin around, looking at his pale face.

"What?" I shout at him, and he grabs my arm, shaking me. It's enough to jolt me. I'm Josef's boss, and he's never touched me like that. He'd never grab me. But his expression is frantic.

"They saw the direction they took Gia. Some of our guys. Come on. Let's go!"

He shouts it all at me, and I nod, my heart in my throat as I follow him. All I can think about is the panicked look on her face, the terror in her voice, the sight of her being taken away from me. After everything, losing her is unthinkable. I can't even stop to think about what Igor did, this fresh betrayal and the future consequences of it or the fact that this was undoubtedly planned, because all I can think about is getting Gia back.

The church is swarming with Bratva, the rattle of gunfire filling the air, the scent of blood thick. Josef and my security move around me, charging forward as they cut down any Bratva man who tries to get in our way, clearing a path towards the door. One of Igor's men pushes through mine, and I pull the trigger again, dropping him in his tracks as my men charge forward over his body. I drop the empty gun, bending to grab a fresh one off of the dead man, and my foot nearly slips in a puddle of blood.

It's been years since I've been in the middle of anything like this, but my body reacts on instinct. Getting out of the church is all that matters, and we plow forward, the Bratva dropping like flies as we burst out into the open air. The doors to the car are open, and Josef and I fling ourselves into it, two more men following as the driver peels away from the curb, heading in a direction further downtown.

"There!" Josef gestures as the car swerves to the left, pointing at a blacked-out town car just ahead. "That's the car that took her."

"Follow him!" I snap at the driver, my voice a hoarse snarl. "Don't you fucking let it get away."

"Got it, boss." The driver's voice is flat, the car lurching forward as he steps on the gas, and I stare at the car, willing us not to lose it. New York's afternoon traffic is thick, and the car weaves back and forth, swinging down a side street and losing sight of the other car before the driver emerges two streets down, close enough to see but not so close that they'll clock us—hopefully.

My hand grips the gun until my knuckles turn white, sweat beading on the back of my neck. I can only imagine how terrified Gia must be, and it makes me feel murderous, so filled with a black rage that I know every Bratva man between her and I is going to have seen his last sunrise this morning.

I'll kill anyone I have to in order to get her back. I'll do anything I need to do.

Nothing matters as much as knowing she's safe.

The car swings down another street, picking up speed, taking a corner so fast that, for a moment, I think we're going to flip. My heart surges into my throat, and I grip the side of the seat, leaning forward as the driver gains on the blacked-out car.

And then he steps on the brake, skidding into an alley and coming to a halt.

"What the fuck are you doing?" I snarl, and the driver turns around.

"They're stopping at that hotel." He points up the road. "Didn't want to get closer, or they might have seen."

"Good work." Josef leans back, popping a clip out of his gun and replacing it with a fresh one, tucking two more into his pockets. "Men, let's go. Salvatore, let me cover you."

"Fine. So long as I get to Gia." I slide out of the car, taking the gun and clips that one of my men hand me. "I need a clear path to her. Whatever that takes."

"You got it." Josef motions to the men. "Let's go."

We make our way up the street, through the alleys to avoid attention, to the back of the hotel. The car is gone by the time we get there, and I clench my teeth, trying not to think about what might be happening to Gia. What could still happen, if we don't get there fast enough.

There are two Bratva men at the back door. Josef drops them before they even have a chance to see us, the silencer on his gun making the sound of the shot nothing but a dull *click* as the bullets find their target. We slink forward through the shadows, the night closing in around us as Josef opens the door and motions the men in, then walks in ahead of me.

We'd been concerned about hotel staff or guests seeing us, but we hadn't needed to be. There's no staff here, no guests—this is clearly a hotel front for a building the Bratva uses for other means. We round the corner only to see five men heading towards us, and in seconds, the hall is filled with smoke as we all fire.

One of my men lets out a pained cry as a bullet strikes his shoulder, slumping against the wall. The dark hallway carpet turns darker still, blood soaking into it as body after body hits the floor. We push forward towards the stairwell, cutting down the Bratva, my hands working on instinct as I empty the gun and shove another clip into it.

Josef yanks the stairwell door open, and we charge up onto the stairs. Halfway up, I hear a choked sound, and turn to see one of my men falling backward, tumbling in a smear of blood and the sound of cracking bones as Bratva rush in, following us and shooting one of mine. Josef and the others turn instantly, releasing a volley of gunfire and mowing them down as I and three more of my men charge up, pushing ahead.

The second floor is so empty that I know Gia can't be there. The same for the third. But the fourth is crawling with Bratva, and I lean back into the stairwell, reloading my gun as Josef and my men do the same.

"There's a hell of a lot out there," I murmur. "It's going to be tough getting through."

Josef nods. "We've got this." He pauses, and I hear footsteps. "Backup," he says. "We'll get her back, boss. Just one more push, and we'll get to her."

When the door opens, we flood out into the hall, gunfire going off the moment we emerge, and the Bratva turn to meet us. Over the sounds of shooting and through the haze, I look down the hall, and my entire body tenses.

I see *him*. Pyotr. Stepping out of a room towards the end of the hallway.

"Josef!" I shout my enforcer's name, and he turns, following my gaze. Without hesitation, he motions to three more of my men, and the five of us push forward, the rest bringing up the rear and clearing a path all around us as we move toward the room where I'm certain Gia is.

Pyotr turns, meeting my gaze, and everything narrows down. There's a sick irony in how similar it is to the moment when I knew how I felt about Gia, when the world disappeared around me, and there was only her. Only her softness, her scent, her body against mine, and the taste of her mouth, everything else vanishing except for what was right in front of me.

Only this time, it's not love that blooms through me like a red cloud of blood; it's hate. It's pure, unadulterated fury, and as my gaze narrows down on Pyotr and the sounds of gunshots and the scent of smoke and blood fade into the background, it's because all that matters to me at that moment is that he dies.

He smirks, as if I'm not coming for him, ready to tear him to pieces if that's what it takes. He says something, but I can't hear it, my ears ringing too loudly to make out the words. It doesn't matter—I don't give a shit what he has to say.

He raises his gun, and I raise mine, a second quicker than he is. That's all that matters, in a moment like this. A split second faster, and the other guy is a dead man.

I feel the trigger sink under my finger, and I see the moment the bullet strikes Pyotr in the shoulder. He recoils, and I shoot again, this time aiming for his knee.

I want him to hurt, before he dies.

He falls, crashing down, the sound of his scream tearing through the ringing in my ears. I stride forward, adrenaline rushing through me, and grab a fistful of his hair in my hand as I yank his head back.

"She's mine," I snarl, and I press the gun to his forehead. I have two shots left.

I pull the trigger.

The second I feel him go limp, I fling him down to the carpet, spinning towards the door. I shove it open just in time to see a tall, bulky man stepping away from Gia's bedside, an empty syringe in his hand.

I don't even hesitate. I fire once more, and put my last bullet squarely through his forehead.

Gia doesn't move when he hits the floor next to the bed, and panic floods me. I toss the gun away, rushing towards the bed, and the sight of her pale face and limp body makes the hand around my heart squeeze into a fist, crushing it.

"Gia." I reach for her, smoothing her hair away from her face, rage flooding me all over again when I see the bruise on her cheek and the blood on her lip. If I could kill Pyotr all over again for this, I would. "Gia."

She doesn't move. I press my fingers to her throat and feel her pulse, faintly.

She's alive, but I don't know what they've done to her, and fear jolts through me. Her hands are cuffed above her head, and I turn to the man's body, bending to rifle through his pockets until I find the keys.

I might have lost the chance to tell her I love her. I might be too late.

The thought echoes through my mind, a punishing loop, over and over as I free her wrists and lift her fragile body off of the bed, clutching her to my chest.

I love her, and it might be too late.

I turn around to see Josef behind me, covered in blood, his eyes instantly on Gia. "Get a car ready to go," I snap, striding towards the door. "Anyone who tries to stop you dies. We have to get her to a hospital, *now*."

Josef nods, following me out, barking orders at the men. I head for the stairwell, cradling Gia as my men and I make our way past the blood and bodies back down, all the way out to where the car is waiting for us. I slide into the back, still holding Gia on my lap, unwilling to let go of her.

I hold onto her all the way to the hospital, until we push past the front doors, past the startled staff. "Clear a floor," I snap at the nurse at the front desk. "I need a doctor, *now*—"

"Who the hell do you think you are—" she starts to say, her eyes flicking between Gia's body and my face, and I lean forward, my jaw tight.

"Salvatore Morelli."

Her attitude changes immediately. She nods, grabbing for the phone. "Floor nine," she says after a moment. "You can head up now. A doctor will meet you."

Fifteen minutes later, Gia is in a bed, with my security spread out over the now unoccupied floor and Josef calling for more backup. Nurses are taking vitals and hooking her up to an IV, asking questions that I answer as best as I can, but all I can do is look at her, my heart heavier in my chest than it ever has before.

I sink into a chair, staring at her still form, and reach for her hand. I can't lose her. Not now, not like this.

And I'm going to stay right here with her until I have her back.

Gia

I wake in a daze.

At first, I have no idea where I am. There's a sharp, antiseptic smell, and when I move my hands, the fabric under them feels rough. At least, compared to what I'm used to.

I blink, trying to clear my vision. The lights above me are bright, glaring, and I reach up to press a hand over my eyes. There's movement to my right, and I feel a large, warm hand suddenly covering mine.

Startled, I push myself up—or I try to, anyway. My body hurts, my head aches, and I mostly want to go back to sleep.

"*Tesoro*. Gia." A familiar voice cuts through the fog, and I blink again, rubbing my hand over my face. When I lower it, my heart squeezes in my chest.

I'm in a hospital bed, I realize. In a hospital room. I feel a sting in my arm, and realize there's an IV there. But none of that matters, because sitting in a stiff leather chair next to me, his hand gripping mine, is Salvatore.

My *husband*.

He stands up suddenly, leaning over me, and both of his hands are on my face as he kisses me fiercely. I gasp, my mouth opening without thinking, and I hear him groan—a sound of near-relief as he cups my face in his hands and kisses me as if he thought he'd never see me again.

When he breaks the kiss, he stares down at me, his hands still pressed to my face. "Gia."

"You're alive," I breathe, blinking past the sudden burn of tears behind my eyes. "You're not dead."

Salvatore looks at me confusedly. "No, I'm not dead."

"Pyotr said you were dead." Most of what happened feels foggy, as if I can barely recall huge chunks of it, but I remember that. I remember how it felt when he said it, how hard it was to hold onto hope that he was lying. But Salvatore is here, in front of me, and I'm pretty sure that I'm not dreaming.

Salvatore's jaw tightens. "He's the one who's dead."

Shock cuts through me, but there's no sadness, only relief. If he's dead, then he can never hurt us again. His father is still a problem, and no doubt will continue to be unless he died too, but all I can think is that Pyotr is gone. He'll never touch me again. He'll never try to hurt me, or Salvatore, or our child. "You're sure?" I whisper, and Salvatore nods tightly.

"I killed him myself."

I close my eyes, a sob of relief bursting out, and I feel tears drip down my cheeks. Salvatore squeezes my hand, his fingers gently brushing my cheek.

"Shh, *tesoro*. There's no need to cry."

I open my eyes again, swallowing hard. "I thought I might never see you again."

Salvatore's face darkens at that. He sits down, carefully, on the edge of the bed, his palm pressed against my cheek. "I thought I lost you, Gia," he says softly. "And I thought I had lost my chance to tell you how I felt for you. I don't want to make that mistake again."

My pulse leaps, my heart beating a little faster in my chest. "And what did you want to say?" I whisper, my eyes meeting his.

His fingers stroke along my jaw, brushing my lower lip, a look of such utter tenderness on his face that it takes my breath away. "I love you, Gia," he murmurs. "I should have said it before this, but I won't make the mistake of not saying it as often as I can, now that I have. I love you. And I'm so grateful you're still here with me."

Fresh tears spill over, rolling down my cheeks as I look up at him. "I love you too," I whisper. "I'm so glad you're okay."

Salvatore gives me a small, thin smile. "Me, too."

"I'm sorry I didn't believe you about the danger," I say softly. "I should have. I understand you were telling the truth now."

"I know, *tesoro.*" His hand covers mine. "It took time for you to see it. And I can understand why."

I swallow hard, trying to speak through the tears. Everything I feel rushes up at once, feelings that I never thought I could have but that all feel right, now, as if it should have always been this way. "I didn't think you could be the one for me," I whisper. "But you've shown me over and over that you *are* a good husband, Salvatore. That you'll protect me, that that's all you've ever tried to do. I trust you. I love you. And I'm sorry it took this long."

He grips my hand gently, leaning in to kiss me, his fingers brushing the side of my face. "We're here now, *tesoro,*" he murmurs against my mouth. "That's all that matters. You, and me, and our child."

I blink up at him, hope surging in my chest. "The baby's okay? You're sure?"

Salvatore nods. "Our baby is just fine. The nurses don't think you'll have any complications. All you need is rest, and then we can go home soon."

Tears of relief flood my eyes all over again, and I press my forehead to his, letting them go. We stay like that for a long moment, until I finally find the strength to wipe them away. Salvatore brushes a thumb over my cheek, his palm cupping my face gently.

"Sleep, *tesoro*," he says. "I'll stay here with you. And then we can go home."

It's three days before we're able to go home. Salvatore stays with me throughout it all, sending Josef home to get fresh clothes and showering in the small cubicle in my room. When the doctor finally gives me the all-clear, Salvatore hovers as I change, doing all he can to help. He doesn't want to be far from me, intensely protective, and where I once would have found it smothering, I now appreciate it.

He thought he lost me, and I thought I lost him. Neither one of us wants to be far from the other right now. And all I want is to be home with him, at last.

I sleep for most of the drive back out to the mansion. I wake to the car rolling to a stop in our courtyard, and I catch the moment that Salvatore's face relaxes, clearly relieved to be back.

"We're really safe?" I ask softly. "The threat is gone?"

Salvatore nods. "I don't think Igor will cross me, after this. Bella has gone back home to her family, and a large number of his men are dead. If he wants to make a move, he'll have to recover a good deal, first. But I don't believe he will. And he'll never again get to you, *tesoro*," he adds. "There will be no more alliances. Igor will go up against me if he wants revenge, and he'll regret it, if he tries."

"Thank you for coming after me." I sit up slowly, reaching out for him, looking at the handsome man across from me. It's hard to believe that not so long ago, I thought I hated him. Now, looking at him, I can't think of anyone I love more in the world.

"I would do anything to keep you safe, Gia." Salvatore pushes open the door, helping me out into the sunlight, his arm around my waist. "I always will."

"I love you," I whisper, turning towards him, and he tips my chin up, his lips brushing softly against mine. He holds me there, in the warm sun in front of our home, the safety of his arms encircling me as I feel all the fear vanish.

"I love you too, Gia Morelli." His hand slips into my hair, and he bends down, kissing me more firmly this time. And then, with one swift motion, he sweeps me into his arms, holding me against his chest as I squeak with surprise.

"What are you doing?" I ask, and Salvatore smiles down at me, a hint of mischievous humor in his grin.

"What I should have done a long time ago. Carrying my bride over the threshold of our home." He raises an eyebrow. "If that's alright with you, *wife*?"

"Always," I promise him, and I mean it.

I never could have seen it coming, but Salvatore is everything I want. Everything I could need.

My lover. My husband. My *protector*.

Now, and for the rest of our lives.

Epilogue
Gia

Three months later

All day long, I've been looking forward to the night Salvatore has planned for us. We had a checkup today for the baby, and the doctor gave me the envelope that would tell us if we were having a boy or a girl. I promised Salvatore we'd find out tonight, when he said he's taking me out to dinner.

I stand in front of the mirror, touching the soft swell of my stomach, still just beginning to show. I picked the black dress that he gave me for our first dinner out for tonight, and it still fits, although the silk shows the curve of my belly. I don't mind, and I know Salvatore won't, either. I have a feeling, if anything, he'll like it enough that we'll come home earlier than expected.

I've made a full recovery, physically, since the attack at the wedding. The baby was completely fine, and so was I. Emotionally, it's been more difficult, but Salvatore has been at my side through all of it, soothing me when the bad memories re-emerge and holding me close when I wake up from nightmares. And they've been fewer and fewer, recently, all of my anticipation for the future outshining my lingering hurt from the past.

My phone buzzes, telling me the driver will be ready soon. I slip on my onyx and diamond bracelet and earrings, grabbing my clutch, and head downstairs to meet Salvatore.

He's waiting for me in the foyer, in charcoal suit pants and a dark red button-down, and my heart leaps a little when I see him. His face lights up when he catches sight of me, love and desire in his expression in equal measure, and I feel a flood of happiness as I walk down to meet him.

I feel lucky to have him, lucky that things worked out the way they did, lucky that he loves me, and I love him in return. And I know he feels the same way.

"You have the envelope?" Salvatore asks as we slip into the car, and I tap my clutch.

"Right in here."

An hour later, the car pulls up in front of our destination, and I can't help but smile. It's the restaurant Salvatore took me to for that first dinner—the small, rustic Italian bistro that he owns. He opens the door for me, giving me a hand out, and smiles at the look on my face.

"Our first date as husband and wife wasn't what I hoped it would be," he says, his hand on my waist as he leans down to give me a light kiss. "I wanted to recreate it. A second chance."

"I love it," I tell him honestly, and he smiles, taking my hand as he leads me inside.

The restaurant is empty except for us, and Salvatore leads me to a table near the kitchen, the same one we sat at that night. He pulls my chair out for me, and then sits opposite, waiting for the server to bring us water and red wine for him, sparkling cider for me before he speaks.

"Do you want to find out now, or wait until the end of the night?"

"Now." I reach for my clutch. "I don't think I can wait any longer."

Salvatore laughs. "Me, either." He leans forward, moving the plate of olive oil and the basket of bread out of the way. "Put it here, and we can look at the same time."

I slip the paper free of the envelope, laying it face-down on the table between us. Our hands touch it at the same time, and I look at Salvatore, at the eager anticipation in his face. It feels like a light, loving moment, one that, once upon a time, I could never have imagined having with him.

But that's how our marriage is, now.

"One, two—three." We flip it over at the same time, and I let out a small gasp of happiness as a smile spreads over Salvatore's face.

"We're going to have a son." He looks at me, his face full of love as he leans in, his hand squeezing mine as he kisses me. "I couldn't be happier."

"It's what we both wanted." I look at the slip of paper, my chest tight with happiness. "I can't wait."

"Six more months." Salvatore chuckles at my expression.

"It's going to feel like an eternity."

"It'll go by before we know it," he promises. "But that's not the only thing I wanted to know tonight."

I blink at him, confused. "What do you mean?"

He stands up, and I stare at him, unsure of what's going on. But in one smooth motion, he goes down on a knee, and my hands fly up to cover my mouth as he takes a small box out of his pocket.

"I didn't ask the first time, Gia," he says softly. "But I'm asking you now."

He opens the box, and I see a beautiful, radiant-cut pink diamond set in rose gold shimmering up from the velvet, a trillion-cut white diamond on either side of it. It sparkles in the low light, beautiful, and exactly what I would have chosen for myself.

"I know it's a bit late," Salvatore says with a small laugh, "considering we just found out the sex of our first child. But I want to ask you anyway, Gia, because I want to go into our new life knowing that you choose me, as much as I choose you. I love you with all of my heart. Will you marry me?"

"Yes," I blurt out, before the last words are even fully out of his mouth. "Yes, I'll marry you. Of course. I love you—"

"I love you, too." Salvatore nearly lifts me out of my chair, pulling me to my feet as he slides the ring onto my finger, his hand on my hip as his mouth crushes against mine. For a moment, I can't breathe; the restaurant and the music and everything else dissolving around us, the feeling of his mouth on mine and his ring on my finger and his arms around me is all that matters. I can feel him pressing against me, hard and solid, his hand on the small of my back roving lower, and he groans against my mouth.

A throat clears, and we jump apart, my face turning bright red. A server is standing there with our salads, and he looks from Salvatore and me, and back again.

"I can come back, sir, if—"

"No." Salvatore shakes his head, looking as if he's on the verge of bursting into laughter, and an embarrassed giggle escapes me as he pulls out my chair so I can sink back into it. "No, thank you. Carry on."

The server deposits the salads, fleeing, and when Salvatore's eyes meet mine, we both start to laugh, hard enough that tears begin to well up in my eyes.

"This is a good start, I think." I smile at him, reaching over for his hand, seeing the way his diamond on my finger sparkles in the light. "Better than before."

Salvatore lifts my hand to his lips, kissing my knuckles softly. "And it will only keep getting better, *tesoro*," he murmurs. "Forever."

And I believe him. With all my heart, I believe him.

We might not have known it from the start, but there's no one in the world I'd rather spend the rest of my life with.

Salvatore is mine, forever, and I'm his.

And we're just getting started.

Thanks for reading!

I'm super excited to let you know that I now have a subscription plan where you can be the first to see what I'm working on, but also read along as I write, with weekly updates to soon-to-be-published works! You'll also get access to exclusive bonus scenes, short stories, and depending on the plan you choose, access to other published books. I'd love for you to take a look here.

If subscriptions aren't for you, I totally get it. **Text *SPICYREADS* to 737-317-8825 for new release information. For a sneak peek into my next book, continue to read below...**

Vicious Temptation

Chapter One (Bella)

The worst day of my life was a perfectly beautiful, sunny day. The kind of day any woman would want to get married on. A quintessential late spring afternoon in New York, with clear skies and a warm breeze. I can easily recall the feeling of the warmth on my skin before I walked into the cathedral, the smell of the sprays of pink and white roses that filled the space, overwhelming the usual wood-and-incense scent, see the glow of that same spring sunshine filtering through the windows and lighting up the interior on what is supposed to be the happiest day of any woman's life.

Three months later, waking up to sunshine still makes my stomach twist and my palms sweat. And this morning, when I'm supposed to meet my father in his office after breakfast to talk, is no different.

I roll out of bed, leaving my hair loose around my face as I slip into a pair of wide-cut jeans and a long-sleeved, light-weight hoodie, shoving my feet into a pair of Vans. Downstairs, I can hear the sound of the few household staff that work for my father moving around, and I quickly scrape my hair up into a messy bun atop my head, wrapping my arms around myself as I head down the hall to the stairs that lead to the first floor of our New York countryside home.

It's not a grand mansion. My father has the D'Amelio name, but only a fraction of their wealth. Lately, things have gotten a bit shinier around here, largely because of what Salvatore D'Amelio, one of the high-ranking mafia bosses in the Northeast, paid my father to get him to sign a marriage contract between me and Pyotr Lasilov, the Bratva *pakhan*'s heir.

Just the thought of his name makes my stomach twist again, a queasy, panicked feeling spreading through me until I'm not sure I'll be able to eat breakfast.

But breakfast is waiting for me in the sunny informal dining room, waiting at a single place setting near the head of the table. My father and I used to have breakfast together, even though he's not the most pleasant man to spend time with, and we don't ever have much to talk about. But with just the two of us living here, it felt necessary. To feel like we're some semblance of a family.

Now, I wake up much later than he does, and he's given up trying to get me to do otherwise. So if I see him at all, it's at dinnertime, where he insists on meals served by our singular household staff member who stays at night.

I sink down into the chair, pulling my feet up onto the seat and tucking them under me. I couldn't do this if my father was here, he'd insist on proper posture and ladylike behavior, but when I'm by myself, I can do what I want. And I feel better like this. Safer, with my knees tucked up against my chest and one arm wrapped around them as I tug the hoodie closer around my neck and reach for the smoothie sitting to one side of the china bowl in front of me.

It tastes like peach, honey, and vanilla—my favorite. There's probably some spinach and avocado mixed in too, but I don't taste it. Gladys, our cook, has been on a mission to figure out how to make sure I get enough vitamins, and smoothies in the morning have seemed to work so far.

For an entire month, I could barely eat at all. I'm just now starting to gain some of the weight back, so I don't look like a scarecrow instead of a person.

There's a bowl of hot steel-cut oatmeal in front of me, too, with a spoonful of brown sugar on top of it, studded with dried fruits and drizzled with real cream. Gladys is really trying to tempt me to eat more in the mornings, but this one especially, I'm not sure if I'll be able to manage it.

Whatever it is that my father wants to talk to me about this morning, the idea of it has a lump of dread lodged in my stomach, making it difficult for me to even choke the smoothie down.

I manage most of it, and a few bites of the oatmeal. I glance at the clock as I swallow a third sticky bite down, seeing it's just after eleven. If I don't go now, I'll miss him before he leaves—for some business lunch, probably—and while it will mean putting off whatever news he has for me, he'll also be pissed at me for stalling.

The thought of dealing with that makes me shiver, wrapping my arms around myself despite the warmth of the sunny room, and I push my chair away from the table, resolutely heading for my father's office.

I knock once, and walk in.

His office has looked the same for as long as I can remember. It's all dark wood, from the floor-to-ceiling paneling, the hardwood floor, the bookshelves, and the desk with the two leather-backed chairs sitting in front of it. There's a bay window behind him, looking out at the small countryside property that our house is located on. The windows are tightly shut, and the air in here is frigid. My father likes to keep visitors to his office a little uncomfortable. It makes him feel powerful, and that's something he has very little of.

Which is why it didn't surprise me that he was willing to sell me off in marriage to the Bratva. It earned him money and the favor of the don, and would have made him father-in-law to the Bratva heir. A huge jump up in status, for a man whose family normally just barely can consider themselves a part of mafia society.

"Dad." I greet him as I walk in, and he looks up from behind his desk—a tall, thin man in his fifties with hair that's gone entirely grey, and a trimmed mustache and beard. He's wearing a button-down shirt with the collar open, the sleeves neatly closed at the wrists, and there's a file open on the desk in front of him. I see a glimpse of a man's picture inside of it, a middle-aged man, and I feel that queasy ripple again.

Some gut instinct, my own intuition maybe, is telling me that I'm not going to like what this meeting is about.

"Bella." He gestures for me to sit down, and I do, sinking into one of the stiff leather chairs. I keep my hands in my lap and my feet on the floor, but my father still gives me a disapproving look as he takes in my choice of clothing.

"You look like a street urchin. It's summer."

"It's definitely barely above fifty degrees in your office, so I think I made the right choice." I purse my lips, feeling my heartbeat ratchet up a notch. "What's going on?"

My father makes a small, disgruntled noise in the back of his throat. "What's *going on*, Bella, is that I think I've finally managed to arrange a new match for you. Tommas Ferrero. Not one of the most distinguished mafia names, but after what happened with your last engagement—" he breaks off, and I feel my entire body go rigid.

This. This is exactly what I was afraid of when my father said he wanted to meet.

"Finally?" The word comes out as a hoarse croak past the tightness in my throat. "It's been three months. Not—years. You make it sound like I'm some kind of—Victorian spinster or something—"

"The sooner the better." My father pushes the papers towards me, the man's photo on top of it. "It's hard enough to find anyone interested, Bella. Our family name has some weight, but you know as well as I do how far down in the ranks I am. And after the incident with Pyotr—well, Tommas is the first who's shown any interest in you at all."

"The first," I say numbly, staring at the picture. There's nothing particularly significant or interesting about the man staring up at me. Dark hair with hints of greying at the temples, dark eyes, a flat expression, a not-objectionable face. "You make it sound like you've been looking for someone since I was brought back here."

My father doesn't respond at first, and that's really all the answer I need. "There's plenty of gossip about your—condition, Bella. You're lucky that Tommas—"

"My condition?" I look up at my father, feeling that tightness in my throat spread, turning into a hot burn of tears behind my eyes. "You mean the result of how I've been ever since I was brought back after the Bratva—who *you* convinced me I would be safe with—"

"We don't need to go over it again, Bella." He cuts me off sharply, and I sink back into the chair, feeling like I've been struck. I know that my father thinks that I'm being dramatic, that the reactions I'm still having to the aftermath of what Pyotr and his men did to me should have stopped by now. But it hurts every time I'm faced with it.

There's a reason I keep to myself most of the time now. Why I spend most of my time in my room and eat most of my meals alone. Why I don't wake up until late, and feel tired all day.

"The deal was presented as genuine," he continues, letting out a frustrated breath as he takes the papers and Tommas' photo and pulls them back to his side of the desk. "I couldn't have known it was a trap, Bella. Or what would happen to you. You can't possibly think that I—or Salvatore, for that matter—believed that was what would happen. Otherwise, neither of us would ever have agreed to it."

I know he's right. Deep down, I really do. My father is a greedy man, and one who would do a lot for more power, but I don't think he would have outright sold me to a monster if he knew what that monster had planned. He thought that the Bratva's promise of my safety, and the additional security that Salvatore had arranged and paid for, would be enough.

It's just that he was wrong, and now I have to bear the cost of it.

"I don't want to get married again," I whisper, feeling panic tangle in my throat and threaten to cut the words off entirely. "I can't. Please—I really can't do it. Even just more time—"

But as I say it, I know it's not true. More time isn't going to fix it. I don't want to marry anyone else. The idea of putting on a wedding dress again makes me feel as if my skin is too tight for my body, as if I can't breathe, and the idea of walking into a church and down an aisle towards another man that my father has told me to marry sends that queasy feeling spiraling through me, until it feels like I might throw up on the gleaming hardwood floor of my father's office. Panic floods me at the thought of someone touching me, at the thought of all the things I would be expected to do with this future husband, and I feel like a trapped animal, on the verge of gnawing my own limb off in a bid to be free.

He takes a deep, slow breath, as if he's trying to be patient with me. "I understand that you're struggling, Bella. I do. I will find someone who I'm certain won't hurt you. Tommas, to my knowledge, is a good man, and I'll do my due diligence to make sure that he will be a kind and understanding husband to you. If not him, then I will find someone else, but you need to marry soon, Bella. Our family needs—"

"You don't understand." I press a hand to my ribs, trying to breathe, trying to make my father grasp what it is that I'm saying. "I don't want to get married at all. I don't want to marry Tommas, or *anyone* else."

The look on my father's face tells me that he's close to losing his patience. "That's ridiculous, Bella. What are you going to do if you don't get married? All mafia daughters marry. That's your duty, in this world of ours. To make a good match, and elevate our family. To ensure that we rise higher, through the generations. If you marry well, then your children will rise further, and so on."

His voice has taken on the note that it does when he's about to lecture me—a lecture I've heard before, on legacies and the importance of building them, and my place in all of that. It doesn't matter that so far as I can tell, this world we live in is shrinking as the one outside of it moves further and further into the modern age, and ideas like my father's will become obsolete.

"I could go to college," I venture. I can feel the panic winding tighter and tighter, heat burning behind my eyelids, but I have to try. "You know how much I love photography. I could get a degree in it, try to have a career of my own—"

"That's a hobby, not a job. Don't be ridiculous, Bella." My father shakes his head, as if he can't believe we're having this conversation. "And you don't need a job. You need a husband, so you can do what you were always meant to for this family. If you were a son, your responsibility would be to inherit after me. Your responsibilities are different, but no less important."

"I can't," I whisper. Tears well up, stinging my eyes. I can't do it. Tommas looks innocuous enough from his picture; probably not someone who would hurt me the way Pyotr and his men did, but I still can't. I know down to the very depths of my bones that doing this is impossible.

I won't survive it. But my father thinks I'm just being dramatic.

"You've done your duty before," he says stiffly, shuffling the papers into a pile. "You can do it again, Bella."

Somewhere in the midst of all the fear and hurt, a rare surge of anger jolts upwards, searing through me. "You should think about where that got me," I snap, lashing out as I realize, somewhere deep within myself, that there's no escaping this. My father will marry me off to someone again, and I have no path out.

He stiffens, narrowing his eyes at me. He knows he should take a large portion of the blame for what happened, but he doesn't want to. He doesn't want to admit that he's responsible for allowing such terrible things to have happened to his only child.

"I have another meeting," my father says tightly. "Go upstairs, Bella. We'll talk about this later."

There's a finality in his voice that brooks no argument. I don't know if I even *want* to try to argue. I'm not going to get anywhere with him, and right now, all I want is to be alone so that I can have my burgeoning panic attack in peace.

I stand up abruptly, shoving the chair back as the tears start to spill over. I don't want to cry in front of my father, not when he so clearly doesn't understand how this feels, or why I'm not over it yet, or why I can't stand the thought of being married again. Here, in this room with him, I feel more lonely than I do when I really am alone.

I bolt for the door, wanting to be out of the uncomfortable room, away from the photo still staring up from my father's desk, away from all the expectations that I know I can't fulfill.

The warm air of the hallway hits me like a slap to the face as I rush out of the cold office. I swallow hard, the tears falling faster as I bolt towards the foyer and the stairs that will lead up to my room, all of my focus on getting behind the closed door of my personal sanctuary as quickly as I possibly can.

I'm so focused on that, that I don't even see the man who walks into my path as I rush down the hall. Not until I run right into him, smacking against a hard, broad chest as he comes to an abrupt halt right in front of me.

Strong hands grab my upper arms, keeping me from falling ungracefully to the floor. He holds me there for a moment, and I smell spice and vanilla, filling my senses.

I look up at the man who caught me, and directly into the greenest eyes I've ever seen.

Click here to order now!

And don't forget to click here to join my Red Hot Diva's reader group on Facebook for exclusive sneak peeks and giveaways.

Made in the USA
Monee, IL
24 October 2024